PRAISE FOR
DEAD MAN'S CREEK

'Utterly brilliant, a darkly simmering mystery - an Australian *Where The Crawdads Sing*.' **Dervla McTiernan**

'Timely and timeless, *Dead Man's Creek* is some of the finest crime fiction out there. Chris Hammer just gets better.' **Dominic Nolan**

PRAISE FOR
OPAL COUNTRY

'Classic Hammer, with the heat and the small town obsession with secrecy and past grievances. A crime novel that will stay with me for a long time.' **Ann Cleeves**

'A complex, twisty thriller, with nuanced characters and a winding plot all set in the oppressive Australian heat.' **Lisa Hall**

'A clever and compelling small town mystery, with an evocative setting and a brilliant cast of characters. This slice of Australian noir sparkles like an opal in the blistering sun.' **Lisa Gray**

'Opal Country is a top-notch Aussie Noir with real heat coming off the pages.' **Christopher Fowler**

'A brilliantly atmospheric mystery.' ***Heat***

'This novel - tighter, tougher, tenser - is Hammer's best work yet.' ***The Times***

'Keeps you stuck to the story like an Outback miner's shirt to his back.' ***The Sun***

'A sharp thriller' ***Woman's Own***

'Chris Hammer is regarded as one of Australia's best new noir crime writers, and this immersive and lyrically written thriller copper-fastens this well-deserved reputation.' ***Irish Independent***

'Gold standard Outback noir [. . .] Chris Hammer's best writing to date.' ***Crime Fiction Lover***

'Nobody does Australian outback crime better. Hammer nails it again.' *Peterborough Telegraph*

'Opal Country is richly rewarding. Hammer is quite brilliant.' *Shots Magazine*

PRAISE FOR TRUST

'A thoroughly entertaining thriller' *Mail on Sunday*

'Once again Hammer provides a gripping, complex mystery' *Sunday Times Crime Club*

'You won't want to put it down. Hammer is superb' *NB Magazine*

'Immersive, pacy . . . one of Australia's best new crime authors' *Irish Independent*

'*Trust* is a fine example of top-notch Australian crime fiction and there is no doubt that Chris Hammer is one of its leading lights now' *Shots Magazine*

PRAISE FOR SILVER

'Hammer is a great writer – a leader in Australian noir' **Michael Connelly**

'I think this is better than the first' **Ann Cleeves**

'Hammer combines Scarsden's backstory with a vivid portrait of a divided community to mesmerising effect' *Sunday Times*

'Richly descriptive, with a large and well-drawn cast, this is an immersive and enjoyable novel that lives up to the promise of its predecessor' *Guardian*

'Compelling, original and brilliantly executed – an excellent thriller' **Charles Cumming**

'A terrific story . . . This is an excellent sequel; the best Australian crime novel since Peter Temple's *The Broken Shore*' *The Times*

'With their small-town Australian setting, brilliantly complex plots involving corruption, cruelty and climate change, Chris Hammer's detective novels are as compellingly written and characterised as they are, sadly, topical. Alongside Jane Harper, he is in the vanguard of Australian noir' **Amanda Craig**

PRAISE FOR
SCRUBLANDS

'Shimmers with heat from the sun and from the passions that drive a tortured tale of blood and loss' **Val McDermid, author of *How the Dead Speak***

'An almost perfect crime novel . . . Intelligent, thought-provoking, great narrative energy, a central character who's imperfect but selfaware, and of course that amazing setting . . . I loved it' **Ann Cleeves, author of *Wild Fire***

'A dark and brilliant thriller, one that lingers in the mind' *Mail On Sunday*

'Stunning . . . *Scrublands* is that rare combination, a page-turner that stays long in the memory' **Joan Smith**, *Sunday Times* **(Crime Book of the Month)**

'A heatwave of a novel, scorching and powerful . . . Extraordinary' **A. J. Finn, author of *The Woman in the Window***

'Incendiary . . . A rattling good read, ambitious in scale and scope and delivering right up to the last, powerfully moving page' **Declan Hughes, *Irish Times***

'Atmospheric, utterly gripping and written with devastating beauty. *Scrublands* is as scorching as wildfire and as hard to look away from' **Gytha Lodge, author of *She Lies in Wait***

'Well-rounded characters, masterful plotting and real breadth; this is an epic and immersive read' **Laura Wilson, *Guardian***

'Set in the parched Australian landscape, *Scrublands* is a brilliantly plotted thriller which reveals a town full of brooding secrets. I couldn't put this compelling debut down' **Sarah Ward, author of *The Shrouded Path***

Also by Chris Hammer and available from Wildfire

The Martin Scarsden series:

Scrublands

Silver

Trust

Detective Nell Buchanan and Ivan Lucic series:

Opal Country

Dead Man's Creek

Chris Hammer

DEAD MAN'S CREEK

First published in 2022 by ALLEN & UNWIN as THE TILT

First published in Great Britain in hardback in 2023 by
WILDFIRE
an imprint of HEADLINE PUBLISHING GROUP

1

Cataloguing in Publication Data is available from the British Library

Hardback ISBN 978 1 4722 9566 8
Trade paperback ISBN 978 1 4722 9567 5

Map by Aleksander J. Potočnik

Typeset in 13/18pt Granjon LT Std by Jouve (UK), Milton Keynes

Printed and bound in Great Britain by Clays Ltd, Elcograf S.p.A.

Headline's policy is to use papers that are natural,
renewable and recyclable products and made from wood
grown in well-managed forests and other controlled sources.
The logging and manufacturing processes are expected to conform
to the environmental regulations of the country of origin.

HEADLINE PUBLISHING GROUP
An Hachette UK Company
Carmelite House
50 Victoria Embankment
London EC4Y 0DZ

www.headline.co.uk
www.hachette.co.uk

FOR GRACE AND JANE – CHAMPIONS!

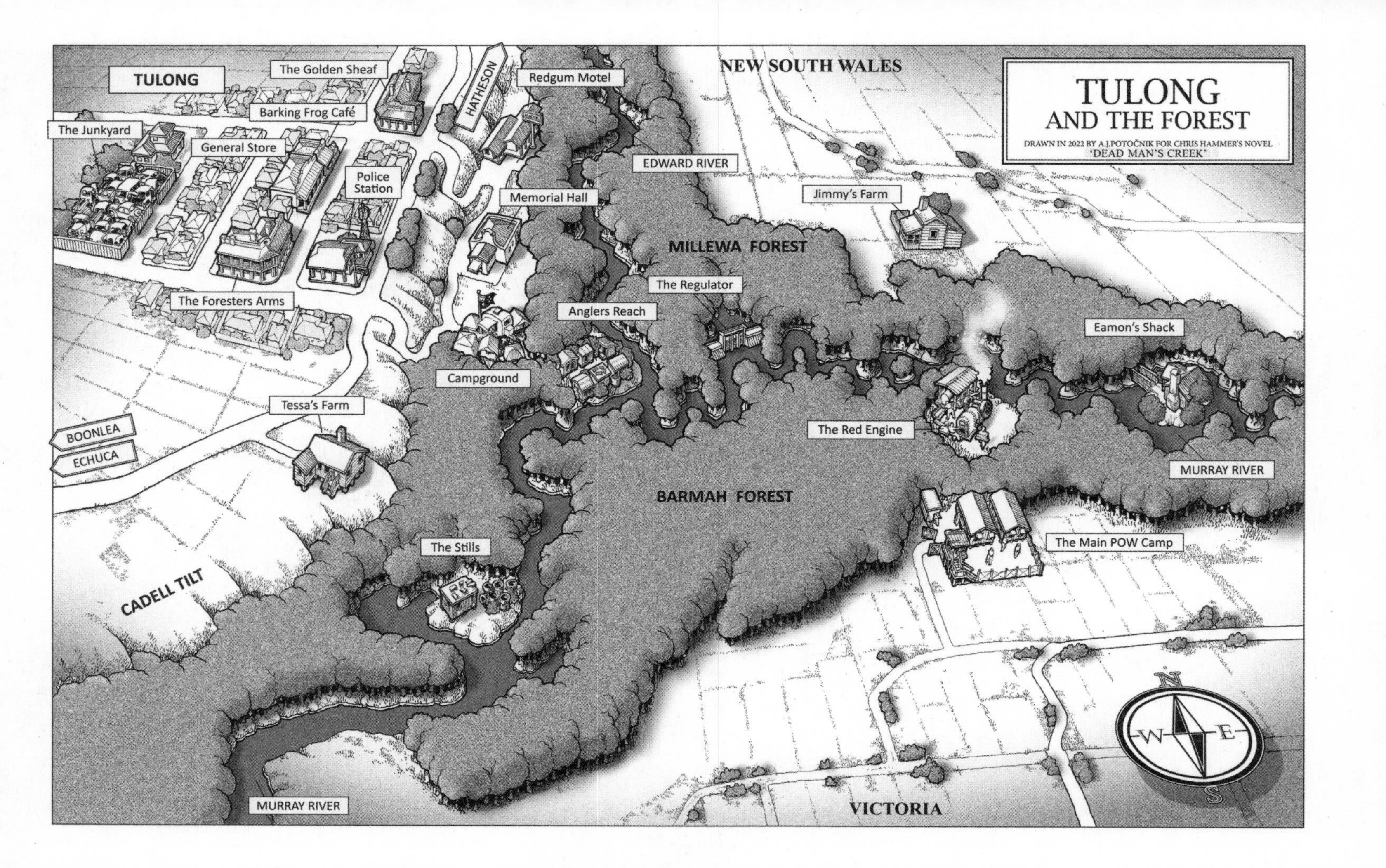
TULONG
AND THE FOREST
DRAWN IN 2022 BY A.J.POTOČNIK FOR CHRIS HAMMER'S NOVEL
'DEAD MAN'S CREEK'
TULONG
The Golden Sheaf
Barking Frog Café
The Junkyard
General Store
Police Station
HATHESON
Redgum Motel
Memorial Hall
EDWARD RIVER
NEW SOUTH WALES
Jimmy's Farm
MILLEWA FOREST
The Regulator
Anglers Reach
The Foresters Arms
Campground
Tessa's Farm
BOONLEA
ECHUCA
Eamon's Shack
The Red Engine
MURRAY RIVER
BARMAH FOREST
The Main POW Camp
The Stills
CADELL TILT
MURRAY RIVER
VICTORIA
N
W
E
S

AUGUST

SHE MOVES THROUGH THE NIGHT, THE FOREST DARK, THE TREES GATHERED AND whispering support. She passes through them, relying as much on memory as the shielded light from her torch. Her mind is alive, her senses alert. A brief hesitation, then the decision to take a shortcut, leaving the ridge and cutting across a small lagoon, now empty, following a wallaby path. Above the trees the sky is dark, clouds skimming low and quick, as if infused with her urgency. An owl swoops, a flash of white against the grey-black, and is gone. She stops, turns off the torch, feels the blackness move in, enfold her. Comfort her. She breathes it in, the smell of it, the odour of this world. She can feel its desire, its thirst, the longing for water. She closes her eyes, then opens them again. The clouds part momentarily and the sky is ablaze with stars, so very bright through the canopy. It seems for a heartbeat as if it's the galaxy that moves and the world that remains static. Then the greyness closes again and the illusion passes.

She reaches the creek and edges down its sides, making her way along its dry bed, the easiest route. There is leaf litter and cracked earth and a few colonising saplings, either struggling or dead. There should be water here, not young trees. At this time of year, with the winter rains in the alps, the water should be above her head, its sustenance bathing the earth, feeding the roots of the river redgums and being thrust back into the sky, breathed out into the misting night. On a midnight so cold, the trees should be wrapped in fog, embraced by it. She breathes out, holding her torch to see her steaming breath. She alone has moisture to spare.

There is no one to see her, no one to witness her passing. Not at night, not in winter, not this far into the forest. Not along the forgotten paths and not in the cover of the creek bed. She leaves no trace: the soil is so hard that even her hiking boots don't leave prints.

She arrives: the last of the water, a putrid remnant, pooling up against the regulator wall, a still and murky pond no longer than thirty metres where there should be water aplenty, water lung-busting deep and stretching away into the woods. In times of drought, she could almost understand it, the authorities robbing the forest of water to keep the farmers afloat, but not this year. This year there is water—storms in the mountains, minor flooding—yet nothing for the trees. And nothing for this last torpid pool, the swimming hole of her youth. A memory comes to her of sleek bodies, sun-touched and hormone-ripened, water beading and eyes alight, before it too passes, clouded over like the fleeting stars. No one would swim here now, not among the slime. Too shallow, too stagnant and, come summer, skinned with blue-green algae, toxic to all who touch it, lethal to anyone foolish enough to drink it.

She scrambles out of the creek bed, moves parallel to it, relieved to see no cars, no last-minute campers, no restless souls driving the access road to the regulator. Past the regulator wall she sees the river, her beloved Murray, and it gives her pause. She moves to the bank and, despite the chill, stands to admire its progress as it eases through the night, a silent god. The sky parts again and the Milky Way shimmers on the water like a blessing. The river flows, sliding, as if in its entirety, towards the sea. Such a mighty thing, quiet tonight, resolute in its movement, a passive observer. She knows it's not real, this river, that its impetus was long ago arrested, constricted by dams and weirs and locks, its lifeblood sucked at by thousands of pumps, the mosquitoes of agriculture, told when to flow and when to stop, when to carry boats and when to water crops, when to supply the towns with water and when, as if no one is looking, to carry away the waste: the slurry from the farms, the pollutants from the factories, the chlorine from the town water, the effluent from a million people, the salt from ancient seas.

The forest is dying without the river, but the river is dying without the forest, like a bloodstream no longer filtered by its kidneys. The annual pulse is no more: the river flooding the forest in winter and spring, the water flowing back as summer progresses. The natural world, her world, subverted for profit and perverted by ignorance. Well, no longer.

She stops dead, her train of thought derailing. What was that? In the distance—what? A gunshot, another. Surely not; not in the forest. Hunting is prohibited in the national park. She strains to hear. Perhaps it's rangers, culling feral animals with no one to witness the necessity. But don't rangers use poison baits for foxes, not bullets? Perhaps it's a farmer, out beyond the forest periphery, taking down wild dogs; sound can play strange tricks at night, travel great distances over water. Perhaps. Perhaps she has just imagined it. But then it comes again, a cackle of gunfire, like fire crackers. That must be it: fireworks at some distant camp site. Risky in the parched forest, but no concern of hers. If anything, it will divert the attention of any late-night ranger. The gods are with her.

The gunfire comes again, closer now. He runs and he runs, plunging through the woods, branches clawing at his face, terror gouging at his guts. He's running blind, the night dark, the scuttling clouds impeding visibility, not daring to use his phone light lest they see him, use it to target him. He's lost, with no idea where he's going, with nothing to run towards, just the imperative to get away from the men with the guns. Another volley rings out, then the unmistakable burst of an automatic rifle. A military weapon, as illegal as it is deadly. Still distant. What are they shooting at? Movements in the bush, imagined sightings? Or are they simply firing for the thrill of it, unable to contain themselves, knowing the terror it will induce?

He runs again, unsure if he's getting away or running in circles. Is that the purpose of the gunfire? Are they mustering him, herding him towards an ambush? But such thoughts slip away as quickly as they come, unable to gain proper purchase, like his boots on the dry leaves.

He hits water, a low lagoon, stumbles, almost falls. It stops him. He starts to back out, then thinks better of it. They have dogs, he knows that. Could they follow his scent? Is that why the shots seem to be getting closer? He plunges ahead, but there is no more water, not enough, just mud, cloying and solicitous. It slows him, tugging at his boots. What a disaster that would be, to lose a boot when he needs it most. He pushes through, comes to a shallow stream a metre across, wades through it, water barely above his ankles but the creek bed solid, the going easier. Then he's up the other side, breathing hard, climbing a low rise. He clambers behind the trunk of a massive tree, dares to check his phone. Still no signal. He looks out from his refuge, back the way he came, can hear nothing. No shots, no dogs. He can see nothing; no torches. And then, in the distance, not behind him, but somehow ahead of him, a soft crump, like distant thunder. Maybe it will rain. Maybe that will save him. He runs towards it, as if it might offer sanctuary. Maybe it's not thunder. Maybe there is someone else in the forest. Someone who can save him.

——

She approaches the regulator. She even hates the name, so technical, so official, with its hard straight lines of concrete and steel and logic, so foreign amid the knotted and twisted tree trunks, its barrier keeping the river from the hinterland. She squats for a moment, listening. There is no sound. She uses her torch, can see the disparity, the river a good three metres above the remnant pool.

Now comes the difficult part, demanding concentration. She removes her backpack, extracts the wires and the detonators. She retrieves the Senatel from its tin, the explosive tubes sourced months ago on a road trip west, contraband from a mine, its provenance disguised by several months and thousands of kilometres. Now she moves quickly. She has rehearsed this, knows what to do. Until this point, she would be able to feign innocence, but not now. Now she is vulnerable—discovery would mean imprisonment.

She inserts the detonators, connects the wires, guarding against an accidental charge. She wraps the two tubes in gaffer tape, waterproof enough to endure the few short minutes required. It would be easier to set the explosives on the forest side, but for maximum effect, the charge needs to be submerged in the river, to recruit its power. The regulator sits some metres back from the river, away from the current; the water will be safe enough. She has been here before, swum in the freezing water, familiarised herself.

She strips naked. Another decision considered and adopted: she can't be caught carrying wet swimwear, so she wears none. The air is cold on her skin, somehow exhilarating, somehow intimidating. She takes the fresh glow stick on its improvised necklace, hangs it around her neck. That is all she wears, that and her goggles. The rest is left on the shore. She eases into the water, feeling the rising chill, resisting the temptation to plunge in. But she needs to eliminate all risk, needs to maintain her discipline. She lowers herself into the muddy water, breathing steadily, letting it lap above her shoulders, acclimatising. She adjusts her goggles, making sure they're sealed. Then she stands, reaches back, takes the hard plastic sausages of the explosives. She inches towards the regulator, takes one last deep breath and pushes gently into the still water of its inlet.

She breaststrokes to the dam wall, explosives in her right hand. The water is starting to gnaw at her, deep and cold. She feels her way across the face of the structure, counting the vertical beams. One, two, three. Even in the dark she knows she has arrived at the centre, the midway point where the regulator will be weakest, the most vulnerable. Now comes the part that needs to be done first time, done correctly. She ducks her head, checks once more that her goggles aren't leaking. Satisfied, she cracks the glow stick beneath the surface, smiles at its luminescence. She ducks her head again, doesn't look directly at the light source, but sees the dam wall clearly enough. It's time. Explosives in one hand, glow stick in the other she moves back from the wall, then duck dives, pushing her legs skywards, feeling her own weight drive her into the depths. She kicks hard, uses her arms as much as possible, gets down two metres, three, enough to feel the pressure in her ears. Working fast, she attaches the explosives to the wall, the gaffer tape holding, a small miracle. It's so quickly accomplished, easier than she had visualised. But now comes the delicate part: resurfacing with the detonation wires, taking care not to wrench them loose.

She breaks the surface, breath gasping, treading water, listening. Nothing. She eases back to her entry point. She is unhurried. This is working; it will work. She wraps the glow stick in cloth, enough light escaping to assist her. She towels herself dry, dresses quickly, takes her time with her socks and boots, making sure all is ready for a quick retreat. The authorities will drive in along the maintenance road, maybe check the paths along the river, but not the forest paths. The water will spread, covering her retreat, remembering the old creeks beds and lagoons, the swamps and the marshes.

She trails the leads as she shelters behind a massive river gum. She attaches the wires, closes her eyes and recites a silent mantra, calming herself with its repetition. The moment is here . . . She turns the dial, feels the detonation deep within her, hears the fluming water. And then, stepping away from the tree, risking her torch, she revels in the sight.

The regulator is all but gone. The two ends remain, but the middle has vanished, and the water is roaring through the gap, roaring with joy, the river spilling into the creek bed. Pushed by the accumulated weight of miles of river sitting above it, all the way back to Yarrawonga Weir, kilometres and kilometres of river. There will be no stopping it now, not easily. She gives herself a moment to take in the sight, knowing that it will live with her for the rest of her days: this vision of life pouring back into the forest. Then she begins to gather the remnants of the leads, pulling them to her, making sure she has left nothing behind, nothing incriminating.

But for a moment she's distracted. She hears it again, somewhere down along the river: fireworks. It sounds wrong. Fireworks, the middle of the night, the middle of winter, the middle of nowhere. She stands perfectly still, but there is no more. She imagines she can hear dogs yelping. Maybe it is a farmer after all, killing dogs that have turned wild and got in among the sheep. Maybe.

She can't stay here, not next to the destruction, not next to the joyous water. She moves away, back into the night, alongside the rapidly filling regulator pond, the water moving down the creek and into the forest. She's excited now; her calmness abandoning her. She's almost skipping with elation, catching the reflections of the sky as she moves, the sky in the water, the sky and earth moving into balance once more.

—

He runs and he runs until he feels he can run no more, and somehow they are still following, the shots growing closer, rifling through the sky, curdling the air. He can hear the shouting voices, still far away. And a dog, maybe two. It must be the hounds; they must have his scent, weren't put off by the muddy lagoon. He scans the darkness and there, suddenly, he sees the flash of a torchlight. They will get him, he realises, eventually they must get him. He is too tired, stumbling and half blind in the night. There will be no outrunning the dogs. Unless he can get to the river. Of course—he should have thought of that before. Could he swim the river? Or let it carry him, take him back down past them? There: a muzzle flash, the sound following. If he can see them, then they can potentially see him. He runs, veering to his right. The river must be there; it has to be. But he knows all too well how it can ramble, folding this way and that in its long bows. It is down to fate, then, whether the Murray will swing close enough to save him.

And now he can hear the dogs. Not one or two. A pack. Baying in the night. Why didn't he think of the river before?

He gets there, the Murray, just in time. There are more lights flickering through the trees, closing in. If they have night sights, they could see him any moment. He keeps low, gets to the bank, is about to plunge in, when he checks his phone one last time, risks the light from the screen, sheltered by the oversized trunk of a redgum. And there it is, the whisper of a signal. One bar, a flickering second. He punches at the messaging app, bringing up the image, the oh-so-innocuous image. He can't think what to say; the adrenaline is too rich, the fear too palpable. *This is it*, he types, but that is all. His eye catches the red circle dancing on the next tree. A laser sight, kissing the trunk, and then it is gone. Something smashes into the wood above his head, followed by the sound of a shot, followed by a yell of victory. Some part of his brain suggests the sounds have come in the wrong order, that a film would do it differently. He hits send on his phone, gets the message away. And then he's in the river, taking the phone with him, swimming desperately for the first few seconds, knowing it will take them some few moments to gain the bank. Before they can, he goes under, stays under, pushing hard, trying to get as far from the bank as possible, out into the main channel, out into the fast water. He comes up for air, dives again. Dives, surfaces, breathes, dives. Once, twice, three times. On the fourth time, bullets smack the water around him, and he dives extra deep, no longer trying to move across the river, just trying to catch the current, trying to survive.

chapter one

NOVEMBER

IT'S A SEVEN-HOUR JOURNEY, DUBBO TO TULONG, MORE THAN EIGHT HOURS including stops, travelling from the centre of New South Wales to the state's southern border, passing through the towns that now belong to them, to her and Ivan. Their patch. Nell is driving, taking them through Parkes and Forbes to West Wyalong, then Grong Grong and Narrandera towards Jerilderie and on to their final destination. The unmarked four-wheel drive has plenty of grunt and power steering, the roads straight.

It's still another hour and a half to go, the days of PolAir planes and charters no longer part of their world. Nowadays they drive the long roads to obscure towns and far-flung shires, distant from head office. And so it is this Sunday, ostensibly their day off. They're based in Dubbo, but it can feel more like Coventry. Not for her, but certainly for Ivan. She's a newly minted homicide detective, still revelling in her promotion. But for him, an established detective sergeant, it's what exactly? She glances across at him, but he doesn't respond, just keeps looking out through the windscreen. He's getting very good at that lately, staring at nothing. She almost misses the days when his intense gaze would fall on her, those piercing blue eyes focused, his mind working hard. Now his eyes seem as unfocused as his thoughts. When they left Dubbo, the stated intention was to share the driving, but almost six hours later Nell is still behind the wheel and he remains staring out into space, his face a blank. The brief she printed for him sits unread on his lap.

'You okay?' she asks.

'Beaut.' He sighs. 'You?'

'Good.'

'Want a break from driving?' he offers.

'Next town,' she says.

The memory of the meeting returns. She considers it once more, searching for implications. She was summoned to Sydney three months ago, the phone call coming at night, the flight down from Bourke the next morning. Superintendent Dereck 'Plodder' Packenham, head of Homicide, waiting for her. What had she thought on that flight? All sorts of wild speculation. That she was in trouble again? Something like that.

The moment she walked into the office, it started becoming clearer. Ivan Lucic was already there, seated across the desk from Packenham. Despite the formality of the setting, despite the looming presence of the Homicide boss behind the desk, Nell couldn't help herself. She broke into a wide smile, so glad to see Ivan again, her colleague from the previous summer, up at Finnigans Gap, where they'd solved a famous case, winning plaudits and garnering media coverage. But Ivan didn't smile back. There was anger in his eyes and resentment and perhaps other things. Was that sadness she saw? So many emotions packed into a single glance, too many to interpret then, only understandable in retrospect.

'Detective Constable,' said Packenham. 'Glad you could join us.'

'Morning, sir.'

'Take a seat,' the senior man said, but Nell's eyes were already scanning the desk. It was covered with printouts of newspaper articles, turned to face her and Ivan. She recognised them immediately. She'd read all of them, studied them with interest. Now she knew what this was about.

'Martin Scarsden,' said Plodder as she sat. 'Good journo.'

'Sir?'

'You ever met him, Constable?'

Nell turned to Ivan. He raised his eyebrows, his mouth crooked and sardonic. 'No, sir,' she told Packenham.

'Spoken to him?'

'No, sir,' she said, voice low. Why do this in front of Ivan, force him to watch?

'Someone has,' said Packenham, voice not unsympathetic. 'But it has to stop.'

She could sense Ivan bristling, but he remained silent.

Packenham smiled at her. 'I've had my eye on you, Constable. That was exemplary work you did at Finnigans Gap. Ivan gave you full credit. Your superiors at Bourke speak very highly of you. And Professional Standards have finally given you a clean bill of health.'

Nell said nothing.

'Ivan is establishing himself as a fine investigator. Especially in rural cases, out where we can't deploy big teams, where the forensics resources are thin on the ground. Places where wit and insight and investigative nous still trump technology. Where a skilled interviewer can get a result. Places like Riversend, or Port Silver, or Finnigans Gap.'

Still, she didn't speak. She knew it wasn't required.

'We've been experiencing some political pressure. The Nats don't think the bush is getting a fair share of the police budget. And the brass see a need for a greater presence out there as well, so they've managed to extract a bit of dough from one of their hollow logs. Potentially it's win-win. More coverage for the bush, a bit more money for Homicide. I've asked Ivan to head up a new rural flying squad. Homicides only. Based in Dubbo, but travelling state wide. Only the challenging cases; not the day-to-day horror shows.'

'I see.'

'You interested?'

'Sir?'

'Homicide, Constable. You ready to step up? Join the A-team? With Ivan at Dubbo?'

She didn't hesitate, not for a moment. 'Absolutely, sir. Thank you, sir.' She looked at Ivan then, saw his wan smile, wondered what it was conveying: gratitude, sympathy, scepticism? None of it dampened her enthusiasm.

'Glad to hear it,' said Plodder, before addressing Ivan. 'Give me a moment alone with the constable, will you, Sergeant?'

'Of course.' Ivan stood, gave Nell another smile, a warmer version, and shook her hand. 'Congratulations. And welcome.' His tone seemed almost wistful. He closed the door behind him.

'Don't let his attitude fool you. He asked for you specifically,' said Packenham. 'You will make a good team.'

'Thank you, sir.'

'To be honest, it's a bit half-arsed, just the two of you out there by yourselves. We'll get you some uniformed support when we can. But it's important you fly the flag. Politics, you understand. Do a good job and we can get you a couple more detectives. Grow it.'

It was a statement, not a question, but still she responded. 'Yes, sir.'

Packenham tilted his head towards the articles still arrayed across the desk. 'I understand why he's been talking to the media. To Scarsden. So do you. But enough is enough. I don't want to lose him.'

Nell looked at the newspaper reports. She'd heard of homicide cops being drummed out of the force for talking to the media.

'Nice town, Dubbo,' said Packenham. 'Very central.'

'I like Dubbo, sir,' she said, which was true, but even to her own ears it sounded weak, as if she was sucking up to the senior officer.

'In that case, welcome aboard.' And he rose, came around his desk and shook her hand.

'Thank you, sir. I've always dreamt of being a homicide detective.'

Plodder smiled at that, a wry grin. 'That's a very strange dream to have.' And then, as she was leaving. 'Look after him, Nell. Shout if you need help.'

There is an echidna unmoving in the middle of the road, snapping her attention back into the present. She brakes hard, unable to stop but slowing enough to slip by behind the spiky ball. She brings the car to a stop.

'What are you doing?' asks Ivan.

'We can't leave it there. It'll get flattened.'

She climbs out, Ivan joining her. The echidna is frozen into place, its instinct to burrow thwarted by the bitumen. Only as Nell approaches does it make for the shoulder, waddling off the road and heading down into a grass-filled gully.

'That was easy,' says Ivan. He climbs back into the passenger seat, offer to take the wheel forgotten.

The plain is flat, the horizon endless, driving effortless. And today there is a blueness to the sky, a purity. It's been a wet spring, talk of La Niña, with a green tinge to the flatness. Off in a field, she sees a tractor ploughing, seeding a summer crop. There must be plenty of moisture in the soil. She looks across at Ivan, who's again contemplating the distance. She wonders what he sees, what he thinks; if he sees any of this or if the landscape is merely the backdrop for his internal dramas. She's grown to respect him, even to like him. She just wishes he would talk more.

She slows down, entering Jerilderie, where Ned Kelly wrote his famous letter of rebellion. She parks outside the town's bakery, next to a lopsided ute with a broken brake light, a peeling Eureka flag, a One Nation bumper sticker and a silhouette of the bushranger's famous helmet. The outlaws are not forgotten inside either; they're there on the bakery walls, immortalised in two-tone portraits: bearded Ned and brother Dan, Joe Byrne and Steve Hart. No images of the policemen they murdered, no mention of that. Nell orders: a pie for him, a salad roll for her, coffees. They sit outside, away from the iconography, not speaking.

Rural Homicide. A huge career leap. And Dubbo is so much bigger than her previous posting in Bourke, with a cinema, a library, a base hospital, air and rail links through to Sydney. Positively cosmopolitan. And now she's not just a detective, but a homicide detective. The crème de la crème. But she's learnt not to let her eagerness show, knowing how it rankles with Ivan. He believes he's been sidelined, warehoused, demoted in all but rank. For him Dubbo is to be endured, survived.

Nell eats her roll, looking past Ivan. The streetscape seems vaguely familiar, the outer reaches of her childhood. But all the towns out here look the same: roads that are too wide, trees that are too far apart, air that is too dry.

She's heading home. Her family is there, unaware of her imminent arrival, but she feels them waiting all the same. She's not sure how she feels about that. She knows she should have called ahead, but in the rush to get going she didn't have the chance. That's what she tells herself. Ivan had only called her this morning, first thing, and she'd rushed to pack. And she doesn't want to call from the car, not with him listening. Better to separate the personal from the professional.

They had been stridently opposed to her joining the police. Her father tried to forbid it; her mother wept at the prospect. They'd wanted her to do something safe, something caring, to be a nurse or a teacher, but all she had wanted was to wear a uniform and get in among it, kick arse and catch crims. Only her uncle Gene had supported her. She can already hear their inevitable inquiries. Has she met a fellow? Is she thinking of a career change? As if policing is some teenage infatuation she'll grow out of. Yet for all of that, she does want to see them.

Maybe she should wear her gun. Not her shoulder holster but the one on her belt, having loosened it a little so it hangs low. She imagines herself striding through the door like a gunfighter entering a saloon. Her mother long ago banned them from wearing shoes inside the house; what might she think of a gun?

Ivan speaks, breaking Nell's reverie. Perhaps he feels obliged, having finished his pie, or perhaps he's starting to engage at last. 'You're from down this way, then? Tulong?' He pronounces the name of the town tentatively, the first words he's spoken since they took their seats.

'Close enough. Half an hour south of there, on the river. Boonlea. Born and raised. I've got a grandmother in Tulong, though, and a grandfather on a farm just outside. An uncle at Hatty.'

'Hatty?'

'Hatheson. We'll drive through it on our way.'

'Good. Having your grandparents nearby might prove handy.'

'I wouldn't count on it. She's a prickly old dear. And he's practically a hermit.'

Ivan sips at what's left of his coffee, disapproving, as if nothing brewed west of the mountains could ever match the artistry of Sydney's baristas. 'What about your parents? They still at . . . what did you call it?'

'Boonlea. Yep.' She sips some of her own coffee. It's perfectly passable.

'Brothers and sisters?'

'Two brothers, two sisters. I'm the youngest.'

'Quite a mob. Any of them still there?'

'One brother, one sister. The other sister just across the border in Shepparton.'

'They must like it.' He sounds unsure, and she knows he can't imagine why anyone would stay in the bush if they had a choice. 'Where's the other brother?'

'Not far. Albury. Greg. He's older by a long ways. Then the middle three. Then me, lucky last.'

Ivan says nothing. If she hoped talking about her own family might elicit some response, some admission of his own, it's not coming unprompted.

'You?' she tries.

'Only child.'

'You can borrow some of mine if you like.'

That does raise a smile, at last. It fades soon enough, though, and they sit in silence once again.

But Nell isn't willing to let it endure all the way to Tulong. 'It's not forever, Ivan. We get the results, you'll be back in Sydney before you know it. Back on the fast track.' There, she's said it. It's only taken her five hundred kilometres.

He stares at her, those piercing blue eyes focused at last. When he speaks, his voice is quiet, considered, any anger long drained from it. 'I know, Nell. I'm not stupid.' His eyes remain upon her, the unwavering gaze not as disconcerting as she once found it. She almost welcomes it now. 'So, this body they've found. In a regulator. You know what that is? A regulator?'

It's the first time he's referred to the case, the purpose of their trip south. She's relieved he's at least looked at the brief. 'It's like a small dam at the mouth of a creek, between it and the river. Regulates the flow. Most of the time, stops it altogether.'

'To stop water flowing into the river? Why?'

'No, the opposite. So the river doesn't flow up the creek. Or only when they want it to: then they open the regulator.'

Ivan frowns. 'I thought creeks flowed into rivers, not the other way round.'

'Not this side of the mountains. Not in the forest.'

'You want to explain that?'

'The land is flat. Some places, billiard-table flat. Back before the dams and the weirs and the regulators and all, the Murray didn't just flow uninterrupted to the sea. In a severe drought it could dry up and stop flowing altogether. Most years, in summer and autumn, it would just dribble its way through. But when there was a lot of water, in winter when it was raining and in spring with the snow melting in the alps, the river would push up the creeks into the forest. Every couple of years or so it would burst its banks, flood the forest. And then later, as summer kicked in, what was left of the water would drain back down the creeks, out of the forest and into the river.'

Ivan is frowning. 'So why put in regulators?'

'To save water. For irrigation. For the towns. For Adelaide. They want to keep it in the river, only let it out where it's needed. And the farmers, the townspeople, the government: they don't reckon the forest needs it.'

'How do you know all this stuff?'

'I told you: I grew up on the river.'

'Any particular reason why someone would dump a body in a regulator?'

'Not that I can think of.'

chapter two

JAMES WATERS–FIRST STATEMENT

I REMEMBER THEM BUILDING THE REGULATORS. HERE, AND ON THE VICTORIAN side. I was with my dad, before the war. Maybe around 1938, before Hitler and Tojo and the whole bloody mess, before I knew anything of Berlin and Tokyo. Sydney and Melbourne were the biggest places I'd heard of, the biggest places possible. 'Course, I'd never been anywhere like that. Biggest town I'd ever been to was Echuca, and that was scary enough. I must have been seven or eight, something like that. I remember Dad standing there, smoking his pipe, watching, a big grin on his face. He liked it, approved of it. It was progress, he told me, and progress was good. Back then it was. No one questioned progress. We were all for it; you'd be mad if you weren't. It was the promise of a better life.

Electricity was still coming through, and it was true: it made life easier. That was progress.

They were starting to seal some of the roads with bitumen and bluestone. Out our way and into the forest there were midden roads in those days, surfaced with the shells the black folk had left behind, great mounds of them, stretching along the river for kilometres. Thousands of years of shells. Tens of thousands. Made good roads, made good cement. But bitumen and bluestone were better, and progress was what was needed and no one complained. There were flush toilets in town, motor cars, steam trains. Radio. Electric power snaking out further and further each year. A field had been cleared outside town and declared an aerodrome. And now they were controlling the river. My dad, he liked the word 'regulator' and he liked the word 'controlled'. It made him proud. He said there would be no more floods, no more droughts. That the forest would be protected for all time, and so would the farms. They were drought-proofing Australia, he said, turning the desert green. It was progress, promising paradise, and we were leading the world. Man taming nature, bending it to his will. It was good and no one questioned it.

We watched the men work. He took me to the Murray to show me. Like it was a great event, one that I needed to witness, our own little bit of history, like building the bridge in Sydney. It affected us, because the lower paddock of our farm was hard up against the forest, so what happened in there was important to us. Back at the start of last century, our land was susceptible to flooding as there was nothing separating the fields from the trees. That's why they built the levee. It's still there, still working, still doing the same job, except no one sees it now, because the regulators do the heavy lifting. But that levee, that's what brought us to the forest, us Waters. My grandfather and his brothers helped build the bank around the perimeter. Have you seen it, the levee? Easy enough to miss, I guess, if you don't know what you're looking for. Right around the outside of the whole forest. Runs for miles. Took years to build. All done with picks and shovels and wheelbarrows. No bobcats in those days. No bulldozers, no backhoes. No gelly. Just hard yakka. Backbreaking. The government paid a shilling a yard and whole families came and camped in the bush, building it yard by yard, shilling by shilling, with nothing but their own muscles, men and women and kids all pitching in. You can still go see it. Close on a hundred years and it's still there. Good as gold. Only knee-high, and easy to miss among the undergrowth, but high enough 'cos the land is so flat. That's the secret of the forest, how flat it is. Even now, after they blew up those regulators, the levees protected the farms, kept the water in. It was a beautiful sight: the fields on the one side and the forest like a lake on the other. The regulators were the next step.

Dad and me, we got a ride in there in the back of a sleeper splitter's cart. It was a big thing back then, cutting sleepers. There were loggers in the Barmah-Millewa Forest. It was quite an industry. They'd fell the redgums, the big fellas, haul them to the river with bullocky teams. They'd stack the logs onto the barges, wait until the flow was high enough and then float the logs down to Echuca, to the mills. But the treetops, the large branches that weren't big enough for milling or had some other flaw, they'd hand-cut them. Sleepers, nine foot long. They exported more than a million of them; the railways of British India had steel tracks forged in Sheffield and sleepers from here. Unbelievably tough wood, river redgum. Naturally water-resistant, doesn't rot. Lasts forever. Go up to Hume Dam, see the skeletons of the old trees standing in the lake, almost a century after it was flooded. The smaller offcuts went to Melbourne. They paved the streets with them. Still there, under the tar, on Bourke Street and Collins Street, on Spencer Street and Spring Street, right outside the parliament. Not cobblestones underneath the bitumen, underneath the tram tracks—redgum. Still softening the ride, not that anyone down there would ever know it. It's all been forgotten.

Anyway, this was before the war in the Pacific, so the sleeper splitters were still working flat chat. Hard men they were. People say 'tough as teak', but teak is a softwood compared to redgum. Put an axe into a redgum and if the blade's not hair-splitting sharp, it'll bounce straight back at you and jar your arms so bad they'll quiver for a week.

They were still building the access road, so Dad and I walked the last bit to the river. There was water in the forest in those days, shallow lakes and ponds, little creeks winding this way and that, lagoons and bogs. Potentially treacherous, but Dad had grown up there, and he knew the tracks, the way through. When we got to where they were building the regulator, there was a steam shovel, this huge thing belching steam and black smoke, its boiler stoked with redgum and box and whatever other offcuts were lying around. Scared the shit out of me. I'd never seen anything like it. They must have got it there on a barge—towed it up from Echuca or floated it down from Tocumwal. No way could they have hauled it through the forest. It was so big, spewing smoke and leaking steam, but I couldn't let Dad know I was afraid. He loved it, pointing out to me how it was turning the wood into raw power. That's what he called it: 'raw power'. He explained how it worked, steam power, said it was same as the trains. 'Look, boy, look at it. That is progress, right there.'

I've got no idea who blew up the regulator, and I know it was wrong, but part of me is glad they did. I don't condone it, but to see the water like that, the life returning, the way it used to do when I was a kid, before the regulators, before it was all controlled. Filling the creeks and lapping up against the levee. It took me back.

I wonder what my dad would think of it. Someone blowing it up like that. Horrified, I imagine. Rolling back progress. But, then, he wouldn't have imagined finding a body like that. A skeleton in the bottom of the regulator. All this time. I couldn't believe it when I read about it. A skeleton. Who could have known that?

chapter three

NELL AND IVAN STAND BY THE REMAINS OF THE REGULATOR, NOT SPEAKING. Crime scene tape flutters in the breeze. It's gone five; the sun is starting to drop towards the trees and the temperature has mellowed. A small pump is chugging away, taking water from the bottom of the works and sending it back into the river. The Murray is on one side, moving like green glass. A temporary dam has been constructed of vertical steel plates, allowing repair work on the regulator to proceed. But nothing is proceeding now—the discovery of the body has seen to that. A small tent has been erected at the base of the hole, protecting the site. The empty creek is deep, maybe six metres, the spread of the empty pool maybe twenty metres wide, narrowing where it meets the river and tapering again as it stretches into the forest a good seventy metres or more away, like a distended swimming pool. But just mud now. No one is here; the local police must have called it a day.

'There's no doubt that the regulator was destroyed on purpose?' asks Ivan.

'None,' says Nell, pleased her partner is finally focusing on the case. 'Blown up. Commercial explosives.'

'Sourced from?'

'Who knows? Probably stolen from a mine.'

'Somewhere close?'

'Nothing obvious. The locals checked quarries, that sort of thing. Nothing reported stolen.'

Ivan frowns.

She knows what he's thinking: there are thousands of mines and quarries in Australia, maybe tens of thousands, everything from globally significant mega mines to farmers extracting a bit of bluestone.

'Why would someone blow it up?'

'Albury thinks it might be environmentalists, wanting more water for the forest.'

'Any claims of responsibility?'

'No. But another regulator went up a couple of nights later, over on the Victorian side.'

'Same M.O.?'

'Seems like it.'

'And this was what? Three months ago?'

'Correct. August. They only found the body in the mud yesterday when the reconstruction work was well underway.'

'So if the regulator wasn't destroyed, the body would never have been found?'

'Probably not.'

Ivan takes his eyes from the hole and looks about, as if expecting the trees to tell him what they know. 'Where's the body now?'

'Most of it's in the morgue at Hatty.'

'Most of it?'

'Skeletal remains. All that's left. They're still extracting the last of it.'

'How do we know it's murder then?'

Nell frowns. So much for him reading the brief. 'The skull has a bullet hole. Entry wound and exit wound.'

'No bullet?'

'No bullet, no gun. They've started going over the site with metal detectors. Finding all sorts of shit, but nothing obviously relevant. Not yet.'

'Clothing?'

'Nothing so far. Early days.'

Ivan looks about again. 'Why dump a body here? Why not in the river?'

Nell shrugs. 'Maybe they feared the currents, that it might wash up somewhere.'

'But the pond here, behind the regulator—wouldn't there be a risk it would dry out altogether, expose the body?'

'Further up the creek, yes. But it's pretty deep just here where it meets the river. Maybe it never dries out. Maybe there's enough leakage through the regulator.'

Ivan looks at her, eyes intent. 'Not everyone would know that. Is it part of your local knowledge?'

'No. I'm only guessing.'

'Why didn't the body float to the surface?'

'They think it might have been weighed down.'

'Think?'

'There's a large rock sunk into the mud, right next to the bones.'

'Rope? Chains?'

'Not so far. Rope might have rotted away.'

He seems to take that on board. 'How old is the regulator?'

'Built in 1938. So the killing must have happened after that.'

'Well that narrows it down.'

'Blake will know more.'

——

They leave the forest, driving first along the dirt access road from the regulator to the fishers' shacks at Anglers Reach and then along the sealed road out through the trees to Tulong and the highway. The sun is setting by the time they reach Hatheson, half an hour north, the closest town with a hospital, the closest with a morgue. It's an innocuous-looking building, functional and no fuss, a glorified clinic, good for emergencies and rehabilitation and not much else. They find Blake Ness, forensic pathologist, typing away at his laptop in the reception area. He's a big man, perpetually friendly, never perturbed. Nell remembers him well, likes him, appreciates that he's waited here for them.

'There's not a lot to tell you so far. It's a man, mature, between twenty and sixty-five. Bullet hole, straight through the skull and out again. Instant death.'

'Identity?'

'Nothing yet. No clothing. Either the body was stripped, or the clothing has rotted away. But we won't begin searching the surrounds properly until we've removed the remains. I only got down at lunchtime. The team from Albury are doing the best they can, but it's a quagmire.'

'What happens next?'

'I'm concentrating on assembling the bones for now, see what they can tell us. I've asked for a crime scene investigator. Carole Nguyen's trying to get down here, bring some proper gear with her.'

'So we've got nothing?' Ivan summarises.

'Quite the contrary,' says Blake with a twinkle in his eye. 'We've got teeth.'

'Tell me.'

'Two gold caps. Top-right front, top-left canine. And a gold filling, lower-left wisdom tooth. Very distinctive. Somewhere, there'll be dental records. Might take a while, but we'll find him.'

'Missing persons database?' Ivan asks.

'Good place to start. I'll leave that to you.'

Ivan turns to Nell, raises his eyebrows.

'Sure,' she confirms. 'I'll ask the Vics as well.'

'DNA?' asks Ivan.

'Probably,' says Blake. 'Should be able to extract something useable from the molars. Send it to Sydney. Needs specialist equipment. I've brought a portable sequencer, in case we locate a blood relation.'

'Very good,' says Ivan, although she can hear the qualification in his voice. DNA is definitive, but only if there's something to match it with. 'Any idea how long the body has been there?'

'More than ten years. Probably more than twenty.'

'Based on?'

'How deep in the mud the skeleton was set. The fact that everything except the bones has rotted away. Possibly including clothing and any rope that was used to weigh it down.'

'Any chance it was buried during the construction of the regulator?'

That gives Blake pause. He stares hard at his computer screen, concentrating before reaching his conclusion. 'I wouldn't think so. No. But I suspect it's been there a very long time.'

'Suspect?'

'When the regulator was blown up, the water would have really torn through. The river was high at the time, the creek low, almost empty. The flow through the breach would have been moving very fast that close to the regulator. Lots of energy, lifting a lot of silt. The bones must have been deep. Decades deep.'

'I see,' says Ivan, and Nell hears the pique in his voice. She knows why: they've driven all this way, on their day off, for nothing. They're homicide detectives, not archaeologists.

chapter four

1973

TESSA ALMOST MISSED THE SCHOOL BUS. HER ENGLISH TEACHER HAD KEPT HER back, telling her yet again in that smarmy voice of his how smart she was, how she was capable of achieving so much more. Same crap, same excuse. She had barely listened. All she wanted was to get away. If she missed the bus, she'd have to walk across to the highway and stick her finger out. She didn't like hitchhiking, not in her school uniform. It made her feel such a dag. Who'd want to pick up a schoolgirl? The bus was better, full of fellow dags. Like a sardine can, cheek to jowl, packed with dags.

The teacher finally got sick of the sound of his own voice, tired of stroking her with his eyes, and let her go. Marcus O'Toole. The Tool, they called him. She grabbed her bag and ran from the classroom, down the corridor past the lockers. The bus was still there, the driver loitering by its door, sucking on the last of his cigarette, his eyes lingering as she climbed the stairs. He and the English teacher could have formed a club. The pervy old deadshits' club. The bus was packed, seats taken, juniors standing in the aisle towards the front, knowing their place. She pushed through, down towards the back, holding on to steel poles and seat backs as she went. The bus was baking in the afternoon sun, hot and fuggy, open windows providing scant relief from the late spring heat, summer already here in every sense except officially. She could smell BO and hair oil and chewing gum. Some tart was wearing 4711 and there was the smell of clandestine cigarettes. Tessa reached her own third form cohort, happy to stand rather than pull rank and evict a junior from their seat closer to the front. A mile or two out of town, after the first few stops, there would be plenty of places to sit.

Gene Buchanan was sitting by a window, showing off his transistor radio, brand-new in its made-to-measure orange vinyl carry case. It was tuned to the local station—Hatty's only station—2HN. It was so small, he was able to swing it gently back and forth, just one finger through the case's handle. She couldn't help but look at it. So tiny, so modern. Battery-operated. She wanted to hear it, hear what was playing, but he was talking over the top of it to the boy next to him. Then, as if by chance, he looked up, caught her eye. 'Ad break,' he explained.

The engine kicked over. A cloud of black smoke belched from the back of the bus, drifted along its side, the smell of diesel wafting through the open windows. How old was this rust bucket? Old enough to break down every two or three weeks.

'Floor it, retard!' shouted some smart-arse from the back seats. 'Gun it!'

There was no response from the driver, just the grinding of gears and the bus lurching into motion.

They weren't even out of town, just heading south on the highway, passing over the irrigation canal, when Gene cranked his trannie up loud as it would go, tinny speaker distorting. 'Shush!' hollered the bloke seated behind him. 'Shut up, you dickheads!' Voices fell silent, not at the command but at the sound of acoustic guitar, drifting treble and distinctive through the throng followed by the all-too-familiar vocals: '*Most people I know think that I'm cray-zeee-yee-ee-eee.*'

'Thorpie!' yelled Larry Doherty—'Larry the Loser'—who immediately started playing air guitar, head down, long hair swaying from side to side, acne-riven face distorted with passion.

There was a moment of silence, and then, from nowhere, someone started singing. '*I know at times I act a little hay-zee-yee-ee-ee.*' Then, as if led by some unseen conductor, the whole bus was singing. '*In every way help me to show-ow ii-ii-ii-it.*' And for a few joyous minutes, the bus was bonded as one as it rumbled along the highway, the out-of-tune and overheated student choir of Hatheson High School. The song ended and a cheer erupted. Gene couldn't wipe the smile from his face, and Tessa thought it made him look like a dickhead. But she liked Gene, liked his shyness, and felt good for him.

By the time the bus had travelled ten miles out of town, Tessa was sitting next to him, the bus almost empty now, the transistor off. Thorpie had been followed by Neil Diamond, and the howls of derision had silenced the portable radio and moderated Gene's grin. Soon they passed out of range but Gene kept holding the trannie, not putting it in his rough canvas satchel.

'I should have asked for a cassette player,' he said.

'As if.'

'Yeah. As if. Have you seen one?'

'Of course.' It wasn't quite true; she had seen ads for them in the *Western Explorer*. She stole a glance at Gene. He was almost finished fourth form, almost a senior, a year above her despite being only a few months older. She could see the man in him, where he had so recently been a boy. She could smell him as well; she could smell everyone in this baking-dish bus. 'For your birthday?'

'Nah. A reward.'

'For what?'

'Next year. Staying at school.'

'You're going to fifth form?' She could hear the surprise in her own voice, couldn't imagine why anyone would voluntarily stay at school.

'Yeah,' he replied, almost sheepishly. 'You?'

'Nah. But I'll be back next year, finish fourth form. Seems stupid to drop out before then.'

'Plenty do.'

'I know. I'm almost sixteen, I could if I wanted. It's legal.'

'Not tempted?'

'Very tempted.' She looked beyond him, out the window. From this side of the bus, the right-hand side, there was nothing to see but the wide flat lands of the Riverina, wheat tall and golden, ready for harvest. Some paddocks were already nothing but stubble, grazed by sheep. A willy-willy carved across a newly ploughed field, red dust flying. 'But Mum reckons I'll be better off with a School Certificate. Easier to get work. Show I'm not dumb.'

'But not seniors?'

'Why would I? Why are you?'

Gene looked down at his transistor, as if to reassure himself, as if embarrassed. 'They reckon I can go to uni.'

'Your parents?'

'Mostly Mum.'

'Uni? You serious?'

'Uh-huh.'

'Fuck. Really? Where?'

'Dunno. Sydney. Melbourne. They reckon there's even one in Canberra.'

'Jeez. Your olds must be loaded.'

'Nah. It's going to be free. Gough Whitlam says that from next year anyone can go, now he's prime minister. It was an election promise.'

'Bullshit. Really?'

'The old man wasn't so sure at first. Says Whitlam's a commie.' He smiled, maybe to show he didn't take his father too seriously. 'But free is free.'

Tessa pivoted around, spotting Gene's brother Grainger, up on the back seat with a couple of other seniors, like small emperors on their thrones, legs spread as if they reckoned someone would be interested. There were only about a dozen sixth formers in the whole school. She turned back. 'What about Grainger?'

'Yeah, he's thinking about it too. He reckons Whitlam's a secular saint.'

'He does?' She had no idea what her own parents thought of the Labor leader. Not a lot, she imagined.

'Sure, ever since Gough canned the draft. Grainger's nineteen next year.'

Tessa couldn't help it: she turned and looked again at Grainger and his friends. They seemed so cocky, so confident. She remembered their older brothers. They'd been the same, right up until the lottery, right up until the plane to Vietnam. 'Good for Whitlam,' she said.

The bus creaked to a stop. Without looking, she knew where they were—halfway between Hatty and Tulong—and who was getting off: the Thompson twins, their mother waiting in their ritzy Valiant at the farm gate. Lucky them.

'What about Tycho?' she asked, referring to the eldest of the Buchanan brothers, almost twenty, the best-looking one; the one all the girls fancied. 'Will he go to uni?'

'Nah, no need,' said Gene. 'He's got a job already. Newspaper reporter.'

'No shit, a reporter? That's so cool. Where?'

'Hatty. The *Western Explorer*.'

'Wow.' Her father got the *Explorer*, but she never read it. Too boring. She just looked at the ads, what was on at the movies. She decided she needed to look out for Tycho's articles.

Half an hour later, the bus was almost empty: just Gene, Grainger and herself left, plus the end-of-the-liners from Boonlea. The ancient vehicle ground to a stop outside Tulong's new bus shelter, brakes squealing. She stood and let Gene exit, then sat by the window and watched as he and Grainger slouched away, shirts out and long hair swaying. She could see the distant wrecks of the Buchanan junkyard shimmering under the afternoon sun. As the bus was getting underway again, Gene turned and waved. She didn't wave back, unsure who he was waving to.

Another six miles, and it was her stop. No one was there to pick her up at the end of the farm drive, no fancy car. There never was. She was grateful for it. It gave her time to herself before having to contend with her mother. Besides, it wasn't so far, only half a mile, although she could do with a drink after the baked-oven bus. She could see the house in the distance, floating on its slight rise above the wheatfields, glowing in the sunlight, framed by the dark treetops of the forest. She started walking towards it, but was halted by a snake, long and sinuous, writhing its way across the dirt drive. She watched it, fascinated. Looked like a tiger. A big one. Full of field mice, no doubt. Good year, plenty of tucker. She edged closer, watched as it carved into the field. Beautiful, really—all the more so for being so deadly. Maybe that was what gave it such presence. That menace, that venom. She reminded herself to wear boots if she went walking at night.

She kept going, but instead of entering the house she continued past it to the edge of the tilt, towards the treetops, their green edging above the incline. The geological fault was like the edge of the world, sitting just a hundred yards further on from the house: the Cadell Tilt. Beyond it the ground fell away, not sharply, not abruptly, but rather gently, the fracture in the land smoothed by hundreds of years of erosion. The great uplift of land, a hundred miles long, was only twenty or thirty feet high, but it was enough. Enough to dam the Murray, enough to divert it, enough to split it, enough to create the great forest. She stood atop it, on the edge, looking out over the immensity of trees. It stretched as far as the eye could see, out to the horizon, like a promise, like a mystery: Barmah-Millewa, the biggest redgum forest in the world, at her feet. She breathed it in, its wildness, its size. A flock of cockatoos, brilliant white and raucous, swooped in, alighting in a treetop almost at her eye level, screeching away irreverently. She longed to be down in the forest. She knew it would be cooler where there was shade, where there was water, where the colours were darker and more muted, away from the razor sun of the plain. She wished she was deep within it, at the river or, even better, at the regulator, swimming in the lush cool water.

University. She shook her head. Just another school. Only bigger. Full of rich arseholes. What was the point of that, putting yourself through that, sitting on the sidelines watching them with their cars and their clothes and their condescension? She turned and headed towards her home, the weatherboard box in the wheatfields above the forest. Her mother would have chores waiting; she always did.

chapter five

THE REDGUM MOTEL, JUST DOWN THE TILT FROM THE HIGHWAY, IS FULL, a no-vacancy sign illuminated in the twilight. It doesn't deter Nell. She parks outside reception and leads the way inside, Ivan following. It's a small room, with no one behind the counter. There's a bell with a sign: RING IF UNATTENDED. Nell rings; rings again. While they wait, she looks about. There's a map on one wall showing the Barmah-Millewa Forest, Tulong sitting at its western edge. There are a few brochures in a dusty stand next to the window advertising forest walks, kayak hires, steamboat cruises. All the attractions are located in Echuca or Boonlea or Hatheson or Anglers Reach. Nothing in Tulong itself.

Eventually there's the sound of a door closing and a crotchety-looking old bloke emerges: unshaven and bleary-eyed and wearing a polo fleece that hasn't seen the inside of a washing machine anytime lately. He doesn't bother with small talk.

'We're full. Whaddya want?' His voice is sibilant, his mouth missing teeth.

'Are you John? The manager?' asks Nell.

'What if I am?'

'I rang this morning. Early. Left a message, booking two rooms. Buchanan and Lucic.'

'I didn't get no message.'

'Did you check?' It's been a long day and Nell can feel her ire rising.

'Why would I? I told you, we're full,' the man says, as if talking to an idiot. 'First time in three years. Contractors working on the regulator, a team from Telstra, a travelling salesman and a gaggle of twitchers.'

'Twitchers?' asks Ivan.

Nell glares at him.

'Birdwatchers,' says the manager. 'Wet spring, river spilling. Birds come from all over, attracted by the wetlands. The twitchers follow. Never seen so many.' He points behind them. 'See?' There is a small A4 flyer pinned to a noticeboard beside the door. *Reward*, it states, above a blurry picture of a seemingly nondescript bird. *Painted Snipe. $200 for a sighting leading to photography.*

'Any other accommodation in town?' asks Ivan.

'The pub. Pretty rough. You might be better off in Hatty or Boonlea.'

'You just full tonight, or all week?' asks Nell.

'Don't know. Leave me your number, I'll let you know if anything comes up.'

'Does the pub serve food?' asks Ivan.

'Yeah, but you want to be quick. Kitchen closes early on Sundays.'

—

The Foresters Arms sits at one end of the main street, a block back from the Hatheson–Boonlea highway. It's postcard perfect, a traditional Aussie pub, two storeys with a wraparound verandah. Nell feels her spirits lift; it might prove better than the motel anyway. A bit of country character. There's a sign promising accommodation, but the door to reception is closed. ALL INQUIRIES AT BAR, says a printed sign taped inside the glass.

The front bar is quiet, no one staffing it, three rough-looking blokes at a table, the one facing them offering a sneer even while struggling to focus above his half-empty schooner. The only other customer sits at the far end of the room: a solitary man with a beard and glasses, wearing an anorak and nursing a small wineglass, perhaps port, perhaps sherry. But it's not the customers that seizes Nell's attention, it's the decor. There's a Red Ensign, framed behind glass, hanging upside down above the fireplace, smeared with signatures. A Eureka flag is pinned above the bar, next to a repurposed Solidarity flag from Poland. There's a television screen mounted above the fireplace: Sky News with the sound turned down, a middle-aged man leaning into the camera, lecturing the world. Elsewhere, among the usual sporting images and brewery merchandise, she can see a STOP THE STEAL sign, a photo of Donald Trump and, behind the bar, a red MAGA baseball cap. There's a placard, souvenired from a rally—OUR KIDS ARE NOT LAB RATS—and another next to it: TRUST GOD, NOT BURROCRATS. She can sense Ivan on alert; the three men at the table have all turned to look at them now, radiating hostility. She recognises it, that unspoken animosity towards police, familiar to her from her uniform days.

She and Ivan are in plain clothes, but the drinkers have clocked them easily enough. In the corner, anorak man raises his sherry glass in a mock welcome, as if amused by their discomfort. Ivan frowns, looking more puzzled than irritated.

'Help you?' It's a large man, appearing behind the bar. He has a face like a slab of marble, white and veined with pink, topped with a strawberry-blond mullet so thickly woven it could be a doormat. His chin has vanished beneath a bright orange beard that has run wild, spreading down and across his barrel chest. He has eyes like blue marbles. Give him horns and he could be a Viking.

'We're after a room and a feed,' says Ivan, apparently deciding Nell is equipped to deal with motel owners but not Eric the Red.

The barman looks at Ivan then Nell, scanning her up and down like he's at a sales yard. 'One room or two?'

'Two.'

'Motel full, then?' asks the barman.

'Twitchers,' says Ivan.

'Plague proportions,' says the barman, dispensing a disparaging glance in the direction of anorak man. 'I've got rooms, but nothing flash. Bathrooms and toilets at the end of the corridor.'

'We'll take them. Just one night for starters.'

'You coppers?'

Ivan blinks. 'That a problem?'

'No, mate. Coppers always welcome here. My old man, my grandfather, both in the force.' And he smiles. At least, Nell thinks he does; his beard badly needs trimming.

'Locals?' asks Ivan, his posture relaxing a touch.

'Old man out at Coota, grandfather in Hatty. Not detectives, nothing flash, but a credit.' He offers his hand across the bar. 'Noel Tankard,' he says.

'Ivan.'

'Nell.'

The hand is huge and meaty, swallowing hers.

'Kitchen is already closed, but I can rustle you up a burger or a steak. Maybe even defrost a schnitzel.'

Ivan selects the steak, Nell the burger.

'Right. I'll get your keys. You can go up, get settled. Food in about twenty.'

—

Nell's room is basic. Just a single bed, springs gone and a mattress like the Bungle Bungles. A wardrobe of pressed wood and peeling veneer. No table, no chair, nowhere obvious for her suitcase. No pictures on the wall, no mirror; just a copy of the Innkeepers Act on the door. She checks the sheets: clean, if worn. She wonders if they might be better off up at Hatty, with Blake and the Albury police, but Ivan had been insistent on being as close to the scene as possible. Maybe he'll change his mind after a night here.

Back downstairs, the bar is empty. The burly men have gone, so too the twitcher. Noel emerges from the back rooms, offers her a drink, and she orders a white wine. He doesn't ask her preferred variety before dispensing from a twenty-litre cask propped inside a glass-fronted fridge, the generous size of her glass compensating for the uncertain provenance.

'Interesting posters,' she comments.

'Yeah. We get all sorts here.'

'Such as?'

'Preppers, hippies, cookers. Harmless enough.'

'Cookers?'

'Anti-vaxxers, conspiracy theorists, gun nuts. QAnon and contrails. Don't know why they're called that.'

Ivan appears, requesting a beer and inserting himself into the conversation. 'Who was that twitcher?' he asks Noel.

'Don't know. Comes in most nights, sits there with a glass of sherry, just one. Does the crosswords. Not staying here. Why?'

Ivan shrugs. 'Looked familiar somehow.'

'Quiet as a mouse. Wish the rest of the punters were as peaceful.' The large man heads back out to finish their meals.

The food is surprisingly good, Ivan commenting more than once on the quality of the steak. It's only when they've finished and returned to the bar, propped on stools for a nightcap, that the conviviality vanishes. The publican brings out the register for them to sign for their rooms, an old-fashioned book, pen and ink. Ivan signs in first, then Nell. The barman reads the names. And freezes.

'Narelle Buchanan?'

'Correct.'

His blue-pebble eyes are peering at her. The shape of his mouth is camouflaged by his beard, but there is no mistaking the belligerence in his voice. 'Tell me you're not related to that old bitch in the junkyard.'

'My grandmother,' says Nell. 'We're not close.'

But if she was hoping that might lessen his hostility, it doesn't work. He looks at her with disgust. 'Fuck me. The Buchanans.

You're one of them.' He's almost spitting his words now. 'Wouldn't have let you stay if I'd known.'

Later, alone in her hotel room, Nell sits on the sagging bed, staring at her phone. Now that she's so close, it feels harder than she imagined. She probably should have called earlier. Too late to worry about that. She dials, manually selecting the digits, knowing the number by heart. The ringtone comes through, somehow old-fashioned, suggesting the outmoded landline handset she remembers so well. She stands, sees herself reflected in the windowpane, image distorted by grime. What's that she sees in her eyes? Trepidation? She's not wearing her pistol; there is no gunslinger swagger, just a young woman with her hair cut short and practical. She can imagine her mother's disapproval: *Nell, you look like a boy.* The call rings out, switches to voicemail. No, not voicemail: an answering machine. She can hear it whirling, the hiss of a tape. Like her parents, stuck somewhere in the past.

'*You've called the Buchanan residence.*' Her father's voice, stilted, straining to sound authoritative. '*Tessa and Grainger can't come to the phone right now. Please leave a message after the beep.*' And then a pause, some fumbling, before the beep finally sounds.

'Dad. Mum. It's Nell. I'm in Tulong. For work. An investigation. I'll try to get down to see you when I have a moment.' She regards her reflection. 'Love you.'

She's sitting on the bed, room growing darker, still holding her phone, when it rings. The screen glows, identifies her parents' number. She keeps her voice official as she answers. 'Detective Constable Narelle Buchanan.'

'Nell, it's Mum. You're here?'

'Close enough. Tulong.'

'Don't be silly. Come and stay with us. Your room is still here. Bed all made up.'

'I'm on duty, Mum. We need to be here. But I'll come down first chance I get.'

'What's in Tulong?'

'A body. Found in the forest. A skeleton in a creek.'

There's a silence. She can sense her mother tensing, holding her breath, before she speaks again. 'The regulator that was blown up by the environmentalists?'

'That's the one.'

'But why you?'

Nell swallows. 'I've had a promotion. Homicide.'

'Oh,' says her mother, and then nothing more for as long as it takes Nell to stand and walk to the window. Outside, beyond the verandah, the street is empty. 'Do you have to . . .' Her mother's words tail off, the implication of the news sinking in.

'Do I have to what?' Nell feels the irritation edging into her own voice. 'Look at the body?'

'Yes.' Her mother sounds small.

'It's the job, Mum.'

Her mother doesn't respond.

'It's just a skeleton. Nothing to see.'

'Nell . . .'

What's that she hears in her mother's voice? Foreboding? Or censure? 'I have to go, Mum,' she lies. 'I'll come see you soon.'

'Please do. We'd like that. Your brothers and sisters too.'

'Of course.'

After the call is finished, Nell sits for another long moment in the gloom. She and Ivan could have stayed at Boonlea; it's just half an hour south. There's the river, the irrigated gardens, Echuca just across the bridge with restaurants and bars and shops, the tourist paddle steamers lined up at the wharf. Modern motels with ensuites and mattresses from this century. But Ivan wanted to be here and she was quick to agree, glad of the distance between her and her family.

chapter six

NELL IS UP WITH THE SUN, TRAINING GEAR ON. TULONG IS STILL ASLEEP; SHE wonders if it ever wakes. The town sits flat and exposed on the long plain above the tilt, its trees punctuation marks lacking a narrative. Beyond the houses to the west there is nothing: no hills, no distant ranges, just endless wheatfields stretching to the horizon. She jogs the other way, to the east. A truck rumbles through on the highway, heading south from Hatheson towards the border. Across the highway, at the town's edge, the land tips over the Cadell Tilt and falls into the forest, the great redgum woodland.

Nell jogs down the incline and finds a different version of the world: shaded, cooler, softer. A sign carved into a solid slab of wood marks the entry to Clarrie Buchanan Park. The lawn is freshly mown, still giving up its scent. There are magpies, searching for breakfast worms or warbling at the sight of a sprinkler. The park sits beside a creek extending all the way from the Murray, a special dispensation for the town. Two black swans and a flotilla of minor birds glide towards her, looking for a handout, their shapes mirrored in its surface. Trees stretch out above the water, a protective canopy. There are barbecues and picnic tables and an old hall of peeling weatherboards and an iron roof. TULONG MEMORIAL HALL, says the sign above the door; TULONG SCOUTS, says the sign next to it. Beyond it, there's a water treatment plant behind wire fencing, a small red-brick bunker without windows but with pipes leading from the creek.

A little further along the creek, across the forest road, she can see movement. She walks over, checks it out. A campground, well patronised even before summer. A few early risers are up and about, preparing breakfast on tabletop gas stoves. There are small tents of red and orange and blue, large family affairs and even bigger ones that look semi-permanent, like small homes, constructed of heavy canvas, tall enough to stand in, decked out with solar panels and water tanks and satellite dishes. It's like a village, with its own avenues and byways, linking clearings with fire pits and logs pulled up for seating. There are Australian flags everywhere, and among them the Southern Cross of Eureka, the Red Ensign, a Confederate flag. Twin-cab utes with oversized bull bars and too many driving lights are parked nearby, bearing bumper stickers and back-window slogans: *Birdsville* and *Port Pirie* and *Bundaberg Rum* mixed with *Stop the Vax!* and *Fuck Off, We're Full* and *Trump 24*. A couple have the letter 'Q' fashioned from a snake eating itself. Cookers. Nell wonders if they've washed up here for good or if it's a temporary refuge.

A woman passes, walking her dog. 'Morning, love. Beautiful day.'

'Yes. Morning.'

Nell returns to the park, starts moving through her martial arts drills, stilling her mind, concentrating on breathing, on flexing. Karate, judo, taekwondo, she moves through elements of each—even a touch of kung fu. Her own mix. She moves slowly, a meditation; she moves quickly, an explosion. It calms her, centres her. She goes through the sequences, feeling all the better for the routine.

She's almost finished when Ivan emerges from a path beside the creek, coming from the direction of the campground. He's running hard, a final sprint to finish his jog, face and arms glistening. That has to be a good sign, she thinks. Maybe he's shedding his malaise at last.

'Check out the cookers?' she asks as he comes to a stop, wiping the sweat from his brow with the back of his hand.

He grimaces. 'Of course.'

'Thoughts?'

Ivan shrugs. 'Nothing to do with us.'

'I can't work out what they're on about.'

He laughs at that. 'If I find out, I'll let you know.' It's nice to hear the humour in his voice, his annoyance at being handed such a dated case apparently eased by a good night's sleep.

'See you at the station?' she says.

He looks at his watch. 'Eight thirty?'

'Sounds good.'

——

The Tulong police station is a repurposed house, small and functional, a one-person station made of weatherboards, painted an inoffensive grey. It's on the highway, only the blue-and-white sign indicating its function. That and its forty-metre radio mast.

The resident officer, a senior constable, is there to meet them. Kevin Nackangara, part Aboriginal, heritage evident in the broad features of his face. His hair is dark and curly and a little long, and he wears an amused expression, seemingly as a default, as if life should not be taken overly seriously. When they shake hands, Nell notices his left hand is bandaged.

'Nothing serious, I hope,' she says.

'Minor run-in at the campground. Drunk and disorderly. Nothing I couldn't handle.'

'Right,' says Nell, but she's thinking of the Confederate flag, a sole officer, the nearest backup a half-hour away.

'You local?' asks Ivan.

'That a joke, mate?' For a moment the air freezes, the constable's face serious, tone challenging. And then he instantly thaws, melting into a smile, indicating he's joking. 'Nah. North Coast. This is a different planet to me.'

Nell can see Ivan struggle to adjust; banter and small talk aren't his strong suit. 'Like it?'

'Fucking cold in winter.'

'So why come here?'

Kevin looks like he might say something flippant, then he appears to think better of it, and his response sounds genuine. 'Good career move. Run my own show. Demonstrate I'm up to it.'

'Fair enough.'

Kevin turns to Nell. 'Heard you were in Bourke.'

'Three years.'

'Tough job. The brothers give you much grief?'

'Some. Same as everyone else.'

'They keep offering it to me.' He shrugs. 'Blackfellas policing blackfellas. They like the sound of that.'

'Happy to talk you through it,' says Nell.

'Thanks. I'd appreciate that.'

He gives them a tour. It takes no time; there's little to see: an office, which is his, and a squad room, which is theirs—three desks, telephones, a television and a bar fridge. As if the place was designed for a four-person team. Just in case. A toilet and a kitchen. A door through to Kevin's private quarters, the back half of the house. There's an interview room and, next to it, a holding cell. And out front, a reception area with a counter and a few tired chairs.

Ivan points to an A4 notice, laminated and pinned to a noticeboard on the wall beside the counter. It has a blurry photo of a youngish man with a blond beard, wearing sunglasses and a baseball cap. *Missing Person. Jean-Luc Hoffner. Have you seen this man? Tulong Police.*

'What's this?' asks Ivan.

'Cooker,' says Kevin. 'Went missing a few months back. Same week the regulators got taken out.'

Nell can see the speculation in her partner's eyes as he asks, 'Any connection?'

'Don't think so. His car was found in Melbourne. Tullamarine.'

'The airport?'

'Yeah, but the last time he was definitely sighted was here. His parents ring every week or so, just to check.'

'Was he with the rest of them? At the campground?'

'Yep. Tent was still there, with some of his stuff. Some in the car, too, and some missing.'

'Sounds like trouble, the whole set-up,' says Ivan.

'Nah,' says Kevin. 'They're harmless enough, most of 'em.'

'Most of them?' asks Nell.

'We get the occasional skinhead. The Vics had real problems in Barmah last autumn. Neo-Nazis. Serious shit. But there's been nothing approaching that here. A few tinfoil hat wearers, that's about it. Think I'm deep state.'

'Any of them likely to blow up a regulator?' asks Ivan.

'Can't see why they would.'

'Any thoughts who might?'

'Albury suspects greenies.'

'Any activists around here?'

'Not unless you count the twitchers.'

Ivan sighs. 'Any theories who the skeleton is?'

'Hang on.' Kevin goes into his office and returns with printouts. He gives Ivan a sheet of paper. 'I've done a bit of legwork for you. Missing persons. Adult men. Every local who has vanished since the regulator was built in the thirties.' He hands over a second sheet. Nell catches a glimpse of the Victorian coat of arms. 'Same thing, from across the river.'

'Impressive,' says Ivan, scanning the lists. He passes the papers to Nell, then addresses Kevin again. 'Tell me about the regulator,' he says, taking a seat at one of the vacant desks. 'The explosion.'

The constable takes a seat of his own. 'Three months ago. Went off in the middle of the night. No one heard a thing. Underwater charge, river side, would have been muffled. Depths of winter, so no campers or bushwalkers or kayakers. Wasn't until dawn that people noticed the forest was filling with water and I started getting calls. River management knew nothing, so I went out. Probably an hour after dawn when I got there. The closer I got, the more water there was. The access road was okay, raised just high enough, but surrounded by water. I guessed it wasn't a planned release; there was too much, too quickly. I thought the regulator must have failed, but when I got there, half the wall was gone. Water was pounding through, pushing up the creek. Nothing I could do about that, of course. But I sealed it off with crime scene tape, called it in. The detectives didn't muck about, came in from Albury, same day. We made sure we gave it a thorough search before letting the water mob in. They didn't get down until the day after.'

'Find anything useful?' Ivan asks.

'One thing. A pair of swimming goggles, sitting behind a big river redgum.'

'Signifying?'

'Middle of winter. Strange time to be swimming.'

'Left by the bomber?'

'That's the theory.'

'You got them here?'

'The detectives from Albury took them. They'll be in their evidence locker.'

'Fingerprints? DNA?'

'Nah, they were clean. Fairly small, though. Might have been a woman. Or a kid.' He grins. 'Or a pinhead.'

'Right. Anything else out there?'

'Nothing useful.'

'And now?'

'Albury came back across yesterday, as soon as I let them know about the body. Staying at Boonlea. They'll be back at the regulator this morning.' Kevin looks at Nell, eyebrows tilted in the suggestion of a frown. 'Contact details are in your brief.' She knows what he must be thinking: Ivan should already know this, know about the goggles.

'What did Albury conclude?' asks Ivan, unperturbed. 'In August?'

'That it was deliberate. Industrial explosives. Same thing happened across the river.'

'The Murray, right? The border. It flows past here.'

Kevin smiles. 'Sure. Through the forest. Winds south, past the choke, down to Boonlea and Echuca.'

'The choke?'

Kevin looks again at Nell; he knows she's local, that she must know this. But he continues, for Ivan's benefit. 'Geological anomaly. An uplift of land. The Cadell Tilt. Runs right past town here, north–south, dams the Murray. The river splits up: the Edward to the north, the Murray to the south. It gets real shallow where it's found its way across the tilt; that's the choke. If they put too much water down, it flows over the banks and into the forest. If there was no choke, there'd be no forest.'

Ivan turns to Nell and she nods her endorsement of the summation. She holds out the sheets of paper with the lists of missing persons. They quickly scan the list from Victoria. There are nine names.

1941—Lawrence Seabourne, age 18

1943—Major Gerard Stannard, age 52

1943—Lieutenant Eamon Finucane, age 22

1952—Harold Ducketty, age 63

1962—Vince Lombardi, age 30

1973—Reginald Waters, age 75

1974—Patrick Jones, age 23

1988—James 'Jamie' Boots, age 46

1996—Trevor Mackingham, age 16

'The pathologist told me not to bother with anyone this century,' explains Kevin.

'Yes. Seems the skeleton has been there for decades,' replies Ivan.

They turn their attention to the New South Wales list.

1938—Glenn Cockburn, age 48

1941—Montgomery 'Monty' Bell, age 33

1943—Brendan Flannery, age 22

1955—Joel Fortescue (1955 floods), age 24

1973—Tycho Buchanan, age 19

1988—Stavros Notaras, age 20

1990—William 'Billy' Dugdale, age 84

2001—Lee Siu 'Johnny' Wong, age 28

Ivan turns his eyes to her, unblinking. 'Tycho Buchanan?'

'My uncle.'

'Seriously?'

'Yep. It's pronounced Tie-co.'

She feels her partner's gaze upon her. Tycho: long gone. More than twenty years before she was born. It hadn't occurred to her that his name might come up. 'He murdered his father—my grandfather, Bert Buchanan—and went on the run. Sighted in Queensland and Western Australia. Not much chance it's him in the regulator.'

'Says who?'

'There was an inquest. Coroner's finding. Bert was found buried in a shallow grave. Shot dead.'

'I see.' Ivan considers the piece of paper. 'Tycho stays on the list for now.'

'Of course.' It makes her think: a bullet through the skull. She recalls there had been another theory, that both the son and the father had been killed by organised crime figures, that Tycho was also a victim, not a perpetrator. Was that the reason for the trepidation she heard in her mother's voice the previous night? Did she think the body might be his?

'Reginald Waters also went missing in 1973. Any connection?'

Nell sighs. 'Not that I know of. He was some distant relative of my grandfather. Other side of the family.'

Kevin whistles. 'Unlucky mob, your lot.'

Nell smiles. 'Long time ago.'

'Your grandfather?' Ivan probes.

'I mentioned him on the way down. Jimmy Waters. Lives in an old farm a few kilometres south of here above the tilt. Pretty much a recluse these days.'

Ivan says nothing; she can see him considering the information.

Kevin fills the silence. 'If you need a hand with anything else, just let me know.'

'We should be right,' says Ivan.

But the young constable isn't so easily deterred. 'I mean it. If I can be involved at all, I'd be really grateful.'

Ivan realises his mistake, that behind the constable's languid manner lies ambition. 'You want to be a detective?'

Kevin shifts his weight sideways, like a footballer sidestepping a tackle, but meets the directness of Ivan's question head-on. 'Yeah. Like to step up. One day.'

'Sure. We can always do with another set of hands. Another set of eyes.' Ivan flicks his head at the missing persons list. 'This is good work. You've given us a head start.'

Kevin beams. 'Well, I'm off to get some coffees then. What do you want?'

Ivan waits until the constable has left with their orders before turning to Nell. 'What do you suggest?' he asks. 'Way forward?'

'Has to be the teeth. Two gold crowns and a filling. Near enough to unique. I'll work my way through the missing persons list. See if I can get a match for the dental records.'

'Sounds like a plan.'

She considers the list again, then looks at her partner. 'Ivan, what are we doing here?'

'What do you mean?'

'This is routine. Albury could do it. They're not Homicide, but they're detectives. They have the training. There's nothing urgent about this. It all happened years ago.'

Ivan shrugs. 'Plodder's call, not mine.'

chapter seven

JAMES WATERS–FIRST STATEMENT–CONTINUED

MY DAD DIDN'T WANT TO GO TO WAR. NOT BECAUSE HE WAS AFRAID, BUT because he was resentful. I didn't understand it at the time, but I worked it out later. His own father had come back from the first war shattered, as if he'd been broken and then glued back together. That's what my mum said. Before he went, my grandfather was a strong man, one of those who built the levee by hand, earning enough to buy our little farm north of the forest. Afterwards, he was damaged and sullen. Not violent, but cowed; hollowed out. Unrecognisable. Two of his brothers died over there, and it wasn't so long after he got back before he was dead too. I never heard it said out loud, but I reckon he must have killed himself. No one talked about that sort of thing back then. It was taboo.

It devastated the family, fell across my dad like a long shadow. There had been four boys before the Great War, the Waters brothers, good at cricket, better at footy, but afterwards there was just my grandfather and Uncle Reg, and then there was only Reg. He was Dad's uncle, not mine, the last of the Waters boys, the youngest. He'd call in every now and then to help us out. I liked Uncle Reg; he was always cheerful. Always whistling or singing some jaunty tune or another. He used to bring me a single strap of licorice in a brown paper bag. It tasted of molasses and aniseed. I could make that strap last a whole week. For some reason, Uncle Reg seemed unaffected by all he'd been through. That's what I thought, but maybe he was just better at hiding it.

Others talked about the Great War, the war to end all wars, but not my father. He'd buried it in the past and kept his eyes on the future and his faith in progress. I think that's why he approved of the steam shovel and the regulator: he thought we could progress beyond what had gone before, that civilisation was outgrowing such barbarities. And then it was back. At first it was like a whisper, a rumour. It wasn't discussed at home, but at school we talked about nothing else, especially after the Germans invaded Poland and we declared war. We sat hushed as our teacher told us about Hitler and Churchill and our soldiers off to fight in North Africa. They even reckoned the cricket could be cancelled, the Ashes, so we knew it was serious. At school, it was like an exciting adventure, something from a book. All that year, 1940, and the next, it was like an unfolding story.

But Europe wasn't Paris and London to our family, it wasn't the Roman Empire and the Napoleonic wars. It was the Somme. I reckon that the men who went to the First World War were full of optimism, thinking it was maps and heroics and medals. Poor sods. Not so those who went to the next war; they knew what they were getting themselves into, that some wouldn't survive and some would be wounded and some would be damaged forever. So Dad reckoned he wasn't going, not with two kids, me and my little sister; not with the farm to work. He said that our family had given enough blood—let the Poms and the Frogs and the Krauts sort it out. But it wasn't easy. There was one night, I heard Mum and Dad arguing. That was unusual. Much later, I learnt what had happened: we'd received a white feather in our letterbox. Dad was angry, simmering, but still he wouldn't go. And he didn't have to: he was a farmer and farmers were exempt. The country needed food, the army needed food, the empire needed food. And that suited Dad fine. 'Nothing to do with us,' he said.

Still, it weighed upon us. We couldn't ignore it, couldn't just shut ourselves off. Men were leaving, rationing was brought in. Those days when he went to town, Dad started buying a paper. He and Mum would study it on the big table in the kitchen, pointing to the maps, talking softly. They'd explain it to me; they wanted me to understand. It all seemed simple: Hitler was bad, Churchill was good. So was Stalin. Funny to think of it now, but Stalin was Uncle Joe, with a bushy moustache and a big smile and he was with us. Dad was elated when the Russians entered the war. 'No need for us,' he said. 'Hitler is for it now.' But Mum wasn't elated. She didn't say anything. I reckon she was worried.

The pressure of not knowing what was happening, between the trips to town and the newspapers, started to get to Mum and Dad. We didn't have a lot of money, but they bought a radio. Uncle

Reg found it for them, got it cheap. A big thing that sputtered and hissed, reception drifting in and out. We must have been on the edge of the transmission area. I remember a valve blew and it took more than a week before we could get it fixed. Cost money, of course, and you needed a technician, and it was the war, so spares were scarce. But they found the money. They were no longer ignoring what was going on; now they needed to know.

The radio was working the day Pearl Harbor was bombed. I came home from school and it was like someone had died. Dad was inside, which he never was in the afternoon. The radio was on, the atlas open on the table. It still seemed so remote to me: Hawaii a tiny dot in the middle of all that blue. I couldn't see why it mattered but I knew that it did, just by my parents' mood. Next day, Dad and I started digging a bomb shelter in the yard, and that night I wet the bed, I was so scared. I'm not ashamed to admit it. In my dreams, the vague and shapeless menace of Europe had been replaced by sharp-fanged yellow men.

The news grew worse, then worse again. Singapore fell and it was as if the entire country went silent. I went to school, expecting the teacher to explain what it meant, but he was gone; he'd signed up, an old guy with a dodgy leg and three kids. A veteran from the first war. Suddenly, the cancellation of the cricket seemed trivial. The Japanese were in New Guinea, they'd taken Rabaul, murdered civilians and soldiers alike. Just like that: walked in and took it, that's what people were saying. And suddenly the distances on the maps didn't seem so large. In the atlas, New Guinea was pink; it was meant to be ours. 'Practically part of Australia,' Dad said. Now it hung over the head of the country like an anvil waiting to drop. My nightmares continued, got worse. Mum and Dad whispered about the Brisbane line.

We finished the bomb shelter just in time, as the Japanese started bombing Darwin—the same battle group that had levelled Pearl Harbor. Day after day they bombed, week after week. The news on the radio was dire, yet somehow we knew they weren't telling us the whole truth. So Dad went to war. He explained it to me, that half our army was in North Africa fighting Rommel, the other half had been taken prisoner in Singapore, that there was no one left, no one to stop them, no one to stop the anvil falling and crushing us all. Just the men who were left, just volunteers, men like him and my teacher: the old, the young and the exempt. And he was gone, just like that.

That summer, before Singapore and before Rabaul, before Dad went to war, he started taking me into the forest with him and we'd camp in there with the cattle. I loved being there with him. It was a different world, away from the war, and he was so strong, so competent. He had a knack of doing things: lighting a camp fire, pitching a tent, tying all sorts of knots. A real bushman. It was a bad year, though, that year: there'd been no rain all summer and there was a severe drought, as if the war wasn't enough. It had already lasted a couple of years and there was next to no feed on the farm. That's why we were grazing the cattle in the forest. Dad told me that in previous years he had just branded them and let them loose, mustering them at the end of summer. But the forest had grown treacherous. All the waterholes were drying up. The cattle would chase the last of the water and get bogged in the mud. We'd already lost a few. So he started going into Millewa with them, and soon he was taking me along.

He showed me some of the safer places: open areas where there was still feed, and a place on the river, Lackmires Beach, with a sandbar, good and shallow, where the cattle could drink. I asked him why they didn't just open up the regulator, let more water into the forest, replenish the creeks and the waterholes, but he said they must need the water elsewhere, for the factories down in Adelaide making munitions and food and clothing. That there was a war on and everything was in short supply, even water. And that seemed kind of right to me: if the world could plunge into conflict, of course we would be in drought. It seemed appropriate. By the end of that summer, before school came back, I was taking the cattle in by myself, camping overnight for a night or two, me and a swag, with the dogs and my pony Lenny.

When Dad enlisted, he said he wouldn't be gone for long. He said he'd be back by Christmas. He was trying to comfort me, but I was horrified. I was ten years old. We'd just had Christmas. The next one was almost a year away; it might as well have been another century. That's when I understood: why he'd been taking me into the forest, showing me what to do. In case I'd have to take the cattle in by myself the next summer. Mum couldn't do everything; she had my little sister, who was just a toddler. The fate of the cattle, of the farm, rested on me. I remember Dad saying to me, 'You'll be right, mate.' Stuff like that. I wanted to cry, but I held it in. Knew it was important. But it all seemed so big: the forest, the responsibility, the cattle. The world. And I felt so small. He was a tough man, my father, a man of strong beliefs, but he looked me in the eye and he pulled me close and hugged me, and in that moment I saw his humanity: his fears and his hopes and his decency. I never loved him more.

After he left for the army, things went from bad to worse. The Japanese seemed unbeatable. They were still bombing Darwin, they shelled Sydney and Newcastle, they put mini-submarines into Sydney Harbour and sank the *Kuttabul*, killed all those sailors. German raiders were lurking in the Bight, picking off our convoys taking food to Britain. The Yanks were edging towards defeat in the Philippines, and we realised that even the Americans couldn't stop the Japs. We were alone, isolated at the bottom of the world. The Poms couldn't help and the Yanks were out of it and Uncle Joe was too busy fighting the Nazis and we were just sitting here, waiting for the anvil to fall.

Mum and I would listen to the radio, but we no longer needed the atlas to explain how dire it all was. We could close our eyes and see the threat coming over the horizon for us. Then one day I came home from school and Mum was crying, tears rolling down her cheeks. Just standing there in the lounge, by the radio, sobbing. I feared the worst, of course. That dread, I carried it with me every day. To school, to my chores, to bed at night and into the forest on the weekends. That's what I felt in that moment: that dread coming down on me, consuming me. Mum couldn't speak, couldn't form the words at first, but her eyes weren't crying, they were laughing. She was weeping with joy.

'The Americans, Jimmy,' she said, when at last she could get the words out. 'They're coming to fight with us. MacArthur is here, he's in Australia.'

And I cried too, and we danced, Mum and me and my little sister, who didn't know why we were so happy. And the man on the radio—they had these very plummy English voices in those days, very proper, but I reckon you could even hear the relief in his voice, like it was cracking a bit—said the commander of Allied forces in the Pacific was to be based in Melbourne. The marines were setting up camp on the MCG. We thought we were saved. We thought my dad was saved. We thought he would be coming home to us.

chapter eight

IVAN HAS TAKEN THEIR FOUR-WHEEL DRIVE AND HEADED ACROSS TO VICTORIA. He wants to see the destruction of the regulator on the southern shore for himself. She's not sure what he imagines he'll find, but Nell knows it's part of his methodology, to walk the ground, to inhale the landscape, to get a feel for things. And to work his way through his mental checklists, eliminating possibilities, narrowing the focus. Establishing a working relationship with the Victorians is only sensible; with no victim on their side of the border, they'll have little incentive to commit significant resources. For them, it's a property crime, a lower priority.

Kevin heads out on his rounds and she has the station to herself. She calls her parents' number once more. Again it rings through to the answering machine. She draws a deep breath, waiting for the beep before speaking. 'Hi. It's Nell again. Can you call me, Dad? I need some advice. Dental records.'

It doesn't take long, maybe a minute, for her father—the recently retired dentist—to return the call. 'Nell. Will we see you? Come to lunch. Today?'

'Sorry, I'm working out of Tulong. I can't just leave.'

'Dinner, then?'

'My sergeant and I are sharing a car. He has first call.'

'I can come and collect you.'

'Dad, I'm working.'

'Okay,' he says, sigh audible. 'Fair enough.'

Is that resentment she hears in his voice? Why is she so hypersensitive to everything her parents say? When did that start?

'What's this about dental records?' asks her father, changing the topic.

She takes another breath, repositioning her attitude: a police officer, not a daughter. 'The body found in the regulator is nothing more than a skeleton. Been there for years. Most likely we'll be relying on dental records for identification.'

'I see.'

She swallows. 'Dad, your brother—Tycho. Did he have gold crowns, a gold filling?'

There is a moment, a pause, a heartbeat. 'No. No way.'

'You're sure?'

'He was nineteen, too young for crowns. And I'd remember gold.'

'Right. Well, that's a relief.'

There's no reply.

'Dad? You still there?'

'You'd think so, wouldn't you?' he says.

'Sorry, I don't follow.'

'You'd think it would be a relief that it's not him. I'm glad it's not, but part of me would like to know what did happen to him. He just disappeared. It would mean a lot to your grandmother if we could bury him. She still wonders about him.'

'Of course. I understand.' She thinks of the inquest, the finding that Tycho was most likely a murderer, a fugitive. Did the old lady refuse to believe it? 'How is Grandmother?'

'Soldiering on. Heart's a bit dicky and she needs a walker some of the time. Hardly leaves the house. But her mind is sharp as a tack. She'd love to see you. She's still there, you know. In Tulong. A two-minute walk from the police station.'

'Right.' She recalls the publican's animosity, decides the subject isn't worth broaching with her father.

'These gold teeth,' he says. 'Were they visible? Usually, you wouldn't bother with gold for the back teeth.'

'One was top-right front, the other the top-left canine. The filling was on one of the lower molars.'

'Memorable then.' She can almost hear her father thinking. 'I've retired, you know that. But you want me to go into the practice, see what I can find in the records?'

'How far back do they go?'

'Way before me. Back to the war at least. Old Henry, the bloke I bought the practice from, he had it for years. Never threw anything out. Even had a foot-powered drill in the storeroom.'

'Jesus. You ever use it?'

'You joking? I'd be indicted.'

'Were you the only dentist in Boonlea?'

'The only practice, yeah. Couple across the river in Echuca. A few more up in Hatty.'

'Any here in Tulong?'

'No. Not that I know of.'

'Thanks, Dad. That would be helpful. I've got a missing persons list—I'll email it through. One or two might have been patients there. You can check them off against the records, let us know if you can rule any of them out.'

'Happy to help. I'm sure the others will be as well.'

'I'll be calling them.'

'Nell . . .' The tone of his voice changes. 'Come and see us. It would mean so much to your mother.'

'I'll get down as soon as I can.'

The call ends. She will visit her parents; of course she will. So why does it feel more like an obligation than a pleasure? Because she knows all too well the mix of unspoken disapproval and concern that will greet her promotion to Homicide? Or is it because she's embarrassed by her mother's affliction, doesn't like to confront it? Surely she has moved beyond that.

She emails her father the missing persons list then starts searching for dentists online; there's one in Boonlea, three in Echuca, four in Hatheson. She makes a list of phone numbers and emails. Then she calls Blake and leaves a message, requesting he send through an accurate dental chart of the victim so that she can pass it on to the dentists together with the list of missing men.

While she waits to hear from Blake, she walks the town. There's not a lot to walk. Along the highway there is a petrol station and a park with a local area map, a toilet block, a bus stop leaning at a precarious angle and a rusting steel sculpture of a Murray cod. The rest of the town is a chequerboard of houses and vacant blocks, fading into fields at its periphery, like an illusion-free Escher.

At its centre lies the main street, Highgate Street, running parallel to the highway, one block long, one block back. It stretches from the Foresters Arms on one southern corner to the Golden Sheaf at its northern end. Nell wonders at the division: did the sawmillers and forestry workers once drink in one pub, and the farmers and their farmhands in the other? If so, there must have been more money in wood than in grain. The Golden Sheaf is one storey, squat, with a bullnose awning, while the Foresters Arms revels in two-storey elegance, its wide verandah boasting iron lacework. And the Golden Sheaf is closed—not just for the day, but padlocked and shuttered. Nell can see there were once more pubs, at least three or four, proud on their street corners, converted to houses now. It must have been quite the town, back when the forest was full of cattle and logging, when it was an important staging point between Boonlea and Hatheson, when machines were yet to replace manpower. Now Tulong has just one pub left and, from what Nell has seen, even that depends in part on the custom of cookers and twitchers.

She leaves the main street and continues west. Two more blocks and the houses are almost gone, giving way to agistment paddocks. The Buchanan junkyard looms large. It sits between the town and the fields, half a block packed with wrecked vehicles. It looks much the same as it always has, a wall of rusting cars piled on top of each other round the periphery, like a fortification. The drive is still there, with its gate, the old sign fading: BUCHANAN'S METAL AND SPARES. It gives the impression the entire block is submerged beneath cars, but Nell knows better. She knows that inside the wall, there are the old work sheds and the broken compactor, and the grand house of her grandmother Rita, like a palace protected by broken steel battlements. She could call in, say hello. But she doesn't. Instead she returns to Highgate Street.

In the block between the two pubs, there's an Anglican church, St Paul's, built of bluestone and, inevitably, across and along, the Catholic St Peter's, built of red brick. Both look in reasonable repair. Not so the rest of main street. There are shops closed, shops for lease, shops slowly sinking, weighed down by too many years and buoyed by too few customers. One or two have been converted to homes. The signage on some of the failed businesses is still evident: a butcher, a fruit and vegetable store. There's a shuttered cafe: the Olympus Milk Bar. She peers in through the windows. The counter is still there, so are the booths, the wide floorboards, an old jukebox. A memory comes to her of sitting in a booth, drinking a milkshake in an aluminium container. The jukebox may be worth something; she wonders why some inner-city scavenger hasn't made an offer.

There are some remaining businesses: a second-hand store, clothes and bric-a-brac, open Wednesdays and Saturdays; a lawyer and accountant; a real estate agent. There are a few cars and farm trucks parked at a forty-five degree angle outside the Tulong General Store and its annexe, the Barking Frog Café.

There's no one in the general store as Nell enters, just the smell of dust and cabbage. Necessities line the shelves: bread and condensed milk, washing powder and toothpaste, breakfast cereal and cans of soup, baked beans and fruit salad. Newspapers. There is a glass-fronted fridge with milk, Coke and flavoured drinks on one side and margarine, bacon and kilo blocks of cheddar on the other. One sad corner of the store exhibits a sign, FRESH VEGETABLES, but the broccoli looks soft and limp, and the beans are starting to blemish. Locals must shop at Echuca or Hatheson; this is for emergencies. Past the food there is a whole aisle of camping and fishing gear, everything from lures to mosquito coils and gas cylinders. The cookers must be good for business. But there are signs on the counter: SHOPLIFTERS PROSECUTED and VIDEO SURVEILLANCE and IF UNATTENDED, PLEASE PAY IN BARKING FROG. She checks the ceiling: sure enough, cameras with red-flashing LEDs. Maybe the cookers aren't always good for business.

She passes through the connecting door into the cafe and finds a different world. Here, planters hang from the ceiling, greenery overflowing, the corrugated iron of the roof largely replaced by translucent skylights. Vines climb a trellis mounted on the far wall. There's a chalkboard advertising wraps and organic breads and vegan treats, and glass-domed plates sit on the counter displaying fresh-baked pastries. There are shelves, old bookcases, stocked with exotic vinegars, homemade relishes and organic olive oil. There is music, English folk, purring from ceiling-mounted speakers. And there are people: a couple of grey-haired women chatting at a table, a long-haired man and his son wolfing sandwiches, and a woman behind the counter fussing away at an espresso machine. The wall beside the counter is plastered with flyers for theatre groups and music and art exhibitions down in the river towns or up at Hatty. There is the one seeking sightings of the painted snipe, another requesting information about the missing cooker, Jean-Luc Hoffner. Nell can't help observing that a sighting of the bird is worth two hundred dollars but the missing man will fetch nothing.

'Yes? Coffee?' asks the woman behind the counter with a European accent.

Nell recalls the coffee Kevin had fetched them, how good it tasted, sees the commercial espresso machine. 'A flat white, thanks.'

'You want to eat?'

Nell scans the blackboard, chooses a wrap: baked eggplant, pumpkin, tomato and zucchini with haloumi, baby spinach and a garlic hummus spread.

'Take a seat. I'll bring it over.' And then, almost as an afterthought. 'I am Frieda.'

'Hi, Frieda. Nell.'

'Police?'

Nell smiles. News travels fast in a small town. 'That's right.'

The man and his son leave. The cafe is empty apart from the grey-haired pair, who must be twitchers: they have binoculars and one has an impressive-looking camera. They're dressed in subdued tones of green. One wears a camouflage vest full of pockets, the other a bucket hat.

'Morning,' says Bucket Hat as Nell passes their table.

'Morning,' says Nell. 'Birdwatching?'

'Heading out shortly, yes.'

'After the painted snipe?' asks Nell.

'Among others, yes.' Bucket Hat smiles, flicking a finger towards her camera.

'Is it worth it?' asks Nell. 'Two hundred dollars?'

The women laugh, and Camo Vest replies, 'We don't want the reward. We want to photograph it.'

Nell grins at the thought. 'Competitive, then, is it?'

'Too right it is.' And the smiles broaden.

'What about the missing bloke? You see him about before he disappeared?'

'That was months ago. We only came up last week,' says Camo Vest.

Bucket Hat shrugs. 'Snakebite. Drowned. A crook mushroom.'

'Should never go out alone,' adds her friend. 'Turn an ankle, out of phone range and suddenly you're in strife.'

As Nell takes a seat nearby, her own phone rings. 'Dad.'

'Found him.'

'Sorry?'

'I've found him. Your dead man.'

'What do you mean?'

'Gerard Stannard.'

'Seriously?' She recalls the lists. Victoria, 1943. Major Gerard Stannard.

'Two gold crowns and a filling,' her father says triumphantly.

'That was quick.'

'He's near the top of your list. Thought I'd work through it in chronological order. His was the first record I found.'

'At the practice?'

'That's right. The new bloke, Than Lee, knew where to look. There's a whole filing cabinet of military records. I'd forgotten it was here. Two gold crowns, front top-right, top-left canine. And a gold filling on the bottom-left wisdom tooth.'

Nell recalls Blake's description: an exact match. 'Outstanding. Where are you? Still at the surgery?'

'Yes.'

'I'll be right down.'

'Meet me at home. I'll bring the file with me.'

'No, Dad. Chain of evidence. I'll need to see where it was filed. And I'll need a statement from you as well.'

'No problem. I'm still here. You remember where it is?'

'Of course. I'll come as soon as I can get a car. I'll call when I'm on my way.'

She considers what Blake had told them. A body, male—a victim. No gun, no bullets, so not suicide. Just two holes in his skull, entry wound and exit wound. She sighs, leans back. Major Gerard Stannard has been missing since 1943. He was murdered, not much doubt about that, but how can they investigate a crime eighty years old? She already knows the answer to that: they can't. Any witnesses will be long dead, as will any suspects. Even a twenty-year-old killer would be pushing one hundred now. If the immediate family are dead, if the suspects have died, where is the incentive to investigate? Plodder will want them on contemporary cases, where the grief is still raw, where the families want answers, where the politicians want results. The murder of Major Gerard Stannard is destined for the cold case file.

She walks across to the counter, asks Frieda to package her wrap and coffee for takeaway. Once she has them, she returns to the station. Kevin is back in his office. She asks to borrow his car, tells him why. Then she calls Ivan.

'Major Gerard Stannard,' she says, then explains what her father has told her.

'Your father?'

'Former dentist. Seems Stannard had work done at his old practice in Boonlea.'

'Stannard was your father's patient?'

She laughs at that. 'Don't be ridiculous. My father wasn't even born in 1943.' And that, as much as anything, emphasises to her just how ancient this case is.

—

Boonlea hasn't changed. Why would it? How could it? The town of Nell's youth. Always the lesser town, dominated by Echuca across the river and all that came with it: Victorian football, Victorian beer, Victorian television. Even the railway, crossing the border and stretching up to Hatheson, is run by the Victorians. She parks outside the dental practice; it, at least, has changed. It's still in the same location, on a side street off the highway, nestled into a row of three shopfronts. The new owner has given it a makeover, filling the reception with blond wood, mass-produced art and a smiling young receptionist with translucent braces. Nell's father is looking renovated as well. Retirement suits him: swimming laps, playing golf, eating well. He's sporting a tan and has lost weight. His hair, once mouse brown and perpetually an inch too long, is now grey, thinning and cropped close to his skull. His teeth, of course, are perfect. He could feature in one of those advertisements for all those things that boomers need: cruise ship holidays, funeral insurance, incontinence pads.

'Nell!' he exclaims, giving her a hug and a large smile. Then he holds her at arm's length, looks her over, offers a quick assessment. 'Looking good,' he says. 'Looking fit.'

'You too, Dad. Younger by the day.'

'Come on,' he says. 'Through here.'

He gives a nod to the receptionist and leads Nell down a corridor, past the doors opening on the two surgeries, past a small kitchen, past a room full of office equipment, past the closed door to a storeroom and out the back. There is a new Mercedes SUV parked under a flimsy carport, sporting *Baby on board* and Richmond

Tigers stickers. Her father opens the door to a separate brick building, a storage shed. It's like walking into a small museum: there are old dental chairs and drilling rigs on retractable arms and shelves of outdated books and obsolete computer programs. Along one wall is a shelf of plaster teeth, moulded from the mouths of long-ago patients. She sees her father's old brass plaque—DR GRAINGER BUCHANAN BDS—removed from the shopfront it graced for decades, discarded next to the teeth. Against another wall sits a line of filing cabinets. There are new models, made of plastic, sitting beside older models of grey steel. And at the far end, one of solid steel, military green.

Her father opens it, explaining as he does, 'The army had a garrison in the forest from 1941 through to 1946, both sides of the river. Looks like this practice did all their dental work.' He pulls out the middle drawer, points to the file. There is a brass label holder, the name in fading blue ink: *Maj. Gerard Stannard* and a service number. The file sits between similar ones identified as Smith and Stirling. She takes the file, rests it on top of a shorter, two-drawer cabinet. There's no doubting its authenticity. It contains a list of appointments, invoices and receipts, the ink translucent, written with a fountain pen or a nib, not a ballpoint. There is no record of the gold crowns being fitted, nor of the filling, only of check-ups. But there is a diagram, still clear after all these years. A printed sheet, showing the top and bottom teeth. The two relevant teeth are shaded, each with an arrow and the insignia *AU 16kt.* The filling is also noted, the dentist colouring only part of the wisdom tooth. Very precise. And an exact match. She takes the file, leaves a receipt.

'Your man?' asks her father.

'I'd say so.'

'When did he die?'

'Vanished in 1943.'

'Long time ago,' says her father. 'Does that mean you'll rule a line through it?'

She thinks of saying something official, something noncommittal, but can't see the point. 'I'd say so. Not my call, of course.'

'Well, make sure you come and see us before you leave.'

'Of course, looking forward to it.'

'Tonight?'

'No. Not tonight.'

'Tomorrow?'

She sighs, relents. 'Yes. Tomorrow night.'

'Beauty. Six o'clock?'

'Sure.'

'You can always stay the night.'

'Thanks. I'll think about it.'

She tells her father she needs to get the car back, that the Tulong policeman will be needing it, that she needs to brief her sergeant, bring him up-to-date, discuss how to advance the investigation. Even as she says it, she feels like she is making excuses, no matter that everything she says is true. But her father seems happy enough; he has her commitment.

chapter nine

1973

THE NEXT WEEK IT WAS BLATANT; THERE WAS LITTLE PRETENCE. TESSA HAD done nothing wrong, given him no excuse, nothing that could possibly warrant detention. Not a snigger, not an eye roll, not an exaggerated yawn. And yet the Tool kept her back. Again. Tuesday, English the final period of the day. He sat her there, banging on about Lord Byron, the Pre-Raphaelites and the libertines. The way he wrapped his lips around the word, 'libertines', he was practically sucking it off, mouth framed by a John Newcombe moustache. He had an outdated mop top and thick-rimmed glasses, like Buddy Holly or that wanker from the Seekers. The first time she'd seen him she'd made the mistake of smiling at him, thinking his dress was ironic, or at least eccentric. Afterwards, she'd decided it was merely accidental, born of neglect rather than purpose, that he had tripped over that invisible line into middle age and lost all fashion sense. Finally, however, she was forced to conclude it was deliberate, that he saw himself as the groovy young teacher. 'Call me Marcus,' he purred, and she just about spewed. He used words like 'groovy' and 'cool' and 'man', like he'd applied for the Monkees and only just missed the cut. She avoided looking at him and stared at the wall clock instead. The bus wouldn't wait much longer; even the pervy driver needed to meet some sort of schedule. The Tool moved on to Henry Miller, whoever the fuck that was, and how Whitlam was ending censorship. Poor fucking Whitlam. If he knew the Tool voted for him, he might toss it in and go back to whatever he was doing before politics.

The clock was moving so slowly she wondered if it was broken. *Fuck this*, she thought. 'I'm off,' she said, standing. 'I'll miss the bus.'

She half expected anger, the assertion of authority. Instead: 'I can give you a ride,' he said, voice like treacle. So that was his plan.

She looked at him then, letting all expression fall from her face, giving him her 'wet fish' look. 'That,' she said, spacing her words for emphasis, 'is never going to happen.'

'Wait . . .' he said.

She didn't wait, though, feeling a shift in power, sensing victory. She strode from the room, not looking back, knowing this was the last time he would ever detain her. The creep. But she was too late. By the time she got outside and around to the front of the school, all that was left of the bus was a receding cloud of diesel smoke and the driver's cigarette butt smouldering on the tarmac. Fuck it.

She didn't pause, though, just kept walking towards the highway, wanting to be out of sight before the Tool emerged. She needed to hitchhike home, there was no other choice, but she sure as shit wasn't getting in a car with the fifth Beatle. As she walked, she rehearsed exactly what she would say if the Tool attempted to pick her up. It made her feel better. She almost wished he *would* pull up, just so she could cut him down to size.

But when she reached the highway, it wasn't her English teacher who stopped to offer her a lift. A bright blue Datsun eased to a stop beside her, and through the window she saw the driver: Tycho Buchanan. Her eyes widened. She wished she was wearing make-up. She wished she'd washed her hair that morning.

'Hey,' he said, leaning across and speaking through the open window. 'Heading home?'

'Trying to, yeah.'

'Jump in. I'm heading that way.'

Her heart gave a double take. Tycho Buchanan knew where she lived.

She got into the passenger seat. 'Cool car.'

'Thanks. Datto sixteen hundred. Fixed it up at the yard. Four on the floor.'

'Ace.' She looked at him. His dark hair was shorter than she remembered it, barely brushing his shoulders. Fair enough, she thought, he was working now, needed to conform. A proper job, a journalist, not manual labour. She was glad to see he still had his long sidies, cut off squarely at the same level as his mouth. And a five o'clock shadow, which she found madly attractive. Chest hair billowed from his body shirt. *All man,* she thought to herself.

'Seatbelt,' he prompted her.

'Sorry,' she said. She knew you had to wear them if they were fitted, but her father's farm truck was too old.

'Let me show you,' he said, voice playful. He leant across and she could smell cigarettes and cologne and something altogether different, and her heart stepped up a little. He pulled the belt from where it drooped down onto the floor, lifted it across her stomach, handing her the buckle. 'This goes in here,' he said, pointing to the clasp. 'Lower belt across your waist, the other across your tits.'

She blushed, but did as he said, grateful that he was letting her put it on herself. There was a moment when she thought she was doing it wrong, then the buckle clicked into place.

'Here,' he said. 'We can tighten it a bit.' He leant across again, pulling it tighter. 'Okay?'

'Good, thanks.'

He smiled at her then, and it was a wonderful smile, a generous smile, his eyes full of humour, so different to the Tool, who bared his teeth through thin lips with calculation and not empathy.

'How come you're hitching?' Tycho asked. 'Miss the bus?'

'Detention,' she said. And told him of her confrontation with the Tool. Not just recounting it, but dramatising it, and the more she exaggerated it, the more Tycho laughed, the more his eyes twinkled, the more he encouraged her lampooning of the hapless teacher.

'You're really something,' he said when she had finished, and she felt pleased with herself, as if she had passed some test.

Tycho put on sunglasses and turned his attention to the road. She thought him a movie star, someone from a magazine. He dropped the clutch and the tyres skidded in the dirt of the shoulder before the car lurched onto the bitumen and he accelerated away, changing the gears with aplomb, the engine sounding like it meant business. The windows were down in the heat, and the roar of the wind combined with the pitch of the engine and the thrum of the tyres. The wind whipped her straight brown hair around her face. It all felt exhilarating.

'Fag?' he yelled, offering a soft pack of Peter Stuyvesant.

'Thanks,' she said. She didn't really smoke, but she took one anyway, in case he thought her stuck-up or uncool.

He leant across, hand hovering by her knee for a split second before pushing in the cigarette lighter. And then, smooth as silk, he slipped a cassette into the player hanging below the dash. An unfamiliar song started to emerge from speakers along the back window ledge and a low rumble came from some deep-seated woofer, audible above the roar of wind and road.

'Cool,' she said.

'Bowie.'

'Great.' She wasn't sure if Bowie was a band or a person, but she decided she liked them/him very much.

Before long, they were on the highway, the familiar road made new by the Datsun's hum, the music pumping. She raised her window, so her hair was no longer whipping her face. She didn't really smoke the cigarette, but enjoyed posturing with it, holding it elegantly, or so she thought, between her middle and ring fingers, keeping them ramrod straight. They roared past the school bus, broken down by the side of the road, driver standing by the back with his hands on his hips like the loser he was, and she felt the thrill of it: the wind in her hair, the cigarette in her hand, Bowie singing there was a star man waiting for them. Tycho was singing along, laughing, she wasn't sure why, but she found herself laughing as well. This was it, she decided; it had arrived, whatever it was.

Tycho dropped the speed back as they reached Tulong, doing something with the gears, the engine revving, its pitch rising and falling and rising again. The noise of the road and the wind dropped and she felt compelled to speak.

'Great car,' she said, not knowing what else to say, the words sounding lame.

But Tycho didn't seem to notice. 'Yeah. Work insisted. Said I needed reliable wheels. That same day, this came into the yard. Two years old, but the fuck-knuckle who owned it melted the engine. Sump plug fell out and the dopey prick didn't even notice. Rest of it was immaculate, so we dropped in a new donk. Runs like new. I'll have it paid off in no time.'

She smiled at that. 'Your old man is charging you?'

'Below cost price. Way below.'

'Good of him.'

'Yeah. And the paper pays for petrol.'

'Deadset?'

'No questions asked. I can go wherever I like. You should come for a ride sometime. If I'm heading out to a story or something.'

'Seriously?'

'Sure.' He offered her a smile and she saw in that smile so many things: the promise of music and freedom. And him.

She fell silent then, as they left town and the bright blue Datsun gathered speed anew, driving the last few miles to the end of her driveway. He slowed, pulled in by the gate, by the repurposed paint-can letterbox.

'Thanks,' she said.

'Any time.'

'Gene says he's staying at school. Might go to uni.' She didn't want to get out, didn't want to walk to the isolated little house, didn't want her mother's instructions.

'Yeah,' he said, looking away out the driver-side window before turning his deep brown eyes back to her. 'Grainger too.'

'Not you?'

He cracked a smile. His teeth were perfect, with just one small chip to emphasise the uniformity of the rest. 'Fuck no. Not with this job.'

'It's that good?'

'Sure.'

'Where you living? Still at the yard?' She asked the question then felt a flutter; was she being too forward?

He didn't seem to notice. 'Nah. Rented my own place in Hatty, near work. But just temporary.'

'Temporary? You going to buy?'

He looked at her and his smile eased and his face became serious. 'No. Not there. It's just a stepping stone.'

'What do you mean?'

'Between you and me?'

'Absolutely.'

'I got the whiff of a couple of big stories. Really big. Not small town stories—big city stories. If I nail one of them, I can talk my way onto the *Border Morning Mail*.'

'Albury?'

'Stepping stone number two.'

'To where?'

'Melbourne. If I crack both these yarns, I could be there by next year.'

'Jeez, really?'

He sounded so assured, so confident, it was hard to doubt him. 'That's the goal. What about you?'

'Me?'

'Yeah. What plans?'

Suddenly her own ambitions seemed so tame, so nebulous. 'Dunno. I want to get out, get a job somewhere. Anywhere but here.'

'Great. Might see you in Melbourne.'

'Cool.' But she looked away from him, unable to match the directness of his gaze, the steadiness of him. She stared out the window. She'd never been to Melbourne. She'd never been anywhere. All she knew of the Victorian capital was what she'd seen on television, and a faded postcard of Flinders Street Station that her mother kept on the mantelpiece for some reason. It seemed impossible.

'I'm heading up to Griffith tomorrow,' he said. 'Want to come?'

The suggestion shocked her. Griffith? It must be a two-hour drive, at least. 'What's in Griffith?'

'A story. One of the big ones. Bloke in a furniture store wants to talk to me.'

'Wow.' She looked across at him, his eyes deep and constant. 'Maybe not. I got school.'

'You care about that?'

She didn't answer. Jesus. Tycho Buchanan. Asking her. He was nineteen, almost twenty. So mature. So dreamy, so fucking good-looking, so fucking everything. She could wag, pack street clothes in her bag.

'Long way,' he continued. 'Might have to stay over.'

'No,' she said. And then. 'Maybe another time. Somewhere closer to town.' Suddenly she felt a need to get out of the car, as if she were wading in the Murray and had ventured a step too far, lost her footing, the current pulling her towards the main channel.

She opened the door, looked back at him as she got out. His eyes were still on her, that unflustered manner of his, his stillness. But he was looking at her face, not her tits or the hem of her skirt. 'Thanks for the lift,' she said.

'Any time.'

--

A week later. It was Tuesday, English last period. She knew what was coming, or so she thought, her response ready to rip. But the Tool didn't even wait until class ended. He invited her to stand, to read. And so she did, her eyes on the page even as she felt his own all over her. The fucker. He'd chosen John Donne's 'The Flea'. They'd already studied it in class, so every dickhead knew what it alluded to, even the morons. And so she spat it out, stripping the poem of its rhymes and inflections, replacing eroticism and longing with contempt and sarcasm.

'That was beautiful, Tessa—such passion,' said Marcus the Tool.

But when the end of the day came, it wasn't Tessa he kept back. It was Becky McGuinn, her dress hitched so high her knickers flashed like white lightning. Tessa regarded her with contempt, and then with pity, and perhaps with some inexplicable envy, but mainly with relief. She picked up her bag, leant down as she passed. 'Don't let the fucker touch you,' she whispered.

Becky looked at her, horrified, reality dawning.

Outside, the bus was waiting. She considered it for a moment before she headed into the library instead.

'We're closing in fifteen, love,' said Mrs Plover, the balloon-shaped librarian. 'Don't want to miss your bus.'

'I just need to check something. For an assignment.' She walked to the catalogue, thin blond wood, pulled a drawer out at random. She loved the library, had started borrowing more and more books these past few years, but she found the Dewey decimal system incomprehensible, invented by a sadist. She flicked through reference cards absently, killing time. Then she walked to the fiction stacks, home to her favourites, but today she couldn't concentrate.

'Time to go, love. I've got bridge.'

'Oh. Sorry, Mrs Plover.'

'You find what you need?'

'Yes, thank you.'

Outside the bus was gone and the street was empty. She wondered how Becky was faring. She'd heard stories about her; maybe the Tool had heard them too. Maybe he'd heard stories about Tessa as well. She dismissed the thought and started walking towards the highway.

Tycho was waiting in his blue Datsun. Cat Stevens was on the cassette player, *Tea for the Tillerman*, playing low and gentle. There were new sheepskin seat covers, smooth on her legs. Tycho smiled. 'Thought I might see you here.'

'Thanks,' she said. 'I shouldn't have told you about him.'

'You want me to sort him out?'

'No, Tycho. He'd dob for sure, call the cops.'

'Not violence.' Tycho grins. 'I could write an article. Ruin him.'

'Maybe. But he hasn't actually done anything. Just leered.'

He shook his head. 'I could, you know—write about him. There's power in this job. See?' He gestured towards the back seat. There was a case of wine sitting there. Not flagons, with their clear glass, their thin metal screwcaps and half-gallon capacity.

These were real wine bottles, dark and mysterious, with proper corks and paper labels.

She laughed at the sight, and when she turned to him she could see he was laughing as well, that he liked her reaction, and she felt at ease. He really was a nice guy. 'What's wine got to do with power?'

'It's a perk. New winery down by Echuca. I'm doing a special report on them, and they gave me a whole case. Reds and whites. Top drop.'

'I wouldn't know.'

'Italians. Smart people. They know the power of the press. That's why they're giving it to me. Because they don't want to get on the wrong side.'

She wasn't entirely sure what he was saying. 'You like wine?'

'Learning,' he said. 'You want to step into the world, you need to know about shit like that. You should come down to the winery with me sometime. Lovely place. Really nice people. River frontage, on the Campaspe.'

She felt her heart expanding and didn't know what to say. Tycho Buchanan and her. At a winery. Like a dream. A vision of a picnic came to her, by the river, on a blanket, with a wicker basket.

He reached into the back and plucked a bottle from the carton, handing it to her. It was heavy, dark green glass. The label was plain, the lettering in dark red: *The River Pirate Claret.* There was a line drawing of the pirate, with a beard, a scar on his cheek and an eye patch.

'Far out,' she said. 'Pirates.'

'You want a taste? We can go to the river. I've got glasses.'

She looked at the bottle, tempted. Not by it, but by Tycho Buchanan and the lure of adulthood. 'Maybe not today,' she said. She'd had wine not long before, at a party at the start of spring, outside, around a bonfire. Gene had brought it, a new thing, wine in a cardboard box with a little tap on it. It was the first time she'd seen one. Gene had called it a 'Hatty Handbag' and laughed, but she hadn't got the joke. Not then. She'd forced herself to drink it, even though the taste was acid and metallic and not as sweet as she would have liked. She'd ended up spewing all over the place. Endless spewing, even after her stomach was empty, only the taste left in her mouth: wine, bile and menthol cigarettes. She didn't want to go to the river and drink wine, just in case it set her vomiting again. Then Tycho would see her as a child and want nothing to do with her. He'd drop her like a mutton bird's turd.

'Fair enough,' he said, unbothered as always. 'You want to give a bottle to your dad?'

'Tycho, I'm fifteen.'

And he laughed, free and easy and untroubled. 'I guess not.' There was no sign he was deterred by her rejection of the wine or the offer of drinking some by the river. 'Sorry. Can't give you a lift tomorrow. I'm in Griffith again.'

'That's okay,' she said. 'The bus isn't so bad.'

His eyes were on hers, somehow deep brown and luminous at the same time. 'But any other day, if you're waiting for the bus and you see me driving by, don't get on. Make yourself scarce and meet me over here instead.'

'Really?'

'Of course.' And he shrugged. 'I like being with you.'

She could feel his deep brown eyes reaching into her and warming her from within. Then he leant across and kissed her, just a brushing of lips, like a waft of air, but like bellows to her heart.

Then he kicked the engine into life, and pulled out onto the highway. She lifted her fingers to her mouth, touching her lips. And in her mind she saw the two of them, hand in hand, in Melbourne together, inserted into her mother's postcard, walking from Flinders Street Station.

chapter ten

IVAN HAS RETURNED FROM VICTORIA; BLAKE HAS COME DOWN FROM HATHESON. Nell meets them in the front bar at the Foresters Arms, then they retreat to the beer garden. There's not a lot of garden, just a concrete slab supporting some trestle tables ringed by a HardiePlank fence. The greenest thing, apart from a few weeds exploiting cracks in the concrete, is a tattered shade cloth hanging above the tables. The air retains some of the day's warmth, and a smattering of fairy lights along the fence top supplies artificial gaiety. They have the place to themselves, apart from the anorak-wearing twitcher, sitting at another table doing his crossword and sipping on sherry.

Ivan has decided to leave. So has Blake. They will drive to Wagga in the morning, returning Blake's hire car to the airport before flying to Sydney. Ivan wants Nell to finish the paperwork, then drive the car back to Dubbo.

'It's your show now,' he says. 'Wrap it up, have a day or two with your family.'

'Sure.'

'Good result,' says Ivan. 'Sorted in record time.'

'Sorted? We've identified the victim, not the killer,' replies Nell.

'It was eighty years ago. The killer will be dead.'

'So we just shelve it? Rule a line under it?'

'Yes.' Ivan's face seems to have hardened. 'Find his relatives if you can and let them know. Tell the army we've found him, let the Missing Persons Registry know, inform the coroner, and then file it. Cold cases.'

Nell sips her wine, the house white. It tastes like sugar, vinegar and pineapple juice, and she wonders if the now-surly Noel Tankard is feeding her the dregs of some long-dead vat.

She knows her partner is right: there are more pressing cases. Maybe the relatives will gain some solace. It's a service rendered, a job well done, with minimum fuss. Yet her wine tastes no more satisfying. It irks her, this knowledge that Stannard's killer will never be known, their name remain untarnished, that they got away with murder.

She turns to Blake. The pathologist is studying a blackboard menu with a gleam in his eye. The guy doesn't have an iron stomach, he's got a titanium one. If he's kept awake at night, it will be indigestion, not unsolved cases.

'Any doubts that it's Stannard?' she asks.

Blake offers a twist of his lip, a raised nostril. 'It's him. Dental records are an exact match. Condition of the bones. Height's right. I've got a good DNA sample; I just need to sequence it. So if you find any blood relatives, let me know. That would put it past all doubt.'

'And shot to death?'

'Almost certainly. In the back, out the front.'

'Close range?'

'Couldn't say. A three-oh-three.'

'Meaning?'

'Meaning the shooter could have been just about anyone. Three-oh-threes were thick on the ground back then. Still are, for that matter. Lee-Enfields were standard issue in the army. Plenty from World War One still washing about the place in the 1940s. The work horse rifle for farmers. Every man and his dog had one.'

Ivan is frowning, repeating the checklist: 'The next of kin, the army, Missing Persons, the coroner. Then file it.'

'So no investigation?'

'What's to investigate?'

'Who killed him?'

He doesn't bother replying; they've already been through this. Unsolved murders are never closed, but the passing decades impose their own statute of limitation.

'See you in Dubbo,' he says, bringing the conversation to an end.

Nell says nothing.

'Beautiful spot,' says Blake, the peacemaker, before explaining himself. 'Not the pub—the forest. Wouldn't mind doing a bit of birdwatching myself. Out in the woods, surrounded by nature. Who knows what you might find?'

Ivan scowls. And stands. 'Which reminds me.' He stalks off towards anorak man, stands next to him, speaks softly.

The twitcher looks up, apparently unperturbed, and invites Ivan to join him. Ivan accepts the offer. And Nell realises he must be truly pissed off if he prefers the company of some pigeon stalker to herself.

Blake gives one more longing look at the menu before apologising. 'Sorry, Nell, but I still need to pack and organise storage of the remains, so I'd better get back to Hatheson.'

'No problem. Understood.'

Nell is wondering whether to switch from the abominable wine to a gin and tonic, or order some food, when her phone rings. A blocked number.

'Detective Constable Narelle Buchanan,' she answers, voice noncommittal.

'Nell! Welcome back.'

'Sorry, who is this?'

'Gene. Your uncle. Don't tell me you've forgotten me already?'

She relaxes immediately. 'Uncle Gene. Sorry.' She likes her father's brother, always has, the quiet friendliness behind the bohemian facade. He'd been the one who supported her interest in martial arts, who argued her case to her parents, who would drive her to regional tournaments, put her wins in his paper.

'Let's drop the "uncle" now that you're a fully-fledged homicide detective.'

Gene, as supportive of her career choice as her martial arts. 'You heard?'

'Of course I heard. Your parents are proud as punch.'

'They are?' She suspects it's a white lie and changes the subject. 'You still at the paper?' Her uncle has been editor and owner of the *Western Explorer* in Hatheson for as long as she can remember.

'Yep. Hanging on. In fact, that's why I'm calling. I'm on deadline.'

'I see.' Nell can hear the caution in her own voice.

'I'm after an update on the body found at the regulator.'

'I'm not sure how much I can tell you.' But running through her head are Ivan's words: *It's your show now.*

'I'm told the body has been identified as Major Gerard Stannard, missing since 1943,' Gene presses.

'Did Dad tell you?'

Her uncle laughs. 'A good journo never reveals their sources, you know that.' But the playfulness in his voice as good as confirms that Grainger has told him all about the file in the Boonlea dental practice.

She sees no point in keeping it secret; the investigation is heading to cold cases. And Gene already knows, anyway—he's just seeking confirmation. 'Yeah, it's him. Gold teeth, an exact match.'

'Is that on the record?'

'Leave my name out of it, if you can. But I reckon police sources would be fine.'

'That's brilliant, Nell. Thank you. It's a cracker of a yarn.'

His statement piques her curiosity. 'How so?'

'Oh, it's one of those mysteries. Stannard and another soldier went missing, ran off with a pile of money. No one ever knew what happened to them. I dust the story off every few years, if it's a slow week. You know, "The Mystery of the Missing Soldiers". There's an internal Defence Department report. I got it through Freedom of Information years ago. I can send it through if you like.'

'Thanks, that would be handy. Save me dealing with the bureaucrats.'

Her uncle chuckles again. 'Tell me about it. But I'd better get on with it now. Need to put this paper to bed.'

chapter eleven

TUESDAY MORNING AND HER UNCLE'S EMAIL IS WAITING FOR HER AT THE POLICE station. Ivan has departed, Kevin is out on his rounds, Nell has the place to herself. The email's subject simply reads *Stannard*, and the body of the text is short.

Nell. Thanks for confirming Stannard. Top job. Report attached. Fascinating stuff. Love Gene.

Nell opens the attachment. It's a PDF, a scan of the original, a manual typewriter on fly-spotted paper. Its age is evident despite being digitised. She imagines holding the page, smelling its age, feeling its fragility. Another reminder of just how long ago Stannard died. She finds the relevant part of the report.

> Major Gerard Stannard was last seen in the early afternoon of Thursday, 28 January, 1943. He lunched at the forward detention camp at the edge of the forest, then, as was his routine,

he departed on horseback to inspect the work parties of Italian prisoners in the forest. There were three such parties, designated 'Alpha', 'Bravo' and 'Charlie'.

Major Stannard first visited work party Alpha, the closest to the detention camp. Lieutenant S. Ackland and Privates L. Lovegrove and S. Smith reported that Major Stannard spent about half an hour with them, between approximately 14:00 and 14:30. They were overseeing a work party of sixteen prisoners who were cutting wood to supply charcoal burners. They were working in an area known as McGilligys Swamp, about halfway between the camp and the Murray River.

Lieutenant Ackland testified that there was nothing unusual in Major Stannard's manner or comportment. He made some minor criticisms and recommendations and encouraged greater effort on the part of the prisoners. Lieutenant Ackland said this was in keeping with previous inspections.

Lieutenant Ackland said Stannard left them sometime around 14:30, stating he intended to proceed to the other work parties. Lieutenant Ackland's evidence was independently corroborated by Privates Lovegrove and Smith.

The alert was raised at 16:50, when Major Stannard's horse returned alone to the forward detention camp. There were indications the horse may have entered water. A deployment of three men led by Lieutenant James McKusker and including Privates F. Seton and D. Ellencamp left the camp at approximately 17:30 on horseback. Lieutenant McKusker says they initially feared the major had been struck by a low-hanging branch while riding or had fallen from the horse while fording a stream.

The lieutenant testified that he proceeded directly to the closest site, Alpha, where the work party was finishing up for the day. He encountered Lieutenant Ackland, who described the visit of Major Stannard earlier that afternoon. The search party then began to make its way towards work party Bravo, which was working closer to the river. He reported that the two privates and himself encountered the prisoners from work party Bravo returning towards the detention camp, the work day finished, under the supervision of Privates K. Tankard and P. Louth. Neither soldier reported seeing Major Stannard.

Lieutenant McKusker pressed the men, seeking information about the whereabouts of the officer in charge of work party Bravo, Lieutenant Eamon Finucane. The men reported Finucane had been supervising the work party by himself when they had gone to survey a prospective work site. This was contrary to regulations—even with a full four-man contingent of guards, only one of the privates should have left—but the work camp was short-staffed. The men were candid in admitting their breach of the regulations and further investigation has demonstrated such a practice was not uncommon across the work parties. McKusker described the prisoners as obedient and docile. Privates Tankard and Louth said that when they had returned to the work detail, Lieutenant Finucane wasn't there and had left no message. They thought perhaps he had been called back to the main camp. They repeated their earlier statement that they had not seen Major Stannard.

Lieutenant McKusker attempted to glean information from the prisoners of work camp Bravo. He reports they were compliant and cooperative, but communication was severely restricted by their inability to grasp even the most basic English. However, he says he gathered that Stannard had indeed visited the camp and that the major had departed in the company of Lieutenant Finucane. He was unable to extract any useful information as to why the two officers would leave the prisoners unattended and why they hadn't waited for the return of the two privates. There was some confusion among the prisoners over the direction in which the two officers had departed.

Lieutenant McKusker's first priority was to secure the prisoners, as there was only about an hour of daylight left. He left Private Ellencamp to assist Tankard and Louth, then he and Private Seton continued. They located work party Charlie shortly afterwards, also returning towards the forward detention camp. The four-man detail reported nothing amiss and said that they had seen neither Major Stannard nor Lieutenant Finucane that day. McKusker and Seton then rode ahead, returning to the forward detention camp. They arrived back at approximately 19:20. Once the prisoners of work party Bravo returned, a translator fluent in Italian was able to confirm and elaborate upon the POWs' account. They claimed that Stannard had arrived at work camp Bravo and that, after some discussion, he and Lieutenant Finucane had left together, possibly towards the south-east, Stannard on horseback and Finucane on foot. Some accounts say the two men had quarrelled, a greater number recounted that the two officers were on good terms and had even treated each other 'affectionately'. It is noted that statements provided by prisoners of war are inherently unreliable, but there is little contradictory evidence. Italians in general are weak-willed and compliant, as attested by their inability to seize the opportunity presented by the absence of guards and make good their escape. All prisoners insisted that Stannard was mounted as he left the camp. Both men were armed, Stannard with a pistol and ceremonial sabre, and Finucane with a pistol and a Lee-Enfield rifle.

A widespread search was instituted across the following days, under the command of Lieutenant McKusker and later by the military police. Black trackers and local dogs were used. Sleeper cutters, fishermen, charcoal burners, loggers, cattle grazers and vagabonds were all canvassed. No one volunteered any sightings of either man.

Late on the afternoon of Saturday, 30 January, Captain Amos Penhurst, the camp commander, returned from furlough in Melbourne to discover that a large amount of cash had been stolen from the unit's safe, calculated to be in the range of £400. Captain Penhurst confirmed that Major Stannard held the key to the safe. Major Gerard Stannard and Lieutenant Eamon Finucane were officially listed as Absent Without Leave, and wanted for questioning about the missing money, with a brief forwarded to the military police.

Conclusion

It is not possible to ascertain with any precision what exactly occurred on the afternoon of 28 January, 1943. There is no evidence any harm came to the two officers, Stannard and Finucane, and the reports of the POWs remain consistent in that the two men departed together. In light of Finucane's problematic record in New Guinea, perhaps the most probable explanation is that the two deserted together, and that Stannard stole the money from the unit's safe in order to finance their disappearance. The military and civilian police continue to seek the fugitives.

Nell considers the report. The two men stole the money and disappeared, deserting together. She goes online, finds a calculator on the Reserve Bank website. She's surprised by what it tells her: four hundred pounds in 1943 would be worth about thirty thousand dollars in today's money. A small fortune; a considerable motive. A new scenario suggests itself: Stannard steals the money, perhaps at Finucane's bidding, and the two men desert together. But Finucane kills Stannard, shooting him with his army-issue three-oh-three, dumps his body in the regulator and keeps the money for himself.

Why the regulator? She examines the map attached to the report. The work camp was inland from the river a couple of miles, situated beside a creek. She immediately spots the obvious: the POW camps and work sites were in Victoria, but the regulator was in New South Wales. So the two men had crossed the Murray, which would make sense if they were deserting. She scrolls back through the PDF: *There were indications the horse may have entered water.* She visualises what happened: the two men reached the river, made their way across it, Stannard holding the saddlebags full of cash above the water, aiming for the regulator, a clearly visible landmark. And it had an access road, a speedy way out of the forest, which would suggest they'd planned it in advance, perhaps had a collaborator waiting with a car. And at the regulator, what? A double-cross? Finucane shooting Stannard, then deciding how to dispose of the body. Burying it would have been time-consuming and difficult without a spade or similar tool, and dumping the body in the river would risk it washing up or being discovered by fishermen. Under those circumstances, the regulator pond would be convenient and opportunistic, provided he could weigh the body down.

She goes online, searches the Defence Department's website for a police liaison number, fails, and ends up calling the switch. Eventually they put her through to the historical records section.

'Janine Collinston, Records.'

'Janine, it's Detective Constable Nell Buchanan, New South Wales Homicide. I'm calling in regard to a missing persons case involving two officers during the Second World War.'

'I see. How can I help you?'

'We've identified the body of a Major Gerard Stannard.' She explains finding the skeleton, confirming it belonged to Stannard, that he was a serving officer and was almost certainly murdered.

'That's thoughtful of you to inform us,' says the defence clerk. 'Can you email through a summary when you get the chance so I can update the file? No hurry.'

'I have a contemporary army record concerning the disappearance. Can I email it through? I have some questions.'

Now the clerk sounds intrigued. 'Sure. If you like.' She recites her email address and holds on the line while Nell forwards the document, confirming a moment later that she has received it. While she reads the report, Nell scans it for a second time, can't help noticing one of the privates was K. Tankard and wonders if he was related to the surly publican.

'Interesting,' says Janine, voice cautious. 'Can I ask how you obtained the report?'

'Local paper down here. The *Western Explorer*. Said they got it through FOI years ago.'

'Fair enough. How can I help?'

'The report raises some questions. Would you have any other records for Stannard and Finucane?'

'I really doubt it. All personnel records from the Second World War are now held at either the Australian War Memorial or the National Archives. You'd have to ask there.'

'Right. So this report, where it mentions Finucane's "problematic record" in New Guinea, you have no way of knowing what it's referring to?'

'Not me. The War Memorial has unit diaries and personal diaries. Archives will have official records, including individual service records. I'd try there first.'

'Okay, thanks. But can you tell me, was Finucane ever found?'

'I don't know. I'd have to check. But if your local newspaper accessed this report, they might know about that as well.'

'I'd still be grateful if you checked.'

'Of course. But I wouldn't be too confident. Desertion was viewed very seriously, even without the theft. But once the war was over and demobilisation was complete, the MPs would have been wound right back.'

'So they'd have stopped searching?'

'Possibly.'

'Right. Thanks for your help.'

'No problem. Let me know what you find out about Finucane. I can amend the file.'

Finishing the call, Nell finds herself staring at the wall. Once the war was over, people would have wanted to move on, put it all behind them. Maybe the military wasn't interested in giving oxygen to an embarrassing incident. They'd want to reconcile it, like an accounting measure, unaware a murder had been committed and a killer was on the loose. Nell thinks about that, what eighty years does to a case. All the urgency has gone, all the passion, all the compassion. Now it's just paper in a folder, a vague curiosity, a footnote to be added. For the records. 'No hurry.' A clerk in Canberra wanting to close the file once and for all.

She is considering whether she should brief Ivan when Kevin comes bursting through from reception, wide-eyed and breathing hard. 'Holy fuck. What have you done?'

'Sorry?'

'Noel Tankard. He's up on the pub verandah, chucking your stuff into the street. He's gone completely ballistic.'

chapter twelve

JAMES WATERS—FIRST STATEMENT—CONTINUED

THE NEXT SUMMER, AT THE END OF 1942 GOING INTO 1943, THE DROUGHT WAS worse. We had no feed on the farm and risked losing the cattle, so I took what was left of them into the forest. The regulators were shut off, the river was low, the forest was tinder-dry. Any time you caught a whiff of wood smoke, you flinched. I was just eleven and had never seen a bushfire, not a big one, but we all knew about Black Friday. Half of Victoria went up. That was in 1939, not long before, up in the mountains and down on the coast. We escaped the worst of it, but we knew all about it. Like a harbinger it was, an omen of the war and what was to come. And with the drought getting worse and worse, we were on edge. If a fire got away in the forest, no one could have stopped it. It was more open woodland in those days, with lots of grass between the trees, and the flames would have raced through it. Grass fires don't burn nearly as hot as forest fires, but they're quicker and they'll kill you just as dead. You can't outrun a grass fire, not if the wind is up. It was always on my mind. If it happened, I would have to leave the cattle and save myself, get me and my pony Lenny and the dogs out of there, or get to the river. If there was time, get the cows into the water as well. I was always thinking of it, always assessing it.

Dad had left by then, was in New Guinea fighting the Japs. He'd enlisted across the river at Echuca, so he was with a Victorian unit. At first, he was at Puckapunyal, doing basic training. He'd write us letters all the time. We'd get one every day, and sometimes two or three would arrive at once. He came back for one last visit. He was wearing his uniform, and he seemed somehow different, as if he were changing into someone else, someone I didn't recognise. He gave me a hug and the uniform was coarse, and smelt of tobacco and beer and cordite. He and Mum were so cheerful that weekend, but I realised later that it was forced, put on for me and my sister. When he left, Dad was still laughing and chiacking, and Mum was attempting to laugh and smile through her tears.

The first few days in the forest were the hardest, trying to remember what Dad had taught me, finding my way about, learning where the cattle were safe and where they were in danger of bogging. Dad had shown me, but it was different when I was by myself. Cows all look the same to an outsider, but with a small herd you get to know each one, their personalities. There was a big steer, a hand or two larger than the rest of them. I nicknamed him Benito, after you-know-who, because he was ugly and bull-headed. He wasn't outright trouble, but it was kind of like he demanded respect. If you treated him okay, he'd do what you wanted and the others would follow, but if you tried forcing him, he'd rebel and things would get tricky, like a contest of wills. The dogs worked it out before I did. They knew he was the key to the herd. Then there were a couple of troublemakers. There was a smaller brown one, I used to call him Tito. Not so much a troublemaker as an independent thinker. Always trying to wander off by himself. But the dogs were soon on to him, learnt to keep an eye on him. Rex would give him a nip. They didn't like each other, Tito and Rex. Sometimes it was like watching a play, a performance put on just for me.

The dogs knew more than I did. Without them, I'd have been buggered. It was strange how it worked, like the cows and the dogs were in on it together, trying to show me up. Rex was a kelpie cross, but my favourite was Pouch. She had more of the border collie in her and a sweet nature for a working dog. The kelpie would occasionally get a bit ratty and give a cow a nip in the heels for no good reason. I don't think it was mean or anything, just in his nature. I never saw Pouch do that, yet she seemed to carry the same authority with the herd, like they respected her more. Dad had warned me not to get too close to working dogs, that they weren't pets, but I was a kid, alone in the forest, so I couldn't help but get close to them. They were smart those dogs; they rarely barked, I rarely had to call. Occasionally, they'd belt off after a roo, but even then they never really lost their heads. They were my friends.

There were about thirty in the herd. They were valuable, of course, because we were at war and meat was strictly rationed.

You heard stories of duffers coming in and stealing cattle, so I usually camped in places you couldn't easily access with a truck. They'd use horses to muster, but then they'd need the trucks to get the cattle away. There were cattle let loose in the forest back then, branded and put in there to feed, so it was easier for the duffers to get them. They just needed to wait by the remaining waterholes, even pull out a few who were bogged. I was scared of them, but thinking back, I reckon I was pretty safe. They didn't need to take from us.

I used to camp with the cows. I had my swag and I'd lay it out under the stars. I had a light tarpaulin to put over me in case it rained, but that whole summer, I can only remember it raining a few times, and only once seriously. I slept out in the bush with the dogs and Lenny to keep me company, but each evening I would ride home for dinner, leave the dogs in charge. They did a good job. The cows never wandered while I was gone, not once. Rex and Pouch knew I'd bring back some tucker for them, so they were almost glad to see me go, but I wasn't so glad to be heading home, even though I wanted to see Mum and my sister. That's because I dreaded what might be waiting for me, what news. News on the radio, or in the paper, or, worst of all, a telegram.

In those days the telegraph boy was like the grim reaper. He wasn't even a boy, I don't know why they called him that; he was a man, and not even a young man. A lanky guy, with a bony head and wispy hair under his cap, and if you saw him on his red bike, you'd cross yourself and say a Hail Mary even if you weren't Catholic. He wore a black suit and it was said he didn't raise a sweat, even on the hottest day. I always feared that I'd see him when I emerged from the forest for dinner; that he'd be knocking at our door. I was always relieved when he wasn't there. I'd have something to eat at home, get some supplies and return to the forest before it got too dark.

I got into a pattern during the day. Leading the cows along the higher ground, past the bogs, to find pasture. I could leave them happily grazing, the dogs supervising, while I went further into the forest, looking for new pasture for the next day or two. Sometimes I rode Lenny, but most days I went on foot. Once a day, I took the cattle down to the river, usually to Lackmires Beach. The cattle got to know it, know the way. It was on the inside curve of the river, on a big horseshoe bend where the water was slow and shallow. They could water there without fear of being stuck. The dogs loved it. They'd splash about in the water. I'd get in there as well. You needed to be careful, of course, swimming by yourself, but the deeper water was further out, by the outside bend where the current was stronger.

One day, I saw a boy on the Victorian side of the river. He waved to me, and I waved back. He shouted something and I shouted back, but I couldn't hear him. And then he stripped off, just like that, and dived straight in. No checking for snags or submerged rocks, just dived in. He didn't care about the current. There was no fear in him. And he swam across the river, not dog paddle or breaststroke or any of that malarkey, the Australian crawl, freestyle. He was a natural, like a fish. He got to the sandbar, stood up, walked out past the cows. He was stark naked, but didn't care a fig, didn't care who saw him. He was nature's son, unafraid, skin brown and eyes clear and a grin from ear to ear, as if he knew the impact he was making.

'Watcha doing?' he asked.

'Minding the cows,' I replied.

'I know. I been watching ya,' he said. 'Wanna swim?'

'Sure,' I said. And that was it. We were friends. And that's how I met Bucky. Best mate I ever had.

chapter thirteen

BY THE TIME NELL AND KEVIN GET TO THE FORESTERS ARMS, THERE'S NO SIGN of Noel Tankard, but the aftermath of his tirade is all too evident. Nell's suitcase lies eviscerated in the street, clothes and underwear and toiletries strewn about like a spatter pattern. A couple of rough-hewn men lean on their twin-cab, smirking and waiting for the second act. She swallows her dignity and scrabbles about recovering her belongings, stuffing them back into the suitcase while the men chortle their amusement. She has one thought: confront Tankard and arrest the bastard.

'Deep-state bitch,' says one of the men, a low-voiced observation, pitched just loud enough for her to hear it. She glares at the men, who stand, arms folded, belligerent and contemptuous.

At this moment Noel Tankard emerges from the pub, arms spread like a pro wrestler, full of anger and aggression. 'Get ya stuff and fuck off,' he says.

Nell says nothing in response, just walks slowly towards him, not intimidated. He moves forward, a huge man, towering above her from the footpath, radiating hostility. She steps up the gutter onto the path, but he's still head and shoulders above her and at least twice as heavy. With his mullet and red beard, he looks like a Norseman intent on pillage. 'Get off my property.' He turns his head, spits into the street.

Nell glances slowly left, then right, taking her eyes from him, demonstrating she is not cowed. Behind Tankard, a couple more of his customers have leaked out of the pub, come to watch the show. She points to the ground. 'Public property,' she says, 'not yours.'

'Whatever.' He smiles maliciously. 'But I can still put out the trash.' And he steps towards her, pebble eyes inflated with confidence. She doesn't retreat, half expecting him to take a swing. Instead he stops mere centimetres from her, planting his feet, close enough that she can smell his meaty breath. He leers, lifts both hands, telegraphing his intention to shove her from the kerb.

It's almost too easy, her judo mind taking hold. For her, it unfolds in slow motion, one well-rehearsed movement. She drops down and under, even as she takes one of his arms, pulling him forward, using his own momentum, gaining leverage, feeling him come across the pivot point, then lifting, surging with her thighs and calves for extra leverage and swinging him over, lifting more to make his fall all the greater, feeling him topple, swinging him so he'll land on his back, not his head, but land with impact. The onlookers see it differently: one moment he is looming over her, the next he is flying through the air, smacking onto his back, an expulsion of air as he hits the road.

She steps down next to him. He's lying winded, struggling for breath like a beached whale. She addresses the onlookers. 'I am not a deep-state bitch. I am a homicide detective investigating a murder. And this man just attempted to assault a police officer. Do not obstruct me as I conduct my duties.'

Tankard tries to speak, but lacks the necessary breath.

Nell turns to Kevin, who is standing wide-eyed and open-mouthed. 'Cuff him, Kev.'

'Hey?'

'Cuff him or give them to me.'

'Jesus, Nell. You sure?'

She puts her hand out. Kevin hands over the cuffs.

'Roll over,' she says to Tankard. 'Or sit up.'

'You can't,' he wheezes.

She squats next to him, face close to his. 'I can and I will.'

But even as Tankard heaves himself to a sitting position, Nell realises defusing the situation might achieve more than escalating it. She doesn't cuff him, standing instead and addressing the crowd once again. 'This man threw my possessions from his hotel. This man attempted to assault me. Remember that.' And she hands the cuffs back to Kevin, picks up her suitcase, directs one last glare at the two Visigoths by the twin-cab, no longer smirking, and stalks back towards the police station, followed by Kevin, who rushes to catch up.

'Shit, Nell. Where did you learn that?'

'Echuca,' she says.

'It's not allowed,' he says. 'Martial arts.'

'It was reasonable force. He went to push me from the footpath. You saw.'

'Even so.'

'Even so, what?' She stops, turns, scowls at him. He looks like he's still trying to comprehend what's happened. She relents a little, her anger beginning to subside, the tension and adrenaline easing. 'Do you have any idea what that was about? Why he did it?'

'Yeah. The paper.'

Nell frowns. 'What paper?'

'Your uncle's. The *Western Explorer*.'

'You got a copy?'

'Not here, but I heard.'

'Heard what?' She feels her anger returning.

'Give me your case,' says the constable. 'I'll take it to the station. Go to the store—they sell papers.'

Nell does what he suggests, feeling a sea of eyes upon her as she stalks back past the pub and down Highgate Street to the general store.

There's still no one at the counter, and the fresh food section looks no fresher. She's about to call out when she sees the papers arrayed along a low display bench. There's *The Age* and the *Sun Herald* and the *Border Morning Mail* and the *Hatheson Post*, but it's the *Western Explorer* that grabs her attention. The headline is bold—IS THIS THE FACE OF A KILLER?—and so too is the by-line: *by Eugene Buchanan*. The story fills the entire front page. There is a photo, old, black-and-white, of a policeman, wearing his cap, smiling at the camera. And the caption: *Corrupt police officer Keith Tankard. Was he also a murderer?*

'Holy shit,' Nell whispers.

She moves through the internal door to the adjoining cafe, walks to the counter.

'Read it outside, love,' says Frieda, as if picking up on Nell's shock and disquiet. 'You want me to bring you out a coffee?'

Nell nods.

'Latte?'

'Thanks,' says Nell, finding her voice, tapping her credit card.

Outside, she sits at a table on the footpath under the awning, oblivious to who might be watching.

In a sensational new development, a decades-old mystery has moved closer to resolution following the discovery of a body dumped in a regulator pond beside the Murray River.

Police sources confirm the skeletal remains belong to Major Gerard Stannard, who disappeared together with another soldier, Lieutenant Eamon Finucane, in January 1943.

There is clear evidence that Major Stannard was murdered, his body weighted down and disposed of in the regulator pool.

The body was uncovered by construction workers repairing the regulator upstream of Anglers Reach in Millewa Forest. It was destroyed by unknown saboteurs using commercial explosives in late August.

According to official Department of Defence documents obtained by the *Western Explorer* under the Freedom of Information Act, Stannard and Finucane were accused of stealing £400—a small fortune—and deserting. But the discovery of the body suggests the men met with foul play.

Despite a massive nationwide manhunt conducted by military police at the time, there is no record that either Stannard or Finucane were ever found.

Stannard was last seen meeting Finucane at a prisoner of war work camp in Barmah Forest on the Victorian side of the river. Finucane was guarding Italians POWs, who later testified that the two men left together but were unable to say in which direction.

An enduring question surrounding the mystery has been the whereabouts of the two soldiers assigned to help Finucane guard the prisoners that day, Privates Peter Louth and Keith Tankard. The men claim to have been absent at the critical time, scouting new work sites, despite this being strictly against army regulations. Louth and Tankard were disciplined over the breach; both were fined a month's pay and had their military records annotated. However, with manpower in short supply, both continued in their guard duties.

Based on the statements given by Louth and Tankard, which were supported by the Italians, the military investigation concluded Major Stannard and Lieutenant Finucane had stolen the money and deserted together. But following the discovery of Stannard's body and confirmation he was murdered, the testimony of the Italians is now cast in a dramatic new light.

These were men who were at the mercy of their armed guards, Louth and Tankard, alone in the forest. This raises serious questions about the veracity of the Italians' evidence and the robustness of the military investigation.

Were Louth and Tankard really absent? Or had only one of them left on a scouting mission, as per army regulations?

There can be little doubt that Stannard stole the money; he held the key to the safe where it was kept. But nothing links

Finucane to the crime, beyond the unreliable and potentially compromised evidence of the Italians.

There remains no proof Finucane survived that fateful day. Is it possible both men were murdered by Louth and Tankard?

Private Peter Louth died in a live-firing training accident in the forest less than a year later. Tankard was in the same training party and close by when the alleged accident occurred.

Which leaves Private Keith Tankard. He survived the war and prospered, becoming a prominent police officer at Hatheson. At the height of his powers, it was said he ran the town like a Wild West sheriff.

But in 1980, following an in-depth investigation by the *Western Explorer*, he was arrested, charged with corruption and jailed for three years, ending his career. He died in disgrace seven years later.

The courts found Tankard to be corrupt. The question now must be, was he also a killer?

Nell stares at the paper. Is that all? She re-reads it, considers the photo looking out from the front page. It's a neat theory, compelling even. But she knows the disdain Ivan would heap upon it: so much conjecture, so few facts.

Frieda delivers her coffee in a takeaway container. Nell takes a sip, then rings her uncle.

'I saw your story,' she says.

'Corker, isn't it?'

'Noel Tankard just threw my clothes from the pub verandah and tried to assault me.'

'Jesus. Are there photos?'

For a moment she's speechless. 'Gene, I'm fucking furious.'

'Why were you staying at the pub? It's a shithole. I thought you were at the motel.'

Nell ignores that. 'What is going on here, Gene? When I registered at the pub, Tankard said he wouldn't have let me stay if he knew I was a Buchanan.'

'What can I tell you? His grandfather was a corrupt cop, his father was a loser and so is he.'

'And you didn't think you might tell me any of this before you splashed it across your paper?'

'I stand by the story.'

The pat line infuriates her. 'I don't care if you dance a jig next to it. I'm conducting a murder investigation. I don't need you setting the locals against me.'

'You have your job, I have mine,' says Gene.

There's a long pause. Suddenly, somehow, a relationship that has endured the entirety of Nell's life has been turned on its head: he's no longer the indulgent uncle; she's no longer the adoring niece.

When he speaks again, Gene's tone is conciliatory. 'I'm sorry, Nell. Truly. If there is anything I can do to help, let me know.'

Nell takes her coffee and the paper and walks to the station, conscious of a couple of stragglers outside the Foresters Arms watching her pass, pointing and whispering. She's almost past the pub, when she reconsiders. She walks back, steps up onto the gutter where she felled Tankard and stalks into the front bar.

Tankard is behind the bar, too surprised by her reappearance to speak.

She holds up the paper. 'I knew nothing of this. Nothing. Got it?' And then, before he can respond, 'Any bad blood between you and my family is your business. I want none of it.'

'Bit late for that,' he says.

Nell doesn't wait for him to elaborate; she turns and strides back out of the pub. What has she got herself into—the Hatfields and McCoys? She's not above the law, no police officer is, but she needs to remain above the fray.

chapter fourteen

1973

SATURDAY CAME, HOT AND OPPRESSIVE, JUST A COUPLE OF WEEKS BEFORE THE end of school and the long summer break. The weather wasn't waiting for the calendar to turn the page on the seasons: the fields were brown and the flies were thick, the cicadas were chorusing and the tank water was growing more tepid with each passing day. Tessa was glad to be in Boonlea, working her weekend job at the air-conditioned newsagency. She sold the *Saturday Age*, inches thick, and the *Australian Women's Weekly* with picture spreads of Jackie Onassis and Princess Grace; she sold *Cleo* with its racy male centrefolds to assertive women and editions of *Playboy* to furtive men. She unpacked Christmas cards and next year's calendars and diaries, lining them up on the shelves where her boss wanted them. Her dad had driven her down, off for his weekend golf. At noon, she collected her pay, the owner closed the shop and she was free. Old and bespectacled, he was a decent guy who kept his hands and his eyes to himself. He'd even given her a copy of the *Western Explorer* for free, which made her feel guilty for pocketing a half-pack of Alpine when he wasn't looking.

She planned to catch the one o'clock bus, the one that ran through Tulong to Hatheson, so she had an hour to kill. Walking to the park by the river, she thought about smoking one of the cigarettes, just for practice, but she didn't have a lighter. She didn't much like smoking but thought she should put in more of an effort; she didn't want to look gauche around Tycho. Sitting in the shade of a poplar, she scanned the *Western Explorer* from cover to cover. Tycho had four articles with a by-line. The first was an update on the Whitlam government's plan to turn Albury-Wodonga into a city the size of Canberra; the second quoted a scientist claiming an introduced fish, the European carp, had the potential to ravage the Murray-Darling Basin; the third was about squatters and hermits living wild in the far reaches of the Barmah-Millewa Forest, including so-called 'preppers', who were convinced nuclear war was imminent. The final story was all about the winery he'd told her about, Camilleri's, the one that made the River Pirate wine. She read them all twice and decided she liked the one about the forest dwellers the most. It seemed somehow romantic to her, the idea of disappearing into the bush, leaving the world behind. She could almost imagine Tycho reading it with his deep and masculine voice.

After folding the paper carefully and placing it in her bag, a keepsake, she thought about walking across the bridge to Echuca.

She wanted to buy make-up, maybe a new top, some shoes; she wanted to become more stylish, more attractive. But it was the weekend and all the shops shut at noon on Saturday. Only the pubs, a milk bar or two and the swimming pool were open. She should have brought her swimmers. She could have sunbathed, worked on her tan. And the chlorine might help bleach her brown hair a touch blonder. Men liked blondes, that's what everybody said.

It was getting hotter and hotter. There were no clouds, no wind, just the sun. She drank water from a bubbler in the park. She walked to the library, wondering if it was open, wondering if it might offer refuge from the heat. She liked books, liked the ones they read at school—at least, she did before the Tool started imposing his manipulative interpretations. She thought of her old favourites, sitting at home in her room—*Anne of Green Gables*, *Little Women*, *Seven Little Australians*—and wondered if she would ever read them again. They were kids' books, and she was no longer a kid. At school, in class and in the library, she'd discovered the Brontës, Jane Austen, Miles Franklin. But they were old, those books, their authors dead. She needed something contemporary, something fashionable, something she could discuss with Tycho to demonstrate her sophistication. She thought of *Portnoy's Complaint*; Whitlam or Gorton or someone had removed it from the banned list. Her mother declared it 'utter filth'—without reading it, of course—which made it madly attractive. Except the Tool had recommended it, which tarnished its appeal. Also, she'd heard it was all about some guy tossing himself off, and she wasn't so sure that lent itself to the chic new image she wanted to cultivate. Chances were the library wouldn't have it anyway—and even if it did, she'd be too embarrassed to borrow it. She needed something a bit safer: edgy but not all about sex. She didn't want to appear overly keen in that regard, lest Tycho thought her loose. *Catch-22.* That would work. Or Kurt Vonnegut. But how to pronounce his name? Von-gut? Von-goot? Vonnie-goot? She'd just have to scour the stacks, not ask the librarian.

But when she got there, the library was closed anyway. Saturday afternoon and the world had shut its doors.

The bus was waiting—right place, right time—but it wasn't going anywhere. The back engine cover was open and the driver was standing, hands on hips, staring at the motor, a hopeless look on his face, as if he had never seen one before or this one had suddenly taken on the complexities of an F-111.

'Sorry, darl,' he said. 'Might be ready for the four o'clock run, but I wouldn't count on it.'

There wasn't much for it; she'd have to hitchhike. But it was so bloody hot. She wished Tycho would come by and pick her up, whisk her off for that picnic at the winery. But that was a pipe dream: she knew he was hundreds of kilometres away, researching his big story in Griffith. She thought of her father. Surely he would have finished golf by now and be watching the cricket in the clubhouse, or whatever he did after the game. She decided to walk to the golf club on the edge of town. If she was lucky, he might be ready to leave, but if he wasn't it didn't matter so much. There was nothing waiting for her at home, nothing she needed to be back for except her mother's harping. She could wait in the golf club. It would have to be cooler than the house on the plain. She could sit in a quiet corner and re-read the *Western Explorer.*

But when she got to the club, she found it bigger and busier than she'd imagined, more daunting, with the men milling about on the deck overlooking the river, their voices loud, the women in their natty golf clothes, chortling and comparing. Some looked like they had already played, others were just heading out. She pushed inside, and there were even more people. She'd heard about this: Victorians driving miles to cross the border and play the poker machines, illegal in their own state. It seemed there were even more drinkers, eaters and pokie players than there were golfers.

Then she saw a familiar face. Her father's Uncle Reg, holding court, a big man with a ruddy face and a big belly, drinking a big beer, surrounded by other men. She wondered how she might approach him, how she could possibly interrupt, when suddenly she saw him excuse himself, head towards the toilets. She skipped across to him.

'Excuse me?'

'Yes, lass?'

'I'm Tessa Waters—Jimmy's daughter.'

'So you are,' he said. 'And what a beauty you've turned into.'

'I'm searching for Dad. He came to play golf.'

'Jimmy?' He looked a bit confused. 'Sorry. Haven't seen him. Might have finished and left.'

She thanked him and moved away. What to do now?

She walked into the bistro, went up to the counter.

'I'm looking for my father,' she told the woman serving behind the counter. 'Do you know how I might find him?'

The woman sounded sceptical. 'In here? Doubt it.'

'He was playing golf.'

'Competition?'

'Pennant.'

'In that case head out to the balcony. There's a table out there where they tally the scores. They'll know what time he's playing.'

Out on the deck, she found the table. A man, with a shirt too small or a gut too big, chins cascading down into his chest, sat behind it. Next to him was a large silver trophy inscribed: *The Reg Waters Cup*. He looked up as she approached, brandishing a friendly enough smile.

'I'm looking for my father,' Tessa said. 'James Waters.'

'Jimmy Waters?' The man frowned. 'Sorry, sweetheart, he's not playing the summer comp.'

'Oh, sorry. My mistake.' She backed away, embarrassed, wrong-footed. Her father, not playing this week, not playing this summer. Where was he, then? He'd driven her in, his clubs in the back.

So hitchhiking it was. At least she wasn't in her school uniform. As she started walking down the club's long drive, heading towards town, she put her finger out, more in hope than expectation. Even if someone stopped, chances were they would simply be going a few blocks. Where was her father? Could he be having an affair? Jesus, her poor mother; no wonder she was so narky all the time.

A car slowed, then stopped just ahead of her, a little Morris Minor. A cute car. An unthreatening car.

Tessa ran up to it, opened the door, and was surprised to see the school librarian, Mrs Plover, behind the wheel.

'Tessa? It is you. I thought I recognised those long legs of yours.'

'Thanks for stopping, Mrs Plover.'

'You heading home, love? Jump in. I'm heading back to Hatheson.'

'Thank you. Thanks so much.'

'Tulong, isn't it?'

'A farm, Mrs Plover. Just this side.'

'On the way then,' said Mrs Plover with a jolly smile. She worked the gearstick protruding from the steering wheel and got the little car underway. Tessa thought it sounded a bit like a lawn-mower. Or a sewing machine. 'What brings you down here, Tessa?'

'I work Saturday mornings at the newsagency.' Tessa was worried that the librarian would quiz her on her presence at the golf club, but instead the old dear started talking about bridge. That was why she was in Boonlea: competition bridge. She explained the games, the tactics and the personalities, growing in her enthusiasm and volubility as she did so. Tessa, who knew nothing of cards beyond Snap and Go Fish, couldn't have followed the conversation even if she tried. Maybe that was something else she needed to do, learn some adult card games. Poker and gin rummy and black-jack. Maybe the school library had books on cards. She waited for a pause, so she could ask, but Mrs Plover's monologue was relentless. Perhaps all those hours of silence had backed up the librarian's conversation and now it was flowing out, unimpeded, like an unblocked drain. By the time they were leaving Boonlea, Tessa was no longer attempting either to listen or interrupt. Instead her thoughts drifted away: to her father, to her mother, to Tycho. Mrs Plover didn't seem to mind. Out on the highway her voice seemed to harmonise with the engine, both put-putting away, both content, both capable of going many miles more.

And yet Tessa was grateful. The day seemed to be getting hotter and hotter, even with the windows wide open. She got dust in her eye, wiped at it, tried to blink it out. That was something else she needed to buy: better sunglasses. All she had were a crappy old pair won in the sideshow alley at the last Boonlea show. They were falling apart, held together on one side by a paperclip. She thought of the *Women's Weekly*: she bet Princess Grace never wore paperclipped sunglasses.

Out the right-hand window she could see the top of the forest approaching, beyond the edge of the tilt. The great forest. She thought of Tycho's article about its inhabitants: the hermits and squatters and the preppers, those who had dropped out of society. She decided she wanted the opposite: she wanted life, to be in among it, to see the world, drink cocktails in Melbourne with Tycho. Maybe she should think about university after all. Not to study, but as a strategy, a way of getting to the big city. A groovy university chick, hanging out with her handsome reporter boyfriend. She looked out across the parched fields and wondered if it could ever be so. She thought of Tycho now, wondered what he was doing. In his car, going fast, going wherever he liked, music loud, windows down, sunglasses on. Classy sunglasses. Sunglasses without paperclips.

Before she knew it, they were almost at the farm. She pointed out the driveway, breaking into the librarian's monologue.

'Here we go, love.' Mrs Plover brought the Morris to a stop.

Tessa was about to open the door, then suddenly decided against it. She thought of her mother, all alone, abandoned by her father, and wasn't sure she could deal with her, what to tell her about the golf club. 'Sorry. Would you mind dropping me in Tulong instead, please?'

Mrs Plover shrugged. 'Sure, love. Your call.'

And before Tessa could reconsider, the little car was chugging on its way again.

Maybe there would be some distraction at Tulong. Maybe she would run into Tycho: Griffith cancelled, down from Hatty to see his parents. Such were her thoughts as she thanked Mrs Plover, climbed out of the Morris and walked the one block from the highway to Highgate Street. There was a handful of shops, two churches, a small park and that was it, with the Foresters Arms at one end and two more pubs at the other, like sentinels—the Golden Sheaf and the Commercial. Beyond the pubs were houses, and beyond the houses were the fields.

The only shops open on the main street were the Olympus Milk Bar and the general store. Inside the milk bar, a couple of kids were playing pinball, thrusting and flipping and tilting. There was a TV showing the cricket, sound off, black-and-white images ghosting, the image rolling all together now and then. The owner's son emerged, gave her a cheesy smile and turned the jukebox to automatic. His father had installed it, hoping for extra income, but soon discovered his customers were too tight to shell out ten cents for a song. They preferred to sit in silence. And once word got out that it could be turned to automatic, playing for free, no one ever fed it another coin. As a result, the records were never updated and were still the same ones that had come with it three years before. 'Boppin' the Blues' sounded as shit as ever, everyone hated 'Sadie, the fucking Cleaning Lady', and the Beatles' 'Hey Jude' had been played so often it was almost worn through. This time it started with Brian Cadd; it could have been worse.

Tessa was hot after the drive, hot and thirsty, and not entirely sure why she'd come here. She'd have to go home sooner or later.

It was six miles down the road; she'd have to hitch out in the mounting heat. She thought about buying a coffee. Tycho might approve of that. Coffee was modern and American, something you drank with cigarettes; that much was clear from the movies. But the last thing she felt like in this heat was a cigarette, or coffee, so she went to the counter and ordered a lime spider instead, a kids' drink. She didn't care: when it came it was sweet and cold and tasty, the vanilla ice cream foaming the GI lime cordial and lemonade. She sat in a booth, pushing the dollop of ice cream around the parfait glass with her straw, thinking that the world was changing, that this was perhaps her last-ever lime spider. She felt a tinge of nostalgia, so she conjured an image of Melbourne cocktails and felt much better. She was sitting there, thinking such thoughts, when Gene Buchanan came in wearing his cricket whites: long pants, grass stains on his knees. He smiled when he saw her, waved. She waved back. He bought himself a Coke and came over to join her.

'How'd you go?' she asked.

'Lost. But not by much.'

'Good.'

He looked up at the ghosting television. 'What's the score?'

'No idea.'

He sipped at his Coke. 'Watcha up to?'

'Killing time.'

'Waiting for something?'

'Life, I guess.'

He laughed at that, got her drift. 'You've come to the wrong place then.' He had some more Coke, frowned. 'How did you get here?'

'Hitched. Came up from Boonlea.'

'Tell me if you want a lift back home.'

'You have a licence? Already?'

'Learner's. But Grainger can supervise. Or he can drive.'

'Wow. That would be ace.' And she wonders if Gene is blushing or is merely sunburned from his cricket.

chapter fifteen

THE FAMILY HOUSE, BACKING ONTO THE MURRAY RIVER NEAR BOONLEA, LOOKS much the same to Nell, proud and clean, sitting on its half-acre block. There's an ornamental willow, some rosebushes, but mainly it's lawn, cut to perfection by her father, never happier than on his ride-on mower. A sprinkler is tick-tocking a bore-water circle, mapping out the endless cycle: sprinkler-mower, sprinkler-mower. Her tyres crunch on the white-pebble drive. Her father's car must be inside the four-car garage, but she's not the first to arrive: a large white SUV is here before her.

On the porch, she removes her boots. There are slippers waiting for her, hard and new and sterile. Some things never change. She rings the bell, hears the faraway chime, a clichéd ding-dong, like in a cartoon. Her father opens the door, smiling warmly, unlatching the security door. Inside, the house is as anticipated: completely spotless. Vacuumed, scrubbed, disinfected. The smells of her childhood permeate the air: chemical pine, bleach, air freshener. Nell knows it's not for her benefit; the house is always like this. She thinks of her own haphazard housekeeping, grateful she has inherited none of her mother's obsessions.

The family is gathered in the lounge, the special room, plastic covers still on the two sofas. Nell's sister Molly and her husband Gary stand to greet her; not so their two surly teenagers, sitting to one side, staring at their screens. Nell embraces Molly, studies her face as they make small talk. Her sister is ten years older, and the first hints of middle age are visible in her jowls. She seems a little plumper, but just as happy. Molly: her perpetually positive sister. Gary gives her an awkward embrace then returns to his seat, nursing a beer.

Nell excuses herself and makes her way to the kitchen, where her mother is preparing the meal.

'Mum.'

'Nell.'

They embrace, but stiffly. There's that familiar feeling, Tessa holding back, always a little too proper, even with her own children, as if they may have unwittingly introduced something toxic from the outside world.

'Looks good,' says Nell, flicking her head towards the half-prepared dishes on the bench, hating herself for the banality of her remark, for playing into her mother's comfort zone. 'Want a hand?'

'Not necessary. I'm almost done. Just salads. Your father is barbecuing.'

'Yum.'

'We thought we might eat outside. On the patio.'

Nell thinks she sees the faintest indication of nerves. 'Nice weather for it.'

'Daylight savings,' says her mother. 'Want to make the most of it before summer heats up.'

Nell studies her mother while trying not to be too obvious about it. There'd been a long period, back when Nell was a child and her siblings were teenagers, when her mother had not dared step outside at all. When the agoraphobia was at its worst, she even confined herself to the same routes within the home. The kitchen had been her citadel. Only her compulsive need to clean took her to the frontiers of the house, competing forces fighting within her. Over the years, she'd grown a little bolder, regained a little more territory each year. The backyard; the letterbox at the end of the driveway on a good day. Small excursions, there and back. These days, she goes for drives with Nell's father. But here, the kitchen, was always the heart of her kingdom, the one place she retained confidence in her authority, even as her influence over her children waned. Nell understands eating outside is a statement, a demonstration of control and achievement. She's glad for her mother, proud of her. And she's grateful she left her gun locked in the car safe, that she didn't opt for her own petty demonstration of independence. Such thoughts now seem unworthy. Her poor mother, captive to her anxieties.

'Nell?'

'Yes, Mum?'

'Congratulations on your promotion. I should have said . . .' Her mother's voice trails off.

Nell can sense the effort Tessa is making. 'Thanks. That means a lot.'

There's a shout from the front door: 'Buchanans!'

Nell moves out of the kitchen. It's her brother Greg, and it's as if the whole place lifts with his arrival. Molly gets to him first, delivering a bear hug. Nell feels a rush of joy; she hadn't been expecting her elder brother, now living in Albury with his boyfriend. Even Molly's teenagers stand, eyes off their devices for long enough to say hello and demonstrate that they can, after all, raise a smile. Her father is there, circling, grin stretching from ear to ear, and then her mother, apron on, hugging her boy. And finally Nell, as if he has left the best for last. He plucks her from her feet, swings her around, an echo of childhood twirlies. He's twenty years older than Nell, into his late forties, wearing it well, still moving like a much younger man, looking fit and lean compared to Gary's beer-belly bulk. Greg has dark good looks, similar colouring to Nell, his features better aligned: white teeth, brown eyes, laugh lines. She loves to see him: they're the two dark bookends either side of the three fair heads. She loves the mischief in his eyes, the vitality of him. And suddenly she feels herself at home, objectivity falling away, embracing the moment.

The celebratory mood continues once they move outside to eat. Her father is cooking on the world's biggest barbecue. 'A six-burner,' he informs Nell, flipping steaks and spiced sausages and homemade rissoles. There's music playing in the background, one of her parents' albums from decades ago, the soundtrack to her youth, so ingrained that she barely notices it. *Rumours,* she thinks. Fleetwood Mac. The conversation has stepped up, flowing this way and that, breaking into smaller dialogues before uniting again. It's the alcohol, the presence of Greg, maybe her own return, mixing together in the warm evening air.

The meat is done and they sit on well-cushioned wicker chairs around a glass-topped table, the setting large enough for at least twelve people. There is the smell of the cooked meat, of insect repellent and mosquito coils and, from the end of the yard, the subtle odours of the river. Why had she been reluctant to come? She looks around the table at her family, feels content to be among these good people. Her mother catches her eye, as if reading her mind, and smiles.

Sitting at the head of the table, her father flourishes a bottle of wine. 'Local,' he says. 'Good drop. Mum and I picked it up at a cellar door.'

Nell looks at her mother, trying to imagine her in the car, entering an unknown building.

'Yes,' says her mother, pride in her voice.

The rest of the table has fallen silent, listening.

'Good for you,' says Nell. 'Where?'

'On the Campaspe River. Near Echuca. Pretty place.'

'Victoria?'

'I read about it years ago. It sounded so nice and I always wanted to go there. So, finally, we did.'

'Mum, that's brilliant.'

'Just in the car, love. One step at a time.'

'Not just the car,' says her father. 'In the cellar door. Next time, we'll walk by the river.' And her father raises his glass in an unspoken toast to his wife, and the family quietly follows suit, no matter if they have anything in their glasses or not. Then her father stands, walks around the table, filling glasses. It's a red, not Nell's favourite, but this is good. Light and aromatic and almost sweet.

'Chianti style,' says her dad, smiling at the approval he must see on her face. 'They're Italians originally.' He hands her the bottle.

'It's good.' She examines the label, dark red printed on parchment yellow. *The River Pirate* it says, with a line drawing of a grinning man with a ponytail, a scar on his left cheek and an eye patch. She reads the label aloud, putting on a posh accent, the family a ready audience: *'A light, flavoursome wine, ideal for drinking now, the perfect accompaniment for antipasti. Honouring the original river pirates, the bushrangers who lived in the Barmah Forest, targeting the paddle steamers of the Murray.'* Greg applauds and she takes a mock bow. 'I never knew there were river pirates,' she says.

'Where there's money, you'll find pirates,' observes her father.

'Says the dentist,' laughs Greg, and the family laugh with him, their father showing no signs of offence.

The conversation drifts this way and that, and then, in a lull, her father asks, 'How's the case? Moving along?'

'Just about wrapped up, thanks to you.' She explains to the others that Blake has officially confirmed the skeleton belongs to Gerard Stannard, a soldier missing since the Second World War, and that the quick resolution is thanks to Grainger. 'Stannard disappeared in 1943 together with a subordinate, Lieutenant Eamon Finucane. They went AWOL after stealing a stack of money.'

'You saw Gene's story?' asks her father.

'I did.' A stiffness returns to her.

'What do you think of his theory?'

Maybe it's the wine, but she sees little reason to hold back. 'To be honest, I think it's far more likely that Finucane killed Stannard and kept the money for himself.'

'How awful,' says her mother quietly.

'What happened to Finucane?' asks Greg.

'Disappeared without trace. There was a manhunt at the time, the military police, but it seems they never found him.'

'Dead by now,' says her father. 'Or a hundred years old.'

'Yes,' says Nell. 'A cold case. Deep freezer.' She looks at her food, a sense of sadness coming over her, of the investigation being too little too late. She changes the subject. 'What's with Uncle Gene and the Tankards?'

There's suddenly silence, just for a heartbeat, the sound of the night. Greg is peering over the rim of his glass, looking amused. It's her father who answers. 'You'd have to ask Gene.'

'But it's not just Gene, is it? Noel Tankard has it in for Grandmother Rita as well.'

'I've never met Noel Tankard,' says Grainger. The celebratory spirit has gone now. Nell can see her mother staring down at the table, kneading her hands. Grainger glances across at his wife before he speaks again. 'We left Tulong fifty years ago.'

'Tell her,' says her mother softly.

Grainger frowns, takes another sip of wine, swallows. 'Your grandmother once accused Noel's grandfather, Keith, of trying to extort bribes from the family business.'

'So what was today's paper? Revenge?'

'We had nothing to do with the article,' her father says, and Nell thinks she catches the edge of anger in his voice. 'Just ignore it.'

'Ignore it? Noel Tankard threw me out of the pub,' she says. 'Chucked my stuff into the street.'

'Why would you stay there?' asks Greg. 'It's full of rednecks and homophobes.'

Tessa stands, looking distressed, starts clearing plates, Molly helping. 'That doesn't mean his grandfather murdered Gerard Stannard,' says their mother quietly.

There's another break in the conversation at her mother's unexpected intervention.

Nell is the first to speak. 'What do you mean, Mum?'

But her mother shrugs, smiling weakly. 'Maybe you should go see my dad. He remembers what it was like back then.'

'Grandpa Jimmy? In the war?'

'He spent a lot of time in the forest.'

'He was just a kid,' interjects her father. 'He wouldn't have had anything to do with soldiers or prisoners of war.' He stands and moves around the table, topping up wineglasses.

'I dropped in to see him last week,' says Greg. 'Fit as a fiddle. And for a recluse, he sure likes a chat.'

'You should have invited him along tonight, Mum,' says Molly.

'I tried. He feels uncomfortable in crowds.'

'So he's all alone?' asks Nell.

'Likes his own company,' says Grainger. 'Nothing wrong with that.'

'Let's go inside,' says Tessa abruptly. 'It's getting a bit cool out here.'

Her father pauses mid-pour. 'Good idea. Dessert inside.'

Nell is about to speak when her phone rings. She's forgotten to put it on silent. She glances at the screen, thinking to ignore it, but it's Kevin Nackangara. She stands, excuses herself, takes the call as she walks out into the yard, away from the well-lit table, beyond earshot, towards the trees and the river and the darkness.

'Hi, Kev. What's up?'

'There's another body.'

The world stops. She looks back at the table, in its circle of light. She can see her mother heading inside, hear Greg's banter as he tries to restore the happy bubble that existed before Nell pricked it. Only her father is watching her, raising his glass in her direction.

'Where?' she asks Kevin.

'At the regulator.'

'Jesus. I'll be right there.'

chapter sixteen

1973

GENE AND TESSA WALKED TOGETHER FROM THE OLYMPUS MILK BAR TO THE junkyard two blocks further west, Gene talking about cricket and how shit Australian music was compared to what was coming out of Britain, how it was controlled by money-grubbing fuckwits and dominated by lack-talents like Johnny Farnham and Olivia Newton-John. 'You wait. Give it ten years and no one will remember who they even were.'

But Tessa was only half listening. Instead, she was scanning Gene's face, picking out those parts that resembled Tycho and those that didn't. He wasn't as handsome, that was obvious, his face pink in the heat and sprayed with subterranean acne, his teeth a little crooked, the colour of his eyes a shallow hazel instead of

Tycho's deep brown. It seemed to Tessa that each flaw in Gene's face served to highlight the perfection of Tycho's. Gene seemed to misinterpret her interest as fascination with what he was saying, so he kept prattling away, talking about Pink Floyd and prog rock and *The Dark Side of the Moon*, the record on everyone's turntable.

'Does Tycho ever come back and visit?' she asked, trying to keep her voice casual.

'Sure, when he wants to,' said Gene. 'Just turns up every now and then, unannounced.' He smiled. 'Dinnertime usually. When he's run out of food.'

'So he's unpredictable?'

Gene looked at her then and she could feel herself blushing. But if he noticed, he was kind enough not to mention it. 'The definition of unpredictable. Or unreliable, depending on how you look at it. When he's with you, he's totally with you and you're the most important person in the world. But when he's somewhere else, he's somewhere else.'

She laughed nervously. Could that be right? 'What about Grainger?' she asked, not because she wanted to know, but because it might seem strange asking about one brother and not the other.

'Opposite. Completely dependable.'

'That's good.'

'I guess. Bit boring, though.'

They walked into the junkyard, through gates of wrought iron, left wide open as always, past a freshly painted sign—BUCHANAN'S METAL AND SPARES—and through an honour guard of rusting and disembowelled cars, some on blocks, some left with their tyres flattening, some without windscreens, some with their hoods up or missing them altogether, tufts of spindly grass growing in between.

Some were wrecks, the violence of their demise sculpted into their forms: here a head-on collision; there the V-shaped indentation from smashing into a roadside tree; on the far side, the crumpled roof of a rollover. Others seemed unblemished, save for dust and rust and powdering paint, brought low by some internal malfunction. After about thirty yards the corridor of wrecks gave way to a more open space and the track forked. To the left it led to the working spaces: a large machinery shed; an industrial compacter/crusher; a crane with a huge electromagnet; a tow truck, red paint fading and chipped, with *Buchanan's Metal and Spares* painted on the door in yellow cursive. To the right was the house, a contrast, behind a low fence of black wire backed by a precisely trimmed hedge. Inside the barrier was a lawn, short and golf-green perfect, with a birdbath and a Venus de Milo. The house itself, two storeys high, was solid brick, with terracotta tiles and a portico. Tessa had been there before, mostly for birthday parties when she was younger, but walking into the yard with Gene it struck her how eccentric the set-up was: the picture-perfect house surrounded by the field of mangled cars, like a chateau in a battlefield. She interpreted it now with older eyes: the house belonged to the boys' mother, Rita, and the yard belonged to their father, Bert. She realised something similar, if more subtle, could be discerned in her own family's farm: the house belonged to her mother and the farm to her father. Except Rita's house was a veritable palace compared to the feeble weatherboard baking on the plain above the tilt.

'Wait here a tick,' said Gene. 'I'll get changed.'

It was hot in the sun and Tessa moved away towards some shade over near the crusher, spotting a tree among the bruised metal, an ash or an oak or an elm, one of those European ones with plenty of leaves. It was then that she heard music. Violin. She thought it was a radio, but as she approached the tree it became clearer: not a song or piece of music but scales. Up and down and up again, drifting on the breeze. Curious, she walked further and the cars parted to reveal another access track, this one only wide enough for walking. Down this path a little way she saw Grainger standing under a second tree playing the instrument, as if to serenade the gutted remains of a Bedford truck. His back was to her; he was intent on his rehearsing, unaware of her presence. She found the sight mesmerising, the way he held himself, the arch of his back, the way he was swaying back and forth as he played, captured by the music. Captured by scales.

'Can I help you, lass?'

The voice startled her. She pivoted around. It was the father, Bert Buchanan, dressed in overalls, hands grease-covered.

'I'm waiting for Gene. He's getting changed.'

The man smiled. 'Goodo.' He was older, of course, but the likeness to Tycho was startling: the same white teeth, the same tanned skin and deep brown eyes. The father looked much more like his eldest son than either Gene or Grainger, although he was shorter, carried more weight, and his face was not quite as well aligned. A prototype, not the finished model. The dark hair was turning grey at the temples, giving him a distinguished look, like a senator in a TV soap, and she wondered if one day Tycho might look the same, growing more handsome with age. Some men were like that.

'Have fun then,' said Bert Buchanan. And he turned and walked back towards the machinery shed.

Grainger must have heard them talking. He came over, holding his violin by the neck, the bow in the same hand. 'Hi, Tessa. Fancy seeing you here.'

'Hi. Gene said he might be able to give me a lift home. He'll just be a minute.'

'I can take you. He's not licensed.'

'Whatever works best.'

'Can you wait a bit? Until I finish my practice?'

'Sure. It sounds amazing.'

Grainger smiled at that, looking almost bashful. 'Thanks.' And he returned to his spot under the tree and his music stand. She sat in the shade of the first tree. Before long, he was playing again.

Gene returned wearing shorts and a t-shirt with a faded image of a long-haired man in a cowboy hat riding an extravagant motorbike. *Easy Rider*, said the logo.

'I said we'd wait for Grainger,' Tessa told him.

'Fair enough,' said Gene. There was something in his voice. Disappointment? 'Could be a while then. He can go on for hours.'

'Seriously?'

'Yeah. But not if he knows we're waiting.' Gene looked about. 'It's hot here. Let me show you something.'

He led her to an old car slowly crumbling in the shade of another tree, just a few yards from where she'd been sitting. The wreck was old, from the 1930s or 40s, with running boards and long curved fenders, dark paint flaking and patched russet with rust.

'Studebaker,' said Gene.

'Classy,' said Tessa.

Gene pulled the back door open for her, like a chauffeur. It opened backwards, the opposite way to modern cars, the hinges squealing in protest. She dipped her head and got in. Inside, the seat was deep and low and covered with dry leather, with so much space she couldn't reach the front seat with her extended foot and could only just touch the roof with an extended arm. With the windows open, the car was almost cool under the tree.

Gene walked around and got in the driver's seat. 'We can wait here for him.' He sat with his hands on the cracked wooden steering wheel, as if he intended driving her somewhere. 'It's where I come sometimes, just to get away,' he said. 'The old man. He can get shitty. Has a drink or two. It's better not to hang around. We call it black Bert.'

'He seems so nice,' she said.

'He is. Mostly.'

She thought of her own father. He was nice too, if distant. Absent. He wasn't violent and he didn't drink much, like she knew some men did, but sometimes she felt as if he'd had the stuffing knocked out of him. He worked so hard on the farm; maybe that was why he had little energy left for Tessa and her mother. Again, she thought of the golf club.

'What's with the scales?' she asked, trying to change the flow of her thoughts. 'Why doesn't he play something?'

'You do them at the start of practice. Gets the fingers working, the mind in tune. He must be almost done with them.' And Gene demonstrated, his voice surprisingly rich and assured. '*Do Re Mi Fa Sol La Ti Do*.' He turned to her and smiled. 'That's a major. Here's the minor.' He sang the syllables again, but there was some difference in the notes, unclear to Tessa. It sounded mellow, almost sad.

'What scale is Grainger playing?'

Gene listened. 'That's D major.' He paused. 'And now D minor.' Another pause. 'And now he's dropped a seventh into it.'

Tessa blinked. 'You can tell that just by listening? How?'

'Perfect pitch. We've all got it. From Mum.'

'Do you play instruments? All of you?'

'Yeah. Tycho did trumpet but prefers the piano. Doesn't really go for classical; he likes improvising, making up his own tunes. Bluesy stuff. I've done clarinet, but I'm a bit like Tycho, just not as good.'

'Piano?'

'Guitar. I'd like to be in a band.'

'A rock group?'

'Yeah.'

'Wow,' she said, recalibrating her opinion of Gene. There was more to him than just the quiet boy she had known most of her life. 'How come I didn't know that? Why haven't I heard you play? At school?'

'I'm working on it,' Gene said, but she could sense the shyness in him, even looking at the back of his head, thought it unlikely he could ever be a rock star, no matter how much talent he possessed. Maybe the guy standing up the back next to the drummer, head down, face shielded by hair.

'What about Tycho? Is he any good?' She could imagine the eldest son, not up the back but out front singing, in the spotlight, like Mick Jagger. No, not Mick Jagger: Jim Morrison.

'Tycho? Tons of talent. But too slack, doesn't practise. Grainger is the only diligent one. Mum's hoping he can study at the Con in Sydney or the VCA in Melbourne. She's got her heart set on it.'

'Are they free? Like uni?'

'Don't know. We're trying to find out. Mum's written to all of them.'

Tessa thought about this for a moment. There was a band at school, trumpets and banged-up trombones, massacring 'When the Saints Come Marching In' and 'Heartbreak Hotel' and other prehistoric shit. But she'd never heard any of the Buchanans play. Maybe they were embarrassed by it. No, Gene maybe, but not Grainger and certainly not Tycho. Maybe they thought themselves too good for the school band. Having heard Grainger, she thought maybe they were right. 'So it's your mum who's into music, not your dad?'

'All Mum. We don't have a telly, but we've got a proper stereo. You know, with twin speakers and a separate amplifier. She listens to classical music all day long. We're even named after famous musicians.'

'Really? I always wondered. Your names.'

Gene looked embarrassed, turning back to the front again, as if he'd said too much.

'So who then?'

For a moment it seemed as if Gene was considering whether to answer or not, before responding. 'Tycho is named after Tommy Tycho. He's a famous pianist, conducts the ABC orchestras and does all sorts of stuff. Pronounced differently: "tee-co". Grainger is named after Percy Grainger, who Mum reckons is this country's greatest composer.'

'Never heard of him.'

'Wrote the Edgell's frozen pea jingle. You hear it on the radio.'

'Deadset?'

'Yeah.' Gene whistled the tune.

The sound surprised her, pure and simple and note-perfect. The melody was instantly recognisable. 'Yeah. It's on the telly too.'

'It's actually called "English Country Garden". It's an old folk tune, but he arranged it into a proper piece of orchestral music. Of course, they've bowdlerised it for the ad.'

Tessa couldn't help but laugh, trying on the unfamiliar word for size. 'Bowdlerised?'

'Means dumbed down.'

'Top word.'

Just at that moment Grainger shifted from scales into a simple melody, and it was like something in the air changed with it. It wasn't classical, and it wasn't anything flash, but some sort of lament. The notes were long and plaintive, evoking a kind of longing in Tessa, surprising her. 'Jesus. He is good, isn't he?'

'If I practised all day long, I'd never be as good as him.'

'So who are you named after? Gene who?'

'Doesn't matter.'

'Oh, come on! Tell me!'

Now he did look embarrassed. 'Promise you won't tell anyone?'

'Who would I tell?'

'Seriously, you can't tell a soul.'

'Shit, Gene, chill out. I promise.'

He laughed nervously. 'Eugene Goossens.'

'Never heard of him either.'

'He used to be Australia's top classical muso. Conductor of the Sydney Symphony Orchestra, head of the Conservatorium. Mum reckons he was the one who had the idea for the Opera House.'

'What happened?'

'He got busted at Sydney airport with a bag full of porn. Then they found out he was having it off with a witch. Satanic orgies.'

'Bullshit. Really?'

'Yeah. In the 1950s. He was run out of the country. Went back to England.'

'Maybe Whitlam will let him back in. Was he back last month? For the opening?'

'The Opera House? No. He died years ago.'

'That's sad.'

'Dad hates him, hates the mention of him.'

'Why?'

''Cos I'm named after him, I guess. Dad won't ever call me Eugene, or even Gene. Calls me "lad" or "Number Three" or "Victor" instead.'

'Victor? Like the record player?'

'Nah. Victor Trumper. The cricketer. It's my middle name. We all have sportsmen for middle names. Tycho's Les, after Les Darcy, the boxer, and Grainger is Cazaly, after an Aussie Rules player. I think it was some sort of trade-off between Mum and Dad.'

'Grainger Cazaly Buchanan. That's something,' Tessa said laughing, and then silently mouthed 'Tycho Les Buchanan' to herself. 'I'm named after my grandmothers: Theresa and Mary. Utterly predictable.'

'I wouldn't complain. There's safety in normality.' He smiled. 'Promise not to tell?'

'What?'

'Me and Eugene Goossens.'

'Cross my heart.'

'Thanks.'

'You should play something on the guitar for me.'

'Maybe.'

'Do you write songs?'

'Sort of.'

'I'd love to hear one.'

'Maybe some time.' And then, awkwardly, 'Maybe I could write you one.'

'That's so sweet,' she said, thinking nothing of the impact her words might make.

Outside there was a pause, just the wind in the tree above the old car and the creaking of metal, before the violin music recommenced, sweet and low and melodic. Another lament. It brought silence to the old car, Gene in the front, Tessa in the back. And Tessa thought to herself how fortunate she was to have such a cultured family living so close. Tycho's family. Maybe a family she would join one day.

chapter seventeen

ONCE NELL IS OFF THE HIGHWAY, DOWN THE TILT AND PAST THE CAMP FIRES and gas lanterns of the conspiracy theorists, the night turns ominous, moonlight flickering through the trees. She drives along the sealed road, passing an old sawmill, trying not to speed, knowing there is no hurry but again and again having to ease her foot from the accelerator. Another body. According to Kev, another skeleton. Is it Finucane? Could both he and Stannard have been murdered by their collaborator, waiting at the regulator with their getaway car? Was Gene right after all when he accused Keith Tankard of being a killer? She's almost at the river, slowing as she approaches Anglers Reach, then turning left onto the dirt access road. The trees close over the track, her lights carving a beam through the darkness, civilisation left behind. The mist is down, early in the windless evening, like some last vestige of the winter passed. Two kangaroos, big greys, better suited to the plains, come bounding out of the bush, leaping in front of the car, startling her, their eyes shining white. In the headlights, they glow like ghosts in the fog. They stop, blinded. She hits the brakes. Still one of the roos sits there, staring her down, a buck male, muscles rippling, flexing. Her mind tells her it's confused; that she's only imagining its defiance. She sounds the horn; it moves back into the forest.

She doesn't drive on immediately. And when she does, she's more cautious. Why has she been racing, anyway? The body is going nowhere. Why, then, does she feel so on edge? It makes no sense. It must be Finucane, Stannard's accomplice. She repeats that to herself, wanting it to be true.

She feels guilty, leaving her family so abruptly, remembering what her father had said on the phone after identifying Stannard: that the family longed for closure. When she had told them that she had to leave, that there was a second body, she had seen the impact, the fragile bonhomie draining away, the descending silence. The unspoken name: Tycho. She'd realised the earlier gaiety had something of the air of a celebration: a celebration that the first skeleton didn't belong to her father's brother. She had left reassuring them that the new discovery was almost certainly Eamon Finucane.

The regulator emerges from the darkness, flickering through the trees, an island of light. There are cars: Kevin's plus two work trucks, identified by the signs on their doors as belonging to an engineering company and to the Murray-Darling Basin Authority. There is the sound of a generator and of birdsong, incongruous in the night, the animals confused by the artificial dawn.

Kevin is waiting. 'Over there,' he points. There's not much to see. A couple of small yellow flags, triangular. 'Crime scene investigators will be here tomorrow.'

'From Sydney?'

'Yeah.'

'Who found the body?'

'Not us. Contractors. Finishing up for the day. Preparing to recommence the repair work. They found a bone, realised straight away what it might be. Poked about a bit more, found a skull.'

She surveys the site, noting the position of the small tent where Stannard was found. 'Quite a way along from where the first one was found, am I right?'

'Yep. This side of the creek, and back away from the regulator wall a good thirty metres.'

'The skull. Where is it?'

'Still there. Half buried. You can clamber down, if you like. But it's as muddy as shit. I figured we should leave it to the experts. Forensics.'

Nell feels an urge to see it for herself. It's her investigation, her responsibility, but Kevin's logic is hard to fault. There is no urgency. Like driving the track; she needs to pace herself. 'Any sign of trauma?'

'It's still half buried.'

'How come it's only just being found now, as they're about to recommence works? How did the contractors find it when we didn't?'

'Albury scanned the area as best they could with metal detectors, but you know . . .' He shrugs; she gets it. No metal, no detection. 'What now?' he asks.

'What's the weather forecast?'

'No rain for days.'

'That's lucky. I'll speak to Ivan. We may have to dig the whole thing up.'

Kevin looks at her, eyes round. 'You reckon there might be more?'

Now it's her turn to shrug. 'Can't see how we can flood it again without checking.'

He looks back at the muddy expanse as though seeing it for the first time. 'Faaaaark.' He lets the expression drain out of him, one long breath. 'A serial killer.'

'Let's not get ahead of ourselves.'

'You want me to stay out here? Guard the scene?'

'You think it's necessary?'

'Up to you. Your show.' He smiles. 'I don't mind. Got my swag. Nice night.'

She looks around her. The whole place feels ominous to her, the lights turning the trees into scarecrows, the darkness beyond like a wall, the mist wisping in and out. 'It doesn't spook you, being out here?'

'This country, it's full of the dead, full of spirits. I won't offend them.'

'You believe that?'

'Sure. They'll keep an eye out for me.' And he winks. She can't work out if he's serious or just having a lend of her.

She looks back at the hole, the muddy grave. 'I wonder about that sometimes. The dead. Do the murdered rest easy?'

'If we find out who killed them, they will,' says Kevin.

—

She's driving back, thinking she might stay in Hatheson, when her phone rings, coming through the car's speakers.

'Detective Constable Nell Buchanan.'

'Constable, it's John here at the Redgum Motel. You left your number in case a vacancy came up.'

'You have something?'

'The engineering crew coming in to work at the river cancelled at short notice.'

'I'll be there in ten minutes.'

—

The motel room has none of the character of the hotel. No high ceiling, no sash window, no verandah. But it has a working bathroom and wi-fi and a lump-free mattress. Sitting on the double bed, she's surprised to see it's only just gone eleven o'clock. It feels later to her, as if the woods were set to midnight. She rings Ivan.

'Nell?'

'You heard?'

'Yeah. Kevin rang. Blake is heading back down, hopefully Carole Ngyuen as well. PolAir, first thing.'

'Stepping it up?'

'Two bodies. Always the chance there are more. Plodder wants to be on top of it.'

'He's across it?'

'Not in any detail. Just wants to know what we're dealing with before the media get a whiff of it.'

'Will you come back?'

'Depends. Certainly, if there are more bodies.'

'We'll have to excavate the whole thing.'

'Carole will bring proper gear. That's another reason for the plane. Ground-penetrating radar, the works. Albury are sending their people back. But tell me one thing: this second body, it's definitely a skeleton? Been there for a long time?'

'That's what it sounds like. I'll know more in the morning. Why?'

'Plodder. He got wind of that missing cooker—Hoffner.'

'Why would he be concerned about that?' asks Nell.

'Search me.'

'Can't see it being Hoffner. He only disappeared three months ago. Kev said this body is skeletal, buried in the mud. Been there for years, not months.'

'Right. Confirm that tomorrow and I can let Plodder know.'

'I reckon it's Eamon Finucane,' she says.

'Who?'

'The lieutenant who went AWOL with Stannard in 1943. They stole four hundred pounds. I thought Finucane must have killed Stannard and kept the money for himself. But maybe not. Maybe they were both murdered.'

'By whom?'

She doesn't want to mention her uncle's newspaper claims. 'I don't know. Maybe a double-cross. Someone they were paying to help them with a getaway. Someone selling them a car or something.'

She knows her theory is entirely speculative, unlikely to impress Ivan. There's scepticism in his voice when he replies. 'One step at a time. Let's see if we can identify the body first. Confirm whether it's Finucane or not.'

'Will do.'

'You still have carriage, Nell. Stay there, stick with it. But keep me posted.'

chapter eighteen

THE NEXT MORNING, HER FATHER RINGS EVEN BEFORE NELL GETS TO THE police station.

'Hi, Dad.'

'Hope it's not too early.'

'All good. Sorry I had to race off last night.'

'We understand. That's why I'm calling. The new discovery.'

Is he trying to probe her for information? 'What is it, Dad?'

'I'm in at the old surgery again, checking the records. There is nothing here for anyone called Finucane. That was his name, right?'

Nell feels a flash of guilt for suspecting her father of ulterior motives. 'Yes. Eamon with an E, surname starting with an F.'

'Sorry, nothing. I've had a good look through. If the practice did all the work for the garrison, it's unlikely any of the other dentists in the district will have a record for him.'

'Okay, thanks, Dad.'

'Good on you, Nell. Let me know if there is anything I can do.' And he hangs up.

—

Kevin is leaving the station as she gets there. He holds up his bandaged hand. 'Just running up to Hatty to get my stitches out. Shouldn't be long.'

Nell frowns. 'How many?'

'Three. It's nothing.'

She remembers what he said about a run-in at the campground. 'You get a lot of grief from the cookers?'

'Nah. Most of them are fine.'

'I saw a Confederate flag down there.'

Kevin grows serious. 'What are you asking? Are they racist?'

'I guess.'

'Sure. Most people are. But petty racism. Gives you the shits, but not physically threatening.'

'So how'd you get the stitches?'

'Couple of aggro skinheads. Out-of-towners.'

'You arrest them?'

'The one who cut me, of course.' And he smiles. 'Remanded in custody.'

'When we arrived, you said the Vics had trouble with some Neo-Nazis.'

'Yeah, but not this side of the river,' says Kevin. 'Why you asking?'

'Some of those blokes at the pub looked like trouble. Called me a deep-state bitch.'

'Well, if you encounter anything, let me know. The brass want to know if I pick up on anything.'

'Because you're black?'

'I guess. Makes sense. If anyone is going to get grief, it'll be me.'

'You don't sound too stressed about it.'

'Of course I'm stressed. But on the other hand, nothing would give me more pleasure than helping put a couple of those fuckers away.'

He raises his bandaged hand in farewell and Nell heads inside.

When she checks her messages she finds an email from the Department of Defence.

Dear Detective Constable Buchanan,

Thank you once again for notifying the Department of the discovery of the body of Major Gerard Stannard. We appreciate your thoughtfulness and I have updated the file.

As per your request, I searched our records, but there is no further mention of either Major Stannard or Lieutenant Eamon Finucane.

However, that is not unusual. As I said, most records from the Second World War are held at either the Australian War Memorial or the National Archives.

I have cc'd in Guy Powell, a researcher at the Australian War Memorial, attaching the contemporaneous army report into the two men's disappearance. Good luck with your investigation.

Kind regards,
Janine

Janine Collinston
Records Branch
Department of Defence—Army, Ph: 1300 333 362

Nell replies with a quick thanks, then calls the Australian War Memorial. The automated switchboard recites the opening hours for the public and then informs her that staff work from nine to five on weekdays. She follows the prompts, finally gets through to an operator, and asks to speak to Guy Powell.

'Guy here.'

'Guy, this is Detective Constable Nell Buchanan from New South Wales police. Homicide.'

'Wow, that was quick. I received an email from Defence mentioning you just this morning.'

'Yes. Janine Collinston. Have you had a chance to read the attached report?'

'Just finished. Intriguing stuff. How can I help?'

'We have located two bodies, skeletal remains, in the Barmah-Millewa Forest. We've identified one as Major Gerard Stannard and we're now trying to establish if the other one is Lieutenant Eamon Finucane.'

'I see. But how could the Memorial possibly help with that?'

'I'm searching for dental records. Also, medical records, to establish if Finucane sustained any wounds or fractures. This could help us to identify the body. And a list of relatives would be good, so we can use DNA.'

'I'll see what I can do, but we won't have any of that on hand. You should contact the Archives. They'll have records of where he enlisted, where he was deployed, any injuries and medical treatment. Promotions, demobilisations.'

'Okay. So the Memorial doesn't have anything?'

She hears the man sigh. 'We do. We have the official histories and histories of different regiments and the like. Also unit diaries and many thousands of personal diaries and hundreds of thousands of letters. I can search to see if he is mentioned in the histories or if we hold any of his documents.'

'That would be useful, thank you.'

'Don't get your hopes up. If he was a private or lieutenant, he's unlikely to be mentioned in the histories unless he was involved in conspicuous action. I can check to see if we hold any of his papers. But even if we do, they won't be digitised.'

'What about mentions in the letters and diaries of his comrades?'

The same sigh. 'No way of knowing. Because they're yet to be digitised, they're not computer searchable. You'd have to come here yourself, or hire a researcher. It could take weeks.'

Nell laughs. 'I can't see us doing that. But thank you.'

'Do you have a service number for him? That would be useful for Archives.'

'No. All I know is that his name was Eamon Finucane and he was twenty-two when he went missing in January 1943.' She spells the name.

'Bear with me a moment. I'm going to do a quick search.'

Before she can respond, he puts her on hold. Radio National is talking to an expert about feng shui. Less than two minutes later Guy is back, just as Nell is suspecting the police station decor is seriously out of balance.

'Okay, I think I've found him. Eamon Patrick Finucane. Born in Bendigo on the twenty-fifth of April 1920.'

Nell does the mental sums. 'Yes, that sounds like him. Can't be too many Eamon Finucanes, can there?'

Guy laughs. It sounds like he's enjoying this. 'His service number was VX76517. Write it down. It might help you with Archives.'

'Do you have a contact there you could put me in touch with?' she asks.

'To be honest, they're severely understaffed. The government has been underfunding them for years.'

'Meaning?'

'It could take days, even weeks, for them to get back to you.'

'Even for a police officer?'

'If you were general public it would take at least a month. At least.'

'What do you suggest?'

'Leave it with me. I'm authorised to access their databases from here. I'll see what they have—and if it looks promising, I can do a physical search myself.'

'That's extremely generous of you.'

'Not at all. I love a good mystery. If we get anywhere, I might write it up for the Historical Society's newsletter.'

Nell can't help but smile at the researcher's enthusiasm. 'Well, let's hope you find something useful for both our sakes.'

She ends the call and leans back in her chair. It's refreshing to encounter such a helpful person, but she wonders if there really is any useful information to be found. Would the National Archives keep dental records? It seems unlikely.

She decides she needs coffee. Best to get some now; the afternoon could get busy. Blake and Carole should be back at the regulator by lunchtime. Hatheson and Albury are both assigning uniforms to help the technicians search the site.

Tulong is still quiet as she walks from the station to Highgate Street. There are a couple of cars outside the Foresters Arms but no other signs of activity at the pub. A woman walks past pushing a pram, smiles to Nell through tired eyes. At the Barking Frog, Frieda is behind the counter, offering a greeting and suggesting homemade banana bread. Nell takes her up on the offer, ordering takeaway. She's heading back outside to the footpath tables to wait when she sees the flyer for the vanished cooker.

She returns to the counter. 'Frieda, do you mind if I ask you something?'

'Please.'

'This missing man, Jean-Luc Hoffner—did you ever meet him?'

'Yes. He liked my coffee. Drank it black.'

'Was he French? European?'

She shakes her head. 'Second generation Australian. French mother, German father. That's what he told me.'

Nell has no idea if that has any significance. 'Anything else?'

'No. A polite young man.'

Nell thanks the cafe owner and heads outside.

As she sits there, a twin-cab ute cruises past, Australian flags fluttering from window mounts. The new fringe, she thinks, in the towns and the cities. Out on the periphery, the conspiracy theorists and the anti-vaxxers and the QAnon adherents are coalescing: preppers and cookers and chancers. She wonders what it is that takes people there, out of the mainstream and off into this parallel belief system. Maybe it's nothing new; maybe the marginalised have always searched for reasons. Once it was religion, people looking beyond the old churches to cults and happy-clapping. Maybe it's the same thing, adapted for this secular age. Maybe.

Frieda delivers her coffee and snack. She takes them with her, dropping into the general store to buy some milk for the station fridge and some washing powder, so she can clean her street-soiled clothes in the motel's guest laundry. She's just emerging when she runs into Noel Tankard. The big man flinches involuntarily.

'You still here,' he grunts.

'I told you, Noel, that article had nothing to do with me.'

'Bullshit.'

She shakes her head. 'I'm sorry for what happened, but I'm going to do my job, then I'll leave. Simple as that.'

'You can apologise all you like—it won't save you.'

'What's that supposed to mean?'

'You'll see. You're fucked.'

'Are you threatening me?'

'Don't have to,' he says, and brushes past her.

She walks to the station, places her shopping on the porch and rings Ivan.

'Morning, Constable. I was going to call you a little later on.'

'Ivan, is there something I should know about?'

'Such as?'

She recounts the encounter with Tankard, explains their confrontation the previous day.

'I'm told you arrested him,' says Ivan.

'No. I let him off with a warning.' A campervan passes along the street, Australian flag in the back window. 'You heard about it?'

'I did. So did Plodder. So did Professional Standards.'

'Tankard has made a formal complaint?'

'He has. That's what I was going to call you about.'

'He tried to shove me off the gutter and into the street. Assaulting a police officer. All I did was defend myself.'

'Using karate.'

'More like judo. Purely defensive.'

'It doesn't help.'

She knows what he's saying. Police officers with training in boxing and martial arts are restricted in how they can use those skills. 'What happens now?'

'It's with Professional Standards. Nathan Phelan.'

'Shit.' Nathan 'Feral' Phelan, the scourge of the force. She's encountered him before. If he gets his claws in, it could get nasty. 'What should I do?'

'Just hang in there for now. Word is that Phelan knew Blake and Carole were heading down on PolAir but decided it wasn't worth his time.'

'That's a good sign,' she says.

'Let's hope so. But Nell, you should know—this bloke Tankard, he claims to have a police witness.'

'Kevin?'

'Yes. I take it he was there?'

'He was.'

'So a word to the wise: do not engage Kevin on this. Even the most innocent conversation could be misconstrued by Phelan as attempting to influence a witness. You understand?'

She does. 'Thanks, Ivan.'

'You want me to come down there?'

That rattles her, makes her feel even more vulnerable. 'Do you think you should?'

'No. That might be interpreted as a lack of confidence in you. That's the last signal I want to send.'

'Okay. Thanks.'

'Don't thank me. Crack on with it. The sooner you wrap things up and leave, the better. If it's Finucane, get out of there and finish the paperwork back here.'

Call finished, she picks up her shopping, looks along the street. The nature of the morning has changed. The clarity of the air has disappeared and a warm wind is starting to blow in from the west. She imagines it's lifting dust, hazing the sky, but she knows it's not. The goodwill of Frieda at the cafe and Guy Powell at the War Memorial has evaporated.

An old work truck sidles past, muffler gone. A yob sticks his head out the window, waving a bong of all things. 'Legalise it!' he yells as an unseen companion hoots with laughter.

She doesn't bother to respond.

chapter nineteen

JAMES WATERS–FIRST STATEMENT–CONTINUED

BUCKY AND ME, WE WERE INSEPARABLE THAT SUMMER IN THE FOREST. HE'D come across the river, help me with the cattle, or I'd swim across and see him. After a few weeks, the dogs and the cattle had settled into a routine and didn't need me as much, so I was spending more and more of my time over on the Victorian side with Bucky. My swimming had improved out of sight and crossing was nothing to me. I could go back and forth without even drawing a breath. It looms large in our minds, the Murray, being the state border and all, but back then, to us, it meant nothing. People talk about it as if it's our Mississippi, but they're having themselves on.

Bucky's dad Clarrie ran a steam engine, over on the Victorian side. It was a brute of a thing. The story was it had been the boiler in a paddle steamer that had run aground and, instead of leaving it there or trying to get it down the river, they'd winched it up onto higher ground by a little lagoon, bolted it to a couple of huge redwood beams, then put it to use powering a sawmill. It had a giant flywheel with a belt driving the saws. Bucky's dad would keep it oiled, the belt taut, and feed it with wood and water.

There was plenty of wood, of course: the offcuts from the mill. He'd set up a kind of flying fox arrangement with these two big buckets, like counterweights, that he used to haul water up from the lagoon. One would dip down into the water, then he would crank it up as the empty one went down. He'd pour the water into a large tank he had there, then he'd feed the engine from the tank. It was a steam engine, so it went through a lot of water. It was hard work hauling the buckets up like that, so if Bucky and I were there, we'd ride the empty one down into the lagoon and our weight would pull the full bucket up. It was tremendous fun, zooming down in the bucket and spilling out into the lagoon, then climbing up and doing it again. 'Cos of that, Bucky's dad was always glad to see me, and we'd get his tank full before heading off on our adventures.

The forest wasn't empty. Don't get that idea. You might think of it as a kind of wilderness, now that it's all locked up in national park, but back then it was crawling with people. Men had left, of course, off to the war, but others had come in to replace them, because the forest was a valuable resource. The nation still needed wood; the war effort demanded it. So the old fellows were still in there, still logging. Still hauling timber to the river or to one of the forest mills. Clarrie's was called the red engine and was on the Victorian side, but there was a similar set-up a few miles down the river on our side: the black engine. There was another—the green engine—over in Barmah. And so it went.

The logs were in demand, and so were the sleepers, but the big thing, the new thing, was charcoal. First it was just the offcuts, then the tops and the branches, then whole logs were being carved up for it. Petrol was scarce and getting scarcer, strictly rationed, going to the military and essential services, but some bright spark had worked out that you could run cars and even buses and trucks on charcoal. You'd put the charcoal in a box next to the engine and warm it up, the charcoal would release its gas, and there was enough energy in it to power a car. Not a lot of torque, like petrol, but enough. Soon it was vital, necessary to the war effort and essential for everyday life. You'd pull up at a service station and they sold charcoal, not gasoline. It was in Melbourne and all over.

They built charcoal stills near the red engine and they'd be working them all day and all night, first in charcoal pits and then, later, they made these huge steel drums on brackets, and every few hours they'd tumble them over to spread the heat. They'd get the fire going, then close off the air just enough, so the wood wouldn't burn all the way through but would turn to charcoal. There was an art to it. They didn't have any instruments, no thermometers or anything like that, just dead reckoning. Some blokes were expert at it, had the nose for the charcoal. Everyone looked up to 'em; it was a much-admired skill.

It was hard yakka, tending the fires in the middle of summer, but those men kept working, day and night. They had to. They were a rough lot, those who worked the charcoal. There were draft dodgers and deserters and criminals on the run, wife beaters and boozers and murderers. That's why they ended up there. You see, after a few days on the charcoal, they were unrecognisable, black from head to toe, and nothing could get rid of it, not a swim in the river, not a scrubbing, not anything. As long as they remained on the charcoal they stayed black and they stayed beyond the law. No one could tell one from the other—and besides, the government needed them, needed the charcoal, so the authorities left them alone. Everyone spoke of how dangerous they were meant to be, but they were always kind to Bucky and me when we were at the engine, helping with the water on the flying fox. I think somehow it cheered them up to see us riding those buckets down into the lagoon, to see two kids laughing and enjoying themselves. I think they liked that.

As the need for charcoal grew, prisoners of war—Italians—were put to work cutting trees over on the Victorian side. They'd surrendered in their thousands to Australian forces in North Africa, back before the Pacific War. The government shipped them here and used them as labourers. I checked the atlas at the farm one evening and saw where Italy was, and where Libya was, and I couldn't work it out. Why they wanted to bring them all the way across the world was beyond me.

It was beyond Bucky as well. He got all agitated. He reckoned the forest was too important, too big and too strategic, to be ignored by the enemy. Here was the source of logs and railway sleepers, here was the source of fish and meat, and here was the source of charcoal. The way Bucky saw it, the whole war effort hinged on the fate of Barmah-Millewa. What if the Italians overpowered their guards, escaped from the camp, and sabotaged the charcoal? The Allied cause would grind to a halt. Bucky was full of terms like 'strategic' and 'saboteurs' and 'infiltrated behind enemy lines' and so on. When he put it like that, I didn't have much choice. I volunteered to help him.

So we started spying on them. The plan was that if we found something, we'd write a letter to General MacArthur. At night, as I slept in my swag, I'd imagine the two of us receiving medals from the general in a big ceremony at the MCG, with us beaming proudly on the Cinesound newsreel and MacArthur removing his corn-cob pipe from his mouth and smiling. 'Well done, young fellows,' he would say. 'You're a credit to your nation.' Maybe even Dad would hear about it in New Guinea.

The trouble was, the Italians didn't look like enemies. They looked like normal men. Bucky was disappointed, but not me; if anything, it made it worse. I hated them. What right did they have—these fascists, as Bucky called them—to be safe and comfortable and carefree in our forest, leaving the dirty work of the charcoal to the Aussies, while my own father was fighting for his life in the jungles of New Guinea? Sometimes, when they laughed, I was sure they were laughing at us. It made me mad and, in my mind, I recast them so they no longer seemed young and full of laughter, but appeared sinister and scheming and murderous. Camping alone in my swag, I had trouble sleeping. It wasn't Japs, or duffers, or even the telegraph boy anymore; I had nightmares about the Italians. What if they learnt we were spying on them, uncovering their secrets? What was to stop them coming in the night to slit my throat, even as they wreaked havoc on the charcoal?

It was around this time that I found an island in the river. Not in the middle of the river, not how you'd imagine an island, but carved out of one bank, where a big horseshoe bend had come back on itself and then, later, had done the same again. It wasn't large, just fifty yards or so long, maybe thirty wide, with some old fella redgums and some higher ground, built up on one of the middens left by the Yorta Yorta. It was a fair way inland from the main course of the river and protected by a delta of smaller creeks, so it was real hard to find if you didn't already know it was there. There was a clearing nearby where the cattle could sleep guarded by the dogs. I felt safe there; it was like a fort, with its own moat. I knew the dogs would bark if anyone was coming, and I had an escape plan. If they kept barking, if it wasn't a possum or a wombat or a koala, then I could slide into the water and make my way to the river, where I'd float with the current and come ashore a mile or two downstream. It was never called for, but it was a good plan.

It was exciting spying on the Italians at first. But once we worked out how to find them and how to get up close without being detected, it was a bit of an anticlimax. If they were intent on sabotage, they were hiding it well. They laughed and joked as they worked, and the guards—the Aussie soldiers—were very relaxed. They had guns, but that seemed to be the only difference. They'd share smokes with the prisoners and sometimes try out a few words of Italian, but otherwise they more or less left them alone. It was getting harder and harder to imagine them as murdering cutthroats. In my mind, they were already different to the Japanese, but although I had ceased to fear them, I still resented them. They were here and my father wasn't.

But that all changed too. Bucky decided we needed to go out on a night sortie. That was another of his words: 'sortie'. He said it was no good spying in the daytime; they'd probably realised they were being watched and were putting on a show to fool us. We needed to go in 'under the cover of darkness' and 'infiltrate', 'deep behind enemy lines'. I agreed, of course. I always did.

It was quite a way from the work camps by the river where they spent their days to the internment camp at the edge of the forest on the Victorian side, so it took a bit of planning. I got through dinner at the farm super quick that evening and returned to the forest well before sunset. I checked on the cattle then swam the river to where Bucky was waiting. We headed off just as it was getting dark.

By the time we reached the edge of the forest, it wasn't hard to get up close to the camp. There was a fence, not so high that you couldn't climb it if you really wanted to, but we thought we should stay outside, at least that first night. There were guards walking around. They didn't seem too attentive, but they had these big Lee Enfields, three-oh-threes. So we sat outside the fence, trying to decide what to do next. And that's when the Italians started singing.

There were funny songs and chants, there were folk songs—all in Italian, of course; we couldn't understand a word of it—and there was what I now reckon was opera. I'd never heard anything like it. At school we'd learnt a few rounds about kookaburras and green bottles, and we sang 'God Save the King' at assembly every Monday, but that sounded like cats fighting.

That night, as the stars throbbed and the night-birds called, the last song was a solo, a solitary voice. It was 'Ave Maria'. I didn't know its name then, but I know it now, and eighty years later it can still send a shiver down my spine. The beauty of it, the loneliness, the longing of it—it made me cry. It was dark, but I reckon Bucky had a tear in his eye as well. And I couldn't see, of course, but I thought the Italians would be weeping too: weeping for their lot and the vast distance to their homes and their loved ones. And it struck me that they had wives and children and mothers and fathers. Maybe sons, boys just like me. And I thought of my father, and wondered what songs of home the Australians might be singing in the jungles of war. I realised there and then the Italians were no different from my dad.

chapter twenty

THEY COME FROM ALBURY; THEY COME FROM SYDNEY. THEY SWARM, LIKE FLIES attracted by the promise of putrefaction. By early afternoon the site by the river is crawling with police. The birds have retreated, the forest withdrawn, as if appalled at what has happened here, at what crimes have been revealed, at what they have been party to concealing. Nell watches from the brink of the regulator, stretching out before her like an open wound, a hundred-metre gash of mud amid the greenery. Carole Nguyen is directing a team of plastic-clad experts, laying duckboards and unpacking machinery. A small tent has been erected over the site of the second body, a match for the first which sits thirty or forty metres closer to the regulator wall.

The sight of all this activity heartens Nell: the investigation is receiving the support it needs. But she also feels the weight of responsibility: all these people are working for her, reporting to her, either directly or through Blake and Carole, and it's up to her to use the information they glean. It's intimidating. Blake and Carole have been doing this for years; some of the Albury police have decades of service. She almost wishes Ivan were here to take charge, but she rejects the thought without giving it a chance to establish itself. She is up to this, she knows she is. And her colleague is just a phone call away. She's not about to let him down; she's not about to let herself down.

A man emerges from the tent, clad head to foot in plastic. He removes his goggles and his mask, pulls the hood of his hazmat-style suit down. It's Blake Ness. He sees her, waves, comes along the duckboards and scrambles up a ladder that is serving as a make-shift stairway. He rustles like autumn leaves, plastic on plastic. His hair is damp and pressed to his skull. The day is already warm, humidity high. Life inside one of the protective suits would be moist and uncomfortable.

'What have you got?' Nell asks.

'Early days, but one initial observation, if I may?'

'Of course.'

'The bodies entered the water from different sides. This one, nearest to the mouth of the creek,' he says, pointing to the tent marking Stannard's location. 'The body would have been placed in the water from the far side. The eastern side. Whereas this new body looks more likely to have entered the water from this side, the western side. It's not absolutely certain; the pond narrows the further it is from the regulator and the river.'

Nell nods, sees what he is driving at. 'So the second body was deposited from this side, the side with the access road, but Stannard must have been brought in through the bush.'

'Or along the river.'

She thinks on that. If the two victims were killed by the same person, why bother crossing the creek to place the second body on the far side? 'How easy would it have been to cross the creek, if it was full?'

Blake shrugs. 'These regulators have a walkway above them, I think. Easy enough to cross. Easy enough for you to check.'

She looks across to where the regulator once stood, but its remains have been demolished in preparation for its replacement. 'Maybe the unidentified man was killed here and Stannard tried to flee across the creek, maybe riding his horse, but was shot dead.'

Blake looks a little pained, as if he is channelling Ivan. 'There's nothing to say that didn't happen, but not a lot to say that it did.'

'Anything else?'

'Early days,' Blake repeats. Then he cracks a grin. 'You want a look?'

She hears the challenge in the words, even if the amiable pathologist hasn't intended it. This is her investigation: she should get her hands dirty, not just remain clean and aloof above the crime scene. So she agrees, backing down the ladder, confident in her balance and physicality. She bounces along the duckboards, waiting outside the tent for Blake, who follows, taking care with his footing.

At the entry of the tent, the pathologist grows serious, respectful. 'So far, we have part of a skeleton. Pretty confident the rest of it is here as well.'

'Bullet holes?'

'Nothing so obvious. Not yet. Here.' He gives her some plastic overshoes, a hairnet, latex gloves and a surgical mask. He holds back the flap of the tent. Nell swallows and enters.

Inside, there are two LED lights mounted on stands, adding clinical clarity to the daylight filtering in through the fabric. The atmosphere is cloying, even without wearing a full protective suit. An investigator is on their knees, rendered genderless by the protective suit, clearing bones with a small trowel. The person eases up to a kneeling position, nods acknowledgement of Blake and Nell's presence but remains silent. Nell looks to the skeleton, the rib cage evident.

'Here,' says Blake. Beside the excavation is a table, with various digging implements at one end, together with a series of sieves and a large camera, and bones and debris at the other. Nell's eyes see one thing: the skull, mud still clinging to it, the lower jaw resting next to it.

'Almost certainly a man. Fully grown. Young,' says Blake.

It's the most sparse information, but it's enough: a wave of emotion and realisation sweeps through Nell. This was once a living person, and this is all that is left. 'Can I see?' she asks.

Blake studies her for just a moment, but his thoughts are impossible to discern behind the goggles and face mask. 'Of course.' Ever so gently, ever so respectfully, he lifts the skull, places it in her hands.

She takes it. It seems so light, the eye sockets so very empty. She looks at it, into the twin voids, as if it could look back. She is not sure why she wants to hold it.

'If you look at the teeth, here and on the jaw, you can see they're intact. No extractions, no fillings, no wear. A very small chip on one of the front teeth.'

Nell examines them. They have been rinsed clean with water, surrendering their secrets. 'Is that why you think he was young?'

'Correct.'

Nell takes one more look, then hands the skull back to Blake, like an offering. There is silence as he gently lowers it back onto the table. The investigator, still on their knees, is watching intently.

'Carole is here somewhere, organising a wider search. Ground-penetrating radar, metal detectors. She's also overseeing the extraction of the body, taking it methodically, photographing as they go. Once the body is cleared, they'll be searching for artefacts. Jewellery, belt buckles, any remnants of clothing. And weapons. Like an archaeological dig.'

'How long?'

'Depends. How deep is the mud? What radius do we search?'

'Who decides that?'

'Your call.'

'Right.'

Blake chuckles behind his mask. 'Relax. Carole will make her recommendations. I've never known a detective to overrule her.'

'Thanks. That makes it easier.'

'One more thing before we go. You can see that the bones are all together? That suggests the body was still intact when it came to rest on the riverbed, not washed down the creek after decay had set in. It had time to settle in the mud, to be covered and protected. So it must have been a time when there was no flow coming through the regulator. Maybe a drought year.'

'Stannard died in 1943, after the regulator was built. But is it possible this body was buried here when the creek was totally dry? A shallow grave. The killer knowing that sooner or later the water would come back through.'

Blake scowls. 'Hadn't thought of that. I'll ask Carole. She'll be able to tell from the way the sediment has gathered around the bones.'

'And no idea of the cause of death?'

Blake just shakes his head. 'Nothing yet. Any other time, accidental drowning would be the most likely.'

'Any other time?'

'If it wasn't for the other skeleton. The one with the bullet through the brain.'

'You think they're from the same timeframe?'

'Can't say, but it's possible. They've both been here for years, probably decades. Nothing left except bones.'

Nell looks again at the semi-exposed skeleton. The technician has resumed the excavation. 'Stannard went missing together with another soldier, a Lieutenant Eamon Finucane. Finucane was never found.'

'He was young?'

'Twenty-two.'

'Well then.'

'There's a suggestion he was in New Guinea before being redeployed down here.'

Blake's eyes twinkle. 'Wounded?'

'I'm trying to find out.'

'Let me know. Anything that could identify him.'

Nell leaves Blake and the technician to their work, returns along the duckboards and climbs the ladder, removing the gloves and other protective items, and putting them in a bin placed there for that purpose. She washes her hands and then washes them again. Just mud, she tells herself, but is unsettled nevertheless. When she closes her eyes, she sees the skull gazing back at her, as if looking for justice. Looking to her.

Opening her eyes, she scans the site. She can see a plastic-clad figure over to one side, thinks it might be Carole helping to set up some equipment, perhaps the radar. Then, as she's turning to go, she sees two men standing back, deep in conversation: Kevin Nackangara talking to the twitcher from the pub, the man in the green anorak. She remembers Ivan's warning, but she can't help herself. Kevin has been talking to Gene at the paper, backed Tankard's formal complaint, and now he's chatting happily to some stickybeak birdwatcher. She walks towards them. Maybe it's something in her demeanour, but when the bird enthusiast sees her coming he ends the conversation and retreats in the opposite direction. Kevin turns, sees her and offers a friendly greeting. 'Hi, boss. All happening.'

But she isn't buying the warmth, or the reference to her as the boss. 'A word, Kevin.'

'What is it?' She can see caution in his eyes now.

'This is a homicide investigation. We do not discuss what we are doing with members of the public.'

The young officer arcs up. 'I wasn't discussing shit with him. I saw him over there with his big camera, taking photos. So I got him to delete them and was in the process of telling him to piss off. Right?'

'Okay. If you say so.'

'Hey, listen, don't come over all high and mighty with me. I've been up half the night saving your arse.'

'What does that mean?'

'Professional Standards, that's what. Some ratfucker named Phelan on the phone from Sydney. Noel Tankard has made a formal complaint.'

Nell takes an involuntary step back. 'We shouldn't really be discussing that.'

'Bullshit we shouldn't. I told Phelan that Tankard went for you, that you were defending yourself, that you used reasonable force and nothing more. I told him you were seriously provoked, what with him throwing your possessions into the street, but despite that you took the deliberate decision to leave your firearm at the station to avoid escalating the situation. That you had every right to arrest him and decided not to.'

Nell says nothing.

Kevin lets it all sink in before adding the kicker. 'And I told Phelan my body cam was not turned on at the time of the incident.'

Nell knows she shouldn't ask the question but can't help herself. 'And was it?'

'What do you think?'

'I see.' Her voice is almost meek, 'Thank you.'

But Kevin isn't finished. 'But don't you, under any circumstances, let Noel Tankard know what has gone down. All the shitheads in this town and down in the forest and for miles around congregate at his pub. I need to keep him onside, help me keep an eye on them.'

'He's an informant?'

'Not formally. But if I have him onside, I stand half a chance. Without him, I'm operating blind.'

Nell nods. 'I understand.' And then, 'I'm sorry. Thanks, Kevin. I appreciate everything you've done. I really do.'

chapter twenty-one

1973

THE NEXT DAY, SUNDAY, WAS WORSE. A HEATWAVE HAD INSTALLED ITSELF, parked over the Riverina, dispensing heat like malice and dust like disease. It was one of those awful times when the temperature doesn't drop at night, so the house accumulated more and more heat, already baking by early morning and getting worse as the day progressed. A high-altitude haze was tinting the blue with orange, as if to banish even the concept of rain. A total fire ban was in place and only the lack of wind prevented conflagration.

Yet that same lack of wind meant there was nothing to mitigate the oppression that enveloped the weatherboard house on the plain above the Cadell Tilt. It baked and it sweated and it cowered, its iron roof shimmering like a skillet. The windows were open, begging for a breeze but delivering only flies. The shaded interior seemed as unforgiving as the sun-blasted yard. Tessa's father was gone, leaving in the early morning, more golf, protesting that it was 'pennant', that he couldn't let his mates down. She hadn't said anything, had watched the farm truck trundle down the driveway as her mother meekly accepted it. Tessa wondered where it was he was going. Who he was seeing. Not long after he had left, a migraine had snuck into the house along with the dust and the flies and laid her mother low, forcing her to take refuge in her bedroom. Tessa wondered if the two events were connected.

The day was silent, except for the complaining roof and the occasional groan from her mother, as if the oppressive weather had turned personal and pressed her into her bed. Which meant Tessa was trapped: trapped in the house, trapped by her filial obligation. She was restless, unable to sit still. So she hung out the washing, abandoned in the tub by her mother at the onset of her headache, felt it drying under her hands even as she pegged it to the line, squinting against the brightness of the whites. Beyond the rim she could see the tops of the trees, the great forest. In her mind it was cool and inviting, extending the promise of shade, the benediction of water.

The washing out, she returned inside and heard not so much a moaning as a whimper. She eased open the door. Her mother was motionless on her bed, a damp towel on her brow, the curtains drawn, thin and ineffectual against the blinding day. There was the smell of vomit. Tessa tiptoed to the bed, took the bowl, removed and washed it quickly. She brought a fresh towel, newly dampened.

'Medicine,' said her mother, voice weak, loaded with pain.

Tessa searched, but there was nothing. No Aspro, no Bex, no Vincent's. How could that be?

'Mum, we're out.'

Her mother opened her eyes, forehead furrowed. 'Get some, love,' she pleaded. 'Take money.'

'You'll be all right alone?'

'I need it, love. Go.'

Tessa thought of ringing the golf club, seeking her father's help, but rejected the idea as quickly as it came. It made her wonder again whether her mother knew where he was.

She wore as little as possible: cut-off jeans, a t-shirt, considered for a moment going without a bra. A year or two ago that might have been okay, but not now. She wore Dunlop Volleys without socks, her paperclip sunglasses and a white terry-towelling hat, a leftover from her father's cricketing days. She soaked it, not with the precious tank water but from the bore cistern, the water with its familiar pungency. She did the same with the t-shirt, feeling it cold and clammy on her skin. She took her mother's old bike, hers now, filling a plastic cordial bottle with tank water and placing it in the bike's basket. It was six miles to town. Whitlam wanted to turn that into ten kilometres, but she couldn't see how that would help.

By the time she reached the end of the driveway, the t-shirt was mostly dry and the hat close to it. She drank some water. It was almost noon. She wished her mother had thought of the medicine earlier, wished the weather was more benign, wished her father had not run from his responsibilities. But the heat would only get worse. And so would her mother.

The road to Tulong was dead flat; at any other time of year it was an easy ride—she'd done it countless times—but today the highway was brutal, the pavement pulsing with heat, the pedals resistant, as if she were pushing uphill or into a headwind. Someone had tossed an old cassette from their window and its entrails stretched along the road, glittering in the sunlight like cut-price tinsel. She smelt death, saw a roo carcass on the shoulder, a cloud of flies and a raven making the most of it. She held her breath as she passed, but the stench had spread too far in the still air and she couldn't prevent herself from sucking it in, gagging even as she was forced to breathe. She wondered how a raven could defy the heat, stand on the baking bitumen, in the sun, with its feathers so black. It seemed unnatural.

She heard a truck approaching, got well clear, off the side of the road. It thundered past, sucking a vortex of air and dust in its wake. She closed her eyes, held her arms wide, the wind a short-lived relief against her sweat-soaked tee. She continued and a different sound, low and rumbling, came up behind her, running slow: the throbbing menace of a V8. She kept pedalling, tried to ignore it, but couldn't help stealing a glance over her shoulder. It was a panel van, a bright orange Sandman, gleaming and lairy. As if taking her glance as acknowledgement, it sidled up next to her, baritone engine gurgling, even as she stared straight ahead.

'Hey, darl. Want a lift? Bike in the back?'

'No, thanks.' She shook her head, looked at the driver. It was a young man, stubble and a blue singlet.

'C'mon, darl. Too fucking hot to be riding.'

She continued to look ahead, ignoring the overtures.

'Show us your tits then.' The friendliness had gone, his tone turned dry and hard. 'Fuck you,' he sneered. 'Stuck up bitch.'

She pedalled. He revved the engine, then louder, as if to intimidate her or perhaps to impress her, then accelerated away, the car melting into the mirage of the road. Tessa realised she'd again been holding her breath. She released it. Under her sunglasses sweat trickled into her eyes. She stopped to wipe her brow with her bone-dry hat, to steady her breathing and to drink the last of the water. She'd already consumed the pint, yet she wasn't much more than halfway to town.

By the time she got to Tulong, her thirst was insistent. She swooned ever so slightly as she dismounted and rested the bike against a tree. She thought of the Olympus Milk Bar, but there was no time for lime spiders. Instead, she swiped at the flies she knew must be clinging to her back, trying to get rid of most of them before entering the general store. Inside, it was like a sanctuary, shaded, with a fan turning slowly in the ceiling. She was standing there, trying to steady herself, when the store manager Mrs McCardle approached with a large glass of water.

'Not the day for it,' she said, voice kind and without admonishment.

Tessa explained her mission and, guided by the shopkeeper, bought two packets of Bex powders and a small brown jar of aspirin. Mrs McCardle also refilled her water bottle for her. Tessa was about to leave when Grainger Buchanan entered the store.

'G'day, Tessa.'

'Hi.'

'That your bike outside?'

'Yep.'

'You're keen. Day like this.'

She shrugged, not wanting to explain her mother's ailment a second time. Grainger had driven her home the day before and she hoped he might offer again, but was unsure how to phrase the request. She didn't want to seem pushy.

'We're going for a swim—me and Gene, maybe Tycho. Want to come?'

She stared. The cool of the forest. Water. Swimming. Tycho Buchanan.

'You okay, Tessa?'

'I can't,' she said. 'I've got to get this to my mother.' She held up the paper bag. 'Medicine.'

'We'll give you a lift then. Take your bike with us.'

'It's not on the way.'

'It's fine. Ten minutes there and back.'

Outside, Gene was leaning up against the car, trying to look cool. 'Hey, Tessa.'

'Hi yourself. Top car.'

It wasn't, of course. It was another bomb the Buchanan brothers had patched together. This one was a Buick from some long-gone decade, only slightly more modern than Gene's junkyard bolthole.

'Registered?' asked Tessa.

'Close enough,' said Grainger, smiling.

The boot swallowed the bike whole, like a hungry whale. Alone in the back seat she sat low, the windows high, her legs outstretched. There was a guitar next to her in a soft case of black vinyl. The car rattled and wheezed down the road, suspension shot, Grainger swinging wildly at the steering, looking more like he was hanging on to it rather than guiding the car.

Back at the house, she crept into her parents' room, found her mother still immobile on the bed. But the smell was no worse and the bowl was empty.

'Mum?'

'You're back.'

'I've got Bex and Aspro. I'll mix you a powder.'

'Good girl.'

'You need anything else?'

'Just that.'

When she returned with the glass, her mother was sitting up. 'I heard a car.'

'It's Gene and Grainger Buchanan. They gave me a lift.'

'I didn't hear it leave.'

'They want me to go swimming.'

Tessa thought she saw a smile play on her mother's lips, fleeting in the dim light. 'Do they now?'

'I won't go if you need me.'

'I'll be fine, now I have this.' Her mother sipped at the drink, as if demonstrating its restorative power. 'You go.'

'You sure, Mum?'

'Go, Tessa.'

They drove back the way they came, almost to town, before turning off to the right and dropping down the tilt into the forest. It was just a few feet of altitude, but the air took on a different quality. On the highway, bucketing along at speed, the wind had rushed through the open windows, dry and dust-laden. Down here, under the canopy, it was cleaner and offered the impression of moisture, if not the reality. The mood lifted. The road turned to dirt and Grainger was forced to drive more slowly. The car no longer had a radio, but Gene had connected his transistor to its aerial somehow, and he turned it up as a new song began. Van Morrison was extolling the benefits of a moon dance. She liked the idea; it sounded cooling.

At the Murray, by the campground at Anglers Reach, the car park was full, the tiny beach crowded out. Small wonder.

'Tycho was talking about the regulator,' said Grainger. 'Reckons they've opened it up for a while, flushed it out.'

'Good by me,' said Gene. 'Tessa?'

'Sure.' She looked out the window, heartbeat stepping up a pace. Tycho. So he really wasn't in Griffith.

The old car was low to the ground, suspension constantly bottoming out, threatening to beach itself on the uneven corrugations of the access track. Grainger took it even more slowly, concentrating hard. The Hollies were singing, harmonising, the song seven or eight years old, already dated, but Tessa still liked it.

There was no one at the regulator, and Tessa felt her heartbeat return to normal. But Tycho had been right about the fresh water; the level in the pool was as high as the river, and the surface clear of algae and duckweed. Like a long narrow swimming pool, seventy-five yards long and twenty wide by the regulator wall, tapering to a few yards up where the creek entered. And they had it all to themselves.

The brothers changed into shorts, not swimmers, and plunged in. She changed behind some bushes into her old one-piece. Part of her was glad Tycho was not here to see it. She wanted a bikini, but her mother wouldn't pay for it, wouldn't countenance it, told her fifteen was too young. Something else to buy with her newsagency money. But such thoughts were forgotten as she slid into the water. She loved this feeling. The water was somehow smooth, somehow silky, unlike the hard chemicals of the Boonlea swimming pool, with its concrete and chlorine. She struck out, swimming to the regulator wall. Gene was there before her, climbing up the bank, edging onto the structure itself, using it as a launching pad, a springboard. She knew what was coming, the inevitable bomb, but just laughed, turning her face away as he hit the water, knees held to his chest. Grainger diligently checked the water under the regulator wall, declaring it free of hidden dangers. After that they were all doing it, climbing up onto the wall, plunging in, bombs and horseys and proper dives. The water was deep; she dived as far as she could go, pushing down and down, kicking her legs, feeling the pressure build in her ears, until it was almost dark around her. She only just managed to touch the muddy bottom before spiralling back up, lungs bursting. It must have been fifteen or twenty feet deep, maybe more.

After that she left the boys behind, went swimming up the pond towards where the creek entered it. Halfway along she rolled onto her back, floating, letting the water lap at her, looking up into the trees and listening to the bush. This close to the river, the redgums were towering, massive things, timeless. Way up high, above the trees, above the river, above everything, she spied a sea eagle adrift on the thermals. A squadron of black cockatoos came screeching into the tree above her, their shape prehistoric, their calls like pterodactyls. It made her wonder how long this forest had been here, how many centuries, how many millennia. The greatest redgum forest in the world, so they said.

She flipped over, resumed swimming, determined to see how far she could get. Behind her, the brothers were laughing and splashing, their noise receding, the forest growing louder, the sound of cicadas in the distance, two kookaburras laughing, and the constant background hum of bees. There was a tree down, its trunk across the pond just where it narrowed, preventing her going further. Beyond it the creek extended away into the woods. She dived once more, the bottom only three or four feet down this far from the regulator. She touched the mud, a stick. She pulled it free, wondering why it had not floated to the surface. But it wasn't a stick, it was a bone. A kangaroo rib. She threw it onto the shore, not wanting to think what else was below her. She turned and swam back to the regulator wall.

Gene and Grainger had finished swimming; she could hear their voices up on the bank. She had the lagoon to herself. She luxuriated in it for a moment, then she too climbed out. Gene had fetched the guitar from the car and was plucking its strings, head down, not making eye contact. He really was a shy boy. She recognised the tune immediately: 'The Needle and the Damage Done'. Every second kid at school tried to play it, those opening few bars. That and 'Stairway to Heaven'. But none of them had ever played it as well as Gene. She wondered again how she had never known he was musical.

'Sing it,' she said to him.

He spoke, even as his fingers kept dancing on the strings. 'I can't really sing.'

'Yes you can,' she said. 'Yesterday at the yard, remember? Major scale. Minor scale. Perfect pitch, you said.'

Grainger was smiling. 'Go on, Gene,' he urged gently. 'It's just us. No one will tease you.'

And so Gene sang. His voice was surprisingly rich, much better than Neil Young's nasal whine. It made Tessa feel mellow. She'd never really listened to the words before, the story of a man dying before his time, and they made her feel sad.

Gene had almost finished and she was summoning words of praise, wanting him to know how impressed she was, when they were interrupted by the sound of a car. Tessa recognised it immediately. Tycho's Datsun. The mellowness vanished together with the half-formed compliment and awkwardness descended. The colours of the day changed, became more vibrant.

The car emerged from the bush track, pulled in next to the Buick, Tycho giving it a final rev to announce his arrival before cutting the engine. He got out, a young god, with his dark hair and his dark eyes and his five o'clock shadow, shirt barely buttoned, chest hair billowing. But he was not alone. There was a girl with him. A beautiful girl. Small and thin, with long caramel hair, braided loosely. A face of ivory and freckles. She wore a cheesecloth dress; Tessa could see her nipples through the thin fabric. But the girl's demeanour belied the boldness of her dress, her head bowed in apparent modesty. She looked older, maybe eighteen or nineteen. She reminded Tessa of one of the paintings the Tool had admired so much, a Pre-Raphaelite, except with pale hair. Next to Tessa, Grainger and Gene were silent, almost holding their breaths. Tessa felt herself plain in her one-piece swimmers.

'This is Willow. Say hi then,' said Tycho, his manner nonchalant.

Grainger spoke for them. 'Hi, Willow. I'm Grainger and this is Gene. We're Tycho's brothers. And this is our friend Tessa.'

'Hi,' said Willow, nodding to each of them in turn, and there was something in the warmth of her voice and the direct line of her gaze that eroded, just a little, the jealousy engulfing Tessa.

'How is it?' asked Tycho.

'Beaut,' said Gene. 'Fresh as.'

'Here. Show us.' Tycho sat down, cross-legged on the ground, hand out for the guitar. Willow sat next to him. Gene gave the instrument to him and Tycho started plucking out a blues, making up the words as he went. '*Got up this morning, I was feeling blue, got up this morning, didn't know what to do. And I tell you, I had those no good regulator blues.*'

It was a performance, a show, with none of Gene's reticence—and none of his finesse—but executed with exuberance and spirit. Tessa loved it and clapped when he finished.

'Not really my instrument,' Tycho said, handing the guitar back to Gene. Then he stood and walked to his car, returning with a bottle of wine. More of the River Pirate. 'Drink, anyone? Willow? Tessa?'

'Bit hot for wine, isn't it?' said Grainger.

'Possibly,' said Tycho. 'Just offering. Manners and all.'

Gene had started playing again, something soft and classical.

'What's that?' asked Willow.

'Pachelbel's Canon,' Grainger answered for his brother.

Tycho pulled a pouch from his pocket, started to roll a cigarette. But there was more than one paper, and Tessa's eyes widened as she realised it wasn't just a rollie but a joint. There was a silence, just the guitar, Tessa watching Tycho's hands, sensing Grainger and Gene stealing glances at her. Willow was lying on her back, looking at the sky. The eldest brother finished rolling the reefer, held it up to examine his handiwork, brushed it through his lips once or twice, then lit it with his Zippo. Tycho drew deep, holding the smoke in his lungs before exhaling. The smell was rich and redolent, somehow familiar to her, as if she had smelt it before without knowing it. Willow sat up and Tycho handed the joint to her. She held it casually between two fingers, drawing in the smoke, then tilting her chin skywards and blowing it out in a steady stream, looking somehow elegant as she did so. She offered the joint to Tessa.

'You don't have to if you don't want to,' said Gene.

Tessa felt a little annoyed then, as if Gene were talking down to her. So she took it. 'It's fine,' she said, but kept her toke tentative all the same.

When everyone had smoked some and it was finished, they lay on their backs and looked at the sky, contemplating its blueness. Gene was still playing guitar, a stupid grin on his face, a song that Tessa didn't recognise about some cafe where you could get anything you wanted. For some reason, it sounded funny and she felt like giggling.

Tycho started talking, a long rambling monologue. Saying they could all go to Sunbury in January, see Daddy Cool and Thorpie and the Captain Matchbox Whoopee Band. Like Woodstock, but with VB, he said. Or they could head north to Nimbin if there was another Aquarius Festival and take acid and smoke peyote and walk around without clothes.

'Hippiesville,' said Grainger. 'Crystals and incense. Everyone starkers.' And he laughed and they all laughed with him, as if he'd said something brilliant and incisive and witty.

'Too right,' said Tycho, and he stood up, as if inspired, and pulled off his shirt, not unbuttoning it but simply easing it off over his head. Tessa stared. The hair on his chest was gathered in tight dark curls, and a snake of it ran down from his navel towards his groin. He kicked off his sandals and then, without fuss, stripped off his pants to stand before them naked and unapologetic. Tessa could feel her mouth hanging open, her eyes sucked to the dark triangle of his pubes, his dick hanging, long imagined and suddenly made real.

Beside him, Willow stood up and let her cheesecloth dress cascade from her shoulders, a move effortless and graceful. She wore no underwear; she was naked, save for a leather bracelet around one ankle and a silver bangle. She removed the bangle, dropped it on her discarded dress. She was perfect, thought Tessa, staring at the girl's lithe form, her body without fat, breasts small and turned up, pubes golden.

'Game?' asked Tycho, looking directly at Tessa.

'Fuck, Tycho, she's fifteen,' said Grainger.

The words made her blush, made her feel so young, so inexperienced. 'Yeah, I'm game,' she said, and without thinking further, she stood, stripped off her bathers and, with eyes averted from the others, not wanting to see their reactions, plunged back into the water.

Then they were all in, all five of them. Tycho was climbing onto the wall, diving in, showing off, while the others cheered and jeered. Grainger and Gene went up together, leaping in. Tessa was glad that Willow didn't follow, felt safe treading water. After a while, Gene and then Grainger got out. Tycho had swum up close to Willow, something between them. Tessa decided to swim to the far end of the regulator once again.

Later, when she climbed out, Grainger turned his eyes from her as she gathered her things. She felt grateful for that. For some reason, she walked away behind the Buick to put her clothes on. Tycho and Willow had disappeared somewhere, although the Datsun was still parked beside the junkyard relic.

'Where's Gene?' she asked, dressed once again.

'Gone for a walk,' said Grainger. His voice was gentle, not judgemental. 'When he gets back, we can drive you home.'

'Thanks.' She tied her hair back. 'Who's Willow? Is she from Hatty?'

Grainger looked at her, as if trying to decide the correct thing to say. 'No. She's dropped out.'

'What does that mean?'

'Lives in the forest. Lives off the forest.'

'Seriously?'

'Tycho found her when he was researching one of his stories.'

chapter twenty-two

GUY POWELL IS AS GOOD AS HIS WORD. THE EMAIL FROM THE WAR MEMORIAL is waiting when Nell gets back to the police station.

Dear Constable Nell,

About Lieutenant Eamon Patrick Finucane:

- Finucane was born in Bendigo on 25 April 1920.
- He enlisted on 20 December 1941, aged twenty-one, two weeks after Pearl Harbor.
- He was a member of the 39th Battalion, service number was VX76517.
- He was deployed to New Guinea in February 1942 and was seriously wounded in late July 1942 during combat on the Kokoda Track.

- He was repatriated to Australia in August 1942, to recover from his wounds at the military hospital at Heidelberg, Melbourne.
- In September 1942, while convalescing, he was promoted to lieutenant.
- In October 1942 he was deployed to the Barmah Forest POW camp, possibly while he completed his rehabilitation and awaited redeployment.
- He was officially reported Absent Without Leave on 30 January 1943, two days after last being seen in the proximity of detainees in the Barmah Forest. The case was passed to the military police.
- There are no further records.

I was unable to locate any reference whatsoever to dental records. I suspect they no longer exist, if they ever did. However, it is clear that Finucane was repatriated because he was wounded in battle and not due to disease or illness (malaria was rife, as were other tropical diseases). So I'm now trying to ascertain if the Heidelberg Rehabilitation Hospital holds records detailing the extent of his wounds, and if he suffered any fractures.

All the best with your investigation. You owe me a beer.
Guy

The email lifts Nell's spirits. She'll buy him a slab if he comes through with anything useful. She fires off a thank-you email, including her phone number, requesting an update if anything of significance comes to light. In response, her phone pings. An unknown number, a thumbs-up emoji. She adds his number to her contacts.

Which leaves her where, exactly? Waiting. Waiting for Guy Powell at the War Memorial, waiting for Ivan to call or, worse, Feral Phelan. Waiting for Blake and Carole to provide more insights from the regulator search. Waiting. But she doesn't want to wait, not with the sword of Professional Standards hanging over her. She recalls Ivan's advice: crack on with it, wrap it up.

She'd almost convinced herself the second body must be Finucane, but now she's not so sure. The soldier was seriously wounded in New Guinea. That meant getting hit by a bullet or bullets or by shrapnel from artillery or mortars or grenades. All the same thing really: hot and jagged metal. What chance of getting hit like that and it not permanently marking bones or depositing small pieces of shrapnel? Possible, but likely? And certainly, if he was wounded in late July 1942 and died in Barmah-Millewa six months later, his bones would still bear the marks. Yet Blake has found no such signs so far.

Nell finds the list of missing people, starts to consider other possibilities. Her eyes come to rest on the name of her uncle Tycho Buchanan. If it does prove to be him in the regulator, then she needs to remove herself from the investigation. That imperative is all the more evident now that Feral Phelan has entered the equation.

The house of her grandmother, Rita Buchanan, is much the same as she remembers it: a grand edifice seated within a bore-watered lawn—built to impress, yet hidden from sight—a high hedge separating it from the remnant wrecks of the old junkyard, the machinery and cars rusting into the earth. It's like a castle: the hedge a battlement, the machinery abandoned siege weapons, the stacked cars an outer wall. As a child, Nell never liked her grandmother, a punctilious old lady, judgemental, with her cat's-bum mouth and the arching of painted eyebrows, always Grandmother, never Grandma or Gran. But Nell is no longer a child, and if an oversized publican with a mullet and a wild red beard can't fluster her, then neither should an elderly woman.

Inside the hedge there is the sound of a sprinkler and a chorus of grateful crickets. Magpies strut the lawn, looking sleek and well fed. Above the house, towering clouds are starting to colour, pink and orange, illuminated by the setting sun. Nell rings the doorbell and waits and then waits some more. She can hear distant music; someone is home. She rings again. Rita is old, maybe deaf. Probably slow. She must be in her late eighties by now. Still living alone, fiercely independent. Just when Nell is trying to decide between ringing again or finding a back door, she hears movement inside. Eventually, her grandmother opens the door, looks at her wordlessly through the security screen. She's no longer wearing glasses, her eyes preternaturally clear. Cataract surgery, thinks Nell.

'Grandmother, it's me, Nell.'

The old woman scans her from head to toe, as if checking the veracity of her claim. 'So it is,' she says. There is no smile, no move to open the security door, just a narrowing of the eyes and an arching of an eyebrow. Nothing has changed. But then a smile starts to creep across the old woman's face and the eyes crinkle, and for once there is affection to be glimpsed in the severe facade. 'So it is,' she repeats and opens the screen door. 'Come in, child.'

The old woman turns and walks away, knowing Nell will follow. It's a slow shuffle, but steady. There's no sign of the walker Gene mentioned. The music is louder inside, classical piano, something almost familiar. Her grandmother leads the way to the lounge, a room Nell was never allowed to enter as a child. It's impeccable: flat grey carpet with a white woollen rug laid upon it. There are leather sofas and armchairs and a red velvet chaise longue. On the mantelpiece, a polished silver candelabra. Rita makes her way to the stereo, turns down the music.

'You will have tea,' she says, more a command than a question.

'Please, don't go to any trouble,' says Nell.

Her grandmother makes a dismissive sound, somehow Germanic—'Pffttt'—accompanied by an equally dismissive and continental gesture. 'This is Australia. In Australia, one must drink tea.' The voice is serious but the eyebrows seem sardonic. Nell can't tell whether she is joking or not.

'Thank you. Just as it comes,' says Nell. 'No milk, no sugar.'

'Hmm.' The old woman regards her. 'Not so Australian then.' And this time Nell is sure she can detect an underlying humour.

While Rita attends to the tea, Nell scans the room. It is like a shrine, the walls dominated by black-and-white photographs. Pictures of Rita's children playing their instruments: Tycho on piano, positively Byronic, his dark hair like a halo and his eyes intense; Tycho playing trumpet, fingers agile and eyes closed. Grainger on violin, face straining with passion; Gene on clarinet, forehead creased with concentration. Nell makes the assessment:

if Tycho wasn't favoured in life, he certainly is in death—there are twice as many photographs of him as his brothers. There are also photos of her grandfather, Bert Buchanan, murdered so many years ago now, the images grainy but clear. Someone in the family must have been a photographer, owned a real camera. The prints look like darkroom originals, not produced by a modern inkjet printer. Nell thinks her dead grandfather looks a bit like Greg; in the monochrome portraits Bert Buchanan's hair is dark and his eyes are black. In one he's wearing a casual shirt, holding tongs as he barbecues. In another, he and Rita look unbelievably young, dressed for their wedding. He's beaming at the camera, bursting with pride; she's looking serious, eyebrows aligned. There are more recent photographs as well, Rita surrounded by her surviving family: Gene and Grainger, Tessa and the five children, even a few with great-grandchildren. Nell can't help but examine herself, young and dressed uncomfortably in a blue dress. She remembers the dress well. Her Sunday best. She never liked it. Then again, she never much liked dresses, full stop. But the recent photographs seem an afterthought, outnumbered three or four to one by those old ones, the ones taken before the disappearance of Tycho and Bert, as if life since then has been less memorable, less deserving of recording.

Rita returns pushing a small trolley supporting pot and cups, sugar in a cut-glass bowl, milk in a silver jug, Tim Tams on a Wedgwood plate.

'Grandmother, really. It's not necessary.'

'Ha. You want me deported?'

But once the tea is poured, once Nell bites into an obligatory biscuit, it's the old woman who dispenses with the small talk. 'Eugene tells me you are now a homicide detective.'

'That's right. Just this year.'

Her grandmother nods in appreciation of Nell's accomplishment. 'Congratulations.'

'Thank you.'

Rita stands, rising with effort, and walks to a sideboard, returning with a copy of the *Western Explorer*. IS THIS THE FACE OF A KILLER? shouts the headline. And now her words contain an edge. 'I have been reading this week's paper,' she says. 'Eugene's story.'

'What do you think?' asks Nell.

'I'm thinking this visit is business.'

Nell hesitates, but then decides honesty is best. 'Yes. I would like your help.'

The eyebrow arches, and a dry smile comes to Rita's mouth. 'A fair answer.' She glances down at the newspaper. 'But I know nothing of that. In 1943 I was still a child, still in Europe. Why would I know anything? Detective.' The way she adds the final word sounds like a challenge.

'Grandmother, we've found a second skeleton. In the same place as the first one.'

The old woman's eyes widen and she looks again to the paper, as if for guidance. 'At this place, this regulator?' The last vestiges of her accent leak through as she shapes her mouth around the unfamiliar word. 'I have never been there.'

'The second body, it's like the first, just a skeleton. It may belong to another soldier who disappeared at the same time as Stannard.'

'So why come here?'

'We want to make sure it's not your son. Make sure it's not Tycho.'

Rita says nothing, then turns away from Nell, stares out of the window. The sky is pink, the sunset in full bloom. There are trees, the hedge blocking out any sign of the wrecks. 'Fifty years, almost. I am thinking of him every day.'

Nell goes to speak, realises it's not necessary.

'You don't have favourites,' Rita says. 'If you become a mother you must follow this rule. Another rule of Australia. But even Grainger and Eugene would tell you there was something special about Tycho. A spark.'

'Can you tell me what happened?'

'You don't have the records?'

'I'll access them if we confirm it is him.'

Rita's eyebrow lifts, as if elevated by scepticism. 'How is it I can help you, then?'

'The pathologist can extract DNA from the remains. I would like to gather a sample from you. See if we can find a match.'

The old woman frowns. 'From a skeleton? DNA? Is this possible?'

'Yes.'

Rita rolls her bottom lip forward, rocking her head gently, gesturing that she is impressed. 'Of course then. Do we go to the hospital? The police station?'

'No. I can do it here.'

And she swabs her grandmother's mouth, wondering as she does so what the old woman is thinking, what all those countless family members around the country think when the police come knocking with their test kits and their nervous reassurances.

Afterwards, they resume the same seats. Rita sips tea, swills it around her mouth and swallows, as if rinsing away any contaminant from the swab. Only then does she speak again.

'They say a mother knows. I knew nothing. That day was like any other day, that night like any other night. The next day the newspaper rang. The editor. Tycho had promised a story but not delivered it. He hadn't turned up at work, hadn't rung, wasn't at his flat. Even then I wasn't bothered. Tycho could be wilful, ill-disciplined. Bert was worried; Bert knew something bad had happened. But I didn't listen. And then Bert was gone as well.' Rita looks at Nell, eyes like flint. 'I hope it is him. I hope it is Tycho they have found. It would be my punishment.'

'Punishment?' Rita's son has been missing for half a century and she desires punishment?

The old woman shrugs. Her eyes have narrowed and she is staring at the teapot, unseeing, as she speaks. 'People do the most awful things. Barbaric things. You think you know them, but you never do. You never see the monsters until it is too late.'

'Grandmother?'

She lifts her gaze, looks directly at Nell, eyes full of sadness. 'Do you know my story, Granddaughter? How I know of monsters?'

Nell feels the emotion behind the words, realises there is no polite way of refusing her grandmother. 'Tell me.'

Rita leans back, as if to gather herself, and then forward again. 'I was a child when I came to Australia. From Vienna. My parents were dead, my brother, my sister. Killed by the Nazis. There was just me.' Rita checks Nell for a reaction before speaking again. 'It's not what you might think: we were not Jewish. But our neighbours were. My family was caught sheltering them. The neighbours went to the camps and the Gestapo executed my family, an example to others. Their bodies were left in the town square. No one dared take them away. I saw them there.' The old woman has a calm to her, a resolve. 'Monsters,' she says, meeting Nell's gaze and holding it.

'I have small memories of my family. They were educated people. Refined people. They saw what was coming and sent me to live with an uncle on his farm outside our town. All I really remember of them is the music. I can't picture their faces, my mother and father, my sister and brother. I can't see them. Imagine that, Granddaughter. Not knowing what your mother looked like, your father. Maybe there are photographs, maybe I could find them. But still, I wouldn't recognise them. They would be photographs of strangers, people I never knew. But I remember the music. Always the music. They all played. I have an image in my mind of my mother, the only memory of her, standing in front of a high window, playing the violin, producing such beautiful sounds. And me realising, because of this, that she too was beautiful. That's what I remember: not her face, not her voice, not her touch. Just that she was beautiful. That's all I have. That and the music.'

Nell says nothing, shocked into stillness by her grandmother's story of loss, her teacup forgotten and held halfway between the table and her lips. Some small part of her mind—the police officer part—wonders where the story might be leading.

Rita seems in no hurry, offering her granddaughter more tea. Nell becomes aware of her cup, places it back on the table, accepting the top-up.

'I have seen monsters. I know what they look like,' says Rita, eyes locked onto Nell's. 'The Nazis, yes. The ones in the uniforms and goosestepping in the streets. But it was townspeople of my village, looking for all the world like good citizens and good Christians, who reported my family. And it was the local police who arrested them and handed them to the Germans. The real monsters.'

'I'm not sure I understand.'

'The Hatheson police told me my son was a monster, a murderer.'

'But you don't believe that.'

'You are telling me what I believe?'

'Yes.' Nell gestures at the pictures on the wall, the pantheon of Rita's family.

The matriarch smiles and lifts an eyebrow. 'You were a plain girl. Not pretty like your mother. Always the rough and the tumble, never the dresses. Always the muddy shoes. But maybe you are the smart girl.' She lifts her other eyebrow, joining the first in exclamation. 'Smart is better than pretty.'

Nell doesn't react, instead leaning forward, not to be distracted. 'What do you think did happen?'

'Your mother, she told the police that it was the mafia. And they laughed at her. I laughed at her. No one listened. But I think maybe Tessa was right. It was the Italians.'

'The mafia? Here?'

'My husband's body was found in 1975. A terrible year. Whitlam lost and Bert was found. Buried in the forest. Fishermen found him, while digging for worms. Shot through the back of the head. Executed. Mafia style.' There is anger in the woman's voice. She looks out the window as she regains her composure. The clouds are losing their colour. 'They had an inquest. Useless.'

'What did it find?'

'That he'd been murdered. Genius. But not who killed him.'

'By a person or persons unknown,' says Nell, mouthing the formal set of words so often used.

'The police claimed it was Tycho who killed him. That he killed Bert and fled. The judge listened, was persuaded.' Rita looks away, distress evident. But her eyes are clear, with no sign of tears, and her voice is resolute. 'So you see, that's why I hope it's Tycho you've found. To show them all that he was innocent, that he hadn't fled. That he didn't kill his father. To punish me for ever doubting him.'

'What did the coroner say about the mafia?'

'She said it was fantastical, and so that's what we thought too. But then, just two years later, that man Donald Mackay was murdered in Griffith. They had a royal commission and said it was the Calabrian mafia who assassinated him. The whole world knew. It was on the television and in the newspapers and in the parliament. But no one wanted to know about us; no one wanted to know about Tycho and Bert. We wanted a new inquest, but it was too late.'

'Why would the mafia kill your husband?'

'Not just my husband. My son.' And Rita's eyes steal an involuntary look at the photos. 'Tycho was a journalist at the *Western Explorer*—like Eugene is now. He was investigating them. He went to Griffith. Maybe he even met Mackay. He found something out.'

Nell frowns. 'Was that presented to the inquest?'

'The judge, what did you call her?'

'The coroner.'

'The coroner was old. She said there was no solid evidence. That the evidence of the police investigator must be given weight.'

'Who was this police investigator?' she asks, already knowing the answer.

Rita looks to the *Western Explorer*, discarded on the seat next to her. 'Tankard. His name was Tankard.'

chapter twenty-three

NELL'S EARLY MORNING WORKOUT, DOWN THE TILT AT CLARRIE BUCHANAN PARK, is strangely disconcerting. She'd considered going elsewhere to avoid the cookers with their flags and their bumper stickers and their conspiracies, but she's determined not to be daunted. However, instead of confrontation, she's met with pleasantries. The people who walk past from the camp are polite and cheerful, waving greetings: a couple of dog walkers, an elderly couple taking their morning constitutional, and a young couple returning from town with coffees and breakfast. A man even stops to chat as Nell is cooling down from her routines, complimenting the beauty of the day. There is no sign of the aggression so evident at the Foresters Arms.

At the police station, a copy of Tuesday's paper lies on a spare desk, challenging her with its headline and the photo of Keith Tankard: IS THIS THE FACE OF A KILLER? She thinks of her grandmother. Rita accused Keith Tankard of swaying the coroner, of persuading the court that Tycho killed his father. And, according to Grainger, she'd separately accused Tankard of attempting to extort bribes. So was that the motivation behind Gene's story: just the latest skirmish in a long-running feud? She picks it up, re-reads it. Two days on, it seems even more speculative, even more marginal. Unethical. She remembers an observation Ivan once shared: the dead can't sue. Was that it? Payback, now that Tankard was dead?

She calls the coroner's office in Sydney, asks for the records of the 1975 inquest into the death of Bert Buchanan. It takes a minute for the clerk to find them: the discovery of the body was 1975, but the inquest wasn't until early the following year. The clerk emails her the lot: the findings, the transcripts, photographs.

Nell starts with the findings: 'Inquest into the death of Bertrand Oliver Buchanan and the disappearance of Tycho Les Buchanan'. It sets out the sequence of events clearly.

Tycho was last seen at the family home and workplace in Tulong on the afternoon of Thursday, 20 December 1973. Bert was last seen the next day in the afternoon, searching for his son in the forest. His wife Rita confirmed he took a .22-calibre rifle with him. The gun was never recovered.

Bert's abandoned truck, keys still in the ignition, was found in the forest the following day, 22 December, by Eugene and Grainger Buchanan, who also located their brother's Datsun 1600. Bert Buchanan's body was found almost two years later, in October 1975, buried in a shallow grave in the forest.

> The discovery of the body elevated the case to homicide, overseen by Sydney but led on the ground by Albury detectives. They followed various leads, but reached no firm conclusion as to who had killed Bert Buchanan.

Nell flicks through to the conclusions. The coroner, a magistrate called Torshack, found that Bert Buchanan was murdered on or about the 21st of December 1973. She made no conclusion about the fate of Tycho, speculating that he might also have died, either by his own hand or that of others, or that he might have deliberately disappeared after killing his father.

Nell's eyes are drawn to the specific passage.

> The whereabouts of the son, Tycho Buchanan, remain a mystery. However, I do find the testimony of Sergeant Keith Tankard informative and persuasive, including his theory that the son killed the father and then went on the run: 1) Eugene Buchanan testified that the two men engaged in a heated argument on 20 December, the last day Tycho was seen alive; 2) The editor of the *Western Explorer* confirmed that Tycho Buchanan was working on an investigative series on criminal activity in the forest; and 3) Sergeant Tankard reported that Bert Buchanan was involved in low-level criminality.
>
> Sergeant Tankard believes Bert Buchanan attempted to silence his son, but instead the son killed the father using Bert Buchanan's own rifle and made good his escape.
>
> Compelling though this theory may be, it remains speculative, with little concrete evidence to support it.

I found the theory advanced by Theresa Buchanan—that both men had fallen victim to organised crime—less convincing. Theresa Waters was an impressionable fifteen-year-old girl in late 1973 and clearly infatuated with Tycho Buchanan. She was incapable of believing anything bad about him. Her assertion that the Italian mafia was responsible for the deaths of both men seems to be self-delusion, influenced by Hollywood gangster films and experimentation with marijuana. Sergeant Tankard testified there was no evidence of the Italian mafia being present in the region, and that the most notable criminal activity centred on the Buchanan's car yard.

Nell is trying to process what this means, when she's interrupted by her phone. A landline, a Canberra number.

'Detective Constable Nell Buchanan,' she answers.

'Nell, it's Guy Powell at the War Memorial.' She can hear the excitement in his voice.

'Hi, Guy. You have something?'

'Sure do. I can put it in writing if you're busy, send it through. It's quite a story.'

'Just tell me.'

'Right.' She can sense him gathering himself, shuffling papers. 'Private Eamon Finucane was wounded in action on July twenty-fifth, 1942, during combat on the Kokoda Track. Seriously. Not expected to survive.'

'Go on,' says Nell.

'He was hit in the head and the body and lost the sight in his left eye. When he was repatriated to Melbourne, they performed basic reconstructive surgery and fitted him with a glass eye.' There's a moment's silence. 'Constable? You still there?'

'I am. Guy, I can't tell you how grateful I am for this. The body can't possibly be Finucane's. I've seen the skull. No glass eye, no sign of injury, no sign of surgery.'

'Terrific. That's two beers you owe me.'

And Nell laughs. 'Absolutely. Next time I'm in the capital.'

'Kind of a pity, though.'

'How do you mean?'

'Tanks my Historical Society article.'

She laughs at that, her exhilaration bubbling to the surface. 'Okay. Three beers.'

Call finished, she looks again at her uncle's newspaper resting on the adjacent desk. It appears even more outlandish; if the second body doesn't belong to Finucane, then who does it belong to? A new scenario suggests itself: Stannard and Finucane desert, stealing four hundred pounds, and swim the Murray to the regulator to rendezvous with an awaiting accomplice. But something goes awry. Finucane kills the accomplice, shoots Stannard with his Lee-Enfield, dumps the bodies into the regulator pool, then makes his getaway using the accomplice's car. Could it be possible?

She's on her feet, pacing. She has nothing substantive, only threads, only suggestions. She needs more evidence, something concrete.

Half an hour later she gets a call from Kevin Nackangara.

'They've found a gun in the regulator.'

'How can there be a gun?' She's trying to keep her voice even, knowing she's in the constable's debt since he defended her to

Professional Standards. 'I thought you went over the whole site with metal detectors?'

'Not me—Albury.'

'How did they miss it?'

'I told you. Amateur equipment. Dr Nguyen has the good gear.'

Nell can hear the irritation in the constable's voice, understands it, knows why. She takes a breath. She was hoping for a break and he's given her one. 'Kev, sorry. I'm not having a crack at you. I'm a country cop too, remember—Finnigans Gap, Bourke, Dubbo.'

'Sure,' he says, but the phone conveys nothing of what he's feeling.

'Where was the gun?' she asks.

'In the middle. Not close to either body.'

'Have they dug it out?'

'Not yet. Doctor Nguyen is in charge. Treading carefully, taking it slowly.'

'So no reason for me to head out, then?'

'No, but it's definitely a rifle, based on the imaging. They'll know a lot more when they get it up.'

A rifle. Nell feels her heart accelerate. This is good. Maybe it's Finucane's Lee-Enfield, the three-oh-three that killed Stannard. Or maybe it's connected to the second body; maybe it's Bert Buchanan's missing twenty-two. 'Fair enough. You know how far they've got with this ground-penetrating radar? Have they scoured the whole site yet?'

'Nah, not even a third. Pretty tricky in all the mud. And they're still getting the last of the second skeleton out.'

'Okay. Keep me posted.' She gives it a heartbeat. 'Thanks, Kevin. And sorry.'

'No worries. The doc is just instructing the team, then she'll come and see you.'

'I'll be here.'

As she hangs up she can't help feeling a touch of excitement. The crime scene is giving up its secrets, almost reluctantly, but giving them up nonetheless. The gun could be crucial. Surely it has to be connected. Why else would anyone throw a perfectly good rifle into the regulator? But she realises that raises its own questions: why the regulator, why not the river? She understands the logic with the bodies: sink them in the river and there was always the chance that, weighed down or not, they might get washed downstream and be found. But a rifle would stay submerged, would never be found. It just increases her conviction the gun is linked.

chapter twenty-four

JAMES WATERS—FIRST STATEMENT—CONTINUED

BUCKY HAD A FEARLESSNESS TO HIM, A CONFIDENCE, AS IF HE KNEW THE forest would protect him. There were dangers there: snakes in the long grass, but he would run through it barefoot; snags in the river, sunken logs, but he would dive deep into the strongest currents and always surface; branches could break without warning, but he would climb to the very top of the trees. He'd call to the birds and they would call back. He would laugh at me, tease me about my caution and joke about my hesitations, but even though I tried, I could never be like him. I was born on the farm; at heart I was of the fields. But he was born there on the banks of the river and had spent his entire life in the forest, his father working the red engine. He'd never been to school and was proud of it. Yet he could read and write as well as I could, maybe better; said his mother had taught him. That was something he never spoke about: his mother. I'm not sure what happened there, whether she had died or left or what occurred. It was the one subject that would shut him down. Maybe it made our bond stronger: his mum was gone and my dad was gone and we missed them. But he was rarely melancholy; most of the time he was bubbling over with life.

He had an affinity with animals, as if they recognised him as one of their own. I saw him tickle a trout in a creek, reach in underneath it, almost lull it into submission, then quick as a flash flip it out onto the bank. We cooked it up and ate it. Another time, he ran a rabbit down. The rabbit saw us and went still, the way they do. Bucky took off after it and the rabbit bolted through the grass and into the trees. Bucky caught it in about two hundred yards. He took a dive at the end, like a rugby fly half, and came up holding it above his head, laughing, as its legs thrashed away in mid-air. He let that one go, thought it uncharitable to eat it, seeing it had provided such good sport.

There was a birder who used to come to the forest every summer. He had this old truck with a homemade canopy made of dirty canvas. Underneath the tarpaulin, it was full of wicker cages. He'd come and catch cockatoos and parrots, even small finches and fairy wrens, take them back to Sydney and sell them as pets. He had these trained cockatoos—'Judas birds', he called them, sulphur-crested cockatoos. He'd set them out feeding in a grassy clearing and they'd call to the wild birds. And sure enough, a flock would hear them calling and come to feed alongside them. The birder would net them, throw them in the cages in the back of the truck. He told us some would die on the trip north but enough would make it. People loved having them as pets. You'd see that often enough in those days, cockatoos in cages. You could teach 'em to talk. Don't see it anymore. I think it's against the law. This bloke offered us a few bob to help out, but Bucky wouldn't be in it. Not for quids, he said.

The next day, when the birder set out the Judas birds, we hid in some bushes and Bucky picked one off with his slingshot. *Pap.* First shot. It gave a soft squawk and died right in front of us. Bucky pinged a second one, and it set up an awful squawking. That brought the birder running. We were hiding: we thought he'd give us what for if he caught us. He didn't know we were there, didn't know what had happened. He picked up the dead bird and started weeping, held it to his chest and cried. We felt bad about that. We slunk off and left him in peace. But Bucky wrote a note—that's how I knew he could write. He put it on the birder's windscreen. He wrote that the law had changed, that trapping birds was illegal, not to come back. And as far as I know, the birder never did.

Not long after that, though, Bucky apologised to me for sending the birder away.

'You could do with the money for your mum. I'm sorry,' he said. 'But I've got a plan.'

He said he'd been spying on the Italians over at the army camp. We'd given up on that by then, that's what I'd thought, but he reckoned he was still keeping an eye on them. More like he enjoyed their singing, but he wasn't going to admit that, even to a friend like me. Anyway, he said he'd learnt that the officers in charge had their own chef, who was always on the lookout for something fancy for the top brass. They had money to feed the troops and the prisoners and buy supplies, but didn't mind dipping into the funds to get something special for themselves. A farmer had sold the chef a suckling pig, a fisherman Murray cod and trout, and a black marketeer claret and brandy. But what Bucky said was this: the chef would pay for yabbies. That sounded good to me; I could already see the look on my mum's face when I delivered her a few bob extra. Around that time, every shilling made a difference to us. Every penny, really.

Now, we already knew the best place for yabbies wasn't in the river but in the creeks, and the best creek of all was by the regulator over on my side of the river, where the water was deep and still and warm. And I knew how to catch them, because I used to go yabbying with my dad in the farm dam, back when he was still around and there was still water in our dam.

The secret to catching yabbies is you need rotting meat. The more pongo it is, the more they like it. And rotting meat was something I had no problem getting my hands on. We had a couple of guns at the farm. All farmers had one or two, usually a rifle and a shotty. We had a three-oh-three, a big heavy thing, too heavy for me, but we also had a twenty-two, a sweet little rifle, a Winchester. I'd take it and shoot roos for dog meat. Dad had shown me how when I was about eight. I didn't like doing it; I always liked roos. But Dad told me they were a pest, eating grass that the sheep needed—and, besides, the dogs needed tucker.

That was the meat I'd bring to the forest to feed Rex and Pouch. So I got some extra-ripe stuff, too far gone to feed the dogs, and brought it in. Jesus, it stank, crawling with maggots, starting to marble over with greens and blues. But jeez, did the yabbies love it. We got a big haul, maybe thirty or so. Only took us an hour, maybe less. I'd brought a big old tin to put them in, and we half-filled it with water to keep them alive. Soon enough we learnt the tin couldn't hold them. Yabbies are good climbers and they staged a jailbreak. After that we kept the lid on. They clattered around in it, making a real racket. I'd brought the tin and the meat, but Bucky had also come prepared. He had a hessian sack, so once we were done, we put 'em in there and soaked it with water to keep the yabbies happy. We tied it off good and he strung it round his waist with a rope and swam back across the Murray. And sure enough, when I saw him the next day he had money for me. Five shillings, a small fortune. I couldn't believe it. That night was the first time I saw Mum smile, really smile, since Dad left. I was proud as punch, walking around with my chest puffed out like a grenadier. I can't tell you how happy it made me.

Even better, we were asked to deliver more the following Sunday. The chef was going to do a big spread, like seafood but river food: cod and trout and yabbies. He told Bucky he'd lined up a fisherman to get the fish and we could do the yabbies. A shilling per half-dozen and he'd take as many as we could give him.

I ripened up a roo haunch till it was blue and rank, and on Sunday I carried it inside the yabby tin to the regulator. Being a bit of a worrier, I was concerned we'd taken too many the week before and there wouldn't be any left, but they were lining up to be caught. Bucky said I was the best rotten meat producer in the whole of eastern Australia, that I should get some sort of medal. But then it rained. Right in the middle of the drought, right when it seemed like it would never rain again. I couldn't believe it. It moved in from the south-west, from down in the Bight, a huge front of black clouds, all lightning and thunder. Like a wall it was.

Early afternoon, Mum came looking for me, she was that worried, riding into the forest on her mare. She found Bucky and me yabbying at the regulator; I'd told her that's where I'd be. By then we already had a good catch, maybe even better than the first lot, as if the yabbies were bored of their pond and were giving themselves up to us, like word had got about that there was a party going on in that old tin of ours. Or maybe they sensed the storm and wanted shelter—but that seems unlikely. They were yabbies, not university professors.

We were so focused on hauling them in we hadn't noticed the approaching clouds. But Mum had a good weather eye, could tell one cloud from another, could feel the changes in air pressure. It's like a sixth sense. Good farmers have it, so do good bushmen. She warned us then headed straight back home to look after my sister while the dogs and I mustered the cattle. Bucky put the yabbies in the hessian bag and tied it to the rope round his waist then swam them back across the river, just like the first time. Said he might get to the camp in time, otherwise he'd keep them till the next day.

The storm came in fast and furious. If Mum hadn't come to warn me I would have been caught out. Straight up above the sky was blue, but as I rode Lenny out of the forest the sun disappeared and the clouds rolled over and it got really dark, like someone turning off a light. The thunder was starting to roll in and the first rain drops hit, big fat ones that hurt when they struck you. Then the wind came out of nowhere. One moment it was still as stone and the next it was trying to knock me off Lenny. The cows really knew what was coming then. They aren't as smart as dogs or horses, but they aren't as dumb as people think. Smarter than yabbies, that's for sure. And they must have picked up on the anxiety in the dogs. Rex and Pouch were hopping around like the ground was covered in bushfire embers. The cattle moved really quickly, with a type of purpose, which was unusual for them. Usually they'd just idle along, grazing as they went, unhurried. It was like they wanted to get home as much as I did, like they wanted to help the dogs out. It was almost like they were mustering Lenny and me, not the other way round.

We made it in record time. Even so, the rain was getting heavy as I got them into the yard. The raindrops were larger and closer together. And they were cold, I remember that: really cold. The cows crowded down into the corner of the yard, where Dad had put up a corrugated-iron shelter. The metal was still hot from the sun and it was steaming as the raindrops hit it. I'd never seen cows afraid of the rain before, but then the hail hit and I understood. The dogs and I got inside before the worst of it. They were working dogs, not allowed in the house, but that afternoon we made an exception. It was a proper storm all right: the lightning cracking, the thunder shaking the house, the rain coming down in sheets. You could feel it in your guts. It was hard to tell who was the most scared, the dogs or my sister. I wasn't scared inside the house; it was exhilarating. But I was glad I wasn't on my little island in the forest, with only my tarpaulin to protect me.

The storm was scary, but it was also beautiful. You have no idea how wonderful it is to see rain in a time of drought. Like a religious experience, it was. It lit up Mum's face maybe even more than the five shillings. You see, we thought the rain was just what we needed, that it would break the drought. But by sunset the front had passed and the clear skies were back. I kept the cattle at home the next day, fearing the forest might be flooded and boggy, but the day after, when I herded them back in, it was as if the storm had never been through. There was no water in the creeks, the ground was firm. The forest had been so dried out it was like blotting paper. It had soaked up every last drop.

I was hoping to see Bucky, to see how he and his dad had fared out there in the forest in the shack by the red engine. But I didn't see him that day, nor the next, so on the third day I swam the Murray and went looking for him. The river was like the forest, seemingly unaffected by the storm, not running higher, not running stronger. I knew the steam engine was made of steel and that metal could attract lightning, so I was starting to get worried. But it was okay, chugging away, powering the mill. The charcoal was up and running; I don't know if the rain had stopped it or not. His father told me Bucky had been caught in the rain and picked up a chill which had built to a fever. I looked in on him, but Bucky was asleep. Under his old blanket, he looked pale and wan, and I was scared for him. His dad saw and tried to cheer me up. He told me the fever had broken the night before and that Bucky was on the mend, but that it might take him a while. I was still anxious. Kids died often enough back in those days. From scarlet fever and rheumatic fever and from things that even the doctors weren't sure of. One week they'd be at school with you, right as rain, playing marbles or cricket or tag, and the next week they were gone. It was just life, nothing you could do about it. But Bucky's dad assured me he'd come through the worst of it and he'd soon be fit as a flea.

There was only a week or so left before school started again and my days in the forest were coming to an end. I was starting to wonder if I might not see him before then, but I finally caught up with him a few days later. I was down at the sandbar at Lackmires Beach watering the cattle when he came floating down the river in a canoe. I'm not sure where he got it from, but I was sure glad to see him.

He was still looking a little frail when he got out of the canoe, but he was smiling and that was all that mattered.

'Not up to swimming?' I asked him. It was a baking-hot day and I'd already been in for a dip.

'Dad reckoned the river might be too cold for me,' he said.

It was true that, despite the heat of the day, the water was freezing; there must have been a release from deep in one of the mountain dams. Or maybe it was water from the storm, getting to us from higher up.

'Regulator?' I suggested. 'It'll be warm there.'

'Sure,' he said, although he didn't sound that sure.

It was clear he still wasn't back to normal. We'd chat away, and then there would be moments when he would fall silent, like he was thinking of something else. I thought being sick must have shaken him up, made him realise he wasn't invulnerable after all. But when we got to the regulator, he was up for a swim. I stripped off and jumped right in, but he took his time. A thing I remember now, though I didn't pay any mind at the time, was that he kept his shorts on. It was like his confidence was shaken.

I asked him about our catch, whether he'd made it to the army camp. He said he got most of the way there and then the storm hit. He'd gone back to the shack at the red engine. He was shivering cold when he got back and he'd given the yabbies to his dad. He reckoned his dad cooked them up for the workers the day after the storm, to cheer them up. I was fine with that. I said he was brave to try to get to the camp, that he should have waited. He just shrugged.

Afterwards, we did some yabbying. Not to make money or anything, but I had a new theory I wanted to test out: that yabbies might like damper covered in lard. He wasn't keen, but I insisted. The yabbies weren't fooled and they weren't biting. Maybe the rain had washed more food into the pond and they weren't hungry. Or they'd got used to meat and weren't going to fall for a substitute. Who knows how yabbies think? Eventually I got one and dropped it in the old tin. Then he got one, but instead of dropping it straight in the tub, he held it up, studying it. They can give you a nasty nip with their big pincer, but not if you hold them right, fingers on their backs.

'You reckon they know what's going on?' he asked.

'No,' I said.

'What about pain? Do they feel pain?'

I thought he meant when you cooked them, tipped them into the boiling water. 'Maybe, for a second or two, but that's all.'

And then he did the strangest, most shocking thing. Swift as could be, he yanked the claw off, the pincer. Just like that. He studied the yabby's face for a moment, then chucked it back into the pond.

I didn't know what to say. But all this time later, all these years, I still remember that day, that conversation, what he did. I can't forget it.

chapter twenty-five

NELL IS WAITING IN RECEPTION WHEN CAROLE NGUYEN ARRIVES. SHE HAS Blake Ness with her.

'I've got something for you,' Carole says.

'I know. Kevin rang. The gun.'

'Not that. This is something else. Maybe just as important.' Carole holds out a clear plastic evidence bag. 'From the second body.'

Nell can see pink strands of fibre, washed and separated. 'Clothing?'

'Rope fibres. We believe it was used to tie the body down. We found a breeze block nearby.'

Nell takes the bag, examines it. 'What does it tell us?'

'Murder or suicide for starters. Not an accidental drowning.'

'What else?' The two technicians wouldn't have come in from their site merely to tell her that.

'It helps with the date. The rope was a mixture of natural and synthetic fibres. The natural fibres have rotted away, the rope disintegrated. But the synthetic fibres settled in the mud, so we could see what it had been—and where. Tied around the body, connected to the breeze block.'

'Signifying?'

'It's not from the Second World War. There were no synthetic fibres back then, not like this.'

Nell blinks. 'So unconnected to Stannard?'

'Decades apart,' says Carole.

Blake remains silent, deferring to his colleague's expertise.

Nell takes that on board. Not only isn't the second body Finucane, but it's not the hypothetical accomplice either. 'Do you have a date?' she asks.

'Theoretically, manufactured from the late 1950s on. But more likely from the sixties or seventies. Much later than that, most ropes would have been purely synthetic or purely organic. I'm going to see if I can nail down the provenance of the breeze block. I reckon that will give us a good indicator of the earliest possible date.'

'Could it have been used more recently?'

'Certainly. People have old rope and old bits of brick lying around in their sheds for years. But the state of the body, fully decayed except for the bones, makes me think it was probably in there for at least a decade. It's hard to tell: water accelerates the decomposition, while the mud might act to slow it. And plenty of animals in there. Yabbies and so on.'

Blake nods his concurrence; the pathologist and crime scene investigator must have already worked their way through various scenarios.

Nell considers the two deaths, separated by decades, only connected by the proximity of their final resting place. And even then, on opposite sides of the regulator. But still, in the regulator, not the river.

'Tell me about the gun.'

'The team are still extracting it. Shouldn't take long. But it's a rifle. Looks like a twenty-two.'

'So not a Lee-Enfield?'

'Absolutely not.'

A twenty-two. Bert Buchanan's missing gun? 'The second body. Still no closer to determining cause of death?'

'Possibly,' says Blake. 'There are marks. Clipping the spine, cracking a rib. It's preliminary. I need to get them into the lab, under a better microscope.'

Nell feels her mind focusing in. 'What do they suggest to you?'

Blake exchanges a look with Carole. 'Gunshots.'

'Shot in the front or the back?'

'It's not confirmed.'

'And if it is?'

'Probably the back.'

Nell stares. 'Shot with what?'

Blake is shaking his head. 'Too early to say. But small calibre.'

'Twenty-two?'

'Most likely. Statistically.'

'The rifle you've just found?'

'Definite possibility.'

'Is there any way of establishing that?'

Blake grimaces. 'No. Not from the markings on the bones. No way. We're looking for bullets. Small calibre, they might not have exited the body if they hit the bone. Once we have all the bones out, that's our next objective. Metal detectors and radar. They may have sunk further into the creek bed.'

Nell frowns. A twenty-two can kill, but not as surely as larger-calibre bullets. 'These marks—if they were bullet wounds. Would they be fatal if fired with a twenty-two?'

'Potentially. The heart, the spine.' There's a moment of silence, of contemplation. Of respect.

Nell's mind works through possibilities, thinks once again of the inquest findings. 'You two have covered a lot of homicides in your time, so tell me: if Blake is right about the bullet wounds, is this killing consistent with organised crime?'

'Organised crime?' asks Blake, frowning, turning to Carole, whose own face reflects his puzzlement.

'No,' says Carole. 'I mean, anything's possible. But not a premeditated hit, if that's what you're talking about. With a contract killer, it's impersonal and it's premeditated. They want to do it quickly and effectively. Walk up behind someone and shoot them, yes. But in the head, not the torso. Or with one in the head to make it certain.'

'That's what I was thinking,' says Nell.

Carole and Blake exchange another look, perplexed by the mention of organised crime, but waiting for Nell to elaborate.

Instead, she summarises. 'This second body, different era, different methodology, different gun. Nothing at all to link it with Stannard. Only the location.'

Carole agrees. 'That's a fair summary.'

'Anything else?'

'That's it for now.'

Once Blake and Carole have left, Nell returns to the squad room and her list of potential victims, eliminating those who went missing in the 1940s, back before the rope was developed. She also puts a line through Joel Fortescue, missing in the floods of 1955, almost certainly drowned. Six left. Although, she reminds herself again, the victim is not necessarily on Kevin's lists. Then she calls Ivan.

'Greetings from the jewel of the greater west,' he says.

'You're back in Dubbo?' She thought he might have found an excuse to stay in Sydney.

'Regretfully.' He grows serious. 'What news from the front?'

She tells him about Eamon Finucane's war wounds, the rope fibres, the victim probably shot, the discovery of the gun, the decades between the murders.

'So not a serial killer?'

Nell returns the attempt at humour. 'If it is, it's a very patient one.'

'And definitely not Eamon Finucane?'

'Definitely not.'

'Okay. We need to go hard at it then. The killer could still be alive, could still be out there. What's next?'

'Blake is confident of getting DNA. I've collected a sample from Tycho Buchanan's mother. If it's not him, we can locate the relatives of the other missing men. Also, run it against our databases and, failing that, maybe private ones. Appeal to those genealogy companies. After that, I guess we can go to the media, ask for community help. Small towns, people know things, remember things. Maybe Carole and Blake will have narrowed down the timeframe further by then, or found bullets or other evidence. But sooner or later, we need his identity. Without that, it's following

Stannard into the unsolved cases file.' She can't believe she's saying it. 'What do you think?'

'Agreed. Identifying the body is paramount. Sounds like you don't need me. Yet.' It's a statement rather than a question. 'Keep me in the loop. Tell me the moment you identify the victim. If you identify the victim.'

'Of course. And Ivan?'

'I'm still here.'

'Any word from Professional Standards? Phelan?'

'No. Not that he'd be telling me anything.'

'Right.'

After the call, she mulls that over. It's her first murder investigation, the first where she has sole carriage. And now, with the discovery of the synthetic rope, she has half a chance of finding a killer. But she needs to identify the victim; she needs something to break her way.

The bell in reception rings. Too late, she realises she should have locked the door when Carole and Blake left. With Kev still helping at the regulator, she'll need to deal with whoever it is. Some local applying for P-plates or reporting a stolen garden gnome or wanting a stat dec witnessed. Or a cooker complaining about contrails.

Instead, it's her uncle Gene. He's still rake thin but looks older, like an ageing bohemian, with his grey hair worn long, scuffed boots below stove-pipe jeans and an elaborate scarf wound above a black waistcoat. He's smiling, eyes twinkling, as if their last phone call never happened.

'Well, look at you,' he says. 'A detective.'

'You have something for me?' she asks, a little surprised at the hardness in her voice.

Gene's smile fades as he picks up on her irritation. 'I'm told there is a second body.'

She stares at him before answering. 'When's your next edition?'

'Next Tuesday.'

'I thought it was twice a week.'

'No, not for a long time. I'm a weekly now.'

There's no point in denying it; by next Tuesday he'll know all about the body, if he doesn't already. 'Yes. We've found a second skeleton.'

'Is it Finucane?'

'No.'

'How can you be sure?'

'Finucane lost an eye earlier in the war, had reconstructive surgery. Glass eye. I've seen the skull. It's not him.'

'Right.' Her uncle shifts his weight, as if discomfited.

'So chances are that it was Finucane who killed Stannard, not Tankard. There's your story.'

The twinkle has gone from her uncle's eyes. Now he does look old. He must be in his mid-sixties. 'I heard Mum gave you a DNA sample.'

'She did,' says Nell.

And now it's not age she sees in his eyes, it's trepidation. And grief. 'Do you think it's him?' he asks, voice sombre. 'Tycho?'

'We'll know soon enough. Well before your deadline.'

Gene tries to smile, but it doesn't really work, lingering for a moment before receding. 'I'm not just here in a professional capacity, Nell. It's personal. He was my brother.'

She can't help but soften. 'Of course.'

His eyes drift about. She wonders what he's thinking. There's a sadness to him as he speaks. 'Tell me if there's anything else I can do to help, then. It would mean a lot to us to have a funeral. Closure, as the Americans say.'

'There is something. I've had a look at the inquest findings. It says you heard the two of them, Tycho and Bert, arguing the last time Tycho was seen alive.'

'That's right.'

'What happened?'

'It should be in the transcripts.'

'Help me out.'

Gene sighs. 'Mind if I sit?'

'Please do.'

He takes a seat, there in reception. 'It was out in the yard. There was a car, a wrecked Studebaker, where I'd sit sometimes. It was my private place, where I could read or play guitar or listen to my transistor. I was lying in the back seat, when the two of them came by. They were really going at each other. They didn't realise I was there, that I could hear.'

'What were they arguing about?'

'I only caught a bit of it. They just stopped walking for a moment before they kept going. But Tycho was really upset, almost shouting. He was saying that Dad had no right to tell him what to do. That he would write the story.'

'What story?'

'He didn't say. But from Dad's reaction, I reckon it was something to do with us.'

'You mean the low-level criminality the coroner mentioned?'

'You saw that?' He pauses, looks at his hands. 'Yes. I guess that was it.'

'What else?'

'That's all. They walked on and I didn't hear any more.'

'So what do you think happened?'

'I don't know. I really don't.' Gene looks as if he has aged ten years since entering the station.

'What's with the vendetta against the Tankards?'

'Vendetta?'

'That's what it looks like to me.'

Gene shrugs. 'Tankard was a corrupt cop. He told the inquest we were criminals, but provided no evidence. And he refused to investigate the possibility the mafia killed them.'

Nell takes the next step. 'Do you believe Tankard was involved in their deaths?'

But Gene shakes his head. 'No. I thought of that. Checked it out. He was in Sydney, on a training course, that whole week.' He sounds deflated.

Nell relents. 'This is off the record—part of the investigation, not for reporting. Maybe by next week you can use it, but not without checking with me first.'

'What?'

'They've found a gun in the regulator. Just now, this morning. They think it's a twenty-two rifle.'

Gene has become very still, staring back at her. 'Dad's gun?'

'We don't know.'

'The DNA. When will you know if it's Tycho?'

'A day or two.'

He breaks eye contact, stares into space, as if peering into the past.

Nell presses. 'The inquest. It said you and Grainger found your father's truck and your brother's car.'

'That's right.'

'Were they together?'

'Yes. Maybe a hundred metres apart. South of Anglers Reach.'

'So not near the regulator?'

'No. Close by where the fishermen found Dad's body two years later.'

chapter twenty-six

1973

'ARE YOU ALL RIGHT, TESSA?'

She shook her head, looked up. The bell had rung, she'd heard it, but somehow it hadn't registered. The Tool was standing in front of her desk, frowning. The last of her classmates had left; she hadn't noticed. She looked at the wall clock: it was gone three thirty—somehow fifteen minutes had vanished since the last time she had looked.

'I'm fine,' she said, getting to her feet.

'You sure?' asked her teacher. 'If you need to talk about something . . .'

'I'm fine.' Tessa found this new attitude of his unsettling; it sounded as if his concern was genuine.

'Well, have a good break. Hope to see you next year,' said the teacher.

'Happy Christmas, sir.'

Outside, the normal listless drift of her classmates had been replaced by a contained energy. It was the last week of school, just two days remaining, and now she was with them she felt some of it herself. The holidays beckoned; it was contagious. Past summers had meant isolation at the farm, but surely not this year. For a day or two, maybe. For weeks, possibly. But not for the entire break. There was too much momentum, too much impetus. She had waited patiently for it to arrive and now it was here: life. She looked about her, sure that her classmates from the third and fourth forms could feel it too. Life. Big and bold and beckoning. In just two months she would be sixteen, an adult, or close enough.

And then, as if in response to these thoughts, she caught a flash of blue from the corner of her eye. Tycho in his Datsun. Circling. She stood and watched the car pass, a steadiness in her gaze. So he had come. So what? The memory of swimming at the regulator came again, of Tycho with the girl Willow, of her humiliation. As she climbed onto the bus she stared down the bus driver with contempt, meeting his eye, forcing him to look away. Satisfied, she moved down the aisle. It wasn't too hot; the weather had moderated. November had experienced weeks of unrelenting heat, building towards the century, and everyone was predicting a brutal summer, but now that it had ticked over into December it seemed it might not be so bad after all.

She sat next to Gene, but he seemed distracted, staring out the window, unaffected by the pre-holiday enthusiasm.

'What's wrong?' she asked.

'Nothing.'

'Where's your trannie?'

'In my bag.'

She looked at his face. 'Gene? What is it?'

He looked at her. 'I said it was nothing.'

She let him be and looked behind them. The back seat of the bus was empty. The seniors were already on study leave, Grainger cramming, aiming for the marks that could carry him into university.

They rode back to Tulong in silence. She attempted conversation a couple of times, but gave up when Gene's replies remained monosyllabic.

At Tulong, Tessa stood, let Gene get out from his window seat.

'Bye, Gene,' she said.

'Bye, Tessa.' And then, 'Sorry. Hope to see you soon.'

'That would be nice,' she said.

—

When she alighted at the end of her driveway, Tycho was there, leaning on his car, smoking, casual.

'Afternoon,' he said.

'Hello.'

'You didn't see me?'

'I saw you.'

He drew on the last of the cigarette, dropped the butt, rubbed it out with his shoe. 'Jump in. I want to show you something.'

She paused for a moment, making up her mind. She looked across the fields to the house above the tilt, all alone. She thought of the approaching holidays, the heat and the tedium. 'Okay,' she said.

'Music?' he asked, once they were seated.

'Sure.'

He put on Joni Mitchell's *Blue.* It was hard to hear once the car was moving, with the wind rushing in, so she wound her window up and, not long after, Tycho did the same, fiddling with the dash to get air blowing in through the vents instead. On the stereo, Joni's heart was crying out for California. Lucky her.

Tycho was heading north and they were soon through Tulong.

'Where are we going?' she asked.

'Not far. You'll see.'

And sure enough, they were only about ten minutes past the town when he turned right, onto a dirt road leading down the tilt and into the forest. The road was graded, not just a logging track. A couple of cars passed, coming the other way, and she was glad the Datsun's windows were up. They went a little further and then crossed a broad river, the Edward, split from the Murray and forced north by the tilt, flowing towards Hatheson. She found she was starting to enjoy this adventure, heading into the unknown.

'What's here?' she asked.

'Stories,' he said.

'For the paper?'

'Maybe.'

She saw a stillness in him now, a seriousness, as if the jester and japer had fallen away. He must have known her eyes were upon him—where he wanted them, no doubt—but he focused on driving, easing the Datsun along, tapping the brakes and changing gears. Only after long minutes did he turn those deep brown eyes to her, meeting her gaze.

She looked out at the passing woodland. 'Is this where Willow lives?' she asked.

The smallest of smiles flitted across his lips, but only briefly. 'I don't know where she lives. In here somewhere, but deeper in. She wouldn't tell me. Too smart for that.'

'Is she one of your stories?'

He shook his head, not in answer but as if he was disagreeing with the assumption behind her question. 'She knows things. All sorts of things. Some she shares, some she doesn't.'

'I read your report,' Tessa countered. 'All the people living in the forest.'

'Yes, she helped with that,' he said, and gave her a wink.

Tessa wasn't sure she liked being winked at, and changed the subject. 'So where are we going?'

'You'll see.'

The road straightened, the land flat, the trees less thick. And then they were out of them altogether. As far as she could tell, they were heading east, the forest to their right, farms to their left, the road marking the northern boundary of the great forest.

Tycho began to slow, bringing the Datsun to a halt. 'First stop,' he said, climbing out.

She followed, but there was nothing to see. Just the forest with an overgrown track leading into it. Tycho pointed—not to the forest but across the fields to a deserted house. It was all but fallen down, windows empty, walls collapsing, only the brick chimney remaining solid.

'What?' she asked.

'The family farm,' Tycho said. 'It's where your dad grew up.'

'Here?'

'Apparently.'

She stared. That tiny place, that sad ruin? Her dad spoke occasionally about life as a kid on the farm. She had always assumed it was the same farm they lived on now. 'What happened?' she whispered.

'Don't know,' said Tycho.

Back in the car, they continued on in silence. The tape had reversed itself, playing the second side. Joni was leaving a mean old daddy called Carey. Tycho slowed again, turned back into the forest, onto a sketchy path, not even a logging track. It wound this way and that, circling old fellow redgums, just two runnels through the grass. They passed through a patch of fire-blackened trees. The earth was bare, grass gone, without enough rain to engender new growth. They must be heading south, she thought to herself, deeper into the forest. The Edward River would be off to their right; if they kept going they would reach the Murray.

Around her, the forest had become its anonymous self. Not featureless, but with little to indicate where exactly they were. There were dried creek beds and there were ridges, there were stands of river oaks and there were solitary giants: redgums and spotted gums. There were wattles and there were little patches of pasture and small fields of moira grass dotted with saplings, and there were places where vehicles had come through, leaving their mark on the country. She studied Tycho's face once more, saw the concentration there, as he inched their way forward. She realised he hadn't smoked since picking her up.

He turned to her, offering a reassuring smile. He pointed ahead and to the right. 'The regulator where we swam isn't far from here. But the creek is in the way, we can't get through from this side.'

'Okay,' she replied, not grasping the significance of this information, or even if there was any.

Joni finished singing and Tessa leant down and ejected the tape. Now that they were moving slowly and off the graded dirt, she opened the window, letting in the cool air and the sounds of the forest. They continued along without speaking, before eventually breaking through to the Murray. There was a small clearing, a fisherman's campground, with a stone ring fireplace and a scattering of empty bottles and cans. They got out, walked to the river. She realised they were miles from anywhere, alone. The track was the only way in and out. That and the river itself. But she didn't feel scared, not for a moment.

'There,' he said, pointing across the Murray.

'There?' she asked, scanning the opposite bank where a creek entered the river. She could see dark shapes: wood beams and metal, half submerged. Large cylinders of iron and rust, black and orange stood nearby. She looked to Tycho for guidance, but received none. He was looking at her. She felt as if he were issuing a challenge, seeing if she could work it out for herself. 'What is it?'

'That's the red engine—what's left of it.'

'What's the red engine?'

'It's where my grandfather died. He was working it when the foundations gave way, trapped him under it and crushed him.'

She listened, saying nothing.

'My father was still a kid. The war had ended, the forest was emptying, the sleeper cutters and charcoal burners were almost gone. He had nowhere to go.'

She began to understand. This was not a newspaper story he was telling her, but the story of his family. *His* story.

'Did he show you this?'

'Dad? No. He's never mentioned it. He never talks about his family, where he came from. It was Willow. She told me the story.'

'You didn't know?'

'No.'

She was unsure what to say. This Tycho seemed so different. Considered, reflective, vulnerable. The impetuous youth gone. 'Does it matter?' she asked.

He shrugged. 'Maybe. Maybe not.' He looked at her. 'I'm sorry,' he said. 'About Willow.'

She nodded, not knowing what to say.

'I'll take you home,' he said quietly. 'There's just one more place I want to show you. It's on the way.'

She smiled. 'Okay.' And then: 'I like being with you.' She meant it, and she sensed his relief.

He drove them back the way they'd come, back along the same track, back along the dirt road past the abandoned farm and across the Edward River to the highway and then south on the blacktop to Tulong, where he turned down into the forest once again, following the road through the woods towards Anglers Reach. She wondered if he was embarked on a grand circle, heading back to the regulator pond from the western side. But no, at the river he headed right, followed the Murray where it turned south towards the lakes and the narrows and the choke and, much further, the twin towns of Echuca and Boonlea. She knew this road a little, knew that further down there was a way through the forest that would take them back to her parents' farm. Maybe that was his plan.

And sure enough, he took the turn, off the graded dirt and onto one of the logging tracks, better maintained than the one that had taken them towards the red engine, although not by much. But just as she was sure where they were heading, he turned again, a hard left, as if he were intending to go cross-country, pushing through a wall of shrubbery, abandoning the tracks altogether. She soon realised that wasn't the case; there was a faint track, rarely used. She didn't even know how he knew it was there. Tycho was forced to slow right down, moving forward at barely more than a walking pace. When she looked across at him, he offered another wink. She liked this wink a lot more.

They reached a low creek, water across the track. Tycho eased the car through it. She knew there was little water in the forest that year, that it had all gone to the irrigators and Adelaide. Water in a creek, water across the track, meant that it must be permanent and that they must be close to the Murray again. And sure enough, soon there was water to the left of them and water to the right, creeks running parallel to the road for a while before running deeper into the trees, still and without flow. They were driving out onto an island, she realised, or a peninsula. She wondered if that was the right word or if there were special words for the landforms of the forest. Several minutes later they entered a clearing. Tycho cut the engine and the sounds of the forest filled the car. They sat looking for a time, not getting out.

Before them, dominating the clearing, was a black metal drum, easily twelve feet across, perforated with holes and caked in rust, hanging from a pair of supporting brackets. There was a second close by, lopsided, one of its supports having given way, and a third lying on its side, decoupled from its supports altogether.

'What are they?' she asked.

'Charcoal drums. They used to make it here during the war.'

'Why?'

'For fuel.'

She recalled the story he had written for the newspaper, the feature on the forest dwellers. Perhaps this was part of some other story. Maybe that was the point of this tour—he was introducing her to his world.

'This place is all but inaccessible. The only way in or out is the way we came or along the river, by boat,' Tycho explained. 'There's a makeshift wharf hidden down there on a creek.' He pointed. 'About a hundred yards that way.'

'Why bring me here, Tycho?'

'There's something else. But you need to be quiet, just in case.'

'In case of what?'

'In case someone is here.' He squeezed her hand, opened the door and they got out.

He led her past the ghostly charcoal drums, standing like watchmen, then on by a thicket of trees. There was a shed, made from metal, like a large garage. Not so new, but surely not so old as the charcoal drums. The steel was not corrugated, but flatter, a dull green. There were wooden boxes stacked outside, holding what looked like wine flagons. He held a finger to his lips, requesting silence. He watched the shed for a few seconds before speaking. 'It's okay. It's all locked up. There's no one here.'

'What is it?' she whispered.

'Come on.' He took her hand and led her across the clearing to the shed. She could see where vehicles had been. He was right: people did come here. The doors of the shed were closed tight and padlocked, but around the side was a slatted glass window, high on the wall. There was a discarded metal milk urn lying in the grass. He manoeuvred it into position beneath the window. 'Here,' he said, standing behind her, hands around her waist, lifting her effortlessly from the ground so she could stand atop the urn. It was exhilarating, feeling his strength, to have him hold her so close. 'Can you see?' he asked.

'Hang on.' She brushed at the window, leaning forward and cupping her hands, shielding her eyes. Inside she saw some machinery, large vats, a coil of copper tubing, stacked bottles, a series of cages made of wicker and steel. 'What's it for?'

He lowered her back down. She swivelled to face him, his hands still on her waist. 'Tycho?'

'I think it's part of my father's business dealings.' His face is serious, eyes troubled. 'Have you ever wondered how come we have such a fine house? From a junkyard on a minor road in the middle of nowhere?'

'Does it matter?'

'I think maybe it does.'

She understood now. She leant into him, head on his shoulder, her arms reaching around him, embracing him. He'd changed. He was no longer some charismatic ideal, but a real person, with his own concerns and vulnerabilities. And he'd let her in, let her see it. She felt herself suddenly older. More mature, more aware.

'Are you going to write a story about it?'

He looked troubled. 'I guess. I just have to work out how to tell it.'

'What do you mean?'

'I think it might hurt too many people. Please don't tell anyone you've been here, that you've seen it.'

'Of course not.'

And Tycho smiled. 'Besides, I've got wind of something bigger. Much bigger.'

'So why bring me here?'

'To show you why I was hanging out with Willow. Will you forgive me?'

She didn't answer, just hugged him and loved him all the more.

chapter twenty-seven

BLAKE SUGGESTS AN EARLY DINNER IN HATHESON: HIM, CAROLE AND NELL. Nell invites Kevin, not sure if he'll accept, but he's keen. It must get pretty lonely being the only cop in a town like Tulong.

They ride up together, Nell driving, Kev full of chat, looking younger now he's out of uniform, dressed in jeans, a t-shirt, a denim jacket. She asks about his hand, now free of bandages.

'Good as gold,' he says.

Blake has found a restaurant covering the whole of North-East Asia, serving Korean barbecue, Japanese noodles and Taiwanese dumplings. The decor is nothing special, with plain laminex tables and cheap pine panelling on the walls, but the smell is convincing: as soon as she enters Nell knows it's going to be good. It's BYO, so she heads back out, buying a bottle of sauvignon blanc for those who want it and a six pack of beer for the others. It's still early in the evening and the place is half empty. The walls are lined with screens showing a K-pop group singing and grinding and dancing. The boy band looks too energetic, too synchronised, too much for a Thursday night in Hatty, but the volume is low and the sound inoffensive in the way of boy bands everywhere. Blake volunteers to order for the table and the others are happy to delegate.

At first the talk is of the case, and Nell detects a sense of optimism. Blake has sequenced Rita's DNA and express couriered a tooth from the skeleton to Sydney for the delicate art of extraction and sequencing. He expects the results within a day or two. Carole says she has left the gun soaking overnight, to loosen the mud and dirt caking it. With luck, it will be giving up its secrets in the morning, including the serial number. After that, the conversation eases away into more relaxed subjects: the best restaurants in country New South Wales, kayaking holidays floating down the Murray, the infamous Hatty ute muster, which Kevin gets roped in to help the locals with every year. He's proving to be quite the raconteur, regaling them with tales of being a country cop, claiming his popularity is seasonal: not so good in summer, because he's shit at cricket, but peaking in winter, heading into the footy finals. 'All us blackfellas are good at footy,' he says. 'You know that, right?' And the others laugh along with his joke, on the same wavelength.

The only slightly awkward moment comes early, when Nell notices he's not drinking and offers him a choice of wine or beer for the second time.

'Nah, not for me,' he says.

'Right. Sorry,' says Nell.

'Don't be sorry. I don't have a problem with it. Just not a good look, me drinking in public.'

'You serious?' asks Carole, suddenly concerned.

'No big deal. My choice. But these country towns, someone sees me having a beer tonight, by the end of the week someone else will be claiming I was falling down drunk.'

'Even nowadays?' asks Carole.

'Maybe I'm being overly cautious.'

'Do you drink at all?' asks Nell.

'Sure. In private, at someone's house. No problem.'

'I had no idea,' says Blake.

By the end of the evening, Nell is feeling mellow. It's not the alcohol: she's only had two wines, conscious of the drive back to Tulong; it must be the company, the opportunity to talk and engage. In Ivan's absence, she's been alone much of the time, feeling the pressure of the investigation and dwelling on the hovering menace of Feral Phelan.

It's dark by the time she and Kevin head back, the half-hour drive unexceptional. There is a moon out, the sky clear and starry. She drops her colleague at his home behind the police station, then crosses the highway, easing down the tilt towards the Redgum Motel at the end of its cul-de-sac overlooking the creek. She's glad it wasn't a late night; she still has time to use the guest laundry. She dips her lights as she swings into the car park, not wanting to disturb other guests. She's just thinking there aren't many cars yet when a flash of movement steals her attention. She flicks on the headlights again. There's something on the ground, dark shapes looming over. A movement: it's a man, cowering, covering himself. One of the three figures lays in with his boot, kicking the person hard, the other two standing, waiting their turn, not bothered by her headlights or who sees them. She goes to high beam, blinding them, even as she brakes, stops the car, gets out, all in one fluid motion.

'Police!' she yells, moving forward, expecting them to scarper.

But they don't take a backward step. 'It's the bitch,' says one of the men.

And now she sees them clearly, sees what she's up against. Two are wearing ski masks, the other a bandana stretched across the lower part of his face, a cowboy hat above it. One has an iron bar, another a baseball bat. So the bashing is premeditated. She notices their boots for some reason, all the same type: heavy and black, steel-capped. Bovver boots.

'Show time,' hisses one of them.

They start moving towards her, slowly, deliberately. She thinks of her gun, locked in the car's safe. There's no time to retrieve it. She does move back to the car, though, reaching in to hit the siren, loud enough to wake the dead. But even this doesn't deter the men, and she feels a surge of panic as they continue towards her at the same measured pace, fanning out as they come. They're big, but it's not their size that scares her, it's their sense of impunity: not deterred by the siren or the prospect of assaulting a police officer or the likelihood of witnesses. She's in serious trouble, with no easy way out.

She takes a step forward, trying not to let her fear show. Behind them, the man on the ground isn't moving, but she sees a red puddle surrounding him, glistening in her headlights. She needs to survive this for his sake as well as her own. She takes a long slow breath, readies herself.

And then they are on her. The first one is almost too easy, underestimating her, wanting to claim his prize before his mates get their chance. He steps within range, arms out, as if she's just some shop mannequin to be manhandled, passive and defenceless. She feints back, feigning fear, reeling him in, but then, with his hands almost upon her, she drops into a crouch, pushing forward low and hard and fast, using her momentum, thrusting with her own booted foot, feeling it smash into the would-be assailant's knee, hearing the crunch of bone, his cry of pain. She continues through, under his reach even as he collapses shrieking to the ground, and she's up again, facing the two remaining thugs.

They look at each other, reassessing. The one in the cowboy hat comes at her. She moves quickly to one side, too easily, and then sees her mistake. The other man is in the car, turning off the siren, turning off the lights. That worries her. The lights are one thing, but who would know the controls for a siren in an unmarked police car? With the noise shut off, the night seems silent, just their breathing and the sobbing of the man with the broken knee. She hears a clang on the roof of the motel. Her car keys. The one with the iron bar speaks low and clear. 'Together,' he says.

She's in her crouch, trying to find an angle in the dim light, but there's nothing obvious. They are too big, too close; she can't outrun them. They come in together, arms raised, weapons ready. She steps outside the one on her right, so now they are side-on to the car. She can't repeat the manoeuvre, or they'll turn on her lights and she will be the one who's blinded.

They come again. This time she moves the same way—then, as the man follows, as he strikes, she moves in and under, taking his arms and throwing him over herself, continuing on as she does, before the other man can target her. It's a good move, but not good enough. The thrown man is back on his feet in an instant, swearing softly. She's not going to achieve much just by tossing them, even if she is lucky enough to do so again. She either needs to take them out, or she needs to escape, get to the bush, get out of sight.

They're coming again, no longer walking, but crouching, on balance, ready for her next move. Here it comes, she thinks.

And then the lights are back, a floodlight. An explosion, then another. Gunfire. Deafening in the night. At the door of the motel, wearing a dressing-gown and sandals, John the proprietor is standing, shotgun in his hands. He pumps the action, reloading, emphasising his seriousness. His voice is low, scared, determined. 'Fuck off. Take your pal with you.'

'No. Leave him,' says Nell. 'I want him.'

'No,' says John. And then to the masked men: 'Get him out of here.'

'You can't let them go,' says Nell.

'I can't let them stay,' says John.

The men decide it, moving to their fallen comrade, pulling him up. Nell moves forward, not sure what she's intending, maybe to take one of them on as they lift the man with the broken knee. But the one in the bandana and cowboy hat reaches behind himself, pulls a handgun from his waistband and points it straight at her. 'Far enough.'

She stops in her tracks, slowly raising her hands, the universal sign language taught by a thousand Hollywood movies.

It only takes a moment and they are gone, hauling the man up the tilt into the darkness. She hears the roar of an engine, sees the lights of a car or truck come on as they get up towards the main road. She thinks of running after them, hoping to see the car, getting the licence plate. But it's no good. They're gone.

'Thanks,' she says to John.

'Sorry,' he says. 'Too risky. If I let you arrest him, they'd be back.'

'If I'd tried to arrest him, they would have shot me.'

'True,' says the manager.

She can see he's starting to shake, wonders why she isn't. Instead she's hyper alert, the adrenaline coursing through. 'Call an ambulance. Triple zero.'

'Hey?'

She points to the crumpled figure of the man on the ground, still unmoving.

'Jesus,' says John.

'Go, ring them. Tell them a man has been beaten. Potentially life-threatening injuries.'

John heads inside, and Nell moves to the dark figure lying in his own blood.

It's the twitcher, the man in the anorak, no longer camouflage green but splattered with red. She checks his pulse, feels relief as she finds it. His breathing sounds a little ragged, as if there may be fluid in his throat. She rolls him carefully onto his side, eases him into the recovery position. She shakes his arm, tries to rouse him. 'Wake up,' she says, 'wake up.' But he doesn't hear, is beyond hearing. She walks back to her car, gets water and a towel, her torch, and starts washing some of the blood from his face, trying to ascertain the seriousness of his wounds. From what she can see, the blood is coming from his head. There's an awful lot of it and it's still flowing. It could be a fractured skull. One of his arms looks broken, no doubt several ribs, but they can be fixed. Brains aren't so easy.

She rings Kevin and he makes it there in minutes, well before the ambulance from Hatty. 'My God,' is all he says.

She explains quickly what happened, even as she continues to tend to the fallen man. She describes the aggressors, three men, big, like security guards, armed and dangerous. One with a cowboy hat and a bandana and a handgun. And their boots, she describes their boots.

'Black twin-cab?' he asks.

'You know them?'

'Seen them around.'

'Couldn't see what they were driving. But it sounded gutsy—V8 at a guess.'

'Anything else?'

'Yeah. They turned my siren off. Knew how to do it.'

'Shit.'

'Shit indeed.'

They hear the ambulance before they see it. First the siren, then the red and blue flashing lights, coming in to land like a spaceship, edging around Nell's immobilised vehicle.

'Blimey. Hit by a car?' asks the first of the paramedics, a silver-haired woman.

'Beaten up.'

The two paramedics set to work, the woman and a man young enough to be her son. They have a neck brace, gently turning the victim as they fit it, immobilising his head.

'Is his neck broken?' Nell asks.

'A precaution,' says the woman. 'How long's he been out for?'

Nell has no idea; time is moving at high speed. 'How long did it take you to get here?'

'Twenty minutes from the call.'

'Must be half an hour then.'

'Thanks.' The woman starts cutting away the man's blood-soaked raincoat, and then his trousers. By the glare of the lights, Nell can see his leg is broken below the knee but it's not compound. The ambulance officers splint it in a foam-lined half-cylinder. They cut away his polo fleece, check his arms. 'Not broken,' says the woman. 'Shoulder dislocated.' She turns to her offsider. 'What would you recommend?' she asks the young man calmly, as if this were nothing more than a training drill.

'Put it back in?'

'Okay. You steady him. Neck and spine.' She looks at Kevin. 'Give us a hand, mate.'

Kevin kneels, holds where he's told, braces the birdwatcher together with the young man. The woman moves so quickly Nell almost misses it. There's a gasp from the injured man, then he relaxes again. The shoulder is back in.

'Goodo. That'll keep him for the moment. We need to get him into hospital, get his head scanned.'

'Can I ride along?' asks Nell.

'You a relative?'

Nell flashes her badge. 'Police.'

'Thought it must have been something like that. Jump in.'

'I'll be right back.' She trots over to reception. John is sitting just inside, staring at the wall, shotgun between his legs. 'Jesus, John. You got the safety on?'

'Huh?'

'The shotty. The safety.'

He looks down at it. 'Yeah. It's on. All good.'

'Maybe unload it then, hey?'

'Good thinking.'

'I'm heading to the hospital. If you can manage it, I need my car keys back. Those thugs chucked them on the roof. Up here by reception.'

John stares at her blankly for a moment. 'I'll see what I can do.'

The paramedics are loading the unconscious victim into the back of the ambulance. Before jumping in, Nell gathers up what's left of his clothes—shredded pants, fleece and raincoat. She feels a weight in them: a wallet, room keys.

'I'll follow you up,' says Kevin. 'You'll need a lift back.'

'Makes sense. Thanks.'

She rides into Hatty in the back of the ambulance, next to the unconscious man, a saline drip in his arm. She's hoping he might regain consciousness, but she's out of luck. The longer he's under, the more serious his injuries are likely to be. She checks his wallet. A driver's licence reveals him to be Torrence Faithwaite of Turramurra, on Sydney's upper North Shore. There are the usual cards: health insurance, Medicare, a couple of credit cards, the NRMA, a membership for the SCG, memberships of BirdLife Australia and Birding NSW.

At the hospital, the paramedics wheel Torrence Faithwaite away on a gurney, tell her she has to wait in reception. It's only ten o'clock but the hospital has a late night feel to it, empty and silent.

Kevin comes in. 'Any news?' he asks.

'No. Still unconscious.'

'You want to wait?'

'Not much point.'

They're heading towards the exit when they're stopped by a nurse. 'Did you just come in with that injured man?'

'I did, yeah,' says Nell.

'Do you know who he is? I need to admit him.'

'Sure. Here.' Nell opens the man's wallet, pulls out his Medicare card. 'This do?'

'Yeah. Hang on.'

The nurse moves behind a plexiglass screen, taps at a computer. She frowns.

'Problem?' asks Nell.

The nurse holds the card up, tilting it backwards and forwards between her fingers so that it catches the light. 'This card. I think it's a fake.'

'You sure?' asks Nell.

'The card reader isn't recognising it,' she says, still staring at the card. 'There's something not right about it.'

'Can I see?' Nell takes the card, withdraws her own Medicare card from her wallet and compares the two. She can't see any difference, but she trusts the instincts of the nurse; she must handle dozens every day.

'I can't enter it manually either,' says the young woman.

'Give me a moment,' says Nell. She finds Faithwaite's driver's licence, takes a few steps away, opens the MobiPol app on her phone and runs it.

Nothing. No Torrence Faithwaite. Nothing even close. It's a forgery.

chapter twenty-eight

NELL WAITS UNTIL IT IS EARLY MORNING, PAST TWO O'CLOCK. SHE CAN'T SLEEP anyway: the adrenaline has left her but her nerves are jangled. Dealing with Noel Tankard at the pub was one thing, but the three men in the motel car park were in a different league. No amount of martial arts skills could counter that, not if they were also trained, not with their pipe and baseball bat, not with the cowboy's handgun. If the motel manager hadn't appeared with his shotgun, she'd be in the Hatheson hospital as well. Or the morgue. So now she has her Glock in the room with her, and she brings it with her as she quietly exits and walks along the row of motel doorways. She's wearing latex gloves, aware that what she is doing is illegal. She has no warrant, no legal justification. The car park is full: where was everyone earlier when she needed them? When Torrence Faithwaite, or whoever he is, needed them? Her own car sits marooned where she left it. There is no sign of John; the keys must still be on the roof.

Using Faithwaite's key, she enters his room and moves quickly to the windows, making sure the curtains are drawn. She flicks on the bedside lamp, its dim light heightened by the circumstances. The room is neat, unremarkable, clothes folded and shirts hanging in the closet. On the counter-cum-desk, between the television and an electric jug, is a laptop. Next to it is a camera, fitted with a long, fat telephoto lens. It looks expensive and, when she picks it up, it feels expensive, the lens heavy with glass. Nearby she can see a tripod and a monopod. Standard equipment for a twitcher, or so she imagines.

She tries the laptop but, predictably, it requires a password. She tries the camera and has more luck. She hits the review button, and a picture of a black swan emerges. She flicks back through the reel. There are plenty more of the bird and its partner, plus a brood of cygnets, small and fluffy, following in their mother's wake. Nice shots, testimony to the camera and its operator. But would a serious twitcher, a man hunting for the elusive painted snipe, be taking photos of black swans? They look to her like the brood down at Clarrie Buchanan Park.

There's a camera bag on the floor, with more lenses, spare batteries, various leads. She brings it up to the counter, searches it methodically. It surrenders two more SD memory cards. She quickly searches the rest of the room as she ponders her choices, but finds nothing more of interest. Decision made, she takes the laptop, the camera and the bag and returns to her own room. She could have left them where she found them; with no warrant, that would have been the sensible thing. But Faithwaite is in hospital, helpless, and there's nothing to stop the thugs returning, taking the equipment themselves. And given there's a fair argument that she saved his life, or at least prevented further serious injury, he may be inclined not to press charges. He might even thank her. If he ever regains consciousness.

Back in her room, she takes the SD cards and tries to open them on her own computer but can't. They're encrypted. Who encrypts camera cards? She takes the card from the camera, tries to open it. This time, she makes a little more progress. She can see the card has two folders. She opens the first, finding the pictures of the black swans. There are others: cockatoos, kookaburras, galahs, magpies. Like the swans, such common birds, easily captured in a single afternoon. The second folder is again encrypted. Eventually she's forced to give up. She falls asleep, still fully dressed, gun by her side.

--

She's woken by a hammering on the door, sunlight bursting around the edges of her curtains. Eight o'clock. She's slept in.

'Who is it?'

'Kev.'

'Give us a moment.'

She goes into the bathroom, splashes water on her face, decides she's not looking her best.

'Sorry,' she says, opening the door.

'Nothing to be sorry for,' says Kev. 'Tough night. I brought you this.' He offers her a coffee and a smile.

'You're a saviour,' she says. She looks around the mess of her room, Faithwaite's camera and laptop on the floor by the bed, and steps out into the car park rather than inviting the uniformed officer in.

'I've rung around the hospitals and GP clinics,' says Kev. 'No one presenting with a busted knee.'

'Right. Poor bastard will be in agony.'

'You don't sound too sorry about that,' he observes.

'Not overly.'

Kevin smiles again, relaxed despite everything. 'John's getting a ladder. I can get up and find your keys.'

She looks across. Her unmarked four-wheel drive is still where she left it the night before, partially blocking the entry to the car park.

'If we don't move it soon, I'll have to give you a ticket,' he says, deadpan.

On cue, John the manager emerges from around the side of the building, carrying a ladder. Kevin moves to help him.

'Sorry,' says John. 'Didn't want to go up last night, not by myself.'

'Fair enough,' says Nell. 'I didn't get the chance to thank you properly, but you saved my skin.'

The manager shrugs. 'Let's hope they don't come back.'

Nell points to a CCTV camera above the door to reception. 'That working?'

John looks up at it. 'Nah. Never worked. Bought it online, got ripped off. Left it there—you know, as a deterrent.' And then he too tries to smile. 'Didn't do much good.'

Once they've retrieved her keys, Kevin mounting the ladder despite her protests, she returns to her room to shower and dress. Then she calls the hospital in Hatty, identifying herself as a police officer, gets put through to the relevant extension.

'I'm inquiring after a patient. I came in with him last night. Torrence Faithwaite. The victim of an assault.'

There's a wait while a doctor is found. 'Yes. Seriously injured. Fractures. Concussion. But he's regained consciousness. Seems quite lucid.'

'The fractures. His skull?'

'No, the head is fine.'

'Thanks. That's all I need to know. Please don't allow him any visitors. I'm on my way.'

--

By the time she gets to Hatty, Faithwaite is in a private room, sitting up in bed. His face is a mess, one eye blackened and swollen shut, arm in a sling, his leg protected by a sort of under-blanket framework. He looks at her as she enters carrying a large cardboard box, the expression in his uninjured eye cautious.

She places the box on a chair beside the bed, flips her badge, saying nothing, just holding it out for him to see.

'I know who you are,' he says.

'But who are you?'

He doesn't reply.

She retrieves his wallet from the box, hands it to him. 'Not Torrence Faithwaite, that's for sure.'

'What interest is it of yours?'

'Well, you weren't conscious at the time, but I'm the person who saved your life. Me, the motel manager and a shotgun.'

'If that's the case, then thank you. I have no memory of that. Last thing I remember is finishing my drink at the pub, picking up some takeaway at the cafe and walking towards the motel.'

'Concussion,' says Nell.

'So the doctors tell me,' says the man.

'Okay now?'

'Getting better by the minute.'

She recounts what happened, her discovering him already down, the three men wading into him. To Nell, he seems remarkably attentive, considering he must be in pain, and remarkably alert, considering he must be medicated. 'I have your laptop and camera here.'

'You broke into my room?'

'I had your key. I wanted to keep them safe.'

He considers that. 'Thank you.'

'Who are you?' Nell asks again. 'And why are your camera cards encrypted?'

The man examines her for almost a minute before speaking. Maybe he's hoping she will fill the silence. She doesn't. And then he smiles, and she sees the pain that closes the expression back down.

'I'm what the cookers would describe as deep state,' he says. And this time he maintains the smile a tad longer.

'What does that mean?'

'Pass my laptop, if you'd be so kind. And my phone.'

She retrieves them, opens the computer, places it on his stomach so he can type in a password. He enters it with difficulty, using his one good hand. Followed by fingerprint recognition. Followed by a confirmation code generated by his phone. Eventually he finds what he's looking for, opens a document.

'Could you sign here, please, Detective Constable? An electronic signature will do.'

'What is it?'

'The Official Secrets Act.'

'I've already signed it.'

'Excellent. Then you won't mind signing it again.'

She complies, trying to keep her face unperturbed, even while her mind is racing.

'Very good,' he says. 'My name is Jack Goffing. I'm an officer of the Australian Security Intelligence Organisation.'

'ASIO?' She blinks. 'A spook?'

'Just so.' He again offers the tentative smile. 'Would you mind removing my laptop and shutting it down for me? My ribs, you understand.'

She does what he asks, waits to hear what he has to say, thinking of Ivan, how he'd chatted with the twitcher in the pub's beer garden. And, later, Goffing by the regulator, trying to glean information from Kevin.

'You want to know what I'm doing here?' he asks.

'I do.'

'At ASIO we do counterintelligence, thwarting espionage by foreign powers—that's the traditional role. More recently, we've been tasked with countering terrorist groups: what we call politically motivated violence.'

'The cookers?'

Goffing smiles, wincing as he does so. 'Not per se. Harmless, if deluded. But hiding in among them, trying to cultivate them, are Neo-Nazis and skinheads. The extreme, radical, violent right.'

'They're here?'

'You met them last night.'

'Why here?'

'Because the cookers are here.'

'You said they're harmless.'

'Until they're not. They're a godsend to the extremists.'

'How so?'

Goffing considers her. 'These right-wing fringe groups have existed for decades. But always small, always isolated. Always struggling to connect to like-minded people. Then along came the internet, and suddenly they could find each other, set up chat groups and forums, use the dark web. Good for us too, of course. Easy to infiltrate, easy to monitor. But now, with the advent of anti-vaxxers and the Trump supporters and the QAnon nut jobs, cheered on by opportunistic politicians and scurrilous media, they've found fertile new ground. The pandemic helped consolidate them; now they're a loose-knit movement.'

'That doesn't make them terrorists,' says Nell, thinking of the people waving to her and greeting her down by the park.

'Of course not. Most of them wouldn't hurt a fly. But many are ripe for radicalisation: they're actively seeking an alternative explanation for what they see in the world. And they're gullible.'

'But Tulong? The forest? Why here?'

'The housing crisis.'

'What?'

'It's not just middle-class kids who are affected, you know, unable to afford their first home. It's also working-class families who can't make rent. In the cities, they live out of their cars; in the bush they congregate at camp sites and caravan parks. The campground at Tulong is free, so it's perfect. They're looking for someone to blame, so they're susceptible to conspiracy theories. Step one. Then they get recruited by extremists. Step two.'

'So it's not just at Tulong?'

'No, but it's a standout. There are bush blocks on the periphery of the national park, scrubland, not much good for anything. But cheap. Popular with preppers. Been there for years. I don't know, but I think that's how it started. And now, with the free camping, it's as good a place as any to coalesce. The word spreads, more come. Self-perpetuating.'

'Noel Tankard. The pub. It seems central. Is that why you're always there?'

'Correct. Tankard's too bright to be sucked in by any of it, but he's more than happy to pander to them. The pub was dying when he took it over two years ago, now it's booming. For him it's just business, a money-spinner.'

'And the twitchers. Your poster. The reward?'

Again the smile, again the wince as the pain suppresses it. 'Perfect cover, perfect information-gathering technique. They're a resolute bunch, the birdwatchers. They're down here in droves at the moment because the forest is filling up with water for the first time in decades. When that happens, bird numbers explode. The twitchers are out in the most remote parts of the forest, wading through swamps, kayaking up creeks, beating their way through the undergrowth, trying to get a glimpse, a photo of the rare and elusive painted snipe, among others.'

'Your eyes and ears. Hence the reward.'

'Hence the reward.'

'But what are you seeking? Just general information? Or something more specific?'

And now the smile is gone. 'You remember what you have signed?'

'Of course.'

'Good. My cover is blown. But I still need eyes and ears. I still need to know what's going on.'

'You're recruiting me?'

'I'm seeking your help. Pass up the laptop again.'

She does what he requests, and he repeats the sign-in procedure, at one point entering yet another password. Eventually he brings up a photograph. It's a shed, green steel, set in bushland, taken at dusk. To Nell it looks utterly innocuous.

'We received this in late August, the same night your regulator was blown up. It was sent as an SMS attachment from a phone somewhere in the forest. That and a message: *This is it.*'

'This is what?'

'We don't know.'

'A shed in the bush? I don't get it.'

'The man who sent the message was an undercover federal police officer, tasked with infiltrating a particularly malignant group of white supremacists. Immediately after he sent the message, his phone went dead and has never been reactivated. The police officer hasn't been seen since. We assume he has been murdered.'

'The missing person—Jean-Luc Hoffner. That's him?'

'Not his real name, of course.'

'That's what you were doing at the regulator, talking to Kevin. Seeing if the second body was him.'

'Correct.'

'Was he killed near the regulator?'

'We don't know where he was killed. There's only the one mobile phone tower at Tulong, so we don't have triangulation. We can rule out areas accessing two towers down near Barmah, and there is a considerable amount of the forest where there is no signal at all, but that still leaves a huge area.'

'Aerial surveillance?'

'We've tried. Look closely at the photo. It's been enhanced, of course. You can just glimpse camouflage netting. We got the Geospatial imaging lads to fly a plane over. All they found were a few illegal camps and some minor dope plantations.'

'So what's in the shed?'

Again the painful grimace. 'Could be a hideout, fugitives on the run. Could be a meth lab, financing their activities. Could be an arms cache. Could be a bomb factory. We don't know—but it's very important we find out.'

chapter twenty-nine

JAMES WATERS–FIRST STATEMENT–CONTINUED

THE LAST TIME I SAW BUCKY IN THE FOREST THAT SUMMER, WE FOUGHT. I didn't know it would be the last time I saw him and I felt bad about it afterwards. What I did know, however, was that Mum was having trouble with money. We were getting Dad's army pay, of course, but it seemed like the farm was costing us more than it was making. That electrical storm hadn't helped. Just the opposite. The hail flattened what was left of our wheat crop. It was already marginal before that, because of the drought. Uncle Reg came and had a look for us, and he told Mum it was barely worth harvesting, and only then to provide a bit of feed for our own animals, not for any sort of income.

And we needed feed. The drought meant there wasn't enough grass for the sheep. I offered to take them into the forest but we couldn't see how that could work, not with the cattle as well. So I went looking for Bucky. I wanted to sell more yabbies to the soldiers. Just because it hadn't worked last time didn't mean they wouldn't buy them now. It wasn't as if another storm was likely. So I got the cattle settled, put Lenny on a long rope to graze and left the dogs in charge. I swam the river and made my way to the red engine.

Bucky's dad Clarrie was there, as always, feeding the engine, him and his men. He was glad to see me. 'I wondered where you two rapscallions were,' he said. 'You want to haul some water with the flying fox? Make my day easier.'

I told him I wasn't with Bucky, that I hadn't seen him for a couple of days. That troubled him, I could see it. Bucky's dad had one of those faces you could read like a map; even covered in grime it didn't need much explaining.

'You seen him?' I asked.

'He's been here for dinner and sleeping nights. Not during the day, though. Thought he was with you.'

'I'll find him,' I said.

'Good lad.'

I found Bucky over my side of the river, sitting by the regulator. He wasn't fishing and he wasn't yabbying and his clothes were dry, so it was a long time since he'd swum the river. He was just lying there on his back, looking up at the sky. I thought he might have spotted a sea eagle. You used to see them quite a bit, still do, mainly down at Moira Lake and at Barmah, but they nest all along the river. I looked up, but there was nothing there.

Not even clouds, so I knew he wasn't playing that game where you imagine what shapes they look like.

'Hey, Bucky,' I said.

'Hey, Jimmy.'

I sat down next to him. 'Your dad's a bit worried about you.'

'That so,' he said.

'What's wrong?' I asked.

He shrugged, kind of defensive. 'Nothing. Nothing's wrong.'

I sat there for a while, looking at the river and looking at the forest and looking at the sky and looking at him. He just kept looking at the sky.

'My mum,' I said, but then didn't continue. It was a bit embarrassing to say outright that we were desperate for money, even when he already knew. There were plenty of poor people back then, but we had our pride. I knew Bucky didn't care about money, living in the forest like he did, cut off from the outside world. And he knew that money and his dad didn't mix, that it only brought trouble. I never saw him wear shoes or socks, although that could have been out of preference, but I also never saw him wear new clothes, or have anything new about him at all. Maybe that was lack of money, or maybe it was because it wasn't something his dad ever thought about and things had simply been let slide after his mum left.

Anyway, I said to him, sitting there by the regulator, 'We should catch some more yabbies, sell 'em to the soldiers.'

He said nothing.

'I've been ripening some meat,' I said. 'Extra pongy.'

'Nah,' he said. 'They've gone off the idea.'

'You checked?'

''Course I checked,' he said.

'Pity,' I said.

Maybe he could see it in my eyes, my doubt. I couldn't work out how he could have got all the way over to the army camp and back to ask them, not being well. So I guess he saw it and there was anger in his own eyes. Anger and something else. Hurt maybe. He got to his feet. 'Stand up,' he said. His voice was calm, despite his eyes.

'Why?' I asked. I had no idea what was going on.

''Cos I'm not going to hit you sitting down.'

'Why do you want to hit me?'

'Stand up and see.'

So I stood up, but I didn't see anything. He just started hitting me. I tried to fend him off. I didn't want to fight back, not if I didn't know what we were fighting about. But it was no good. He was too quick and too mad. He worked me back a few yards, to the edge of the regulator. I'd started talking again, after the initial shock, telling him to settle down. But he wrong-footed me and pushed me backwards, into the regulator. I couldn't believe it.

He stood over me from the bank while I trod water. 'You're not my friend, Jimmy Waters. I never want to see you again.' And he walked off. By the time I'd scrambled out he was running along the river bank, running fast, as fast as that time he caught the rabbit. Maybe faster.

Then he was gone and I just sat down. I had a good cry, I don't mind admitting. My days in the forest were ruined, as if the real world had decided to punish me for daring to enjoy myself, for escaping while my dad and all those other men were suffering in the jungles for us. And so I cried. My friend was lost to me, my dad was off fighting the Japs, my mum had no money and my time in the forest was spoilt forever. I don't know how long I sat there and cried. A long time. But you can't cry forever, even if you want to. It gets to a stage when the tears won't come, even if you try to make them. You've got to think of something better to do. I knew I couldn't do anything about my dad, and I couldn't work out how to make amends with Bucky, but I thought I might be able to help Mum a little with the farm. I knew looking after the cattle was a big deal, that she was relying on me for that. But it sounded like she needed cash, not cows.

So the next day, I started yabbying by myself. It was a hot day, real hot, nudging a hundred for sure. The meat stunk to high heaven. Bloody awful it was. Half the flies in Australia were there with me. But Jesus, did the yabbies go for it or what? I don't think they have noses, not like us, but they can smell a bit of rotten meat a mile away. I reckon I could have just left it in the yabby tin and they would have crawled in to get at it.

I'd made plans overnight, as I camped on my little island. I decided to try a new spot, give the regulator a break. There was another creek a little further along, heavily wooded and hard to access. It only went a few hundred metres into the forest, so the government hadn't bothered putting a regulator in. I don't reckon too many people knew it was there. I gave it a crack and, sure enough, the yabbies started biting straight away. I got a couple of huge ones. Freshwater crays. Bigger than yabbies; more like lobsters. A foot long, maybe more. I reckoned that army chef wouldn't be able to resist them. Anyway, they all went into the sack. And I don't like to admit it, but I felt vindicated, even if that was a word I didn't know back then. I felt like I'd proved myself, proved that I didn't need Bucky.

Now I knew where the big army camp was all right, because Bucky and I had been over there to spy on the Italians and listen to them sing. It was a fair hike, though, and I could tell by the sky it was already afternoon. I didn't want to be home late for dinner and cause Mum to fret. So I decided I'd try this new work camp that was much closer to the river. I thought maybe I could cut a deal with the guards. They could take the yabbies back to the big camp and give them to the officers' chef, the way Bucky had explained it to me, and I could go over there the next day and get paid.

I did the same as Bucky: tied a hessian sack around my waist and swam the river where it was a little narrower, doing a kind of sidestroke with one arm and holding the yabby sack with the other. It sounds easy, but the sack was heavy and swimming with one arm isn't easy. And the yabbies, once they were back in the water, were trying to swim around. I was afraid they might cut their way out of the sack with those big nippers of theirs and then where would I be? But I made it across okay.

Sure enough, the Italians were at the new camp. They were working hard, shirts off, cutting wood for the charcoal. I remember seeing their skin, how tanned they were, even darker than Bucky, how handsome they were. Not like me, with my pink English skin and my freckles. They looked like real men. I couldn't see any guards, though. I thought it a bit slack, you know. Here they were, sworn enemies of king and country, and they were being left to their own devices.

One of them saw me and whistled. He said something to his companions and they all laughed. I'm not sure what he said, but they seemed friendly enough. So I walked over, still holding the yabby sack, and asked for the guard. The man who whistled, who made the others laugh, he just shook his head, not understanding. But another man, older and starting to go bald, he pointed. 'There,' he said, indicating a small hut. It looked freshly made, out of hand-cut timber. The wood hadn't faded all the way to grey yet.

I walked over and, sure enough, there was an Australian soldier sitting with his back against a tree, smoking a cigarette. He had light hair and a moustache, but the most distinctive thing about him was his eye patch. It was made of black cloth, just like a pirate's.

'Hello there, sonny Jim,' he said. 'What have you got there?' He flicked his eyes at my yabby sack. They were squirming about a bit.

'How do you know my name?' I asked him.

'Sonny Jim? I guess you must be famous.'

'For what?'

'For catching stuff in sacks. What's in there?'

'Yabbies. I want to sell 'em to the officers.'

'I ain't that sort of officer,' he said, but he said it with a smile, so I figured he wasn't taking offence.

I was about to lay out my eat-now, pay-tomorrow idea, when he swore. 'Fuck me rone,' he said and scrambled to his feet. I remember that. It sounded funny, even though I didn't know what 'rone' meant. 'Careful,' he said. 'It's that prick Stannard.'

I turned around and saw a soldier approaching on a big white horse. I could tell he was an officer, and not just by his cap. He wore a tie and had long dress riding boots, polished leather, almost up to his knees. The leather shone and matched that of his belt and his holster. I thought he looked magnificent, kind of like a knight or something. He even had a sabre. He was older. The soldier with the eye patch looked like he wasn't much more than a teenager, but the officer was middle-aged and stout—I could see that when he dismounted. On the ground, he didn't look so much like a knight and he had a limp.

'Finucane,' the officer said. He had a voice like a dog's: he barked his words. He saluted and the soldier saluted back. 'Where are the others? Tankard and Louth?'

'Tankard is crook, sir. Can't stop shitting himself. Louth has taken him to the infirmary.'

The officer looked disgusted. 'Watch your tongue, soldier.' And then, 'You mean you're guarding this lot by yourself?'

'Hard workers, sir. Doing their bit.'

The officer harumphed. Seriously, that's what it sounded like, like one of those cartoon balloons. 'Harumph.' Then he turned to me. 'Who are you, boy? What do you want? This is an army camp.'

'I have yabbies to sell, sir. Crayfish. For your chef.'

'Do you now?'

The officer smiled then, and I didn't like the smile, although I couldn't think why.

'Lieutenant,' said the officer, 'round up the Italians. Get them on the way back.'

'Still pretty early in the day, sir?'

The officer got angry then and drew himself up, puffed himself out. 'You're not in New Guinea now. Do as I order.'

That got my attention. This soldier, Finucane, had been in New Guinea. I wondered if he knew my father. But I could tell it wasn't the right time to start asking questions, not with the officer insisting on obedience. And there was something in Finucane's eye, his good eye, as if he wasn't taking the reference to New Guinea well.

'Where is your gun, soldier?'

'There, sir.' Finucane pointed to the tree where he'd been having his smoke.

'Well, it's not doing any good over there. Any one of these eyeties could grab it. Then where would you be?'

The lieutenant said nothing. It looked like he was biting his tongue.

'Answer me, soldier.'

'Yes, sir. Understood, sir.'

'Fetch the gun, Lieutenant.'

Lieutenant Finucane looked daggers at me before walking back to get the gun, and his glare made me realise that part of this was being put on for my benefit, the officer displaying his power, belittling Finucane in front of me and the Italians. Meanwhile, the prisoners had stopped working and had drifted in a little closer to see what all the fuss was about. I guess they were bored.

Finucane returned with the gun.

'Hand it to me.'

He gave Stannard the rifle.

The officer moved the bolt back and up. It was a very quick action, making it obvious he was familiar with the rifle. 'It's not loaded,' said the officer. His voice was soft but there was menace in it.

'My mistake, Major. It won't happen again.'

'See that it doesn't. Now get moving. I want all these eyeties back and locked up where they belong.'

'Yes, sir,' said Finucane, and he saluted, although there was something in the way that he did it, or kind of overdid it, that hinted at contempt for the officer.

But Stannard's attention had already returned to me, as if dismissing Finucane from his presence. 'So you have yabbies for me, is that right?'

'Yes, sir.'

'I must say, you're an enterprising bunch, you forest urchins. I do find them delicious.'

I guessed he was referring to the catch Bucky had delivered that first time. 'These are even better, sir,' I said. 'I've got two big ones in here, freshwater crays—like lobsters.'

'Excellent.' And he smiled. 'Come over to the foreman's shack and you can show me what you have.'

And so I walked over to the shack, him following me. It was only afterwards that I realised the other men hadn't moved—not Finucane and not the Italians.

Inside the shack, there was a table, two benches, nothing more. He didn't hesitate, this officer. This monster. 'Kneel down, son.'

'Sir?'

'Leave the yabbies and kneel down. I am an officer of the King.' That's what he said.

I knelt down. I thought he wanted to say a prayer, that's how stupid I was. And then, as if it meant nothing, as if it was just a pleasant stroll in the park, he dropped his pants and there it was, this huge, ugly rod of a thing, all pink and purple and disgusting. I must have screamed, because he hit me across the face. Then I definitely did scream.

The door burst open, light flooding in. I thought it must have been Finucane, come to see what the fuss was about, but instead it was one of the Italians, the one with the dark face and thick hair, the one who had whistled at me.

'No,' he said and grabbed me, yanking me away and out the door. He was so strong, I couldn't believe it. He picked me up and pulled me out with one hand, so only my feet were dragging. Others were coming closer. They had heard my scream.

The door to the shack swung open. Stannard had pulled his pants back up and strode out. He was holding his pistol. He was pointing it straight at the chest of the man who had hauled me out.

'You,' he barked. 'Kneel.'

The Italian said nothing, looking perplexed, and terrified.

'Kneel!' bellowed Stannard, holding the pistol above his head and firing into the sky. 'Kneel, you fucking maggot.'

The prisoner looked around, as if disbelieving, or looking for interpretation.

And now Stannard walked towards him, pointing the gun directly at the man's forehead. 'Kneel, or I will shoot you where you stand.'

And what did I do, God help me? I gestured for the man, my rescuer, to kneel. He nodded. He understood. He kneeled.

Stannard held the gun to his head, just an inch or two away. 'Now let this be a lesson to all of you, what happens if you assault an officer of the King.'

'No!' I screamed, closing my eyes, but there was nothing I could do. There was an explosion; I could hear the crack of bone and the shlock of brain, smell the gun smoke and the blood. But when at last I opened my eyes, the Italian was still kneeling and

Stannard was sprawled in a bloody pool, part of his head missing. I'll never forget it. And standing behind him was Finucane, rifle still at his shoulder.

The gunfire had set off the cockatoos. They were screeching and squalling and flapping about in the treetops, but down on the ground not a word was said. The prisoner stood. He had wet himself, but there was no shame in it. I understood why. Finucane put the gun down and fetched the major's horse. He and the Italian hauled the body up onto the horse, helping each other without a word being said, as if they both knew what needed to be done. Finucane took the gun and started leading the horse away, towards the river. He didn't look back.

The Italians watched him go. And then the one who had saved me, the one whom Finucane had saved in turn, held a finger to his lips, signalling silence. I nodded, comprehending. He nodded too. And he smiled. I'll always remember that smile. It had everything good in it; it was the opposite of Stannard's leering grin. For some reason I was very calm then. The Italians started to talk quietly among themselves. Some came from the river with a tub of water, sloshed it where Stannard had fallen, washing away the blood. Others had shovels, were covering the area with dirt, and then leaves. The man who had saved me walked to the river and started to wash the blood off himself. I realised what they were doing, and as they began to move away, I went into the hut and I got the bag of yabbies. I didn't want to leave any evidence either.

chapter thirty

BEFORE LEAVING THE HOSPITAL, NELL TELLS GOFFING SHE'LL ASSIST ASIO, IF only to help catch the bastards who attacked the two of them. She'll pass on anything she gleans, any news of Jean-Luc Hoffner or a sighting of a green shed. But she also tells him it can't be her priority. She needs to focus on her own investigation; she needs to get Feral Phelan off her back; she needs to identify the second skeleton. She'll soon get the DNA results, and learn more about the gun found in the regulator. But until then, there's little appeal in returning to the Tulong station, staring at her computer, waiting on her phone. Seeing she's already in Hatheson, she decides to visit her uncle and probe him: maybe he's heard something about Hoffner.

The *Western Explorer*'s shopfront is small, a couple of blocks back from the highway, the paint on its signage peeling, a vacant block on one side, a service station on the other. Nell knows there's a bigger paper, a daily, the *Hatheson Post*, with offices on the main street. She wonders how her uncle manages to survive. She pushes through the door; the air is flat, without air-conditioning. There are hard carpet tiles on the floor, a basic sofa against a wall, a water cooler with an empty flagon. The counter is unattended, with forms for various types of classified ads in a wire-framed holder: birth, deaths and marriages; rentals; for sale and public notices. There's a bell. She rings it, waits. Maybe there is no one here.

While she waits, she scans the walls. The framed front page from this week's paper confronts her: IS THIS THE FACE OF A KILLER? There are awards going back decades—regional prizes for the most part, but also two Walkley Awards. She knows Walkleys are a big deal for journos, that Martin Scarsden won the Gold Walkley a few years back. It never occurred to her that her uncle was in that sort of league, him and his one-man band in the middle of nowhere. She examines them more closely.

There's one from 1993, Best Suburban, Country or Rural Report. *Million-dollar Black Hole in Council Accounts.* Next to the award certificate, in its own frame, the yellowing front page:

> The State Government is threatening to assume control of the Hatheson Shire Council following a *Western Explorer* investigation that uncovered allegations of widespread fraud.

But it's the Walkley from 1980 that catches her eye. Best Story in a Provincial Newspaper: *Hatheson Policeman Charged, by Eugene Buchanan*. And the front page: CORRUPTION CHARGES AGAINST HATHESON COP. The accompanying photo is identical to the one on this week's edition: Keith Tankard.

> A prominent Hatheson police officer has been charged with seven counts of criminal activity, including corruption and assisting criminal activity. This follows an extensive investigation by the *Western Explorer.*
>
> It is alleged Sergeant Keith Tankard, 62, had widespread connections to organised crime groups, including the Italian mafia. He has been suspended without pay awaiting a committal hearing.
>
> Sergeant Tankard has pleaded not guilty and been released on bail after surrendering his passport and agreeing not to travel more than 50 kilometres from Hatheson.

Keith Tankard. The police officer who initially investigated the disappearance of Tycho and Bert Buchanan, the officer who influenced the coroner at the 1976 inquest. The same Keith Tankard who was reportedly absent that day in 1943 when Gerard Stannard and Eamon Finucane went missing. Noel Tankard's grandfather.

Nell feels like kicking herself; the reference to Tankard's 1980 conviction was in Tuesday's paper. She'd assumed the original investigation was conducted by some other reporter, that it was too long ago for Gene. But here was his by-line, in black and white. It helps explain why the Foresters Arms publican hates the Buchanans: it was Gene's reporting that got Noel's grandfather jailed. What it doesn't explain is her own father's obfuscation: when she asked Grainger about the Buchanan–Tankard feud at dinner in Boonlea, why hadn't he mentioned this, that Gene was instrumental in putting Keith Tankard in prison?

There's a noise. Gene emerges from a door behind the counter, face communicating concern. 'Nell. You okay?'

'Sure. Why?' Is her unease so evident?

'I heard you were in a blue in Tulong. Taken to hospital.'

'Not me. A birdwatcher. Beaten up by a bunch of rednecks.'

'Really? What can you tell me?'

She realises this is the reporter asking. 'Not a lot. The birdwatcher is in hospital, the thugs got away.'

He says nothing, but she can see the doubt in his eyes, the suspicion that she's holding back information.

She pushes on before he can frame another question. 'Have you done any reporting on this missing cooker, Jean-Luc Hoffner?'

'You think it could be him? In the regulator?'

It's not the reaction she was expecting. 'No. That body has been there for years.'

'Of course,' says Gene. 'What's your interest in Hoffner, then?'

'Off the record?'

Gene frowns. 'Do I get the story when it can go on the record?'

'Depends on how helpful you are,' says Nell. 'There's a possibility Hoffner met with violence.'

And now Gene really is attentive, reporter's instincts fully engaged. 'Why do you think that?'

'These thugs last night—the birdwatcher might not be their first victim.'

'Is that right?'

'What can you tell me?'

He looks uncertain. 'I haven't heard anything like that. But there are a few hard cases in among the cookers down in the forest. Did young Kevin tell you about his run-in?'

'He did. Other than that, no reports of bashings or violence?'

'No.' But then he frowns. 'There were rumours, a few months ago now, sounds of gunfire in the forest. Kev looked into it, thought it was illegal hunters.'

'What do you think?'

Gene shrugs. 'He's probably right.'

'Nothing else?'

'Nothing on this side, but the Victorian cops encountered Neo-Nazis down past Barmah earlier in the year.'

'So I heard. Who were they?'

'Not locals. Up from Melbourne for the weekend. The cops thought it was some sort of paramilitary training, but the Nazis claimed it was just a blokes' weekend. They all buggered off back to Melbourne or wherever. I haven't heard anything else about it, except something similar happened in the Grampians. Same thing. Out-of-towners. But I can't be sure it was the same group.' He changes the subject. 'Any news on the second body? The DNA?'

'Today or tomorrow,' she says, then points to the yellowing front page, the Walkley Award-winning story. 'This story. Keith Tankard. What happened?'

Gene grins. 'He was found guilty. Two years in prison. It was the end of him, the corrupt bastard. Never saw him again.'

'The end of him?'

'End of his career. The end of his reputation. The end of his pension. Died a few years after he got out of prison.'

She can hear the hardness in his voice, the lack of sympathy, keeps her own even. 'You don't sound too sorry for him.'

'I'm not. He was crooked through and through. The stuff he went to prison for was only the tip of the iceberg.'

'He investigated the disappearance of Tycho and Bert.'

'Yes. But he wasn't much interested in doing his job. That time, or any other time.'

Nell looks at the story, at the Walkley certificate. 'Is that why you went after him? Because of Tycho and Bert?'

'No. I went after him because he was a corrupt cop.' Gene cracks a wry grin. 'But Mum was happy.'

'Okay, he was corrupt. But I still don't see how you get from that to him killing Gerard Stannard.' She flicks her head at this week's front page. 'And the second body isn't Finucane.'

Gene looks chastened. 'I still reckon Tankard was involved. And I wouldn't be surprised if he had something to do with the disappearance of Tycho and Dad.'

'I thought you said he had a cast-iron alibi? That he was in Sydney that week?'

'That's true. But he certainly had a motive.'

'Such as?'

'Tycho was investigating crime. Organised crime at Griffith, crime in the forest, crime in Hatheson.'

Nell looks at the old stories, the award winners, mounted on the wall. 'How far back do your records go, your back issues?'

'All the way. Back to the start, the 1920s.'

'Can I see what Tycho was working on before he disappeared?'

Gene shrugs again. 'Good luck. I've been through those editions a dozen times.'

'You still have copies then?'

'It's on microfilm. We only fully switched to digital about ten years ago.'

'Microfilm? Sounds very cloak-and-dagger.'

'Ha. Works well enough, but isn't searchable the way digital files are. We could get it all scanned, but we don't have the time or the money. I'll donate it all to the National Library when I'm through.'

'Right. But you have a way of reading it?'

'We do. There's a reader in the back. A projector. I'll set you up. What issues are you interested in?'

'How long did Tycho work for the paper?'

'Only about three months. He went missing in December 1973. The week before Christmas.'

'I guess those three months then, up to the time he went missing. It was twice a week back then, right?'

'Wednesdays and Saturdays. Four journalists and a dedicated photographer. The glory days. Our own press.'

Gene leads her past the counter, through the door. The newsroom is bare. His desk is in the middle, a hand-painted sign leaning against an in-tray—EDITOR. They continue through to a back room, full of broken furniture, a long-defunct telex machine and filing cabinets, a door with DARKROOM still painted on it.

While Gene sets up the reader and searches out the microfilms, Nell takes the opportunity to again broach the subject of her grandfather Bert. 'The coroner's reference to your father's low-level criminality. What was that?'

Gene is standing with his back to her, looking into the map drawer housing the microfilm. He stands perfectly still for a moment, then turns, looks her directly in the eye. 'Grainger hasn't ever mentioned it?'

'No.'

'I don't imagine he has.' Gene takes a deep breath before continuing. 'We grew up in Tulong. In a pristine house completely surrounded by a junkyard. A car-wrecking yard.'

'I was there Wednesday evening, visiting your mother.'

'How many prangs do you think you'd get a year near Tulong?'

Nell blinks. 'Go on.'

'There were no computers back then, no national databases. Cars were registered by state authorities, still are, but back then there was no easy way of checking across state borders.'

'Stolen cars?'

'Yep. Cars stolen in New South Wales would be repurposed and sent to Victoria, Victorian cars sent into New South Wales. Engines and other components mixed and matched, engine numbers and compliance plates altered, bumper bars mixed up, body work resprayed. Tulong was perfect: off the main roads but close to the border. We'd get semis coming in, full of wrecks, but with stolen cars in among them. The wrecks would get stacked higher and higher, the stolen cars rebirthed and moved on through.'

'Quite the operation.'

'Yes and no. Lucrative enough to build Mum that house. All the other stuff, fencing stolen goods and the rest of it, I think that was small beer. He was only involved because he was sending and receiving car parts all the time—it was the perfect cover for a distribution centre.'

'Distributing what?'

Gene shrugs. 'Bits and pieces. But the cars were the main game.'

Nell feels as if she is starting to understand. 'And Keith Tankard knew all about it, didn't he? Dad did say he tried to extort bribes from Bert and Rita.'

'That's right. And it explains Tankard's evidence at the inquest. He wanted all of that kept under wraps. I think that was why he was so keen to blame Tycho. A smokescreen.'

'And before he disappeared, did Tycho know about the car rebirthing?'

'He must have.' Gene takes a breath, as if considering what to say next. 'We all did, to some degree. I was only sixteen when they were killed, but I wasn't stupid and Grainger would tell me things. We were close.'

'Were you involved?'

'Not in anything criminal; Dad kept us clear of that. We'd help around the yard, though, doing odd jobs, earning pocket money. But Mum and Dad, they were keen for us to escape it all. They were obsessed with us going to uni. Grainger and me.'

Nell thinks of her father, his degree in dentistry from Melbourne University, one of the country's best. A stickler, Mr Clean. Rotary, the Chamber of Commerce, the Echuca Club. Maybe he's spent his life distancing himself from his family's shady past. And her uncle's awards, the Walkley hanging so proudly in the foyer, uncovering crime and corruption. What was that? Gene, not distancing himself from the past, but compensating for it?

'Did Tycho write about any of this?'

'No. Maybe he intended to, maybe that's why he and Dad argued that day. There was also some evidence that he was on to the mafia set-up in Griffith. He went there a few times. Might have even met with Donald Mackay at his furniture store.'

'You think Tycho approached your father, asked him if he had useful information?'

'I don't know. It's possible. But what Dad was doing, it was different. Linked into old-school crims in Sydney and Melbourne for sure, but not the Italian mafia.'

'And you? Have you ever written about this?'

A barely perceptible smile flickers on her uncle's face. 'Yes. I've written about it. Extensively. Just haven't published it yet.'

'Yet?'

'I'm saving it for my last edition. The one before I retire. The one before I shut the place forever.'

Nell feels the emotion behind the statement, but she doesn't back down and hears the steel in her own voice. 'I understand. But if the body is identified as your brother, then you must surrender any relevant information to our investigation.'

'Of course. If it is my brother, everything I know will be splashed across the front page of the *Western Explorer*.'

Nell nods. An impasse. 'Let's have a look at the microfilm, then.'

'What are you looking for?'

'I'm not sure.'

—

The microfilm reader is simple. Two aqua-coloured plastic spools, surprisingly light, the thirty-five-millimetre film wound back and forth through a gate over a light source, the image projected up onto a screen. Completely analogue. Old school. It takes her a few minutes to get the hang of the focus, the film threaded through upside down and back to front. She spools to December 1973, the film wheeling and clacking as it passes under the focus plate. She moves to the date that Tycho disappeared. His last stories, on the Wednesday before he vanished, filed in the days before he disappeared: a council meeting, a preview of an upcoming cricket match, planning for the agricultural show, a review of *The Godfather* screening at the local drive-in.

She winds the film back a couple of editions, to an earlier Saturday. Tycho had stories about the Albury-Wodonga growth centre, a warning about European carp, and a colour piece about squatters in the forest. She is interested to note it mentions preppers. So they were around even back then. But it's a story on the lifestyle page that catches her eye.

FORMER POW MAKES GOOD

by Tycho Buchanan

A former Italian prisoner of war who was detained in the Barmah Forest has returned to the district and made the most of his new country, launching a new range of table wines.

Gino Camilleri is part of a new wave of winemakers establishing themselves in the southern Riverina and northern Victoria. But just 30 years ago, he was an enemy soldier.

Mr Camilleri was captured by Australian soldiers in North Africa during the early years of the Second World War. He was transported to Australia and saw out the rest of the conflict as a detainee working in the Barmah Forest.

'It is a strange thing to say now, but it was the best thing that happened to me,' Gino said. 'Without getting captured by the diggers, I would never have met my wife, and I would never have moved here.'

He met his Australian-born wife, Irene, during this time. She worked as a nurse in the army garrison stationed near Barmah.

After the war, Gino and his fellow detainees were repatriated to Italy. But Gino, who had learnt basic English during his internship, continued to write to Irene and romance blossomed.

'I think it was destined, somehow,' said Irene, an active partner in the wine business. She is behind a new concept the couple are pursuing: 'a cellar door', at which tourists and locals can sample and buy wine directly from the vineyard at discount prices. Irene sources Italian-style bread, cheeses and smallgoods such as olives to complement the wine. 'It makes for a more genuine experience,' she said.

In 1950 Gino migrated to Australia and returned to the area. He worked as a labourer constructing the Hatheson irrigation district and installing the last of the regulators in the Barmah-Millewa Forest. He and Irene married in 1955. Then, in 1957, he started growing grapes on land owned by his father-in-law, George Sunters. For many years, he supplied grapes to a variety of commercial wine producers.

'But all that time, I was keeping some grapes for myself, making my own wine, making experiments. At first it was terrible, but over the years it got better and better. I started selling to local restaurants. The reception has been very good. Now we are taking the next step.'

That next step is to launch his own range of wines under the River Pirate label.

'It's a reference to the legend of the bushrangers who would target the paddle steamers, not just the stagecoaches,' said Gino.

'I wanted to honour the outlaws who helped shape the country. And I wanted to honour those people who did so much to help me in those early years, who showed me friendship when I was still officially an enemy soldier.'

The River Pirate wines have a distinctive label, the face of a pirate, complete with eye patch.

Gino laughed when asked about it. 'The story is very Australian, but the wines are Italian in style. We have a chianti, we have a lambrusco, we have a frascati. They suit the Australian climate and appeal to Australian palates.'

The article is accompanied by a photo, black-and-white and not so easy to make out from the microfilm projector: Gino and Irene and a couple of teenagers standing around a barrel with bottles of wine arranged on top of it.

She prints the article. Considers it.

The winery must still be there: the wine her father was serving, the cellar door he and her mother had visited. Run by Italians. Italians, like the Griffith mafia. And something else: the guy was a POW, detained in the forest during the war. Stannard was guarding POWs, so was Finucane. So was Keith Tankard. And Finucane had lost an eye in New Guinea. He'd been fitted with a glass eye, but was it possible he wore an eye patch?

She shows the story to Gene. He frowns, then laughs. 'It's bullshit. There were no river pirates. Plenty of bushrangers, holding up stagecoaches, stealing payrolls and bank transfers and gold coming out of the mines. But not those old river steamers; they were carrying bulk items, towing barges full of wool bales and rafts packed with redgum logs, floating them down to the railhead at Echuca. If the river ran dry, they could sit for months before being re-floated. What would a river pirate do? Wool bales were a hundredweight. You could hardly chuck one on the back of a horse and ride off with it. And if you had a boat, where were you going to head? Down to Echuca? Before Federation, every boat was stopped and inspected by customs officials. There were no river pirates. It's a great label and it's a great story, but it's not based on fact.'

Still, although she has no idea what it means, she can feel a resonance, a hunch. She looks at her watch, then at Google Maps on her phone. The winery is down near Echuca, on the banks of the Campaspe. An hour's drive from Hatheson. If she's quick, she can get there for a late lunch.

chapter thirty-one

1973

TESSA WAS OUT OF THE WINDOW AND AWAY, RUNNING TOWARDS THE HIGHWAY, the setting sun in her eyes. She didn't like daylight savings when it first came in, it made no sense to her, but now she was grateful. It gave her time. Time to finish dinner, time to do the washing-up. Time for her mother and father to park themselves in front of the TV set, the flickering grey ghosts of *The Graham Kennedy Show*, live from Melbourne. Time for her to get out to the highway well before dark, well before the drive-in movies started.

The blue Datsun was waiting at the end of the drive. Tycho Buchanan, unbothered by who might see him. The windows were down and he was smoking. Cat Stevens was on the cassette player singing 'Wild World'. It was a concession to her, she knew from seeing Tycho's favourites piled into the glove box: Led Zeppelin, Cream and Hendrix.

'Not too late?' she asked, buckling her seatbelt, eyes on him, taking him in.

'Right on time.' He smiled and leant across, kissing her on the cheek, more like a brother than a boyfriend, then leant back, studying her breathless reaction, taking another draw on his cigarette. She noticed he was smoking Dunhills now, a step up from Peter Stuyvesant, a mile above the Winnie Blues favoured by the kids at school. A man of the world. James Bond in a blue Datsun 1600. 'Let's get cracking.' He started the engine, gave it the obligatory rev, then made a U-turn, heading north.

She feared she might ruin the evening, yet she couldn't help asking about Willow.

'I thought we settled that,' Tycho replied, sounding more puzzled than irritated.

'Who is she, though?'

'Lives in the forest somewhere, with her dad.'

'You haven't seen her recently?'

Tycho laughed. 'Not since the regulator. She's a friend, a contact, helping with a story.' And then, 'Not like you.'

And that was enough: enough to suppress her doubts, enough to swell her hopes.

A block from the Hatheson drive-in, the Stardust, Tess was forced to get out and climb into the boot. She'd been hoping the film would be something romantic, maybe *The Way We Were*, Barbra Streisand and Robert Redford, which she had seen advertised in the *Western Explorer*, but Tycho insisted on *The Godfather*, some sort of gangster movie. He said he was going to review it for the paper, that he could get free tickets. But the movie was rated R and audience members had to be eighteen or over to see it, so she needed to sneak in. It felt undignified but also exciting. More rule-breaking. Like smoking the joint at the regulator. The thought gave her a flutter.

The movie was long. And violent. The colour gave it an awful immediacy, so unlike the shaky monochrome of television. She winced when a gangster was garrotted, and even Tycho recoiled when Vito got gunned down, leaning towards her, away from the tinny speaker hanging from his window. He held her hand and she felt frustrated by the bucket seats preventing her from sliding into him. For a moment, she almost wished they were in her parents' daggy old farm truck.

At intermission, when it was fully dark, he fetched a bottle of champagne from an esky in the back seat, told her it was better than the French stuff. He had two glasses, proper wineglasses, and a plate of Jatz and cheese. He explained the cheeses to her. There was a soft one with a French name that sounded different from how it was spelt. She didn't know cheese could be soft, or that it didn't have to be bright yellow, or that it could taste good. She hadn't had champagne before either. She sampled it tentatively, expecting it to be sweeter, more like soft drink, but she liked the bubbles, the way it fizzed on her tongue. She drank some more and felt sophisticated, sitting in the drive-in, Tycho by her side, eating French cheese and drinking champagne and watching an R-rated movie. He smoked his Dunhills and she smoked an Alpine and he leant across to light it with his Zippo, his arm brushing her breast, his hand taking a strand of her long hair and gently placing it behind her ear, taking the opportunity to skim her cheek with his lips. She felt the future so close she could almost touch it.

By the time the movie started again, she was on to her second glass, deciding that she liked champagne, she liked it very much. Again the image of Melbourne came to her, the one from the postcard, the two of them walking hand in hand from Flinders Street Station. And now she knew where in the city they would be walking: to a hotel, with a lobby of elegantly dressed people drinking champagne, little fingers extended in timeless elegance, and smoking cigarettes in ebony holders. And upstairs a suite would be waiting, with velvet curtains and its own bathroom with a claw-foot bath.

They'd finished the bottle by the time more gangsters started getting gunned down, and she began to enjoy the film. Tessa admired Michael Corleone, how he'd embraced his inner beast. She almost cheered when his henchmen hit the rival dons, spraying them with bullets. 'They're going to get it!' she squealed and hid behind her hands, as Tycho laughed and put a protective arm around her, overcoming the bucket seats and the gearshift. And she did nestle into him then, breathing him in as she decided she liked gangster movies just fine.

After the film finished, he didn't even ask her to return to the boot. They simply drove out with everyone else, the dust rising as fifty cars edged their way towards the exit. She felt exhilarated, the warm air flooding about them as he directed the car out onto the open road heading south. The moon was up, the night was clear, she could see the ghosting light of the wheat fields, smell the summer in the wind.

'Let's go see the river,' he said.

'The moon,' she said, thinking of how it might look bouncing from the water.

He turned off the highway, dropping down the Cadell Tilt, into the trees and into the forest. They were on a dirt road, maybe the one that led to her father's childhood farmhouse. But before they got to the river, Tycho turned off to the right, onto a lesser track. He eased the Datsun past potholes, past dried-up puddles, past fallen branches, taking it slowly. She could imagine him driving fast, like a rally driver, but not tonight. Tonight, he was in control. There was no hurry. Time had paused, giving them room. Carole King was on the cassette player, *Tapestry*. It seemed perfect. *I feel like a natural woman*, she thought. A mob of kangaroos were loitering on the track, spectral in the headlights, but they parted as the car approached, as if wishing them well, standing aside and watching them pass, like an honour guard, like wedding guests alongside an aisle.

Tessa was starting to feel a little unwell on the dirt track. Perhaps it was the champagne and cigarettes, and maybe the cheese, but Tycho took it slowly and they were there soon enough. A campground, deserted, right by the edge of the water, the Edward River, wide and silent and glistening. The moon was indeed bouncing off it and the sky was sprayed with stars. There was a firepit, a ring of stones. Tycho got a fire going and Tessa wondered if he'd prepared it earlier, if he'd been planning this all along. Maybe. He took a rug from the boot, laid it out by the fire, opened more wine. She liked the fire; it was unnecessary in the warmth of the summer evening but it was romantic, creating a cocoon that only the light from the moon, the stars and the flickering of the river could penetrate. Otherwise they were surrounded by darkness, alone in their own world, like a Seekers song. And once they started, she never wanted it to stop. He was kind and he was gentle and he was considerate and he was all that she imagined he might be.

Afterwards, hours later, when it was well after midnight, he eased the car to a stop out on the highway, across the fields from her home. When she got out, he did as well, and held her close, kissing her deeply and with longing.

She would remember that kiss, that embrace, for many years to come, cherish it for decades. She would savour the evening by the river, revisiting it again and again in her mind, until she was no longer sure what was memory, what was longing and what was dream. But no matter how variable the memories of the night by the river grew, she would also remember with startling clarity the comment he made as they were leaving the drive-in that night. 'They're here, you know,' he had said, almost offhand. 'The mafia. In Griffith. That's my big story.' And she would remember her laughter, her schoolgirl tittering at an assertion so obviously ridiculous—as if anything like Francis Ford Coppola's Don Corleone could be found lurking in the Australian bush.

chapter thirty-two

THE WINERY EMERGES FROM THE SURROUNDING VINES LOOKING MORE LIKE AN oil refinery than a family business, its towering fermentation tanks and stainless-steel piping glinting in the early afternoon sun. Nell had imagined weathered brick; instead there are metal sheds the size of aircraft hangars. Vines radiate from the complex in neat rows, glowing green with health. Indeed, the whole place exudes an air of success. This is no hobby farm.

She follows the signs to the cellar door, where a large car park is sheltered by trees. There's a tourist coach and a half-dozen cars, yet when she enters the tasting room, there is only one couple sampling wines. It's a small space, connected through an archway to a barn full of serious-looking barrels. There's a counter backed by bottle-laden shelves and fridges, with glasses hanging from racks above it. A sign atop a barrel inside the door lists tour times. That explains where the people from the coach must be: touring the complex. Like Disneyland with booze. She walks over to the counter, where the couple are being served wines by an attentive young woman wearing a black apron with the familiar River Pirate logo and *Camilleri Wines* printed in an elaborate font.

Nell apologises and interjects, flashes her badge and introduces herself simply as Detective Constable Buchanan, not mentioning that she's from Homicide. The young woman is suddenly alert, the winetasters curious. 'This is purely routine,' says Nell. 'But I wonder if I might speak to the owner?'

'My father,' says the young woman. 'What's this about?'

Nell smiles. 'Is he here?'

'Yes. I can get him. But can I tell him what it's regarding?'

Nell admires her persistence. 'A missing persons case. From years ago.'

'I'll be right back.' The daughter tops up the glasses of the tourists and heads off to fetch her father.

Nell doesn't want to wait with the tasters, who seem primed to ask questions, so she turns to face the wall, the one separating the tasting room from the cellar. There are framed posters recounting the history of the winery, complete with sepia photos and captions. The first one is all about traditional Italian winemaking and the styles and regions of Italy. Before she can get on to the history of the winery itself, a man enters from the car park. He looks to be in his sixties, lithe and tanned, as if just returned from skiing. Or Tuscany.

'G'day. How can I help?' he says, his accent as broad as any wheatfield.

She flashes her badge, introduces herself again. Includes the 'Homicide' this time.

It has no noticeable impact. 'Lorenzo Camilleri,' he replies cheerfully.

Nell regards the tourists, their eyes wide. She can imagine them already reframing the encounter as a dinner-party anecdote. Lorenzo must see her discomfort as he says to his daughter, 'Gina, take these good people and give them a barrel tasting. They look discerning.'

'Yes, Pa.'

Once they have been left in private, Nell shows the winemaker the printout of Tycho Buchanan's fifty-year-old newspaper story.

'Ah yes,' he says. 'Do you see? We have it framed here.' And sure enough, there it is, on the wall, just along from the poster she was studying when he entered. 'A good story. The first of many.'

'Gino Camilleri,' says Nell. 'Your father? Grandfather?'

'Father.'

'I assume he's passed away?'

'Thirty-five years ago. But he built all of this, from nothing.'

He points to another poster, one explaining the foundation of the winery in the 1950s. There's a photo of the original farmhouse and a low shed, a woman pressing grapes in a barrel with her feet, skirts hoisted, a smile on her face.

'Thirty-five years? You must have had a bit to do with it as well.'

Lorenzo grins broadly, accepts the compliment. 'Come and sit at the counter.' He leads the way, positions himself on the other side of the divide. 'Care for some wine? Something to eat? We have antipasti here: olives, cheese, grapes, prosciutto, whatever you like. Nibbles for the tourists. Or something more substantial, if you're hungry.'

'Just some water, if you don't mind.' And then, by way of explanation, 'I need to drive back to Tulong.'

'A glass won't hurt,' he says, mischief twinkling in his eyes. 'That way I can join you.'

Nell acquiesces. 'Okay. A small one.'

Lorenzo goes behind the counter. 'A light red?'

'Maybe the River Pirate,' says Nell.

Lorenzo smiles again. 'Our signature wine. But here—a special pressing, a special year.'

'Don't open it on my account,' says Nell.

'No problem. My wife and I can finish it with dinner.' He cracks the bottle, pours two glasses. He holds his up to the light, swishes it about, smells it. Then he tastes it, nodding appreciatively. 'I'll spare you the spiel,' he says.

Nell holds the glass up to the light, not sure what she's meant to be looking for, but she likes the look of the ruby liquid, clear and not too dark. She takes a sip. She likes it, but isn't sure what elevates the special pressing above the wine she drank at her parents' barbecue.

'So, how can I help?' asks Lorenzo.

'The reporter who wrote that newspaper article back in 1973 disappeared shortly after it was published. His name was Tycho Buchanan. We might have found his body.'

Lorenzo's smile has become more of a grimace. 'And?'

Nell takes the bottle, shows the label. 'There never were any river pirates. Do you know what your father based the name of the wine on? And who this is on the label?'

Now even the grimace has gone. 'I know of no connection with this Tycho Buchanan, but . . .' Lorenzo sips some wine while he ponders his response. 'You are from Homicide. Does that mean he was murdered?'

'We're investigating that possibility.'

The grey eyes are serious now, the bonhomie gone. This is a completely different man; in no way hostile, but serious, focused, intelligent. 'My father. He didn't talk about it, not for years, but when he was getting older, when he knew he didn't have much time left, he started telling me things. He was starting to find it more difficult to drive, so I would take him places. He had an old Cadillac, beautiful, but no good on dirt. Every six months or so, I'd drive him in a work truck, together with two cases of wine—one red, one white—out to a friend of his in the Millewa Forest. His place was hidden away, deep in the woods, so deep I never would have found it without my father to show me the way. A little freehold block up along the river, on an island formed by a horseshoe bow in the river, on an old midden. We had to walk the last bit, across a bridge, through the forest, across a smaller bridge. An old man lived there, a lot older than me, similar age to Dad—but a lot slimmer, lean like a greyhound, whereas Dad always liked his wine and good food. This bloke called himself Alf Jones. After Dad died, I still did it, every six months, on his instructions. Two cases, one red, one white, twice a year, right up until Alf died about five years later. That was in the late 1980s. More than thirty years ago.'

'You've lost me,' says Nell.

'Here.' The man shows her the bottle they've been drinking from, the River Pirate label. 'It was him. The River Pirate. Alf Jones. He wasn't a pirate, but he looked like one. He wore an eye patch, had a scar. Dad named the wine after him.'

'Do you know how he got the eye patch?'

'Wounded in the war, that's what Dad said.'

'Why did your father name the wine after him? Why did he give him wine all that time?'

'He wouldn't tell me, not for a long time. He was strange, my father. Very Italian. In public he was all smiles, very loud, very demonstrative—like a performance. But in private he could be quiet, very reserved. He relented a little, when he knew he was failing, when he made me promise to continue delivering the wine. He said the man had saved his life when Dad was a POW in the war. He said he owed Alf a debt he couldn't repay. So he named the wine after him, took him cases of it all those years.' Lorenzo sips a little more of the wine before continuing. 'He said it was Alf who convinced him of the goodness of Australians, who gave him the idea of returning here after the war, here near the forest. And my mum, of course.' Lorenzo smiles, just for a moment, before becoming serious again. 'There was a bond between them. It was real, I saw it. And it wasn't just the wine. After Dad died, I took over the winery, the company and all that went with it. I went back through the accounts. I'm pretty sure that, right at the start, he received seed money from somewhere. And later, there was money going out as well. All cash.'

'A loan being repaid?'

'I couldn't say. There is a record of amounts, but that's all. Very unlike my father. He was meticulous with his bookkeeping.'

'And did you ever learn the precise circumstances, how this wounded soldier saved your father's life?'

'No. He never said. Later, much later, after Alf died, I tried to find his war record, but there was nothing. It didn't seem to exist.'

'I don't think Alf Jones was his real name,' says Nell. 'I think he was a man called Eamon Finucane. He fought in New Guinea, he was wounded, then he guarded prisoners of war in the forest. And then he deserted.'

Lorenzo nods. 'You think he was hiding there? That's why he was in the forest?'

'It seems likely.'

'Can you wait here, Officer?'

'Why?'

'There is something I want to show you.'

Lorenzo goes behind the counter, retrieves some biscuits and cheese, sun-dried tomatoes, olives, fresh bread. 'I might be a while.'

But he is not so very long. Five minutes at most, enough for Nell to try some cheese and bread. It's perfect with the wine.

'Here,' he says and hands her a sheet of paper.

She unfolds it. A hand-drawn map: the forest, the river, tracks. A cross.

'It's the location of Alf's shack,' says Lorenzo. 'I don't know if it's still there, or whether the tracks still exist. I haven't been there since he died, not since we scattered his ashes. But if what you say is true, that he was a deserter, a fugitive, it would be the perfect hideaway. If you didn't know it was there, you would never find it.'

'Why would I go there?' she asks. 'There can't be much left, can there? Not after all this time.'

'There was a daughter. Very pretty. About the same age as me. If I wasn't married . . .' And he smiles.

'You think she might still be there?'

He shrugs. 'I couldn't say.'

'What's her name?'

'Willow. Her name was Willow.'

The sun is not much lower as she leaves: it's still early afternoon. Before getting into her car, she follows a sign, walks down to the banks of the Campaspe, no more than a hundred metres away. There is lawn and there are picnic tables, weeping willows. This must be where her mother wants to come. She likes the idea of it, her parents in this beautiful place.

She feels she has found something important here, but she is unsure what it is. The same edition of the *Western Explorer* that featured the winery also carried a feature on the hermits and eccentrics living off-grid in the forest. Maybe that was Tycho Buchanan's big story. Maybe he had stumbled upon Alf Jones, a murderer hiding in the forest.

—

She's driving back to Tulong when her phone rings, the caller identified on the dash as Ivan Lucic.

'Nell, hi. How are you?'

'Good. Making progress. Maybe.'

'I'm coming back down,' he says. 'I've just landed in Sydney. Fly to Wagga tomorrow morning, pick up a car, be there by lunchtime.'

She pauses before speaking, feeling a flash of irritation; just as things are breaking her way, just as she's sensing momentum, Ivan is coming back. 'Why?' she asks. 'Why now?'

'You haven't spoken to Blake and Carole?'

Of course. The DNA results. 'No, not yet.'

'I asked them to let me speak to you first.'

'What is it, Ivan?'

'The DNA matches. The second skeleton is Tycho Buchanan.'

She feels the impact of the knowledge, a dull thudding in her chest, and wonders why. She's ruled out Finucane, knows it can't be Hoffner, has even begun investigating Tycho, and yet it hits her, the certainty of it, the knowledge that this will rock her family. 'Right.'

'The gun,' says Ivan, voice somehow soft, as if not wanting to trespass. 'Serial number easy enough to read. It was registered to Tycho's father. Your grandfather, Bert Buchanan.'

She swallows. 'Jesus. You think he killed his own son? Threw it in the regulator pool?'

'It's not so clear. Carole thinks it may also be the gun that killed Bert Buchanan.'

'So a third party? Someone killed both of them?'

'That's one possibility.'

'Shit. There was a bullet found with Bert's body, right?'

'Correct.'

'She can run ballistics?'

'Maybe. The barrel may be too corroded.' And then, as if to rule a line under the conversation, 'I'm sorry, Nell, but Plodder has instructed me to take over. We can't have you investigating the deaths of your relatives. You must understand that. We'd get laughed out of court.'

She says nothing.

'I know it's not easy, but please don't tell your family yet. Not until I'm with you.'

'Of course,' she says. She changes subjects. 'Did you hear about Jack Goffing?'

Now it's Ivan's turn not to respond. At last he speaks. 'I heard.'

'You knew, didn't you? When you were here. You recognised him.' Another break in the conversation. 'It's all right,' she says, irritation growing. 'I've signed the Official Secrets Act.'

Ivan relents. 'Yes, I recognised him. From Riversend, from Sydney.'

'But you weren't going to tell me? Your so-called partner?'

'He explicitly instructed me not to.'

'He instructed you? What the fuck, Ivan? You're taking orders from a spook? I almost died last night. Did you know that? Walked straight into the middle of it, unaware of what I was dealing with. Blindsided.'

'Look, Nell . . .'

'Fuck off, Ivan. Just do me a favour and fuck right off.'

She hangs up. And the tears come, as the accumulated stress and tension and fatigue of the past twenty-four hours catches up with her.

chapter thirty-three

IT'S SATURDAY. SHE SHOULD TAKE THE MORNING OFF. THE WHOLE DAY. SHE'S worked eleven of the past twelve and Ivan has instructed her to stand down, told her that it's his investigation now. But Nell can't sleep in. She's up early, jogging down the tilt to the park by the creek in the forest. There is mist, kangaroos nibbling on the grass by the memorial hall, looking up as she moves towards them. But she can't avoid taking in the cookers, camping off along the creek. She knows what Goffing says is true: most of them are well-meaning, if naive. But in among them could be the violent men she encountered two nights ago. It lends an urgency to her martial arts routines; she wonders if they might even now be looking on, assessing her moves. Her brain tells her they won't come after her, not without good reason. Why would they attack a police officer, draw attention to themselves? But such logic doesn't calm her. Instead, it amplifies her sense of frustration. She'll probably never know who they were. And if she does, it will be because of someone else's detective work, not her own. Ivan knew about Goffing. Did Kevin? He'd been talking to Goffing by the regulator. Maybe the ASIO agent had recruited the local policeman. It made sense. So Ivan and Kevin. Just not her. And now she's been taken off the murder investigation. She wishes she were in a real gym; she badly wants to hit something, to lash out and practise her high kicks against a heavy bag. It's not as if she can thump a tree.

She calls Carole, then Blake, but neither picks up. It's not yet seven; they're probably not out of bed. So why does she feel as if she's being ghosted?

Five minutes later her phone pings: a calendar appointment, an invitation from Carole to meet with her, Blake and Ivan at the hospital in Hatheson at one o'clock. So once Ivan has arrived from Wagga. And now she really does want to hit something. A calendar appointment, for God's sake, not even a text. Shit a brick. For the first time, she wonders if she *has* done something wrong, breached protocol somehow, if Professional Standards are calling the shots. Surely not—it was Ivan's decision to leave her here, leave her in charge.

By the time she's finished and returned to the motel, has showered and dressed, it's still only eight. Five hours to kill. She can't just sit here, staring at a wall. She takes the car, stops for a coffee and a takeaway muffin from the Barking Frog, then drives down the tilt into the forest.

She can't investigate the murders of her uncle and grandfather, but surely there's nothing to prevent her pursuing Gerard Stannard's killer. She's not related to either Stannard or Eamon Finucane. The only connection between the two cases remains the co-location of the bodies in the regulator, dumped thirty years apart. And she has the map Lorenzo Camilleri gave her, directions to the shack in the woods. If nothing else, it will be a distraction, something to fill the hours, some way to keep her frustrations at bay.

At first, the map is easy to follow. She takes the main forest road, past the abandoned sawmill, almost as far as Anglers Reach before turning onto the now familiar access road to the regulator. But then, guided by the map, she turns again, north, back away from the river onto a fire track. The forest is darker here, quieter. Thicker. The sun has gone behind a cloud. The track winds this way and that, and she starts seeing water on both sides of the road, shallow sheets of it. The track runs over a wooden bridge, old and in disrepair, the creek beneath it still and full.

The path runs deeper into the forest; she senses that it has turned again, heading east. The trees grow closer together. She flicks on the sat nav, which confirms her suspicion but tells her little else. There is the symbol of her car surrounded by nothing but green. She expands the view and she can see the Murray, running east–west below her on the screen: she's moving roughly parallel to it. The track keeps going, twisting and turning, kilometres passing slowly, before swinging north.

She stops and checks the hand-drawn map. It's just a sketch, not drawn to scale. It indicates there should be another turn-off here, but it takes her a couple of attempts to find it, reversing backwards and forwards. She almost gives up, thinking the shack has been abandoned and the access to it become overgrown and unrecognisable. It's only by luck that she finds it; without the map she would have stood no chance. It's off to the right, just a slight break in the underbrush beside the track. It barely seems passable. She double-checks the map, decides she's got nothing to lose.

She takes it slowly, walking pace at best, trusting the off-road capabilities of the police car. The trail is barely visible, the brushes scratching at the side of the car, the vegetation between the two wheel ruts scraping the underside. Can this really be it? She stops, checks the map again. She can't be sure; there should be a gate. She eases forward, around a slight bend, and it's there, the gate, a remnant from way back before the national parks. She gets out, is amazed by the sound. The forest is alive with a natural music. There is a dull roar, a humming, loud and all around her. Bees, she realises, revelling in the wet spring, the blooming flowers, their buzzing overlaid with squawking wattlebirds, chirruping bowerbirds, and the twittering of finches and wrens. She can see tiny birds, darting this way and that. A wallaby, small and dark, fur puffed up, different from the sleek grey of the kangaroos, watches her approaching and then bounds off into the scrub, as if to warn the natural world of her approach.

There is no lock on the gate, but its hinges are gone and it takes an effort to lift it and shift to one side. Before returning to the car and driving through, she checks the twin tracks. There is no sign of recent passage, although any tyre marks could have been erased by rain. She eases through, doesn't bother to replace the gate. There can be no stock here; the fence has all but gone.

She edges the car forward, the strip between the wheel tracks bursting with growth, green plants with purple flowers. Around her, the forest thins again, the trees well spaced but larger, redgums reaching for the sky. The land dips ever so slightly and there is water covering the track. She checks the map again. It suggests she still has some way to travel. Ahead of her she can see where the trail emerges again, maybe thirty metres away. She inches forward, the four-wheel drive handling the water easily enough. It's no deeper than the wheel hubs, the base more sandy than muddy. She moves through it steadily, reaches solid ground once more. The map was most likely drawn in a dry year, not a wet one; not a year when the regulators were open. She wonders how far she might get, if the way will become completely submerged.

She's finding it hard to maintain her bearings, the track zig-zagging through the trees. She tries Google Maps, but she has lost phone reception. She's deep in the forest, much deeper than the regulator. The sat nav still shows only the symbol of the car, like a boat adrift on a sea of green, the track not shown. She zooms it out. She's still about two kilometres north of the Murray. She zooms out again, but there is no more detail. She hadn't realised just how far the forest stretches, how very large it is.

Increasingly, she finds herself driving through water, not so much small creeks and rivulets as large sheets of still water. She starts to read the landscape, to pick up on the clues. If there is growth around her, young trees sprouting, then the water is ephemeral, unlikely to be deep, the ground likely to be flat. The water itself is still and clear. Nevertheless she proceeds at a snail's pace. She really doesn't want to get bogged. The vehicle has a winch fitted, there are plenty of trees to attach it to, she's confident of her ability, but the lack of phone reception bothers her. She wonders if she has become too dependent on it; her and the rest of the world. She recalls what the twitchers said, back at the Barking Frog: how venturing into the forest alone is risky. She pushes on.

Another wallaby. Just sitting in the track defiantly, unsure of this mechanical interloper. Nell moves closer, and closer again, and still the animal stands motionless, staring at her. She sounds the horn and it tenses, then leaps away, bounding off. She watches it go, threading its way through the trees, small splashes here and there as it springs through the sodden forest. She looks in all directions: only the access track is clear of the water, and only by a few centimetres, with puddles and mud becoming more common, even though she's kilometres from the river.

She advances again, only to find the path blocked by a fallen tree. A closer inspection reveals most of it has fallen adjacent to the track, not across it, and only a single branch lies in her way. She's easing it off the road when she sees tyre tracks beside a muddy puddle. Not left by a car, but by the knobbly tyres of a pushbike. The track is being used; maybe someone is living out here after all. Or maybe it's just enthusiasts, out for a weekend ride. She clears the rest of the branch, gets going once more, windows down, senses alert.

She rounds another bend and the track ends. Sitting in front of her, just as the map depicts, is a low-slung suspension bridge, a pedestrian bridge stretching out over a well-defined creek, supported by towering redgums on either side. And beside the track, a green tarp covering something. She puts on latex gloves, wonders why. Is she hoping not to contaminate evidence, or to prevent herself leaving fingerprints? Under the tarpaulin is a mountain bike, modern and well maintained. There is someone out here.

The bridge is dilapidated. The steel cables seem sturdy enough, but the wooden slats are grey and crumbling. Many are splintering; a few have vanished altogether. It swings back and forth as she ventures onto it. She pauses halfway across. This is a much deeper creek, clear of trees, permanent-looking. There is even the slightest flow, surface weed easing away from her, away from the river. So water is still finding its way into the forest. There is the sound of frogs, adding a bass note to the bees, a counterpoint to the birds. Bellbirds have joined the chorus and in the distance twin kookaburras laugh with the joy of it. She closes her eyes and listens. It's an orchestra.

Over the bridge there is a walking track and she starts along it, ferns and grass brushing her legs. But she doesn't get far. She reaches water again, and this time there is no end in sight. The forest is flooded, the water still and silent, giving nothing away, a tree-dotted lake, a swamp. Aquatic plants are patched across it, bright green here, dark red there. Sunlight is shafting down through the canopy, water lilies tilting their heads to follow the rays. She stands and looks. It explains why the bike is on the other side of the bridge: not much point bringing it across. She checks the map. Somewhere on the other side of this swamp, somewhere in the middle of this sweep of water, is the old house of Eamon Finucane. She can't think of any way of getting to it. She can't possibly start wading through the water. She'll get lost, risk turning an ankle.

She gets out her phone. Still no signal. She takes some photos, a long panning video. She wonders why. Not for evidence. Maybe just for the memory. It is so very beautiful here, so very peaceful. In her mind, she'd always thought of the forest as either hostile or, more often, boring. A wilderness. Not anymore.

She returns the way she has come, but as she crosses the bridge, movement catches her eye. It's a canoe, coming towards her from the north, the opposite direction from the river. She stands and watches it approach. There is a woman guiding it with practised strokes. She has long grey hair, gathered in a ponytail, coming over her shoulder and down her chest. She lifts the paddle, lets the canoe glide the last thirty metres, frictionless and silent against the mild flow. It comes to rest beside the bridge, on the same side as the bike. Nell makes her way off the bridge as the canoeist ties her boat to a tree.

The woman is petite, thin, standing erect. She examines Nell, but doesn't break the silence, as if she's not used to speaking.

'I'm Detective Constable Nell Buchanan.'

'So you are,' says the woman, studying Nell's face. 'Tessa and Grainger's youngest.' Her own face is weathered, tanned and lined, the eyes grey and gentle and somehow wise. There is a stillness to the woman, a serenity. 'I heard your car horn. Thought you might be in trouble.'

'Moving on a wallaby.'

'That explains it.' The tone of her voice is light, but her eyes are serious. 'Why come here?'

Nell retrieves the map from her cargo pants pocket, steps forward, hands it to the woman. 'I was given this.'

The woman examines it with a frown. 'Looks old.' She returns her gaze to Nell. 'Who gave it to you?'

'Lorenzo Camilleri. A winemaker on the Campaspe.' She waits, but the woman doesn't respond, so she adds, 'They used to bring wine here.'

'That right?'

'Twice a year.'

The woman scrutinises the map, as if giving herself time to think. She reaches some internal decision. 'Yes. I remember them.'

'They say—the map says—there is a house in there.'

'More of a shack than a house,' says the woman. And abruptly, from somewhere, a smile. 'You want to see it?'

'Can I?'

'I think you should.'

The woman assists Nell into the front of the canoe, then walks into the water, slowly turning the vessel to point up the creek, the way she came. She climbs in behind Nell, barely rocking the boat as she takes her seat, and starts to propel it on its way. Nell realises her back is to the woman, a woman she doesn't know, a woman holding an oar, heading into the middle of nowhere. And yet there is something in the gentleness of the movement, the rhythmic ease and the quiet with which they pass through the water, that reassures her.

'Let's go through here. Usually it's not deep enough,' says her guide, turning the canoe perpendicular to the channel, heading into the flooded forest, weaving through the trees and past bullrushes as the frogs sing their welcome. The water here is so still, Nell feels she is skimming a mirror. An ibis takes flight, followed by its mate, calling as they lift into the air, Nell able to hear the power of their wings. There is a deep silence here, none of the background noises of civilisation, so that the birdsong resonates all the more clearly, like bells in a cathedral. She trails her hand in the water: cool and clean. There is clarity to it; she can see the bottom, spots a fish, then another. She lifts her finger to her mouth, tastes the water's purity. They pass an old man redgum, a remnant from the original forest, many hundreds of years old, branches gnarled.

Two red-and-green parrots swoop so low that Nell can almost touch them. The sun is coming through in beams, penetrating the canopy like spotlights from heaven. For a moment the woman stops paddling, the canoe eases to a standstill, there on the mirror in the forest, amid the silence and the birdsong. Dragonflies pass, one settling on the bow of the canoe, right in front of Nell, iridescent wings aglow, caught in a shaft of sunlight. Nell can hear her own breathing, her own heartbeat.

Moving again, they emerge into a clearer channel, another creek, water as still as set glass, past a small island of green, dotted with flowers of purple tinted with red and yellow and spotted with white, abuzz with more of the industrious bees. There is the smell of blossoms, subtle and transient. Nell looks up through the canopy, checking the position of the sun, realising she has somehow lost her way: she thinks maybe they have come in a loose semicircle, tracking back towards the submerged walking path. And just as she's thinking this, they pass some sort of exotic tree, an oak or an elm standing like a defender, and there before them is the shack, sheltered by trees, sitting a few metres above the water, alone on its island.

The woman turns the canoe expertly, pushes it into a small beach of sand and mud and shell. Nell clambers out, helps pull the canoe higher.

'It's magnificent,' she says. And it is, as if the air is cleaner here, richer.

The shack is old, she can tell, with walls of redgum slabs and mud, but with wide-enough windows. The roof is new: corrugated iron. 'Solar panels,' she says.

'Off-grid.'

'It doesn't flood?'

'Not since the fifties it hasn't. This far from the river, it gets the water, but not the current, nothing strong enough to cause erosion or wash it away.'

'Protected by the forest.'

The woman looks her in the eye. 'You could say that.'

She stores the canoe, squats, runs her hands through the sand and holds it out for Nell to see. There are small shells, the shards of larger mussel shells. 'A midden. Repurposed.'

'Who are you?' asks Nell.

Again the benevolent smile. 'Willow Jones.'

Nell returns the smile. 'Thank you for bringing me here.'

'Come inside, let me show you.'

The shack has been extended, sometime long ago. The original single room has spawned another of similar size. The first has a bed, bookcases, a kitchen in the corner with a small gas cooktop, windows overlooking the lagoon, a two-person table and a pot-belly stove. There is no ceiling; the rafters arch up with the pitch of the roof. Nell can see a bird's nest in the crook of the beams.

The newer room, still decades old, is north-facing and has more glass. There are plants here: herbs for the most part, and canvases and an easel. She looks at the artworks, sees in them the shapes and colours of the forest, clearly recognisable now she has traversed the real thing. She wonders what she might have thought had she seen them in Dubbo, without the resonance of experience. 'They're beautiful,' she says. To one side there are a couple of self-portraits, Willow as a young woman, hair honey-blonde and face serene. There is a Tesla battery, too, looking out of place in the time-worn comfort of the improvised.

Willow Jones leads her through the studio and out through a set of recycled French doors. There is an area of paving, no more than two metres wide, with a handmade bench of rough-hewn redgum and a table of similar construction. The view is out over the lagoon, stretching away into the trees. Nell thinks how calm it is, how peaceful.

'I'll make some tea. No milk, I'm afraid. Honey?'

'How it comes is fine,' says Nell.

'Feel free to look around,' Willow tells her.

There is a small greenhouse by the water. Nell sticks her head inside: tomatoes and lettuces, more herbs. A couple of very healthy-looking marijuana plants. Next to the greenhouse, a small shed, the walls made from wine bottles, brown and green, cemented together by some concoction of straw and dried mud. Inside, the sunlight refracts through the bottles to form a kaleidoscope of colour. A little past the outbuildings, the island comes to an end. There's a suspension bridge leading to a smaller island, with what looks like a drop toilet. Nell smiles.

She returns to the house, where Willow is finishing making the tea. The place is simultaneously messy and clean. There is a corkboard, made from wine corks sliced in half and glued to the board. Nell sees a bill, a bank statement, a couple of old photos pinned to it. But it's the corks themselves that draw her eye. Some are branded with faded ink: *Camilleri*, they say, in a flourishing font. One of the photos, black-and-white, shows an old man with an eye patch holding the hand of a young girl, her hair blonde, turned pure white on top by the glancing sunlight.

'Who's this?' Nell asks.

'My father and me.'

'Alf Jones,' says Nell. 'Eamon Finucane.'

That stops the woman, who examines Nell more closely. 'Yes. Eamon Finucane.'

They return to the outdoor setting, sit side by side.

Willow starts talking, not looking at Nell but out through the trees. 'You're seeing it at its best, how it used to be. Once upon a time, back before the dams and the weirs and the regulators, it would be like this most years. The winter rains would come, fill the river, then the snowmelt in the mountains would swell it to overflowing. The water would come over the banks from the Murray, come up the creeks, fan out into smaller and smaller tributaries. Like capillaries. People think of it as a forest, but back before the engineers, for three or four months a year it was a wetland. The birds knew it: they would come from the coast, from the Northern Hemisphere, from Siberia. The water would soak into the ground, saturate it, protect it from the hard summer sun. Only the ridges would remain out of the water, the secret and shifting byways, the tracks the animals knew, the wombats and the quolls and the dingos. The Yorta Yorta would burn it, keep the saplings under control, so that between the fire and the floods only the big trees flourished and it was more like a tree-dotted parkland. Unique. There are smaller versions further down the Murray, but nothing like this, nowhere in the world. Nowhere. There was a time when there were floods so big that they would reach all the way out to the tilt, to the edge of the forest and off into the plains where the farms are now. Even the largest trees would get their feet wet, one or two, three or four metres deep. This isn't like that; this a temporary soaking, an echo, a memory, a reminder of what we have lost, not what we have saved.'

Nell says nothing. She's looking out across the water, captivated.

'Sorry about the lecture,' says Willow.

'Not at all. Thank you,' says Nell. 'Have you always lived here?'

For some reason that causes Willow to look away. 'No. I grew up here, as a kid, came back later when Dad was ill, but I didn't return for good until . . .' The woman's voice trails off, as if the memories are playing in her mind but not her voice.

'How come?' asks Nell, curious, wanting to know more about this woman. For once, she's not focused on her job and her investigation; she is simply intrigued.

Willow sighs. 'I lived here until I was about seventeen. But I wanted to get out, see the world. Thought I needed to. Went north. Nimbin and the Aquarius Festival. I came back for about six months that year—1973. Dad injured his leg and I needed to stay here while he mended. Then I was off. Up the coast again, then overseas. The hippie trail. Goa. Afghanistan. Marrakech. I was gone more than a dozen years that first time.' She shakes her head and there is sadness in her voice.

'What brought you back?'

'Dad. He was getting old. And then he was dying. Obstinate old bugger. Left it too late for any kind of treatment.'

'Cancer?'

'Yeah. He wasn't that old. Sixty-eight. About the same age I am now. Tough as nails, as spry as a kelpie. But he smoked. Rollies. Drank a little wine too, but it was the ciggies that did for him. We cremated him and spread his ashes in the river.' She looks off to her right, across the lagoon, in the direction of the Murray. 'Same for me when my time comes.'

'Sounds like you were close to your father?'

'Yeah, I was. Eventually. Particularly that last year or so. I'd grown up by then, appreciated him.'

'Must have been hard.'

'Oh, it was at the end. Of course. But before that, in the months before he became terribly ill, we had a marvellous time, sitting out here, talking and eating and drinking wine, or off in the forest, fishing and trapping and picking native plants. He taught me how to live here. He knew he was dying, wanted to leave this to me.'

'So you stayed here?'

'No, I went away again. I loved it here, but the world . . . you know.' And now there is regret in Willow's voice. 'To be honest, I couldn't handle it. Too much baggage, too much addiction, too much responsibility.'

Nell shrugs. 'Not unreasonable. If your father was dead, there was nothing to keep you.'

That brings a smile to the woman's lips even while the sadness lingers in her eyes. 'Oh there was. There very much was.' Willow nurses her teacup. 'My daughter. I had a daughter, Nell. Her name was Amber. The most beautiful child. She was here, living with my father. I left her here. Abandoned her, I guess. She was only fifteen. Had spent her whole time here in the forest. I got to know her, to love her. And then I left again.'

'Why?'

'I don't know. I think about it all the time. As I go about my business, as I garden, or cook or paint or fish or mend, it's what I ponder. But I have no clear answers.'

'Where is she now?'

'Dead. Long dead.'

'I'm sorry.'

The woman reaches out, takes Nell's hand, not quickly or abruptly, but it still seems strange to Nell. 'No, I'm the one who is sorry. More than you can ever know.' She turns back to the view, takes her hand away. 'All those wasted years, those stupid years. I should have been here. I didn't even know she was dead until six months after it happened. Can you imagine? She was living out here by herself by then; Dad was dead. No one really knew she was here. She never went to school, just lived here with my father, and then by herself. When I learnt she had died, it was another two years before I could bring myself to come back. Before I realised this was where I was always meant to be.'

Nell drinks her tea, looks out into the magnificence, its splendour diminished by the woman's sorrow. She doesn't know what to say, so changes the subject, hoping she doesn't sound callous.

'Do you know why your father went by the name of Alf Jones, not his real name?'

Willow nods. 'Some of it. He told me. Near the end . . .' Again the woman trails off.

'He was a deserter from the army, Second World War.'

'He said he was wounded in New Guinea. Lost his eye.'

'That's true. He almost died. Probably deserved a lot more credit than he got.'

'That's good of you to say. It's good to know.' Willow sips her tea. 'Trauma like that, you can't blame him for deserting.'

'There's more to it than that,' says Nell. 'He disappeared at the same time as his superior officer, a Major Gerard Stannard. The theory back then was that the two men had stolen a large amount of money from the army and absconded together. Did he tell you what happened?'

Willow is frowning. 'Stannard, you say? No.'

'Someone blew up two regulators. One on this side, one on the other.'

Willow looks uncertain, as if she doesn't know why Nell has changed subjects so abruptly. 'Yes. I heard about that.'

'Close to here?' asks Nell, feeling almost guilty pursuing the line.

'Not really, no.'

Nell sees nothing in the woman's reaction, looks out across the lagoon. 'So this water, it's not from there? The broken regulator?'

'No.' Willow smiles. 'The whole forest looks like this now. That's the irony of it. Ever since the regulators were broken, back at the end of winter, the rains have come and the water with them. La Niña, God bless her. The authorities have opened all the remaining regulators, but it wouldn't have mattered. The water was coming over the banks anyway, down at the narrows, at the choke, too early in the year to be much good for the irrigators.' She gives a little laugh. 'That regulator is probably the only place in the whole forest not benefitting. They've erected a temporary dam.'

'They found a skeleton,' says Nell. 'While they were repairing it.'

Willow's eyes widen. It's clear she hasn't been expecting this; that she didn't know. She really must be a hermit. It's been a week since the repair workers found the first body. 'On this side?'

'Yes. It was Stannard. Shot through the head with a three-oh-three, body dumped in the regulator.'

Now there is an intensity in Willow's face, a narrowing of the eyes. 'And you think my father had something to do with it?'

'He didn't say anything?'

'No. Never.' She takes a mouthful of tea, considers the expanse before returning her attention to Nell. 'I knew he was running from something. That he had changed his name. But only in those last few months, in 1988. It explained a lot: why he was living here, why he shunned society. I'd always thought he was just made that way. By the time I was old enough to know him, he seemed perfectly suited to this place. He rarely left.'

'And yet the Camilleris would come every six months or so and deliver wine to him. Do you know why?'

'No.' There's a pause, Willow searching her memories. 'He and Gino Camilleri were close. Like brothers. Gino would bring the wine himself. All sorts of wonderful Italian food. Antipasto and whole meals, baked in iron pots. Osso bucco. Rabbit. They'd sit, they'd drink. Sometimes others would join them, but always those two.'

'Gino was a prisoner of war in the forest, on the Victorian side,' says Nell.

Willow leans back, thinking. 'So that's how they knew each other. From the war.'

A cockatoo comes screeching through, a flash of white, followed by two more, as if playing tag, dodging through the trees, missing by centimetres, their calls deafening, shrieking with pleasure.

'You've seen the wine labels?' asks Nell. 'The River Pirate?'

'You think it was Dad?'

'Don't you?'

Willow nods. 'I always thought so.' She looks at Nell. 'You think they killed Stannard together, Dad and Gino, and stole the money?'

'What do you think?'

Willow is shaking her head, at first in disbelief and then in rejection. 'No. It's possible my father might do it—at that age, carrying whatever trauma he brought home from New Guinea—but I can't see them celebrating it: sitting here laughing, drinking wine, toasting the money. Not if they'd killed for it. That wasn't him. My father wasn't that man.'

Nell looks out across the peace, wondering why she's persisting. It hardly matters now.

'Is that why you've come here, Nell?' Willow asks. 'Investigating an eighty-year-old murder?'

'I guess I am.'

'Why? They're dead now—all of them.'

Nell shrugs, is about to deliver a line, something pat, like 'justice never rests'. Instead, she tells the truth. 'I don't really know. It just feels important to me.'

Willow bites her lip, sympathy in her eyes, the inverted curve of her eyebrows. 'I'm not sure how I can help.'

'This house. Are you squatting here?'

'No. It's mine. Inherited from my mother when I was a child. She died.'

'I'm sorry.' Nell takes a breath, feels like she is trespassing. 'Do you have papers?'

'Somewhere. Why?' And then, answering her own question, 'To see if it was bought with stolen money?'

Nell grimaces and Willow must see the affirmation in the expression.

'I'll have to search. Might take me a while. Does it have to be today?'

'No,' says Nell, and wonders why she's allowing the woman to check the papers in private. She moves on, as if to put the thought behind her. 'There was a second body. A second skeleton in the regulator. It was only found on Tuesday. Identified yesterday.'

Willow says nothing, but Nell can see the trepidation in her face, the fear in her eyes, the tension in her shoulders.

'We thought it was your father, that he and Stannard had died together. But your father's injuries ruled him out.'

'Who is it?' whispers Willow, and Nell is sure she hears foreboding in the older woman's voice.

'His name was Tycho Buchanan. My uncle. Last seen in 1973.'

'Tycho,' Willow whispers. Her eyes leave Nell, drift off to the lagoon. 'Tycho.'

'You knew him then?'

Willow is staring, thoughts far away. This is a shock to her. 'Yes. I knew him.'

'Do you have any idea what happened?' asks Nell.

'No. None at all. I'd left by then.'

'How well did you know him?'

And now Willow turns to her, looks her in the eye. 'Nell, there is something you should know.'

'Go on.'

'I'm your grandmother.'

Nell searches for words, but there are none.

'You were born here,' says Willow. 'In this forest, in this house.'

chapter thirty-four

JAMES WATERS—FIRST STATEMENT—CONTINUED

THAT NIGHT, THE NIGHT AFTER EAMON FINUCANE KILLED THE OFFICER, I DIDN'T know what to do, so I did what I always did: I went home for dinner. I swam back across the river, hauling the yabby sack behind me. I got the cattle settled, left the dogs in charge and rode Lenny home. The yabbies were still alive in their hessian bag, but not so feisty. They'd had a big day. Or maybe they knew what was waiting for them. I'd thought of chucking them, or putting 'em back where I found them, but I reckoned—as they and their relatives had got me and Bucky into so much trouble—they shouldn't get off scot-free. Besides, that would have been a waste, and that wasn't a summer for waste. I figured if I couldn't get money for Mum, at least she and my sister could have a decent feed, something different from mutton stew and damper.

It was late afternoon when I was getting home, a bit later in the day than normal. It must have been about six, something like that, with only a couple more hours of daylight for me to eat and get back to the cattle. I wasn't too worried about that. Lenny and I were used to the forest by then, knew it well. We could find our way back to the cattle in the dark if we needed to. I thought Mum would have cooked something else already, but if it was stew it could always hold another day. Or the yabbies would be fine if we put them in a tub of water, they'd last until the next night. Some people reckon they're better like that; it rinses out the muddy taste.

Anyway, that was what I was thinking about as I rode Lenny up to our farm. What I was trying to think about, instead of Stannard's thing, and the gunshot and his dripping corpse. And that's when I saw him, the telegraph boy, coming out of our gate. He looked at me without looking at me, not meeting my eye, and climbed on his old red bike and rode straight past me, heading off into the sun. He didn't say anything. He didn't have to. He was the telegraph boy.

That night, after my sister was in bed, Mum and I ate the two big crays. She cooked them up special. She had a bottle of wine that she opened. I hadn't ever seen it but I knew what it was. It was the bottle that she and Dad were keeping for the night he got back from war. So she opened it and we drank it. I'd never had wine before, and I really didn't like the taste at all. But I forced myself to drink some. I had to drink it because I knew what it was and I knew she needed to share it with me. We ate crayfish and drank wine and didn't speak a word.

I didn't go to the forest again after that, not really. I spent that night at home in my bed, first time in months, but it was a night of tears and terror. The bed was too soft and I couldn't sleep. The next morning, I got the dogs and we mustered the cattle. It was the last time. School was starting in a week and it was always going to be difficult to keep the cattle fed until Dad got back. And now he wasn't coming back. Not ever. So Mum sold them. Uncle Reg looked after the sale and we got a fair price. They were in good condition, well fed from the moira grass. Mum told me how proud she was of me, called me a life saver, and tried to smile to show me she meant it. I guess that made me feel a little better, although I knew her smile wasn't a real one, that she was putting it on for my sake.

It was only a few months later that she sold the farm altogether and we moved down to Boonlea and lived with her mum, my gran. I was really upset about that, but I was upset by a lot of things that year. I couldn't help but think about my dad, that selling the farm was some kind of betrayal. My grandad had bought it from the money he'd earned building the levee and Dad had worked so hard to make it successful, to grow good things, to build it up for us. It felt wrong to walk away. It was our home. But Mum explained how it wasn't really her choice to sell, it was forced upon us by the bank, that we owed too much money, even with the sale of the cows, and it was better to get some money for it rather than hanging on another year and getting nothing. So I understood, even if it still didn't feel right. Uncle Reg found her a job working in a shop and we started to mend. Her mum looked after us, and Reg would drop in every now and then and give us a treat—a nice bit of bacon or a slab of butter or a couple of cans of condensed milk. My sister loved that; it was a favourite of hers.

As the year went on, the war started to go our way. The Japs were getting pushed back. Same with Hitler. People started to smile again, the tension went from the air, and the air-raid drills stopped. For the first time in a long while people started to make plans for the future. But not us. We didn't feel any better and I reckon there were a lot of people like us, smiling in public and weeping in private.

chapter thirty-five

NELL IS IN A KIND OF SHOCK. EVERYTHING WILLOW HAS TOLD HER, SHE believes, knows it to be true. That her mother, Willow's daughter Amber, gave birth to her all alone in the shack on the island in the forest. That Amber became sick, an infection, was found trying to walk out with her baby, seeking help, but couldn't be saved. Willow said she died of sepsis in the hospital at Hatheson, aged just twenty-one. Willow cried to tell it and Nell cried to hear it: Willow for the daughter she'd lost; Nell for the mother she'd never known.

And then Willow told her the rest. That Tycho Buchanan was her lover, the father of Amber, that he had not lived to see his daughter, had not even lived long enough to know Willow was pregnant. Willow recounted how after Tycho disappeared she'd fled back to Nimbin, and had given birth to Amber there. And she cried again, suddenly old and vulnerable, all of her peace and all of her serenity gone.

Now Nell is driving back to town, the car almost steering itself, her thoughts adrift like leaves on a creek, flowing with the currents. Memories of family life at Boonlea pass through her mind: she sees herself playing with her brothers and sisters, her mother ever attentive, but she's no longer certain what it is she remembers. Nell is no longer sure who she is; she is untethered.

It's only as she pulls into the Hatheson hospital that she makes the effort to reconstruct herself, to don her facade, to dress herself in an imaginary uniform. It's quarter to one, fifteen minutes until her meeting. She stares at the building, at this hospital where her mother died, where Tessa and Grainger must have found her. This hospital where her grandfather, Tycho Buchanan, what's left of him, lies in the morgue. She'd held his skull in her hands, looked into those hollow sockets. Not knowing. It's like she is retracing her first days: her birth at the river shack, her care here in Hatheson, her adoption, her grandfather. Full circle. She closes her eyes, steadies herself. Time to front up; time to put on her game face. Time to be a detective, not a daughter. Ivan will be here, and who knows what sort of mood he will be in? Possibly not a receptive one; she winces at the memory of telling him where to go the previous evening.

Blake and Carole are waiting inside the hospital, installed at a table near reception. They look like normal people, living in a normal world. And Ivan. He stands, comes to her, reaches out, touches her arm, says nothing. She sees no anger in his eyes, only concern. She struggles to respond, to say anything.

He sits, she follows his lead, the four of them at the table, Carole frowning, Blake studying her face silently, as if to determine what she's thinking, what she's feeling. She's not sure she knows herself. Numb maybe.

It's Blake who takes the lead, although Nell can see the doubts shading his face, 'I believe Ivan told you the second body belongs to Tycho Buchanan,' says the pathologist. 'I'm sorry.'

Nell shrugs, but something inside her is aching, her words sounding as if someone else is voicing them. 'He died long before I was born.'

'Indeed,' says Blake.

'We haven't informed anyone else,' says Ivan. 'Not yet. Would you like to be the one to tell your family?' His voice is solemn. 'If it makes you uncomfortable, I can do it. Or Kevin.'

'No. It should be me.' And now she feels a little put out, them wanting her to break the news but not wanting her to investigate. She is about to voice her objections, but something stops her, as if her intuition is a step ahead of her logic. And then the logic catches up: if she is the one to break the news, it gives her a legitimate excuse to ask them what happened that year she was adopted. 'I'd like to do it,' she says.

'There's something else,' says Blake, hands wide in a gesture of . . . what? Apology?

Nell looks to Ivan, sees the concern is still in his eyes. Whatever this is, he already knows. 'Tell me,' she says to Blake.

'The DNA match is clear and incontrovertible. It's Tycho Buchanan, the brother of Grainger and Eugene. Your uncle.'

'Tycho was my grandfather, not my uncle,' says Nell, brain now engaged.

Blake takes a breath, surprised, looks to Ivan then back to her. 'You knew?'

'Not until this morning. I just met my grandmother. Eamon Finucane's daughter.'

'His daughter?' Ivan lets out a long breath. Is he amazed? Relieved? Nell can't tell.

'We didn't set out to uncover any of this.' It's Carole, her head lowered. She looks up, looks at Nell. 'Your DNA is on file. We needed to rule out contamination. You'd handled the skull.'

Nell has a creeping feeling. 'Do you know who my father was? My biological father?'

Carole looks confused. 'No. Not that. Something else.'

'Please tell me.'

'We've discussed this, the three of us. It's hard to know what to do, but it's likely you will find out sooner or later, so perhaps it's best coming from us. You have a right to know.'

'What are you talking about?'

'We tested Tycho's mother Rita. You took the sample.' Ivan pauses, as if unsure how to proceed. 'Your brother Greg also requested to be tested.'

'Why would you need his DNA?' Nell asks, perplexed.

'We didn't. He insisted, thought it might shed some light on the case.'

'And did it?'

Carole shrugs. 'Not directly. But he must have suspected. It reveals his father was Tycho, not Grainger.'

Nell says nothing, does the sums. Greg, twenty-two years older than her. The same age Amber would have been had she lived, his half-sister.

'At a guess, the three middle children, Gail, Molly and Simon, are all the natural children of your parents Grainger and Theresa Buchanan. But Greg is your uncle, not your brother.'

Nell feels her thoughts cascading once more. 'So that's why they adopted me. Mum and Dad. Because of Tycho. Because Mum'd had his child.'

chapter thirty-six

1973

FOR ONE GLORIOUS WEEK, THEN A SECOND, LEADING UP TOWARDS CHRISTMAS, Tessa lived in a world of bliss, elevated above the ordinary: bliss anticipated and bliss delivered. She met with Tycho often, clandestine assignations down in the forest. She would head off in the mornings, saying she was going swimming, or walking, or picking flowers, or not saying anything at all, just taking the bike and riding down the tilt, opening and closing the first gate, riding along to the second gate, where she would wait for him or he would already be there, waiting for her.

Beneath her the world spun as if powered by destiny, the sun moving towards solstice, the calendar towards 1974 and her sixteenth birthday, the year the world would finally be hers. The hot weather had ripened the wheat and the contractors had taken it off, and summer was truly here. If her parents noticed the difference in her, they showed no sign. Perhaps they were happy; perhaps her mother was secretly pleased for her. But they said nothing to her and she said nothing to them, and if they did notice the change in their daughter, then their daughter was too preoccupied to notice their attention.

She found she loved everything about Tycho: his body and passion and sex; his personality, with its quirks and complexities; and his mind, with its curiosity and its intelligence. They would talk for hours and then hours more, about themselves, about their world, about their future. And hour by hour, day by day, she found herself growing into him and felt him grow into her, so that they started growing together, more like one entity than two, growing from the rich soil of adolescence into the skies of adulthood, of love and partnership and commitment, so that after a fortnight she felt herself a different person. She knew how special this was, how fortunate she was, and she cherished every moment. They told each other everything, intimate and embarrassing, so that there was nothing left between them. He told her of his previous relationships, of conquests and experiments and mistakes, and, with head low, of his dalliance with Willow. He laid it all out, let her examine it; she forgave him and felt her love deepening. She shared her fears, her hopes, and he listened. And so it was they grew. And in her mind, schoolgirl daydreams became real and transformed into adult plans: she wanted to be with him, she wanted to go where he went, and so they mapped their future.

It was Tycho who suggested she continue her studies. At Hatheson High, but later in Albury, maybe Melbourne, wherever fate took them. And then university.

'Uni? Why?'

''Cos you have the brains for it.'

'No, I don't.'

'Of course you do. If Grainger and Gene are smart enough, then you're a natural. Even that dickhead teacher of yours could see that.'

She wasn't sure about university, but she was sure about Tycho. And she was sure about them. And because he was sure about her and their future together, she began to believe in herself. The great card game of life was being dealt and she was a card or two away from an unbeatable hand.

--

Six days before Christmas, she had the house to herself, her mother out tending to the garden. Tycho was at work in Hatheson; the mid-week stock sales were on, the last of the year, and it was important he cover them. She drifted from room to room, carried by boredom and restlessness, afloat on dreams.

The phone rang. She was on it by the third ring.

'Waters' residence.'

'Tessa.'

Her breath, the inevitable intake. 'Tycho. Are the sales finished?'

'I'm in Griffith. My big story. Heading back to Hatheson soon. I'm coming to Tulong tomorrow to see the family, sort out a few things. Thought we might catch up.'

'I'd like that. You want me to come to town?'

'No. Meet me in the forest. By the second gate.'

'What time?'

'Maybe about three? We can go for a swim. Whatever.'

'Yes, see you then.'

A little later, her father came in. 'Who was that on the phone, Tessa?'

'Oh, you know—destiny.'

He glowered at her then, a knowing look. 'You be careful.' It was all he said, but she didn't care. Who was he, with his phantom golf games, to tell her what to do?

That evening, after dinner, the sun yet to set, the summer almost at its solstice, she walked down into the forest, towards the second gate, as if to check that it really existed, it wasn't just her imagination, that nothing could go wrong. He had met her there before, following the track from the river. She sat and she dreamed, only seeing the growing storm at the last minute.

It advanced quickly, not so much a front from the south-west but materialising into the air, the cloud blooming, white and glorious, rising higher and higher, backlit by shafts of gold and pink, like the heavens themselves were singing. She saw the lightning first, and then heard the sound of thunder. She started back, not hurrying, not worried, impervious. The tops of the clouds were white and pink and ruffled, Botticelli clouds, but the underside was grey and darkening, lightning snaking. She could see the wall of water coming towards her, a solid sheet of rain. The still of the air broke and the wind swept through, cool and urgent, the temperature dropping, her ears popping as the pressure fell with it. And still she didn't hurry. The rain came and she stretched her arms wide, revelling in it. For what is rain, if not a promise of new beginnings?

--

The next day, the morning dragged. She was so restless she offered to help her mother around the house, attracting a raised eyebrow, and vacuumed the living room and mopped the kitchen and bathroom. After lunch, she left early, walking down the tilt, deciding the bike might be tricky in the mud left by the storm. She was full of excitement, full of anticipation. Full of love, for that was what this was, she was sure. Ardour, love. Lust. The real thing. She felt it, the bond so strong; she felt him, as if they were communicating across the ether. She could picture him driving the highway from Hatheson, wind in his hair, cigarette in his hand, the cassette player pumping music. A song inserted itself in her mind as she walked towards the first gate, the boundary between forest and fields. She couldn't remember who it was by, but the chorus looped in her mind again and again, encouraging her to seek freedom. The sentiment lifted her as she passed through the gate and closed it behind her.

The sky was so blue on this day, cleansed by the storm, made new just for them, and the forest was alive with possibilities. For her and Tycho. The marvellous adventure, come at last. She arrived at the second gate, a remnant from an earlier era, always left open now, a marker in the forest and nothing more. She was, she realised, happy. At long last, she was happy. Around her, the forest shared her joy.

While she waited for Tycho she picked wildflowers, the yellows and purples in abundance, the blues and reds harder to find, all brought to new glories by the rain.

But Tycho didn't come. She didn't own a watch, but she knew the time well enough, could tell it by the arc of the sun in the sky. Time, which had moved so slowly towards the rendezvous time, started to accelerate, as if flowing downhill, starting to move so quickly she might not be able to catch it, the moment speeding away from her until it was forever out of reach. An hour passed, then another, and a sense of dread descended as the sun moved lower and lower, placing more and more time between the world she was entering and their meeting time.

And still Tessa sat, ears alert to the faintest sound of a car engine, her eyes on the sky, estimating the time. He was late, nothing unusual in that. Tycho had a watch, of course, but seemed unconstrained by it. As she sat, she looked at the forest. It was their place, she decided. She picked more wildflowers.

That evening, late home for dinner, she asked if she could use the phone.

'Local call?'

'Yes.'

'Okay. Don't be too long.'

The phone was in the hall. There was no privacy; she knew her mother was likely to eavesdrop, but there was no escaping it. She rang his apartment in Hatheson, but there was no answer. She called the newspaper office, on the off-chance he had uncovered a scoop, was working furiously to meet a deadline. The exciting world of the journalist. But the phone cut through to a machine, the click and clunk of the mechanism, the hiss of the tape, the rehearsed voice reading out the office hours, the stilted invitation to leave a message. Then a beep. It was her first encounter with an answering machine, but she left no message. She hung up.

Next day she rang his apartment twice. Nothing. Then the paper. The editor sounded irritated, said he hadn't seen Tycho, and if she did, please get him to ring in. Afterwards, she wondered if there was already concern in the editor's voice beneath the displeasure.

She walked down into the forest, the track dry, small puddles from the storm already evaporated. She got to the second gate, walked past it, checking the ground, but there was no sign. No car had been past here, no blue Datsun with music throbbing and a whiff of tobacco. There were only the wildflowers she had left by the gate, already wilted.

Then, in the distance, she heard a low rumble, the sound of a vehicle, and for a moment and an eternity she was filled with hope. The engine sounded low, and portentous, not the enthusiastic pitch of the Datsun, but that hardly dented her hope. No one else used this track. Even when she saw the tow truck edging towards her she wasn't prepared to accept defeat. She recognised it, the Buchanans' work vehicle. Maybe something had happened to the Datsun; maybe Tycho had borrowed it.

But when it pulled up next to her, she could see it was the father, not the son; it was Bert Buchanan who climbed down from the truck.

'Morning, lass,' he said.

'Morning, Mr Buchanan,' she replied, then couldn't prevent the words from spilling out. 'Have you seen Tycho?'

'No. I'm looking for him.'

'So am I,' she stated boldly.

'Here?' he asked. 'Why here?'

'We were going to meet near here. Yesterday.'

'You're Tessa, then? Jimmy Waters's daughter?'

'That's right. I met you at your yard.'

'So you're the one. He told me about you.' He was looking at her, not unkindly, but objectively, as if judging her. 'You're pretty. I'll give you that.'

'I'm worried,' she said.

'So am I, lass. So am I.' And she could see that he was. 'Did he always come this way? Up through the forest, not along the highway?'

'Both. We drive this way sometimes, when we're going swimming, or he's showing me things.'

'What things?'

She said nothing, remembering Tycho's injunction not to speak of the clearing with the green shed and the charcoal drums.

'It's all right, lass. You're not in trouble here. Neither is Tycho.'

'Can I come with you?' Tessa asked.

But Bert Buchanan shook his head. 'Better not.' Then he made his way back to the truck. 'I'll let you know if I find anything,' he said over his shoulder. 'Call me if you hear from him.'

Back at the farm, she was beside herself, a jumble of emotions she could barely untangle. Tycho was missing, no doubt. Bert Buchanan himself was looking for him, didn't know where he was. Something terrible must have happened. She gathered her courage, rang the Buchanans' house. The mother answered, said curtly she had not seen Tycho and hung up. Tessa checked in the phone book: there was a separate number for the junkyard itself. She called it, hoping Grainger or Gene might answer, but it rang out. She was dimly conscious of her own mother's hovering concern, aware that she hadn't asked to use the phone, sought the customary permission.

That evening, as Tessa set the table for dinner, her mother asked her what was the matter, but she was unable to answer. Instead, she said she wasn't feeling well and excused herself, going to her room. And it was partly true: her appetite had deserted her as abruptly as the joy of the previous weeks had. In its place a pit had opened in her stomach. She was late, she realised. Days late. She checked the calendar, realised it had passed her by unnoticed. She went back over the squares, looked in her diary, but the arithmetic refused to correct itself. The night at the drive-in, three weeks ago. The following days. He had been careful, she knew he had, but she had been so eager, so rushed. Her own fault. So stupid—schoolgirl stupid. But what did that matter now, whose fault it was? How could that help? All that could be corrected, all that would be okay. She just needed to find Tycho Buchanan.

--

The next day, at breakfast, her father was waiting.

'Tycho Buchanan is missing,' he said.

'Yes.'

'You haven't seen him?'

'Not for days.'

'Bert Buchanan didn't come home last night. His wife is worried sick.'

'I saw him. Yesterday.'

'Bert?'

'On the track to the river. He was looking for Tycho.'

'What time?'

She shrugged. 'Late morning.'

'Good girl,' he said, and headed out to search.

She couldn't sit at home, not after that. The telephone had proved itself a tenuous link, unreliable and fractured, incapable of connecting two people who had been so well connected. Calls to his apartment had gone unanswered, the editor had been gruff and angry, there had been no sign, no message. Nothing. She recalled their last conversation, when he called from Griffith. He had said he would visit the family in Tulong. So she rose early, rode the bike into town. That early in the day, it was not so hot, not yet. And she was energised; she needed to see him.

The junkyard was empty, Saturday quiet. The gate was open, as always. Now she had arrived, she felt the nerves, the momentous nature of the occasion. There would be no going back.

Coming towards her was a large car. It washed up to her in pneumatic splendour: a Cadillac, low and purring, Turtle Wax shiny. A thing of pride, a thing of wealth. It eased to a stop and the driver's tinted window slid down. An electric window; she'd heard of them, never seen one in real life. The man was swarthy, with olive skin and a pencil moustache.

'*Ciao, bella,*' he said, smiling. 'Have you seen Tycho?'

'I'm looking for him,' she said.

'Good. The boys, they are not here. They are looking too. In the forest.'

'Did they find Mr Buchanan?' she asked.

'No,' said the man. 'Not yet.' And he was no longer smiling.

The window ascended and the car moved past and away. The sound of the tyres was louder than the sound of the engine. His words hung in her mind. *Ciao, bella.* It reminded her of the movie, *The Godfather*, and Don Corleone. And it reminded her of Tycho's words as they left the drive-in. *They're here.*

She continued down the driveway. She had come so far, the long ride from the farm, she couldn't just turn around and go. She went to the junkyard. It was quiet, not a sound. She pricked her ears, but there was no violin, no transistor, only the wind. She walked to the Studebaker, but Gene was not there; she walked to the far tree but there was a music stand and nothing more.

The truck was gone, the father with it. Perhaps he'd been called to an accident out on the highway, a car to retrieve, no time to tell anyone. She imagined the blue Datsun smashed against a tree, and an ache engulfed her heart, so intense it stopped her walking. Then she summoned her courage, continued to the house, knocked on the door. The mother appeared, Rita, dressed in black, like a widow. 'What are you doing here, girl?'

'Gene? Grainger?' The words stumbled from her lips.

'No. You should go.'

'Tycho?'

The old woman looked at her, a gaze like a spotlight. 'No. Tycho is not here.'

'Where are they?'

'Eugene and Grainger? Swimming.'

'What?'

'Somewhere. Some secret spot.'

'Right. Can you tell Gene I was here, please?'

The woman studied her. 'Eugene? He's not interested in you, girl.'

'What do you mean?'

'Go.'

Tessa had more questions, many more, but the door was already shut.

She stopped in at the store next.

Mrs McCardle was stacking the shelves with biscuits from a carton. 'Hello there, Tessa. How's your mum?'

'Much better, thank you,' Tessa said, feigning normalcy.

'How can I help?'

'Have you seen Gene and Grainger Buchanan?'

'No, love. Not today.'

'How about Tycho? Has he been in lately?'

'I thought I saw that little blue car of his just the other day.'

'Thursday?'

'Might have been. Why?'

'I wanted to tell him something. For a newspaper story.' The lie came so easily, so readily.

'If I see him, I'll let him know you're looking for him.' And there was something in the woman's face, something that suggested she understood, that she too had once been young.

Tessa was about to leave, but then another thought came to her. 'Mrs McCardle, do you know a girl called Willow? She lives in the forest.'

The shopkeeper examined Tessa's face before answering. 'Aye. I do. She and her father. They don't mix, don't come out much.'

'From where?'

'No one knows. Somewhere deep in, somewhere inaccessible.'

'So you don't know how to find them.'

'Sorry, love. No one does.'

Tessa left the shop, but she didn't consider returning home. How could she? There was nothing there. Rita Buchanan had said Gene and Grainger were swimming; the foreign man in the foreign car said they were searching. But where? The forest was so very big; Tycho had shown her that. Rita Buchanan had mentioned a secret spot. Did she mean the regulator? Perhaps Tessa would find the brothers there.

Riding to the swimming hole wouldn't be so difficult. The road to the river was probably six miles, and it was maybe another two to the regulator. Not that much further than the ride to the farm, but easier. No semitrailers, the shade of the trees. And then, from there, she could follow the river road, along the way Tycho had taken her when he showed her the shed, the one with the illegal stills and the bottles. She thought of that place. Could he have gone there on the way to meet her? His father had come that way looking for him the day before when she had encountered him by the second gate. Now she wished she'd told him. That decided it for her: if the brothers weren't at the regulator, she would ride that way home and see if she could re-locate the clearing with the green steel shed and the charcoal drums. She got on her bike, rode down the tilt into the forest.

She was maybe halfway, just past where the sealed road gave way to dirt, when she saw the truck coming towards her, the tow truck from the yard, with its cracked windscreen and high aerial. She waved, moved to the side of the track, expecting Bert Buchanan. But as the truck came closer she could see it had a car on the back. Not a wreck: Tycho's blue Datsun. She waved her arms, desperate and careless, needing to know, but the truck wasn't slowing. And as it passed her, she saw it wasn't Bert behind the wheel, it was Grainger. She saw him and she saw that he saw her, no matter how quickly he averted his eyes. And yet he kept driving, reluctant to stop, to acknowledge her, the brake lights only illuminating when the truck was well past, coming to a stop almost a hundred yards back the way she had come, as if he had arrived at the decision late. It just sat there, engine running, making no sign of reversing. Tessa dropped her bike and walked to the truck in a daze. Before she reached it, Grainger opened the driver's door and climbed down.

'Where is he? Where's Tycho?' she asked, a rising panic in her voice.

Grainger shook his head. 'We don't know. We've been looking. We found his car.'

She looked past him to the back of the truck. If there was any damage to the Datsun, she couldn't see it. 'Where was it?'

'Up along the river, inland.'

'Heading towards my place?'

He looked at her. His face was sombre, eyes full of pain. 'I guess.'

'Where is he, Grainger?'

'He's gone, Tessa. We don't know where he is.'

'I need to speak to him,' she said.

Grainger looked at her, as if seeking something in her face, his own pale and threatening to fold in upon itself. 'I understand. Let's get your bike. Give you a lift. Get you out of here.'

And it was only then that she saw the blood on his shirt and on his forearm, above his too-clean hands.

'Grainger, what is it? What's happened?'

He glanced down, saw where she was staring. 'I hit a kangaroo. Had to put it out of its misery.'

chapter thirty-seven

NELL AND IVAN DRIVE SOUTH FROM HATHESON IN SILENCE, LEAVING BLAKE AND Carole to their work. Ivan is at the wheel; Nell stares into space, realigning the model of her world, reimagining it. Her mother had been Tycho's lover, then had married Grainger before Greg's birth. An arrangement, face-saving. Perhaps the only way, back then, she was able to keep her baby. Then another nine years before the birth of Gail, then Molly and Simon in quick succession. It explains the long gap between children, just as it suggests so much more. And then Nell, born seven years after Simon. Nell, dark like Greg, dark like Tycho. Was that the key to it, her parents seeing the resemblance in her, alone in the hospital, a baby lost in the world? Their decision to take her in, to call her their own. A last devotion to her mother's lover, her father's brother.

'Nell?' It's Ivan, breaking her reverie. 'Tulong.'

'So it is.' They've made the half-hour trip without her noticing.

'You don't have to do this,' says Ivan.

'Yes, I do,' says Nell. 'It's just around the corner, four blocks in. She's still in the same house.'

Rita, Nell's grandmother. Another rearrangement in her mind: her adoptive grandmother, her biological great-grandmother. Tycho's mother, Gene and Grainger's mother. Bert's wife. Alone in her junkyard castle.

'Strange place,' says Ivan, easing the car through the gates, passing through the honour guard of rusting hulks, on through the hedge, driving towards the house and its oversized portico.

'True,' says Nell. The pristine house with its immaculate, minimalist gardens, shielded by the corroding cars, like some strange counterpoint to Willow's shack, protected by water and trees.

Rita answers the door in a dressing-gown, as if she's been sleeping. But there's nothing sleepy about her as she shows them in. Her eyes are fierce and knowing. Perhaps she's anticipated this visit. Perhaps she's been expecting it for fifty years.

In the living room, Nell sees the photographs of Tycho, of Bert, of Gene and Grainger. They're the same images from a few days ago, but they look different now.

'Do you want tea?' Rita asks.

'No, Grandmother. But please sit. We have bad news.'

Rita sits, then Nell. Ivan steps back, giving them space.

'Grandmother, the body I told you about—the DNA matches. It is Tycho.'

Rita nods her comprehension, eyebrows steady. 'Thank you,' she says after some time. 'It is good to know.' And she closes her eyes, breathes, unmoving. Then she opens them, looks across to the framed photos of her son. 'At last, rest,' she says.

They sit in silence. For some reason, having told Rita about the identification of Tycho, Nell is unable to tell her the rest, the family tree made evident by the DNA. She turns to Ivan. He tilts his head, understanding. He tells the old woman quietly, sympathetically, that her son had fathered two children but had not lived to see them: Amber Jones and Greg Buchanan. And that Amber Jones had a daughter, Nell. It's only at this, at the last, that Nell feels the tug of emotion, the suggestion of tears.

Rita turns to her. 'I knew about Greg. They didn't say, but I knew, deep down. But you? Is this true?'

'It is.'

And a smile comes across the old woman's face, broadening as she detects the echoes of her son in Nell. 'I believe it. I see him in you.'

Ivan lets the moment sit a while before speaking again. Nell can hear the subtle change in his voice, the professional edge. 'Mrs Buchanan, now we know the body is that of your son, can you share any further information about what happened to him?'

She lifts an eyebrow. 'The mafia. I told Nell already. He knew too much, had discovered too much, so they killed him.'

'We found a gun near the body. Your husband's gun.'

She shakes her head. 'My husband was shot. The mafia got him as well.'

Nell wants Ivan to stop. It seems unfair to her, this unofficial inquisition in her grandmother's moment of vulnerability. But she knows better. She bites her tongue, stares at the images on the walls, even as she listens intently.

'That's not what you told the inquest,' Ivan says. Nell realises he must have read the findings, maybe the transcripts, on his way from Sydney. She turns to appraise him.

'I was foolish. I believed the police instead of Tessa,' Rita says.

'What changed your mind?' asks Ivan.

'The death of Donald Mackay. The royal commission.'

Ivan looks at her, gaze unwavering, and then to Nell and back again. 'Thank you, Mrs Buchanan. And my condolences for your loss.'

Rita appears emptied, the hollowness of the years upon her. 'Thank you for coming. I will sleep better for knowing.' And her eyes drift once more to the photographs before returning to Nell, and she smiles.

--

Back in the car, driving from Tulong to Boonlea, Nell is no longer distracted. Instead, she tells Ivan of Eamon Finucane, of Tycho's article on the River Pirate wines, of her visit to the Camilleris' winery, of her encounter in the forest with Willow. She tells him of the shack's remoteness, but not of its magic. And she doesn't tell him of her own birth, her biological mother's death, the circumstances of her adoption. She knows he must be wondering, that forensic mind working, but he has the sensitivity not to press her on it. She is grateful: he has been good, her sergeant, her colleague, her friend, listening rather than probing, letting her say what she wants to say. Not reminding her of her outburst the evening before.

And when he does talk, it's a neat summary. 'You think Finucane and Stannard stole the money. Finucane killed Stannard, kept the money. Used it to buy the land for his shack, changed his name.'

'Maybe. I've asked Willow for title deeds. For financial records.'

'Hmmm,' says Ivan. 'Won't actually prove anything. Circumstantial at best.'

'True.'

They're forced to slow right down. There's a harvester on the road ahead of them, slow and wide, Ivan concentrating, trying to see if it's safe to overtake. From her window Nell sees the old farmhouse on the rise above the tilt. Grandpa Jimmy's place. Her mother's childhood home. Where Tessa was living when she met Tycho Buchanan. When she fell pregnant, when he was lost to her. It looks so small. Shrunken.

They arrive in Boonlea. The house sits by the Murray, expectant. Objectively it looks no different, but to Nell her childhood home has taken on an entirely new character.

'You up for this?' asks Ivan.

She grimaces. 'I guess we'll find out.'

Everything is quiet, the yard tidy. Her father opens the door with muted formality, introducing himself to Ivan, leading them into the antiseptic lounge where Tessa is waiting. Her parents sit side by side, holding hands, as if they already know there is bad news coming. She wonders if they know that Greg insisted on being tested as well.

Nell addresses her father, and doesn't know why. Tycho was his brother, but also her mother's lover, Greg's father. Surely, that is more important. And yet it's to Grainger she looks, maintaining the pretence. 'I'm sorry. The DNA results are conclusive. The second body, the one in the regulator pool—it's Tycho.'

Yet there is no pretence on her mother's part, not now. Nell can see the tears approaching, ready to spill. Grainger speaks for the two of them. 'Thanks, Nell. It's a relief to know, once and for all.' He turns to his wife, stroking her back, murmuring words of comfort.

Nell gives them a moment, then steels herself. 'About the DNA tests . . . I'd handled the skull, so they needed to run my DNA to rule out contamination. It's routine.'

And now her parents' eyes are upon her. Knowing eyes.

Nell keeps her face neutral, her voice even, but her composure only lasts two words: 'I know.' And then a sob comes from somewhere and claims her for a moment. Ivan reaches across, his hand on her arm in support. She bites her lip, continues. 'I know about me, I know about Greg. I know about Tycho.'

Her father simply nods; her mother stares at her hands.

It's Grainger who speaks. 'It's better that you know.'

And she feels what? Relief? Anger? Pity? Betrayal? All of those things.

Later, Nell joins her mother in the kitchen as Tessa fidgets her way through making more tea.

'Mum, why didn't you ever tell me that I was adopted?'

Her mother turns, suddenly still. 'We always intended to. We decided we would do it when you turned sixteen. But that year you were troubled, excitable, erratic. It's a precarious age. We thought it better not to destabilise you further.'

Anger flares. She says nothing.

'Oh, Nell . . .' Her mother moves towards her, as if to hug her, but Nell lifts a shoulder, the smallest gesture, draws back. Her mother regards her, shock on her face, then a kind of resolve. 'I will always be your mother, Nell. *Always*.'

Nell doesn't know what to say, what to feel. 'What about Greg? Why didn't you tell him?'

'That's different.'

Nell says nothing, but can feel her anger seeping out. 'You understand, don't you? We need to investigate, we need to find out what happened.'

Her mother's voice is softer, more hesitant. 'Are you saying we are suspects?'

That stops Nell. She struggles to find the right words. It isn't what she'd been driving at. It's like she's always the last one to know things, the last to realise their implications. 'You'll need to be interviewed.'

'By you?'

'Not me. Ivan. I can't be involved.'

'I told the police at the time: Tycho was investigating the mafia.'

'Just tell Ivan what happened,' says Nell. 'You have nothing to fear.' And in that moment she is grateful for her fellow detective's decision to remove her from the investigation, to keep her at arm's length.

'All right,' says her mother.

The kettle has boiled and Tessa moves to fill the pot, the same pot Nell remembers from her childhood, white glazing with birds painted in blue, two shades. It wasn't so very long ago that she lived here, that she saw it every day. And now it seems foreign. Her mother seems foreign.

Tessa turns. The tears are there at last, not streaming, just glossing her eyes. 'I loved him, Nell. I really did.'

'I know, Mum.'

And her mother starts to tell her the story of all that happened that year, that summer, when life and love came so suddenly and so early, when the world lifted. It was 1973 and she was on the cusp of sixteen. 'It all started when I missed the bus home from school,' her mother says, and for a long time Nell stands unmoving, just listening. In the kitchen, then on the patio and, later, down by the river as the afternoon stretches into sunset and sunset into twilight and twilight into dusk. At one point, the men come out, Grainger to say he's driving north to stay with Rita, Ivan to say he's returning to Tulong, that he will come back to fetch Nell whenever she's ready. And then the two women are left alone; alone with her mother's story. It's not a story of murders and missing men, of mafia intrigues and coronial inquests, but of her and Tycho Buchanan. And eventually, as the first stars are appearing, she tells her adoptive daughter of Bert at the second gate and Tycho's blue Datsun on the back of the tow truck and Grainger with blood on his shirt.

Nell doesn't summon Ivan; doesn't feel she can abandon her mother. Instead, she stays in her childhood room. It's been preserved, like a time capsule: the outdated computer is still on the desk, the posters of Bruce Lee and Jackie Chan on the walls, her trophies on a shelf. Memories of her uncle Gene encouraging her to take on the world, her parents advising her to shy away from it. There's even a calendar from her last year of school, dates still marked: the formal, the speech night, one last judo tournament. Parties, a band at a pub in Echuca, an eighteenth birthday at a farm out of town. She'd been so keen to leave this place, to escape the constraints of her agoraphobic mother, that she hadn't bothered to take it down, and Tessa had kept it.

She'd been reluctant to come back here, to visit her parents. And as she tosses and turns in her childhood bed, she wonders if she'd had some inkling, some intuitive understanding, that there was something wrong with her family, deep down and unacknowledged. She wonders about her parents, the decisions taken in the wake of Tycho's disappearance: to marry, to keep Greg, to adopt Nell two decades later. Their conspiracy to keep the truth from their children.

But that's not what keeps her awake: not the knowledge of her adoption and not the circumstances of her parents' marriage; it's her mother's final revelation that Nell can't put to rest: Grainger, sprayed with blood, driving his dead father's tow truck, with his dead brother's Datsun on the back.

chapter thirty-eight

1974

TESSA GAVE BIRTH IN MELBOURNE, AGED SIXTEEN, SIX MONTHS AFTER MARRYING Grainger Buchanan. There was pain and there was joy, there was the intensity of the moment and there was the memory of moonlight on a river, there was Grainger hovering and attentive, and there was the ghost of Tycho. And then there was the baby, uniting it all.

At first, the boy's eyes seemed wrong to Tessa, a murky blue. She sensed a malaise, that she was teetering on the brink of an emotional well, only to be lifted back as her son's eyes turned a deeper brown day by day, richer and richer, arriving at that same beautiful polished mahogany as his father's. Every day, when she woke, she would look for the change and glory in it. Greg laughed and burbled and sucked at her breast, and after all of it, for all of the grief, for all of Grainger's sacrifice, the child carried her from sadness and restored her to life just as surely as she had given it to him.

They took their baby and retreated to a rented apartment near the university, Grainger working two jobs while he studied dentistry. He played the violin less and less, and finally not at all. There was no time. It saddened her—she would have liked the child to grow up to such a soundtrack—but she couldn't say anything, didn't feel she could impose upon her husband. He'd already given so much. He supported her, brought home money, brought his quiet affections, but he was rarely at home, either studying or working. It was Greg who reignited her own love. More and more she retreated into the world of her child, cocooned in their small flat. Sometimes she wished her mother would visit, tell her what to do, but only her father ever came, bringing clothes and her mother's best wishes. Lotte was too frail for the long drive, he said. She sent her love.

One blue-sky day when Greg was about nine months old, almost crawling, his deep brown eyes sparkling, she put him in the old stroller Grainger had found in a second-hand store and went walking. She knew it was good for her to get out of the flat, good for the baby, and such days were rare in a Melbourne winter. Her husband encouraged it, told her she was pale and commented on the dark circles under her eyes. She'd planned a short walk to the park, but it was such a fine day she just kept walking, along Lygon Street, marvelling at the shops and cafes, at the people, smelling the coffee and tobacco smoke. As she waited to cross a street, an old woman peered into the stroller and smiled so broadly at her chortling boy, and then at her, that Tessa felt a surge of pride.

Buoyed, she kept walking into the city, her son asleep and untroubled. She decided Grainger was right: fresh air was what she needed, what Greg needed. She walked past bluestone and she walked past brick, past glass and steel, past churches and pubs, past colonial and art deco and modernist, through the press of people, guiding the stroller over the tram lines, stopping to watch two policemen riding their motorbikes abreast, lights flashing, escorting a black car bearing an unknown flag. She had a vague intention of reaching the river. She could sit by the Yarra with her child. He would like that.

But when she reached Flinders Street Station she stopped. There it was, unchanged from her mother's postcard, as if the image had been taken yesterday. She stared at it, but she could no longer see herself dancing down the steps, or walking hand in hand with Tycho Buchanan, or strolling to a luxury hotel and drinking champagne in a lobby filled with glamorous strangers. At the age of seventeen she felt beyond that; she'd lost her chance. She felt so tired then, so exhausted, that the river was too far, even though it ran just the other side of the station. She caught a tram home, the conductor lifting the stroller for her, getting her seated, not charging her, for he saw something in her eyes that warranted charity.

After that, she kept more and more to the flat and Grainger grew more concerned. He was a good father. She could see his love for Greg, his brother's child. She saw Tycho in the boy's eyes and she loved him all the more for it; she saw Tycho in the shape of Grainger's face and it haunted her. Grainger's sacrifice was so evident, what he had given up, his violin unattended in its case, she felt she could ask nothing more from him. For wasn't this all her fault? Only Greg pulled her from her self-recriminations and erased her incremental despondencies—for he truly was a marvellous child, sparkling and joy-filled. Some days were better than others; she felt herself on the edge.

The tipping point was the inquest. They'd been in Melbourne eighteen months when the body of Bert Buchanan was found, and early in 1976, she and Grainger and the child travelled to Hatheson for the inquest. She'd already told the police about the mafia, of Tycho's investigations, of the story he believed would carry them to Melbourne. She repeated this in a low and steady voice for the coroner. But Grainger had begged her not to speak of the day she'd encountered him driving the tow truck in the forest with blood on his hands from a dead kangaroo. So she didn't. She didn't lie: she wasn't asked; she didn't volunteer. But it brought that day to the surface once again and she struggled to suppress it. It vexed her when she heard the police evidence, their claim that Tycho killed his father, that Tycho was on the run. She didn't believe it. Tycho was dead; she was sure of it. She would never believe he could kill his father, or that he would desert her, or turn his back on their life together. It distressed her, this inquest, the lies and the half-truths.

They were staying at the house in the junkyard, Rita's empty palace, when she summoned her courage, asked her husband what had really happened to Tycho. Grainger said he didn't know, but that he too believed his brother was dead, killed by criminals. He told her to let it rest, that no good could come of it. She felt isolated after that, more alone, more intimidated by the outside world. She started to have trouble sleeping, her dreams haunted by a faceless man with blood on his arms. The abyss was beckoning and she resisted. Back in Melbourne she stayed inside their apartment, where it was safe, where she could keep her son safe.

The years passed and the time came for Greg to enter the world. She'd resisted play groups, feeling herself inadequate among the older mothers, felt their eyes judging her. Tessa turned eighteen and nineteen and twenty. Greg started preschool. He cried the first day, clinging to her. But within days he loved it, running to the gate by himself, eager to get started. She would stand at the fence, watching him play with other children, or sitting in the sandpit engaged in earnest conversation, or pushing toy trucks, or finger painting. She would linger as long as possible before drifting back to the apartment. She wondered if this was what life was: a long goodbye.

Grainger graduated, got a job, and for the first time money was easier. But she found herself unable to change: there was satisfaction to be found in scraping the value out of every cent, of doing what she could to repay the unpayable debt. For she knew if Grainger hadn't married her, then the nameless authorities would have taken her baby. She owed her husband everything. He started talking about buying a small house, somewhere nice. She voiced her support.

One day, she was walking to collect Greg from preschool when she saw a tram hit a car, pushing it along the tracks, tyres squealing, the wheels of the tram shrieking. It was a slow-motion drama, a shunting rather than a smashing, but it filled her with dread. In the weeks afterwards she found it increasingly difficult to leave the flat, for only within its walls could she exert control. And yet she forced herself into the world, to take Greg to preschool and to fetch him home, and to do the shopping. She ventured out for him and she ventured out for her husband, but never for herself.

One evening, a year after graduating, Grainger came home wearing a smile and carrying flowers and wine. The wine was an echo of home, familiar with its River Pirate label.

'We're moving back, Tessa,' he told her. 'I've found a job at Boonlea. The practice needs a junior. We'll be happy there.'

She hugged him then and wept a little. It occurred to her how very fortunate she was, and she realised after five years of marriage that she had come to love this kind and good man, that gratitude and indebtedness had been overtaken by something more profound. And that night, for the first time since Tycho, making love was a joy and not just an obligation. And so her world expanded just a little, and she hoped for something better.

They rented a house in Boonlea for the first six months, then bought their own little place on a side street. For a girl who had wanted to see the world, homemaking filled her with an unexpected pride as she created a sanctuary for her family. And then, with Greg already at primary school, Gail was born. Blonde and pink and plump and jolly, except for a rough few weeks of teething. Molly followed—plagued by colic, but Tessa didn't mind—and then Simon, jaundiced at first but healthy once that passed, quiet in the company of his raucous sisters. A flotilla of children, she their admiral. Grainger took over the dental practice, they moved to a half-acre block fronting the Murray, and the past retreated, leaving her happy for days, even weeks, on end.

And yet the melancholy was never entirely gone. In a quiet moment she would watch the river and wonder what did happen to him, to Tycho and his father. Had the mafia got them both? Or was the truth closer, more terrible still?

One day she thought she saw Tycho at the shops. A flash of dark hair, a visceral response, her heart responding, overruling her brain. She followed the man, tears already forming, only to find the inevitable: it was a stranger with a shock of hair, the curve of a jawline and nothing more. After that, she asked Grainger again what had really happened that day, and he repeated the same story: he and Gene had searched the forest, found Bert's truck with the keys still in the ignition and, later, Tycho's blue car, but no sign of the men. Then he'd hit a kangaroo and was forced to administer a mercy killing.

That was the last time; they never spoke of it again, and she closed in on herself more and more, venturing from the house only to do the school run and the shopping. She knew she should do more, and she tried: volunteering at the school canteen, watching cricket and netball from the sidelines. But she was never comfortable with it; by the time she returned to the refuge of her riverside home, her face would ache from delivering false smiles. Only her family gave her joy; only her home gave her control. She lay awake at night, worrying, always worrying, anxiety preventing sleep, hoping her children would be safe, that they would be sensible, that they would never put themselves in harm's way. But even her obedient three were growing older, heading towards their teens, spending more and more time away from the house. Her mind told her this was what she should want, that she should aspire for them the way she had once aspired for herself, but dread weighted her heart. Her own teenage wants and wildness were nothing but a long-gone error.

The day came when Greg left home. Off to study art at Albury, a man, although she could still see the child in him. It scared her, knowing he was almost as old as Tycho had been when she'd lost him. And he was so much like Tycho. His looks, his charisma. She saw the girls following him with their eyes, her son seemingly unaware of their interest. She saw the boys watching him too, and saw him returning their glances. Secretly she was pleased; she was not sure about sharing him with another woman. Grainger drove him to Albury, full of pride, leaving the younger ones with her. And that night, alone in bed, Grainger still not back, she cried herself to sleep.

After that, she felt herself sliding once again, becoming more and more protective of her remaining three, keeping them close, insisting they pursue safe and secure careers. She spent her days cleaning the house, turning it into a fortress, fearing to venture outside where bad things stalked. And at night, with Grainger snoring beside her, she tossed and turned, wondering what would become of her once the younger children followed Greg into the world, until only exhaustion and tablets brought her the release of sleep.

And then, like some sort of miracle, heaven sent: a baby girl. Found crying in the woods, her mother dying. A baby girl with dark hair and dark eyes. The daughter of Amber Jones. The granddaughter of Willow Jones. The granddaughter of Tycho Buchanan, for Tessa could see it in the child's murky blue eyes, the same shade her Greg's had started out. Grainger agreed to her suggestion, staring at the floor, thoughts unreadable, and the girl was theirs. There was no one else: the mother was dead, the father unknown, the grandmother long gone, probably dead.

Nell. Dearest, sweetest Nell, the world making reparations, compensating Tessa for a life half lived. She had a new mission: to protect her, this last echo of Tycho Buchanan. It was her chance, her last chance to rebalance her world.

chapter thirty-nine

THE SUN HAS BARELY CREPT OVER THE HORIZON WHEN NELL IS OUT OF BED. She walks to the river, but there is nothing calming about the Murray, nothing soothing in her martial arts routine. She feels disorientated, like she's hungover, like her sense of balance is askew. Daylight has failed to dispel the horrid imaginings of the night, fuelled by the image of her father, blood spattered, driving the tow truck from the forest. Her father. Is it possible? Her loving, attentive, conservative father? Was Grainger somehow involved in the deaths of Bert and Tycho? She looks at the river, its insistent push towards the sea. Is her father a killer?

She's still grappling with her thoughts and emotions, neither under control, when her mother walks outside to join her, bringing two mugs of tea. Nell watches her come, astounded, Tessa apparently at ease as she leaves the gravity of the house. Nell half expects her mother to abandon the journey halfway, return to safety, but she doesn't.

'Here,' says Tessa, handing her a mug.

'You okay, Mum?'

Her mother smiles, shrugs. 'It doesn't seem so scary this morning.' And she regards the river, as if seeing it for the first time. 'I slept well last night.'

Tessa has broken her silence after years of secrecy. Nell realises a weight has been lifted from her mother—and transferred to her. A weight she cannot carry, a secret she is unwilling to keep. It is too big, too awful. So she broaches the subject, asks her mother, and Tessa gives her permission and her blessing. So when Ivan arrives to pick her up, Nell is authorised to tell him about Grainger and the tow truck and the blood.

They drive north in Ivan's rental towards Tulong, but Nell doesn't know where to begin, so she just starts talking, recounting the evening's conversation in no particular order, skipping bits, going over things, trying to keep to the salient parts and failing. Ivan listens, saying nothing, although she can see he's baffled by this gush of words. Whenever she glances across at him, his eyes are on the road, a slight furrow in his forehead, a small twist on his lips.

She continues to circle around what she needs to say, talking about her mum and Tycho, about Tessa's search for him, his comments as they left the drive-in, about her belief the mafia was involved, the Italian in the car. And then she is at the heart of it, almost without knowing it, telling Ivan her mother saw Bert Buchanan, down at the second gate, desperate to find his son. And how, the next day, she encountered Grainger driving the tow truck, with Tycho's car on the back; Grainger with blood on his shirt and his arms. And with that, she runs out of things to say.

They speed on, just the sound of the engine, the tyres on the road. Ivan waits, perhaps to see if there is any more, and then takes her through the relevant points calmly and methodically. And he asks, 'Why didn't she tell anyone this at the time? Or when they found Bert's body, at the inquest?'

'Loyalty, I guess. And gratitude. He saved her; saved her from having to give up Greg.'

'Do you think she actually knows what happened to Tycho and his father? What role Grainger played?'

'No. She's convinced herself it was the mafia, accepted his story about the kangaroo. Suppressed what she saw.'

Ivan is silent after that. They close in on a car in front of them, a new SUV with an L-plate, moving slowly. They pull out and overtake. Nell sees a young girl behind the wheel, eyes set straight ahead, not daring even to glance at the overtaking car.

'Okay,' says Ivan. 'She may not know what happened. But Grainger must. It's time I spoke to him.'

To their right, she can see the tops of trees, the beginning of the forest emerging over the lip of the Cadell Tilt. And up on the ridge, like a small wooden lighthouse, her mother's old house, alone and isolated. Where Tessa's mother once lay crippled with a migraine, where Tessa ran down the drive to venture to the drive-in, where she had waited in vain for news of Tycho. Nell wonders about her grandfather, Grandpa Jimmy. Practically a hermit nowadays. Her mother had told her that night at dinner that she should go and see him. She promises herself she will, explain that she's his granddaughter by adoption, not by birth. Another difficult conversation. They pass the house and her thoughts move on.

Ivan drops her at the motel in Tulong and heads to Rita's house. Nell changes into clean clothes: she'll work out of the local station while Ivan confronts her father, armed with her mother's information. Half of her is frustrated, the other half is relieved; half of her wants to be there, half of her doesn't. She's not sure she could trust herself to be in the same room with her father, so she can't see why Ivan should. If it moves to a formal interview, which is likely, it's important that she's kept well clear of it lest they make themselves vulnerable to legal challenge. Ivan is a skilled inquisitor, more likely to give a suspect enough rope to hang themselves rather than coming on heavy, but she knows he'll do whatever it takes. And if that means breaking down an interviewee psychologically, so be it. It's better she doesn't have to sit and watch.

She thinks of her father. The immaculate house, the pebble driveway, the well-tended lawn. No politics or religion discussed at the dinner table, everything buttoned down. Striving for what? Normality? To distance himself from his father's criminality and sink into the anonymity of life? While his brother, Gene, had always been the opposite: kicking against the pricks, winning awards for exposing police corruption, revealing fraud on the town council. And always encouraging Nell's martial arts and her desire to become a police officer, to kick arse. Two brothers, living equidistant from Tulong, one half an hour north, challenging the establishment, the other half an hour south, defining it. But both of them shaped by events that took place near the town half a century ago.

At the station, she tries to stay busy, sending a bulk email to the local dentists, thanking them for their cooperation, informing them the two bodies have been identified. She sends an email to the Missing Persons Registry, telling them they can wipe Tycho Buchanan from their list of sorrow. Another to the coroner's office, informing them of his fate. It's a distraction, something to occupy her mind and nothing else. And all too soon it's done, and she can't avoid speculating about what's taking place between Ivan and her father. It's too much for her: she can't just sit and wait; she needs to do something.

--

She takes the car, heading down the tilt and into the forest. She wants to see Willow again, Tycho Buchanan's other lover. The forest woman has a right to know what the family tree really looks like, that her daughter Amber had a half-brother. Nell wonders what Willow will think of Greg. She and Tessa must have given birth within weeks of each other.

It's mid-morning, but there is still mist in the forest, under the canopy and out of the sunlight, tendrils spread amid the trees and the ferns, following the water into the forest. Despite the beauty, Nell feels none of the previous day's wonder: life has become too pressing for that. Soon, she has left the bitumen, then the main tracks, and is back on the winding paths, seeing the evidence of her own passage the day before. The redgums are there waiting for her, silent and massive, the box trees motionless in the still of the day. She catches a glimpse of a sea eagle drifting on the thermals, high above the world, and she envies its perspective.

She no longer has the map—she'd left it with Willow—but she's confident she can find the house again. She'll drive to the suspension bridge and then sound her horn. It worked before; surely three long and deliberate honks will bring Willow.

But she doesn't get as far as the suspension bridge. She's at the fallen tree when she spies her grandmother coming towards her on her bike. There's some trick of the light and, for a moment, she thinks it might be a young girl, summer dress floating, the long hair golden not grey. Certainly, Willow seems agile enough, bringing one leg over the saddle, dismounting gracefully as she cruises to a stop and waits for Nell to emerge from the police car. 'Hello, Granddaughter,' she says, smile as wide as the forest itself.

Nell feels her own smile pallid by comparison. 'I was just coming to see you.'

'Evidently.' Willow looks around, takes a seat on the trunk of the fallen tree, patting the place next to her, an invitation to sit and talk. 'Are you okay?'

'What do you mean?'

'You look a little strung out.'

Nell tries to shrug it away. 'I didn't sleep well last night. The investigation has uncovered some uncomfortable truths.'

The concern is evident on Willow's face. 'Anything you can talk about?'

'Yes,' says Nell, and sits on the trunk next to her grandmother. 'The DNA analysis we used to identify Tycho's body—it's revealed more about our family tree.'

'Does it matter?'

'My brother Greg—Tycho was his father as well.'

Willow doesn't seem surprised. 'I thought that might have been the case. Tycho was utterly smitten with Tessa.'

'Really?'

'You sound surprised.'

'I thought . . . you know.'

'That she was just a conquest?'

'Something like that.'

'No. That was me.' And she smiles, as if to show she takes no umbrage at the idea. 'Tycho was no saint before he met your mum. Quite the hedonist, in fact. I never thought he felt much for me. Lust, I guess. Plenty of that going about back then.' And then, seeing the look on Nell's face, 'Don't worry, I was a willing participant.' She smiles again, lets it drift away, looking at her hands. 'And I was a source of information. He was always asking questions. But the man had a heart. A soul. Tessa was lucky to have him.'

'I'm glad to hear it,' Nell says. 'What kind of information did he want?'

'Different things. One time he was doing a story on the people who still lived and worked in the forest—preppers and back-to-earthers and hermits. Thought I might make a good photo.'

'Did he now?'

'I declined.' Willow gives a knowing look. 'Later, he wanted to know about any criminal activity occurring in the forest.'

'Did he ever mention the mafia?'

Willow frowns. 'No. Not him. I only heard those rumours years later, when I came back.'

'Were they here? In the forest?'

'Not that I ever heard of.'

'What did you tell him?'

'Not a lot. He wanted to talk to my father.'

'About what?'

'I'm not sure exactly. The wine, I think. I told him he should talk to his own dad.'

'Bert Buchanan. How did he take that?'

'With good humour. He may have said "touché", or something to that effect. He was very good with banter, you know.'

They don't speak then, surrounded not by silence but the sounds of the forest. Bees and frogs and, above all, birdsong, bouncing above the water and flowing through the trees. Butterflies—dusty white ones, and golden ones freckled with black, and larger black ones with white dots—drift around them, a cloud of beauty and wonder. Nell holds out a hand, temporarily mesmerised, thinking perhaps one might alight upon it. But they drift on by, leaving the two women with their thoughts.

'Willow, tell me about my mother. Amber.'

Willow looks at her, eyes simultaneously glowing and sad. 'Oh, she was gorgeous. Wild, of course, although I could hardly fault her for that. She and my dad were devoted to each other. She knew him as Alf, knew nothing of his past.' Willow is perfectly still, sorrow in her words. 'I think she was happy. Happy when I was here, but happy when I wasn't. She was very strong, very independent. I have a feeling you might take after her in that respect.' The light shifts, a passing cloud, and Nell's grandmother looks her age. 'I don't have many regrets. Just one. That enormous, overbearing, ever-present one: I wasn't here when she needed me.'

'What about my father? Who was he?'

'I don't know. I wasn't here. She never had the chance to let me know.' Willow reaches across. 'I'm so sorry, I wish I could tell you.'

The sun passes behind a second cloud before flaring again.

'I'm glad you came along,' says Willow. 'Saved me a ride.'

'You were coming to see me?' asks Nell.

'After your visit, I started going through Dad's things. There's not a lot there; he wasn't a hoarder. He never really left the forest, but he travelled light all the same. Didn't keep anything from his previous life—maybe because he didn't want to, or maybe because it could incriminate him. I found nothing about Eamon Finucane, the man before the forest.' She fossicks in her bag. 'But there is this.' She hands Nell an envelope, the deep yellow of officialdom. 'Title deeds.'

Nell opens the envelope, unfolds the certificate. 'Henrietta O'Reilly?'

'My mother,' says Willow.

Nell reads the document. 'They didn't buy the land until 1957.'

'I guess they just squatted up until then. I was born at the shack in '54.'

Nell scrutinises the certificate. It appears authentic. A forgery would be pointless; the state land titles office is the ultimate authority. 'It says it was previously Crown land—even before the national park.' She turns to a second page, a map. The title refers to the islands, that of the shack and the outhouse. The surrounding waterways remained government property.

'Any use?' asks Willow.

'More curious than useful,' says Nell. 'It eliminates, or at least discounts, the theory that your parents bought it with money stolen from the army. Seems unlikely he would wait fourteen years.'

Willow gives a little snort. 'Maybe. If he did take the money, he sure as hell didn't spend it on anything else.'

'Frugal?'

'No. Just not engaged with money.'

'So how did they buy the land?'

Willow shrugs. 'Does it say how much it cost them?'

Nell searches. 'No. It doesn't. But it says the land is unencumbered.'

'Meaning?'

'That there was no mortgage. She owned it outright.'

Willow hands Nell a second identical envelope. 'And here's mine. After Mum died.'

Nell opens it, withdraws the certificate showing ownership transferring to Willow Jones in 1959. 'Is that your real name?'

'It's the one on my birth certificate.'

'And the land was transferred to you, not your father.'

'I guess it couldn't go to him. Alf Jones wasn't his real name.'

'True.'

'Here,' says Willow. 'I found this as well. There were more—of me, of the forest, of the river—but this is the interesting one.' And she hands Nell a photograph: small, square, black-and-white. It feels so old, reminding her how far in the past they are discussing. It shows four men standing in front of an old truck in the bush, smiling at the camera.

'I don't see your father,' says Nell.

'Behind the camera would be my guess,' says Willow.

Nell flips the photo over. Written on the back in fading pencil: *Sly grogging—the Stills—1972*. She turns it back over, studies the faces. Three of the men are middle-aged, in their prime, with a much older man on the far left holding a rifle, its stock resting on his expansive belly. The sight of the weapon raises the hackles on her neck and she wonders why: hunting and shooting are enmeshed in country life; such images would be commonplace. She doesn't recognise him, but the other three all look somehow familiar. 'Who are they?' she asks.

'Far left is Bert Buchanan,' says Willow.

Nell looks closer, sees that it is indeed Bert Buchanan, her biological great-grandfather. She can see similarities to Greg.

'Next to him is Gino Camilleri.'

'So it is. From the River Pirate winery.'

'And next to Gino—you don't recognise him?'

'He looks so familiar, but I can't place him.'

'Your grandfather. James Waters. Tessa's father.'

Nell squints. Willow is right. The old man in the house above the tilt, the man no one seems to bother with. But fifty years ago, here he was, smiling at the camera, apparently among friends. 'And the big man on the right with the gun?'

'I don't know. I never met him.'

'You met the other three then?'

'They used to come to the shack occasionally, when Gino delivered the wine.'

'So Bert and Jimmy would be there too?'

'Sometimes.'

Nell looks again at the image, half a century old. 'Can I keep this?'

'Of course. Do you need the title deeds?'

'No. I think we might leave them out of it.'

'Thank you,' says Willow, putting the envelopes back in her bag. 'What's happening with the investigation?'

Nell shakes her head. 'Now that we've confirmed it's Tycho, I pretty much have to recuse myself. Stay in the background.'

'I wish I could help,' says Willow. 'I wish I could do something.'

Nell gestures at the photo. 'Who knows? Maybe you have.'

——

Nell leaves Willow and heads back to Tulong. They hugged for a long time before parting, as if this might be the last time they saw each other. How strange it seems to Nell, to feel so close to the woman, this stranger, to embrace her so effortlessly and naturally, whereas she's felt distanced from her own mother for so long. She wonders at that, whether there is some deeper biological connection. She doubts it. Tessa had been all cuddles and hugs when Nell was small, but had stopped sometime around puberty. Not just hugging—all touch, really. Was it her mother's agoraphobia, her obsessive cleanliness and fear of germs, or was Nell responsible as well? The surliness of a teenager? The insistence on risk-taking? She doesn't like where this line of thought is leading and is almost glad when her phone chimes with an incoming call. She must be back in range.

'Ivan. How's it going?'

'Not well. Your father's lawyered up.'

'What happened?'

'Took a while to find him. He and Gene were having coffee at the Barking Frog. He was happy to come back to the station and talk, seemed totally relaxed, but as soon as I mentioned him retrieving the tow truck and Tycho's Datsun, he clammed up.

When I said he'd been seen with blood on him, he told me that he'd run over a roo, administered a mercy killing. And then he demanded a lawyer.'

'Do you believe him? About the kangaroo?'

'He didn't hesitate; he came straight out with it. But it could be a prepared line, kept in reserve all these years.' Ivan takes a breath. 'So no, I'm not sure I do believe him. Although he seemed shocked that we knew about it.'

'What now?'

'He's agreed to talk, but back in Boonlea with the lawyer. He's well connected, knows all the local professionals, so hopefully it shouldn't be long. I'm about to head down.'

'Okay. Thanks for letting me know.'

'You keeping busy?'

'Trying to. I informed Missing Persons and the coroner that we've identified Tycho, thanked the dentists.'

'And then?'

She can hear the concern in her partner's voice. 'I went to see my new grandmother, Willow Jones, to tell her about the DNA, and to see if she could shed any new light on what happened to Stannard.'

'And?'

'Nothing as yet.'

A lull, as if he wants to say more. 'Okay. I'll let you know when I'm done,' he says instead, and ends the call.

She's almost back to town, just passing the old sawmill. She can't bring herself to return to the station; there is nothing there. So when she gets to the highway, she drives south, to her grandfather's house, the farm ten kilometres from town, sitting atop the tilt, overlooking the great forest. The old man lives there alone, seemingly forgotten, disconnected from the family. Now a fifty-year-old photograph is taking her to visit him.

She pulls up at the driveway entry. There's no longer an actual gate, just a cattle grid, but she stops the car nevertheless, gets out. She regards the house as she might a memory, sitting on its rise, a white cube in the distance, fields on either side, the forest beyond it. The wheat has been harvested, only the stubble is left. She recalls her mother's story from the night before, imagines Tessa getting off the school bus here, walking to the house, or riding her bike down the drive, on a mercy dash for medicine. She looks about her, sees the old tin-can letterbox, rusted through and in need of replacement. Was it just along there, where the highway shoulder is a little wider, under that lone gum tree, that he parked the famous blue Datsun? How strange to think of it now, that it's his blood running in her veins and not Tessa's. The past is not so very distant here, she realises: if the shack in the forest was the teenage home to her biological mother, then this was the same for her adoptive mother.

At the house, she parks directly outside the front door and finds her grandfather is already standing there, perhaps alerted by the sound of her car. He looks very old, shrunken and hunched, pants hitched high, but there is a glint in the blue eyes. His hair is a fine white mess, like spun cotton.

'Hi, Grandpa. It's me. Nell.'

'Hello, Nell.' His smile lacks no warmth, just a few teeth. 'That a police car?'

'Sure is.'

'And you a detective and all.'

'Homicide.' She pulls out her badge, hands it to him.

He admires it with wonder and pride. 'Well, you'd better be coming in, then.'

He leads her down a small hall into the living room. It's neat but dusty, in need of a vacuum. There's an air conditioner on the wall, a large television, lots of books. It looks more prosperous than her mother described it. He offers her a seat as he eases into his own. 'So, Detective, what are you investigating this fine day? That skeleton found in the regulator?'

'What do you know of that?'

'It's all in here,' he says. He holds up a crumpled copy of Tuesday's *Western Explorer.*

It sounds like the old man isn't aware of the discovery of the second body. No one has bothered to tell him that Tycho Buchanan has been found at last. That makes Nell feel a little sad.

'Gene Buchanan wrote the story,' the old man continues. 'Bucky's son. He says the body was found in that regulator that got blown up. Is that right?'

'Bucky? You mean Bert Buchanan?'

'My nickname for him. When we were kids.'

'I'm told you knew him?' she prompts, thinking of the photo.

'Very well. But tell me, the body—is it true? It's really Stannard?'

That stops her. She's come to ask him about the photograph Willow gave her, but in an instant that is forgotten. 'What do you know about Stannard?'

The old man grimaces. 'I'm probably the only person still alive who remembers him.'

'And what do you remember?'

'Plenty. Plenty about him. Plenty about that regulator too. Plenty about everything, if you have the ears to listen.'

'You want to share it with me?'

'Oh, I don't know. It's a very long story. Take a good while to tell it properly. And you're busy—a detective and all.'

She thinks of Ivan down in Boonlea, waiting to interrogate her father, her own inability to be involved. 'I've got all day.'

'Well then. Where should I start? With Stannard?'

'That sounds good,' she says.

He seems to think that over. 'If I'm going to tell it properly, I'd have to start before then. I'd have to start with the regulator.'

She smiles. She has the sense the old man has been rehearsing this, deciding what he wants to say, sitting here these last few days, re-reading Gene's report. She sets her phone on the arm of his chair, and he nods his permission as she starts the recorder. 'Tell me about the regulator, Grandpa,' she says, like a child asking for a bedtime story.

And so he starts. 'I remember them building the regulators. Here, and on the Victorian side . . .'

And he talks and he talks and he talks some more. And the more he talks, the more spellbound Nell becomes. It's a story of the regulators, a story of the forest, a story of the war, the story of a boy and his friend. A story of events unfolding so very long ago they seem to belong to another world. It's late afternoon by the time he reaches the end of his tale, and by then she has stopped thinking of him as her aged grandfather, or even as James. Instead he is a young lad, eleven years old, minding his family's cattle in the forest. Young Jimmy Waters and his best friend Bucky.

chapter forty

JAMES WATERS—FIRST STATEMENT—CONTINUED

AFTER MUM SOLD THE FARM AND WE MOVED DOWN TO BOONLEA, I LOST MY WAY a bit. I couldn't settle into school. It was a lot bigger of course, after our little one-teacher school out there on the plains, but that wasn't the problem. It was losing the farm, losing Dad. I stuck it out till I was fourteen, which doesn't sound like much, but it was better than some. There were kids who never made it to high school at all. After that, I worked on the wharf for a while. Odd jobs, carpentry mostly. It was quiet back then, nothing like it is now. There were a few enthusiasts, fixing up the old paddle steamers, trying to attract tourists from Melbourne, people coming up on trains and people with their own cars. Once the war was over, the money started to flow. People were scared that the Depression might return, but it wasn't like that at all. There was plenty of work, good wages. I liked being by the river, but I missed the forest. And I missed the farm. It still felt like we'd let my dad down, selling like that. So I took a job on a farm down at Nathalia.

That's where I met your grandmother, Lotte. Lovely girl she was, with eyes that sparkled and a mouth that curled more on one side than the other. When she smiled and her mouth curled, you knew she was up to mischief. We hit it off right away, as soon as we discovered we were both from up here, from farms on the forest edge in New South Wales, ours north of the levee, hers up on the tilt. We got married, had a honeymoon in Melbourne. Her dad wasn't well, the farm was running down, so we bought him out, him and Lotte's sister, and moved into this very house. That was in 1955. It wasn't much, but we were full of hope. I reckoned my dad would have been proud of us.

It was a tough life for Lotte, mainly because she was plagued by poor health and we didn't have much money. She'd get awful migraines that would send her to bed, twisting her up with the pain. If it wasn't for the headaches and the money, life would have been sweet. Her greatest joy was your mum, Tessa. And her greatest concern too. Of course, Tessa has her own problems, but not like that, and not when she was with us, not when she was a kid. It was terrible when Lotte died, but she kept that smile of hers, right to the end. I was scared it might fade from my memory, the way my dad's face seemed to after the war. But now it's come back to me in my dreams. I'm starting to see Dad again too. And my mum, and Bucky as a kid, and even Bucky's dad working on the red engine. I guess they'll be seeing me as well, soon enough.

That was when I encountered Bucky again, when Lotte and I moved back to the district. He'd married a foreigner, a refugee. Rita was her name—your grandmother—and she was small and fierce and proud. They already had a little boy, Tycho, a real rapscallion.

Bucky's father had died in the last year of the war. The supports under the red engine collapsed and he was crushed by it. But by the time our paths crossed, Bucky was going okay. Better than okay. He knew about milling, of course, growing up there with the red engine, and he'd been able to start up a small sawmill on the edge of the forest, a proper one with a proper rig, down by Tulong Creek. Later he sold it, and used the money to build that house for Rita and set up the wrecking yard. I was happy to see him, happy to see that life had treated him well, but at first he kept me at arm's length, like he didn't really want to know me, like he wished I hadn't come back. I guess I knew why and left it at that. I'd see him at the Golden Sheaf and the general store and wherever, but that was all.

Then I saw the one-eyed soldier again—Finucane. The one who shot Stannard.

I was fishing down on the little wharf there at Anglers Reach. Those were the days before the carp got into the river and spoilt it, before the bag limits and the licences and all that malarkey, when you could still pull out a Murray cod big enough to feed half a footy team. I was sitting there when this bloke in a little tinnie came putt-putting down the river, and tied up at the wharf next to me. Of course, I recognised him immediately, because he was wearing that eye patch, so I said g'day. But he didn't recognise me and didn't want to talk. You couldn't blame him; I'd been a kid last time he saw me and then only for a few minutes. He was going to pass me by, so I spoke up. 'I remember you.' That was all I said, but it stopped him. He glared at me. To be honest, he looked scary, with that one eye of his and the scar down his cheek. And then he twigged who I was and all the aggression went out of him.

'You're the boy,' he said.

'I'm the boy,' I confirmed.

He glanced about then, before speaking. 'You can't tell anyone I'm here,' he said. 'You can't tell anyone what happened. Not now, not ever.'

'You saved me,' I said. 'You and that Italian. I'll never tell a soul.' And I haven't, Nell, not until today. And I'm only telling you now because they're all dead.

After that, he relaxed, and he sat on the wharf with me and I gave him a line and we fished together, talking as we watched the lines in the river. We didn't catch much, we were too busy talking—and, as anyone will tell you, fish don't like talkers. He was the opposite of Bucky, like he was relieved to have someone who knew what he'd done; someone he could talk to about it. He told me what had happened.

After he shot Stannard, he took the body, still tied to the major's horse, and swam it across the river into New South Wales and disposed of it here, figuring the army was less likely to look on this side of the border. He didn't say where he dumped it, but I guess now he sank it in the regulator pond. Then he swam the horse back across the river and let it loose. All the blood had been washed off and he was assuming the army would think there had been some accident, that Stannard had fallen off his horse crossing a stream, like the pompous arse he was.

He told me he was set on returning to the camp, pretending nothing had happened, that Stannard had never shown. He figured he could trust the Italians. After all, he'd saved one of them. But as he was swimming the horse back, he saw the two privates from his unit, and they saw him. They'd skived off to make some money on the side, left him to guard the prisoners by himself. He'd let them go, done them a favour, but he didn't trust them. He knew there would be an inquiry into Stannard's disappearance and they had little reason to lie for him, that they'd report what they'd seen if it shifted attention from their own absence. So he went AWOL. Said it wasn't hard, and he thought that the army owed him after what he'd been through in New Guinea.

When he deserted, he didn't leave the forest. He knew the MPs would be after him, and with that one eye of his and the scars on his face he'd stand out like dog's balls. Instead, he went on the charcoal. Clever of him. He stopped wearing his eye patch, which was the most memorable thing about him, and used the glass eye the army had fitted him with instead. He didn't like it, said it itched, but it made him look more normal. And after a couple of days on the charcoal he was black as night, indistinguishable from the rest of that ratbag brigade. He called himself Alf Jones and no one questioned it. Why would they? The government needed the charcoal, so as long as he stayed there he was safe. No one knew who he was and no one cared.

When the war was over and the charcoal finished, he retreated further into the forest. He'd been there a couple of years by then and he knew his way about. He was living off the land, hoping it might all blow over, that the army would forget about him. That was when he found my little island, the place I first set up camp when I thought that the Italians might come for me in the night. He made that island his home, built a shack. Just squatted there, not bothering anyone. That's where he was living when I met him fishing that time. I'd visit him every now and then. I knew the way, of course, one of the few who did.

The other reason he stayed was a woman. Her real name was Henrietta but he called her Henry. She had a posh accent, English or something. I never knew her story, but I gather she was also running from something. Her family, something traumatic in her own past. So living there, on their hidden island, suited her as much as it suited Alf. She was quite the bohemian, liked making pottery and collecting things in the forest. They weren't properly married—I don't think they could be, because he was living under his false name and it was too risky to formalise it. 'Common law,' was how he described it.

They'd built their one-room shack and they had a daughter, Willow. A beautiful girl. When she was little, she'd run around in the nuddie, barefoot and at home in the forest. She reminded me of Bucky, how he was when I knew him that year in the forest, before it all went wrong. That worried me sometimes. I knew the world wasn't always kind to the kind-hearted, but Alf and Henry never tried to rein her in. They revelled in her, their wild child.

This was in the days before your mum was born. It was selfish of me, leaving your grandma like that, but sometimes I just needed time away. Don't think too badly of me for it. And I liked Alf, and

I liked going back to my secret island. It was a place where I'd felt safe, and I was glad he felt safe there too. He was a lovely man, gentle despite everything he'd been through. He wasn't all that much older than me, only ten years or so, but he'd seen a lot more by his early twenties than I've seen in a lifetime. He was haunted by the war, his memories. Not killing Stannard; I don't think that bothered him at all. But the Japanese. I think that troubled him, having to kill those young men so far from home. He told me about how an officer had messed up, almost got him and his mates killed, how they'd had to shoot their way out. Afterwards, he'd given this officer some lip and ended up getting disciplined for it, his promotion to lieutenant put on hold. They only approved it after he was shot, when they thought he might die.

I wasn't the only person who knew he was there. The Italians knew. Some of them came back to Australia after the war, including the man Alf saved that day Stannard tried to molest me. His name was Gino Camilleri. He grew grapes down past Echuca, later on he became very successful making wine. Sold it all over: Sydney, Melbourne, even England and America. He'd come into the woods and deliver a case or two to Alf. Gino never forgot what Alf had done, never forgot that he owed him his life. I was there one day when Gino visited. When he found out that I was the boy he'd saved, the boy who'd almost cost him his life, he hugged me and I hugged him back and we had a bit of a cry. He used to drop me a few bottles of his homemade wine as well. At first it was just home brew, but later it was the proper stuff. The River Pirate it was called, named after Alf. You should try it sometime. A bit steep nowadays, but worth it.

Then Bucky turned up on the island one day. He knew where it was, of course, from when we were kids. Alf looked horrified, went to brush him off, but Bucky saw me. 'Hi, Jimmy,' he said.

'Hi, Bucky,' I replied.

'I'm Bert now. Long time since anyone called me Bucky.'

So that was the last time I called him Bucky.

Alf was furious, thinking I'd broken my word to keep the shack secret. But Bert walked right up to Alf, took his hand, looked him in the eye and thanked him, like Alf was a saint or something.

'What the hell are you thanking me for?' said Alf, trying to get his hand back.

'I heard you killed that bastard Stannard,' said Bert. 'I needed to thank you myself.'

And Alf, he just stared at Bert for a moment, and then he stared at me, as if remembering what happened on that day. And I reckon Alf understood. He calmed right down. All he said was, 'We'd better drink some wine, then.' By the time we'd finished a bottle, the two of them were firm friends. Alf said to Bert, 'You're always welcome here.' After that, we were like a band of brothers, the three of us and Gino.

From then on, Alf was pretty well set. Gino would bring him wine and fancy food—cured hams, that sort of thing—and Bert would bring the rest. And every year, before Christmas, I'd butcher a couple of fatted lambs and drop one at the winery, one at the junkyard, and then deliver a few choice cuts out to Alf. After all, I was the one who owed them, not the other way around.

Years later—decades, I guess; after Bert was killed and Gino had died from a heart attack and Henry from cancer—when it was just me and Alf left, him and his girl Willow, we were sitting overlooking the lagoon one time. Gino's boy had dropped off some wine and we were a little drunk. More than a little. Alf and me were listening to the birds, the sunset chorus. Somehow, that day came up, the day that changed our lives. We hadn't really spoken of it much before then. I asked him where he'd buried Stannard, but he wouldn't tell me. 'Nowhere nearby,' that's all he said.

I asked him how he'd managed to keep the shack, keep the island. It was hard to find, almost impossible, but I figured if I found it, how come the forestry blokes never had, how come they hadn't tossed him off?

'Can't,' he said. 'We bought it. In Henry's name.'

'How much?' I asked.

'Four hundred pounds,' he said.

We were close enough friends by then that I thought I could ask him, so I did. I asked him where he'd got that sort of money, living off the land the way he did. He could have lied, said it was Henry's money. After all, she'd had a posh accent and I would have believed him. Instead, he told the truth. 'Bert Buchanan gave me the money.' That's what he said. 'And Bert saw to it that the purchase of the land got approved by council.'

'Bert?' I asked.

'Aye, Bert. When he sold the sawmill.'

'He just gave it to you?'

'He did.' Bert was dead by then, there'd been the inquest and all, so Alf wasn't too troubled telling me. 'You ever wonder where he got the money to set up that sawmill in the first place? A penniless kid from the forest? He stole the money, Jimmy. From the safe in Stannard's tent. He'd been in there before, knew where Stannard kept the key. When he heard he was missing, he snuck in there and stole it. And years later he passed it on to me. It was his way of thanking me for killing Stannard.'

chapter forty-one

THEY DRINK TEA, AND THEY EAT LUNCH, AND ALL THROUGH THAT DAY JIMMY Waters tells his granddaughter Nell Buchanan about his summer in the forest with Bucky, his decades on farms at its edge, and the day he witnessed the death of Major Gerard Stannard. And she feels a satisfaction, the mystery of Stannard's murder solved at last. Enthralled by the tale she doesn't interject, letting him finish. Only when his story is at an end does she broach the subject that has brought her here. She shows him the photo that Willow gave her, the four men smiling into Alf Jones's camera lens.

He nods, concentrating and sombre. 'I remember that day. Not so long before it all went belly up. Alf took it. Bert and Gino, and that's me, next to them.'

'And who's the older man, the one with the gun?'

'That's my uncle, Reg Waters. My great-uncle really—my grandfather's brother.'

'Waters?' She comes alert at the name. He's mentioned his uncle Reg several times in recounting his tales of the forest, but only his first name. Now she remembers the missing persons list: Tycho and Bert Buchanan weren't the only men who vanished in 1973—so too did Reginald Waters. 'What were you all doing together? You four and your uncle?'

But Jimmy is still gazing at the photo, a faraway look in his eye. 'They're all dead now, Nellie, all gone. I'm the only one left,' he says wistfully.

'They won't mind you telling me what you were doing then.'

He regards her, his eyes narrowing in concentration, as if coming to a decision. 'Better than that. If you drive me, I'll show you.' And he flips the photo over. 'The Stills. That's what we called it. That's what it was all about.'

Jimmy goes to find some boots and Nell walks out to her car, wondering if she should call Ivan, tell him what she's learnt. Her handset chimes, makes the decision for her. It's her partner calling.

'Where are you?' he asks. He's on speaker; it sounds like he's driving.

'With my grandfather. I've had a breakthrough. He witnessed the shooting of Gerard Stannard by Eamon Finucane. He'll make a formal statement.'

There's a moment of silence while her partner recalibrates. 'Geez, Nell, that's outstanding. Brilliant. Well done you.'

'How about you?' she asks, voice tentative.

'That's why I'm calling. Your father is sticking to his story about hitting a kangaroo and now your grandmother Rita has walked into the Tulong police station and surrendered herself to Kevin. I'm on my way to question her.'

'Rita? What's she confessing to?'

'To shooting Bert. According to Kevin, she's claiming that Bert killed Tycho. An accident. Tycho was threatening to expose his father's trade in stolen cars and they were arguing, then fighting. Somehow it got out of hand, and Bert killed him.'

Nell finds it hard to comprehend, doesn't know how to react.

Ivan fills the space for her. 'She told Kevin she tried to tell you.'

'What?'

'Some story about monsters. That Bert was a monster.'

Nell feels the earth shifting under her. 'You want me to come in?'

'You can't participate in the interview. You know that.'

'So why call me?'

'To get your opinion. Do you think it's possible?'

Nell recalls meeting Rita, the story about her family and the Nazis. Who knows? After what she'd been through, perhaps she was capable of killing her husband. 'And Gene? And Grainger?'

'Accessories after the fact. She says they helped bury Bert, collect the cars. That would explain the blood.'

'I don't know, Ivan. She has pictures of him on her wall. There's a lot of Tycho and the others, but there are plenty of Bert as well. If he was such a monster, why memorialise him like that?'

'True. But it does explain one thing—the gun.'

'What do you mean?' asks Nell.

'I'm getting this second-hand from Kevin, but she claims Bert broke down, confessed to her what had happened. Said that he'd dumped Tycho in the regulator. So after she shot Bert, she got the boys to bury him. And they threw the gun in the regulator. She says it was Gene's idea, to show Tycho he had been avenged.'

'Do you believe that?'

'I can't see any other way Bert's gun could have ended up in the regulator.'

And neither can Nell. 'So what do you want me to do?'

'I'm not sure. Maybe you can come in, monitor the interview remotely.'

She turns to see Jimmy emerge from the doorway, ready to go. She thinks of the words on the back of the photograph: *sly grogging*. Illegal alcohol. Bert Buchanan involved. Maybe that was what Tycho was threatening to expose, not the junkyard and the stolen cars, the argument that Gene overheard the day Tycho vanished. 'No, Ivan. I need to check something out. I'll review your recording when I get back.'

The silence is long and Nell can't be sure what he is thinking.

'Okay,' Ivan says eventually, and ends the call.

—

Jimmy shows her the way, upright and alert in the car's passenger seat, like a kid on an excursion. He doesn't direct her down the drive to the highway; instead, they turn towards the forest. Nell's thoughts are initially of Rita and her confession, trying to pick the story apart, but as they descend the tilt and enter the trees she returns to the present. The old man is still spry enough, still observant enough of country etiquette, to get out, hobble to the first gate and open it for her.

It's well into the afternoon now, the sun losing some of its potency. She drives through, stops, waiting for the old man to close the gate and resume his seat. And again she experiences that strange sensation, as if she's seeing this place through her mother's eyes.

She has never been on this track before, and yet it seems familiar to her. Tessa's description from the previous night still resonates. This was the way to the river, to the regulator, to Tessa's meetings with Tycho Buchanan. Nell wonders, could the light be so very different now, the forest have changed so very much?

They drive on. It's an old track, not much used nowadays. Not since the national park was declared. There's timber on the road, fallen branches. Termite mounds sprout among the trees. The country is still dry, the water not yet reaching this far from the river. And presently they reach a second gate, askew on its hinges, stuck open, the steel rusting but the redgum fence posts erect and strong. Any other time, any other place, Nell wouldn't give it a second glance. Now she eases the car to a halt. The second gate. Where Tessa waited that day when Tycho never came.

'You right?' asks Jimmy.

'Just a moment,' she says, climbing out. The light is starting to turn golden as the afternoon deepens. She looks about, half expecting to see a dried bouquet of wildflowers, wonders what she's doing. Time is pressing; she cannot linger here. She gets back into the driver's seat. 'Straight ahead?' she asks.

'For a bit. I'll show you where to turn.'

Without him, she would never have found it. For beyond the second gate, water starts to infiltrate the landscape, first in creeks and then in shallow lagoons and then spreading across fields. They've crossed some boundary, the water from the river penetrating further and further into the forest with each passing day, now the regulators are open, now the river is spilling. Jimmy points to the right. 'Through there.'

'Where?'

'Between those two trees. The bushes will give way.'

'You sure?'

'Through there.'

She inches the car forward, driving into a line of bushes, pushing through and out the other side, the foliage scraping at the windows and the doors and the underbelly of the four-wheel drive.

Past the barrier, the path is so overgrown she can barely make it out, but there's no doubt in the old man's voice. How he can be so assured, she can't say. But there is a track here, or the remnants of it, fading in and out of existence. One moment it seems clear and she's confident in her guide; the next she's driving cross-country, through grass and low scrub, through puddles and shallow waters, slaloming between trees, hitting larger and larger patches of mud and wondering if her grandfather is making it all up. They come to a low creek, water across the track. She stops the car.

'You'll get through,' says Jimmy. 'Looks worse than it is.'

She makes sure the four-wheel drive is in low range and inches forward, only to discover he's right. Even after all these years, the flow patterns of the forest remain unaltered. As they move through, she can see the creek widening to the left and to the right, as if they have passed across a natural ford, or crossed a moat, a drawbridge to a hidden land. There are more trees here, many more; she needs to circle round a copse of saplings. And still Jimmy knows the way.

They reach a clearing, grass green and long. A mob of kangaroos graze, looking up with curiosity at the interlopers. And at the centre of the clearing are huge black drums, patched with the burnt orange of rust, lying on the ground, beginning to disintegrate and melt into the earth next to poles of grey and splintering redgum. 'What are they?' she asks.

'Charcoal drums,' says Jimmy. 'From the war.' He points off into the bush. 'Down there, by the river. The black engine.'

She drives the car slowly forward. And then she sees it: a large shed, green steel, rusting now, bricks on the flat roof to guard against high winds. It looks old, many decades old. She recognises it immediately from her mother's description of the place Tycho once showed her—and from Jack Goffing's photograph, the image the undercover cop sent, the one he might have died obtaining.

'This is it,' she whispers.

'Hey?'

She gets out, looks more closely, sees the shiny new padlock, sees the camouflage netting strung between the trees, overhanging the shed's flat roof. She checks her phone. No signal. Just like Hoffner, the federal agent. She looks back to Jimmy, still in the car. An old man in his nineties. Frail, like a bird, nothing to him; an eggshell, easily broken.

She gets back in, starts the engine. 'Jimmy, we need to hide the car. If someone sees us here, it could be dangerous.'

'Nah, Nellie. They're all dead. I told you. Hasn't been used for years.'

'Yes, it has. We need to hide the car.'

Jimmy seems to catch on, made aware by her urgency. 'Only way in and out is the way we came. But keep going a little further towards the river. There was a bit of scrub down there.'

Nell starts to follow his directions, moving past some trees, then sees a better option. The water of the past few months has spawned a field of bullrushes. She can't risk driving in; even the four-wheel drive could get bogged. But just beyond the rushes, the land rises, then falls. She parks the car there, out of sight. They're safe enough for the moment. Only someone searching would find it.

'What did you do here, Grandpa? Were you making grog or smuggling it?'

'Making it. Uncle Reg ran it. Not just moonshine but counterfeit. Bundy rum, Corio whisky, Gilbey's gin. All the classy stuff. In the shed we had two stills, copper-bottomed, made from war surplus. Printed our own labels; they looked the business. We did other things down here as well. Sidelines. Trapping birds, snakes, lizards. Goannas, platypuses, echidnas. If it moved, we trapped it. Dug up plants as well. All against the law, even before the national park, but not much harm in it. That's what we thought, what we told ourselves. But sly grogging was the main thing. Took a twisted pride in it, reckoned our grog was better than the genuine article. Maybe it was; wouldn't take much.'

Nell remembers the inquest report, the allegation that Bert Buchanan had been involved in illegal activities. 'So, Bert was involved in all this too?'

'He was. The junkyard was a good cover. Bert was always ordering in parts and mailing parts out. He ran a bit of a distribution centre for Reg.'

'Jimmy, do you know what happened to them? To Bert and Tycho?'

But the old man shakes his head. 'One week they were alive and hearty, the next they'd disappeared off the face of the earth.' His demeanour is grim, his mouth a hard line. 'They found Bert, of course. Murdered. They say it was the mafia.'

She looks at him. 'We've found Tycho's body as well, not just Stannard's.'

Jimmy stares back. What is it she sees in his eyes? Horror? Fear? 'Where?' he says, voice a whisper.

'The regulator.'

'The regulator?'

He turns away, eyes hidden from her. Then he gets out of the car, walking a few steps. He looks very, very old, as if struggling to support himself, as if his very bones have grown weary. He stops by a redgum, leans against it. She gets out too, walks to him.

He shakes his head, appearing confused or disbelieving. 'The regulator? That makes no sense. Only Alf knew what happened to Stannard's body. Gino and I saw him kill Stannard then carry his body away on the horse. I told you that. But he never said what he'd done with it. I asked, but he never breathed a word. I told you.'

'Is it possible that Bert knew? That he found out somehow?'

'Bert? No. Why would Alf tell him and not Gino or me?' And now Jimmy is starting to look even more distressed. 'Why ask me that? What's Bert got to do with it?'

'Rita Buchanan has just confessed to killing her husband. She claims Bert killed Tycho and dumped his body in the regulator, so she shot him, then her other sons buried him in the forest.'

But Jimmy is shaking his head again, more vigorously this time. 'No. He never would have harmed that boy. Never in a million years.' Jimmy looks like he's really struggling now; she doesn't know whether to press harder or to let him recover.

She relents. 'Stay here with the car, Grandpa. I want to have a look at that shed. And then we need to leave.'

But Jimmy is just staring, off into the distance.

Nell takes her gun, strapping it on. And, from the back of the vehicle, she fetches her tactical vest, not worn for months, and an extra magazine of bullets for her Glock. The heft of the weapon, the solidity of the magazine in her hand, reinforces the seriousness of the situation. If the black-booted men turn up, all the martial arts in the world won't amount to a hill of beans. If they killed a federal policeman, then they wouldn't hesitate to silence her—and Jimmy. She walks around the rushes, alert for movement, for sound. There is nothing unnatural in the air: birdsong, bees, the wind in the trees, frogs in the rushes. A small group of choughs are grazing unperturbed in the clearing, their feathers black like crows but their mannerisms more like a morning tea group: fussing and clucking and pecking. They scatter, taking flight, as she walks through them to the shed.

Nell checks the padlock. She desperately wants to break in, shoot off the lock. It's not the law and search warrants that stops her; it's the fear the gunshot might be heard. Or that the extremists, upon discovering her break-in, will come after her. She circles the shed, sees a window high in one wall. There is a discarded milk urn to one side, but it's crumbling into rust, of no use. At the back of the shed she finds some forty-four-gallon drums, used for fuel by the looks. She taps at them and finds an empty one, wheels it around to the window, scrambles on top. But she has no luck: the window of dusty glass louvres is covered on the inside by a sheet of black plastic. She doesn't hesitate; bugger the warrants. She starts working at the louvres, trying to prise them open. They move a little, but not enough to reach through to the plastic. She extracts her multipurpose tool from its pouch on her belt and sets to work on trying to worry loose the clips holding one of the louvres in place.

Soon she has it. She wishes she was wearing latex gloves, but her need to know overcomes her caution. What's the old saying? Forgiveness is easier to obtain than permission? She wonders if Professional Standards would agree. Or a judge. Then, with a snap, the clip surrenders. She takes the glass, works it back and forth, eases it out. She bends, placing it carefully between her feet on the barrel. She needs it intact, wanting to replace it, to cover her tracks. Standing again, she pushes at the black plastic. It's been gaffered to the frame of the window, but the tape peels back easily enough.

She peers into the darkness of the shed, unable to pick out much detail at first, just picking up an unhealthy stench, the acrid notes of vomit, the sordid smell of shit, the odours of blood and fear. The hairs on her neck rise. She hears a muffled sound. An animal? She takes her phone, uses the torch app, shines it in. And sitting there, tied to a steel frame, mouth gagged, face damaged, eyes squinting into the light, is Noel Tankard. And surrounding him are boxes, heavy-duty cases, dark green stencilled with white lettering. She knows these boxes, has seen something like them before. Ammunition: military-grade ammunition. There are cases of guns. Two orange plastic cases, separated from the others, marked DANGER—TNT. And against the far wall, dark green cases, like thin coffins. Surface-to-air missiles or rocket-propelled grenade launchers. Or both. Her knees threaten to buckle; it's almost too much to take in. An arsenal. Enough for a small army. She has the presence of mind to take two, three, four quick flash photographs. *Here it is*, all right.

Her course of action is clear: she needs to get the car, shoot off the lock, rescue Tankard and get the hell out of here. She speaks clearly through the window to the bound man: 'It's Nell Buchanan. Two minutes. I'm getting a car. I'll be right back.'

In the gloom, all he does is squint.

She can do this, she tells herself. But as she scrambles down from the barrel, she hears what she's been dreading all along: the sound of an approaching vehicle.

chapter forty-two

NELL RUNS ACROSS THE CLEARING TOWARDS THE COVER OF THE TREES, TOWARDS Jimmy and the car. They can hide there all night, if needs be. But then she stops. No. These men are killers. They almost certainly murdered the federal agent, and they probably intend to kill Tankard too. If they see any evidence of her car, they will hunt them down, her and Jimmy. Her own grandfather. What has she done? There is enough firepower in the shed for a minor war, and who knows what they're carrying with them? Her handgun would be hopelessly inadequate, her martial arts a hollow joke. She and Jimmy will die and the truth will die with them. Does she gamble? Hope the men don't see evidence of their presence? The sun is close to setting, but there is still too much light. Surely they will see the tyre tracks of the police car, the crushed grass.

She hides among the trees on the other side of the clearing from the shed, draws her gun, checks the safety is off, that it's fully loaded. This could go one of two ways. If the men are distracted, miss the signs of her car, then most likely they will park at the shed, open the door. She could stay hidden. Or it might give her the chance to move in behind them, get the drop on them.

But no sooner does the black twin-cab ease into the clearing than it comes to a standstill. A man emerges from the passenger side, the man with the cowboy hat, instantly recognisable from the skirmish in the motel car park. He's holding a rifle with casual menace. Crouching, examining the ground. Her heart sinks; they are discovered. Cowboy speaks to the driver, then starts walking, eyes on the ground again, tracking the police car. The ute crawls forward and follows him. They pass behind the trees, heading for Jimmy. Can she get around the other way, behind cover? But what would that achieve? They'll have Jimmy, will take him hostage, force her to surrender.

So instead she breaks for the shed, sprinting across the open space. There she waits for a moment—a long moment. She wants the black ute as far from her as possible before she fires her Glock. She waits an eternity, and then another. But she can't wait too long. She wants her shot to bring them running before they reach Jimmy. She directs her gun not at the lock itself but the clasps it's threaded through. She holds it close, fires, feels the recoil, the spit of hot shards, the reverberation in the shed wall. Above, cockatoos screech as they launch themselves into the air, as if the shot hasn't been enough to announce her presence. She has a minute, maybe two at most. She yanks the door open, runs to Tankard, rips the gag from his face, the cloth from his mouth. 'They're here,' she says. Then she moves behind him, checks his bonds. Plastic ties, three or four of them around each wrist, laced through the metal frame. She gets her multipurpose tool out, slashes at the ties with its knife, gets him free. He stinks of fear and shit. She can hear the roar of the ute coming.

Tankard tries to stand, falls, ankles still bound, moaning with pain.

'Here,' she says, offering him the tool. But he can't even raise his hand to take it.

The ute. It's here. She drops the tool next to him, takes hold of her gun.

'Come out, you dumb bitch,' comes a voice, low and unhurried and full of menace. 'We have the old man.'

Shit. She peers around the edge of the door. Just the two of them then, standing a good five metres apart; their mate with the broken knee must be convalescing. The one in the cowboy hat is holding Jimmy by the scruff of the neck, as if he were a child. She sees the face of the other man for the first time: a big man with a Zapata moustache, a neck tattoo, aviator glasses—a poor man's Chopper Read. Two against one. It wouldn't be such bad odds, except Cowboy has his hunting rifle and Chopper a military-grade assault rifle. Highly illegal, highly lethal. Cowboy shoves Jimmy to the ground, dropping him like a bag of garbage. The old man swears at his own impotence.

She steps out, gun still in hand but with arms wide, the muzzle pointing limply to one side, offering little resistance. She tries to bluff them. 'The others are on their way.'

'Good,' sneers Chopper, brandishing his weapon. 'Let them come.'

Cowboy takes two steps towards her, reaches behind himself, pulls a handgun from his belt and shoots her. Just like that. No warning. She feels the bullet hit her, right in the middle of her chest, right in the centre of the tactical vest. Her breath catches; not winded, just shocked. And some small part of her brain admires the shot, the precision of it: a pistol, held in one hand, like a real cowboy, hitting her fair and square. The slightest error, and it could have taken her head.

The cowboy laughs. 'Fuck, I always wanted to do that. See if those Kevlar jobs are up to scratch.'

But Chopper isn't laughing. 'Are you fucking insane? You know what's in there?'

Of course. TNT. Ammunition. An advantage?

She steps back into the shadow of the doorway and fires a shot in the air, shifting back and forth as she retreats, clouding the possibility of the cowboy reeling off a more deadly shot.

But they aren't stupid: they don't need to shoot her; they don't need to fire towards the shed. 'Drop the gun, Detective, or the old fuck gets it in the head.'

Checkmate. If she walks out, they'll kill them both. But if she retreats to the shed, they'll simply kill Jimmy and then come for her.

'Go,' hisses a low voice behind her. She steals a look. It's Tankard, looking like a soiled rag doll in the gloom. He's holding his own SLR, liberated from one of the boxes. She has no idea whether he's threatening to shoot her or rescue her. But only one course of action might save Jimmy. She throws her pistol ahead of her then walks out of the shed, arms raised. Cowboy has his pistol on her, his rifle in his other hand, pointing down at Jimmy.

'Move towards me,' says the Chopper impersonator, the big man, the boss. 'Away from the shed.'

She complies. Advancing as slowly as possible, trying to stretch time.

And then it all happens at once. She sees Jimmy frown, tilt his head. The big man takes a step forward: he must have seen the same movement. Tankard.

Jimmy makes a grab for Cowboy's rifle, taking the barrel with both hands like he's grabbing life itself, distracting the gunman.

'Down!' says a voice behind Nell.

And as she drops to the ground, she sees the shock on Cowboy's face and the momentary indecision on that of Chopper, whether to fire into the shed or not. And then it's too late. Tankard's gun brays, a short spray, deafening in its judgement, shredding the big man, aviator specs tumbling as he falls. But at the same moment, the cowboy, still wrestling for control of his rifle with one hand, fires his pistol with the other, the bullet slapping into Tankard.

Tankard swivels, but too late. The cowboy has dropped his pistol, using his freed hand to haul Jimmy erect. Now he uses him as a shield.

The stalemate holds for an instant, then Jimmy, summoning some vestige of strength, pulls the rifle free, falls away, exposing his now unarmed assailant. The cowboy raises his hands. A red stain is spreading across Tankard's stomach, but he keeps his gun directed at the cowboy as he limps forward, eyes full of loathing.

'No!' yells Nell, up and running towards the cowboy, getting into the line of fire. She scoops up the handgun and throws it clear, takes the rifle from Jimmy and does the same.

Tankard is still shuffling forward, dripping, the assault rifle trained on his now defenceless adversary. 'Get out of the road,' he spits, voice dripping menace.

'Don't do it,' yells Nell, walking slowly towards Tankard.

'The cunt shot me!' says Tankard.

'Please!' begs Nell.

'I saved your life,' he says, as if this gives him the right to take the cowboy's.

'And I saved yours,' says Nell.

A sound seizes her attention, makes her turn, in time to see the cowboy fall, Jimmy standing over him, holding the rifle barrel, stock forward. He's clobbered the man, knocked him out. Argument ended.

The fight goes out of Tankard, like a fire doused with water. He lowers the gun and eases himself inelegantly to the ground. She moves to him. She pulls off her shirt, compresses the wound, tells Jimmy to take over.

Then she's back with the cowboy. He's lying face down. His hat lies beside him. He's bald, the back of his head bearing a swastika tattoo and the beginnings of a bruise. She checks his pulse, relieved to detect it. She finds his handgun, gives it to Jimmy, takes the rifle in exchange. 'Stand guard. There's a first aid kit in the car,' she instructs her grandfather. 'Don't let them kill each other.' Tankard is still clutching the automatic rifle with one hand and doesn't look keen to surrender it.

So she runs. Never has she run so hard, through the trees, around the bullrushes, into the driver's seat. She guns the engine, speeds back to the clearing, and is relieved to find little changed. The cowboy is still unconscious. Jimmy is still tending to Tankard. The pub owner is still conscious but seems hazy. His shirt is now soaked through with blood despite the old man's best efforts.

'Can't stop the bleeding,' says Jimmy.

Nell does what she can. She cuts away the publican's shirt, can see that the bullet has passed straight through him, hitting his liver and who knows what else. No major arteries, but the hole is too big to close. She wipes the entry and exit wounds with alcohol, packs them with gauze, dresses them with self-adhesive bandages. She takes some compression strapping—designed for ankle sprains and snake bites—and wraps it around his girth. Still the blood finds a way of seeping through.

She leaves him with Jimmy, the old man looking grim.

She stalks to the cowboy, cuffs his hands behind his back, then kicks him. 'Get up,' she orders.

But he remains unconscious. Or fakes it. She doesn't have time to muck about: Tankard is fading. She gets down, links her prisoner's ankles together with plastic ties. Then she runs back to the car, reverses it quickly until it sits idling alongside one of the fallen charcoal burners. Out of the car again, she releases the winch line, threading the hook through the ankle ties. 'Last chance,' she says to the cowboy. 'This will hurt.'

She gets no reply.

Back at the car, she starts the winch, reeling him in like a tuna. Halfway in he wakes, starts yelling. She takes no notice, keeps winding.

'What the fuck?' screams the cowboy.

She doesn't respond. She unbuckles the winch, sits him up and fastens his arms: not to the crumbling steel of the charcoal kettle but to its wooden uprights. Redgum. Doesn't rot. Practically everlasting.

—

Driving back towards Jimmy's house, she picks up phone reception just past the second gate. Tankard is sprawled across the back seat, drifting in and out of consciousness, Jimmy nursing his head on his lap. She keeps driving another minute, then another, until she's confident of her two-bar signal, before calling triple zero, instructing an ambulance to meet her at the farmhouse.

Noel Tankard is unconscious by the time they reach it. She cares for him as Jimmy hustles as fast as he can into the house, searching for bandages and anything else that might help. Blood continues to ooze through the dressing.

Jimmy returns to the car with clean face washers and tea towels. She holds them against Tankard, trying to keep the pressure on, to delay the encroaching crisis. The man needs surgery and he needs fluids. And yet he squirms under her ministrations. She takes it as a good sign. She continues to kneel there, awkwardly applying pressure, hearing the approaching siren, hope starting to rise. Jimmy is standing outside, waving the ambulance in like an airport worker guiding a jumbo into a gate.

And then the paramedics are there, the same two from the night at the motel. They recognise her but say nothing. Their task is clear and they set about it with practised calm and ingrained assuredness.

Only then does she ring Ivan.

'Nell, where have you been?'

'I need backup—armed officers,' she says, still breathing hard. 'Tell Jack Goffing I found his shed.'

Two hours later, the sky is dark, the stars a spray of light across the sky. Tankard is in hospital in Echuca, undergoing surgery; the cowboy—real name Floyd Pohls—is in custody. A helicopter has come through, flying low, buzzing the rooftop of the farm, bringing a squad of federal police, armed to the teeth and encased in body armour. Nell is in the kitchen at Jimmy's farmhouse. The old man himself is in bed, utterly spent; Nell's brother Greg has come from Boonlea to help get him fed and bathed.

Nell is sitting at the kitchen table, face and arms washed, wearing a sweatshirt Jimmy has given her. She's drinking a second cup of tea, feeling somehow calm, as if the world has slowed enough for her to catch up. Ivan is on the other side of the table, listening intently as she recounts what she has found, what she's been through. The first cup of tea covered the shed and the armaments and the extremists. Now, with the second, they've returned to her own investigation.

'So Finucane shot Stannard to save Gino Camilleri,' Ivan summarises.

'Yes. My grandfather was there. He saw it all.'

'What about Bert and Tycho Buchanan?'

'Says he doesn't know.'

'I might have to charge Rita Buchanan,' says Ivan. 'I was almost finished interviewing her when your call came through.'

'You're convinced?'

'Not really.'

'Is she in the lock-up?'

'There's no one to watch her. I sent her home.'

Nell stares at Ivan, wondering at this place they find themselves.

They're interrupted by a voice from the doorway. 'She's just protecting her boys.' It's Jimmy Waters, an old man in pyjamas.

'Gramps? Are you okay?'

'No, I'm not. Couldn't sleep.' He sighs. 'It's time you knew the truth.'

chapter forty-three

TYCHO BUCHANAN'S FUNERAL IS A SAD AFFAIR, HELD IN TULONG'S ANGLICAN church five days after Rita Buchanan's confession and the shootout at the Stills. The weather seems disinterested, unable to conjure much warmth even this late in the spring, the cloud cover enough to obscure the sun without offering rain, the day neither hot nor cold, the wind neither strong nor absent. It's as if Tycho died too long ago for it to care. The church on Highgate Street is musty, tinted by a lack of use. The minister travelled down from Hatheson early to air it and some volunteers have dusted the pews, so that now motes hang in the air, floating and expectant. The floral tributes seem too gaudy for the faded interior. To Nell, it seems too little, too late, the mourners too few and too old, emotions eroded by time.

Perhaps it's the coffin, polished and glistening and new, on its pedestal by the stage. It seems overly large, knowing as she does that it contains bones and nothing more. Tycho Buchanan's skeleton could be placed in a casket the size of an esky. She can visualise them, those bones that lay in the mud for so long, the skull she held in her hands, with its chipped front tooth, recalling how she looked into those empty sockets and imagined they looked back at her. But anything smaller than a full-sized coffin would be worse. For Tycho was a full-sized man, living life large; to Nell he is no longer a family ghost, no longer mentioned in whispered asides. She feels a connection to him, this man who died so long ago, who died so young, on the cusp of so much. Her grandfather. The unfairness of it lingers: all that promise unfulfilled, the young man on his way to Albury, to Melbourne—who knows?—maybe to London and New York. They will never know and that is the tragedy of it. And so she finds herself grieving for this man she never met.

He must have had many friends. He was popular, charismatic, but there are none here now. They have drifted away, carried on the tide of years, and only his family is present, united and divided in their grief. To the left of the aisle, Rita and her two surviving sons, Gene and Grainger, sit in the front pew. Rita looks frail, the men sombre and stiff. Across the aisle sit Willow Finucane and Tessa Buchanan, side by side: Tycho Buchanan's lovers, his teenage widows grown old, united in sorrow. Tessa is wearing widow blacks, Willow a tan linen suit. It makes Nell wonder, seeing the two women together like this. Some small consolation. As she watches, she sees her mother's shoulders shake and Willow taking her hand in comfort. Fifty years on and the grief lives, no matter what the weather may think. Nell wishes her parents were together, not on either side of the aisle like this, but understands their divergent needs and responsibilities. She wishes she could be at the front with them, but that isn't possible either.

Behind Rita and her surviving sons sit Molly and her husband Gary, their teenagers even now scanning their smartphones. Behind them her brother Simon sits alone, his wife absent. Across the aisle, Greg is in the second row with his partner, a slim man respectful in his kilt, silent behind Tessa and Willow. A couple more pews back sit Nell's other sister, Gail, and her husband, their own children excused. There is little talking, just the occasional whispered greeting, Molly trying to engage her children.

Nell looks again at the coffin, tries to imagine what Tycho might think of this. Maybe he would be touched by the grief; maybe he would be concerned about the unexpressed tension.

Next to her, Ivan reaches across, hand soft on her shoulder, just for a moment, letting her know he is here for her. She is grateful for it, grateful for him, his understated support. She has felt much closer to him these past few days, her emotions surfacing unpredictably, leaving her exposed and vulnerable and raw. She's not been able to see her family, at Ivan's insistence, but also her own. She can't risk the case the two of them are building. So she and Ivan sit in the back pew, distanced. Only Jimmy Waters sits with them, still unable to force himself upon his family. He looks diminished, too small for his mothball-impregnated suit, a shaving plaster on his turkey neck, his mop of fine white hair refusing to sit flat.

The priest is professionally sympathetic, reading the room, realising this is no pro forma ceremony, that there are live emotions for a man so long dead. Then it falls to Grainger to deliver the eulogy. He makes no mention of how Tycho died or the circumstances surrounding his death. There is no theorising about who killed him, no reference to any argument with Bert Buchanan, no acknowledgement of Rita's confession. Instead, he gives a quiet speech of dignity and compassion, recalling the Tycho he admired and loved, just as his brother was admired and loved by all who knew him. He does emphasise how he was adored by their father, Bert Buchanan. And in this moment, Nell feels enormous pride in her own father. The investigation has separated them for now, but she hopes he sees her teary smile as he descends from the pulpit to rejoin his mother and brother.

Tycho is buried in the cemetery, a few blocks inland from the highway. That is how Nell has come to think of it: inland. As if the forest is the ocean and Tulong a harbour town and the plains the solid and unmoveable continent. Tycho has come back, a sailor lost at sea, found at last and laid in the ground.

Rita had wanted to have the reception in her home, the palace built for her by Bert Buchanan, to fill it with her family one last time. But it didn't seem right, not with her confession public knowledge and yet to be retracted. Ivan hasn't charged her after all, not even arrested her, but she remains a person of interest, under active investigation. Instead, the reception is held in Clarrie Buchanan Park, down by the creek, inside the Tulong Memorial Hall, near where Nell has exercised most mornings. The cookers' camp has greatly diminished, a series of armed raids sending shockwaves of reality through it. At first, some had thought it was the police state, come to get them at last, but as word filtered out about what had been found in the forest, that the extremists had shot the sympathetic publican, a schism had formed. Some saw the errors of their ways, or at least wanted to distance themselves, and had left. So it's only a few stragglers who remain to witness the mourners.

The hall seems a good choice to Nell: a venue for dances and town meetings and fetes and deb balls and scout groups. Grainger and Gene had suggested it, and Willow and Tessa had agreed. A trestle table has been set up by the stage, supporting a battered urn, cups and saucers from the CWA, white bread sandwiches of ham and gherkin, of curried eggs, of processed chicken and mayonnaise, their crusts cut off.

Family members circle each other, hobbled by politeness and restraint, not wanting to mention the subject on everyone's mind: the police still investigating, down in the forest, digging and searching. Word has spread, as it must in such a town, that the forensics people, in their white plastic suits and operating their complex machines, have moved on, away from the regulator pool, re-establishing themselves many kilometres south, not far from the river; not far, so they say, from Jimmy Waters's house. Furtive eyes keep sliding across to Nell, but each time she tries to meet them, they look away again. She is here by rights—Tycho Buchanan's granddaughter, no less. She's even wearing a dress for the first time in months, but that's fooling no one: they see her as a police officer first and a relative second. She has discussed it with Ivan; they will stay just long enough to register her presence and her respect, then leave. Only Willow makes the effort to hold her gaze, to offer a reassuring smile, while Tessa gives her a forlorn look. And then Grainger comes across to her. She can feel Ivan slipping away, giving her space.

'Lovely speech, Dad,' she says.

'Thanks. How's your mother?'

Grainger has been staying with Rita, lending support to his own mother. 'I'm not sure. Good, I think. Molly is staying at the house with the kids. Filling the place up, keeping her busy. How's Grandma?'

'Stoic.'

'As always.'

'When this is all over, Nell—the investigation, trials—whatever happens, you will come back, won't you? To visit?' He swallows, looks around. 'You won't disown us?'

'Of course not.' And then she adds, almost as an afterthought, 'Dad.'

That elicits a smile from him, a small relief. And she realises it's true: whatever her biological origins, whatever the DNA may insist, Grainger and Tessa remain her real parents.

'Well, see you soon,' says her father, stealing a glance at Ivan, hovering by the sponge cake.

'Yes, see you,' says Nell.

She looks around, spots Jimmy on his own. He's standing over by the windows, studying the honour rolls, one for the First World War, one for the second, wood-panelled and yellow-varnished, gold-leaf lettering, carved scrolls along the top. Nell walks across to him.

'There they are, Nell. No funerals for them.' He's pointing to the roll for World War I. The four Waters brothers are listed together: Clarence and Walter, James and Reginald. Clarence and Walter have asterisks next to their names, small and almost apologetic. Her eyes drift to the bottom of the board, to another asterisk: *Killed in Action*.

'James. Your grandfather?'

'That's him. Made it back, but made it back damaged. Reg was the only one who got out of it in one piece.'

They regard the names in silence. Then Jimmy points a little higher on the board. 'Can you see? There he is. The bastard.'

Her eyes run up the names until she sees it: *Gerard Stannard*. So he was there as well, the first war, caught in the mincing machine of history.

Jimmy shuffles across to the companion board, the roll for World War II. Stannard is listed again. And so is Jimmy's father, another James, another asterisk. Standing next to her, the old man is staring, inscrutable. Nell places a hand on his shoulder. He raises his own, holds hers for a moment. His fingers are bony, his skin dry.

'I went to Bert's funeral,' he says. 'Held there, in that same church. The place was full. Rita crying a flood of tears. The cricket team, the footy club, the council. Rotary. Everyone was there. People forced to stand outside.'

Nell nods, understanding.

'Has she recanted her confession?' asks Jimmy.

'No.'

'Understandable,' says Jimmy. 'But Bert loved those boys, all of them. He was so proud of them. He'd never been to school a day in his life and yet he kept telling us, Alf and Gino and me, how Gene and Grainger were going to study at university, how Tycho was going to become a big city reporter.'

'That's what Mum says too,' says Nell.

They're still standing there, offering up their thoughts to the dead, when Kevin comes in, holding his broad-brimmed hat before him, awkward with respect. He looks at Ivan, nods at him and then at her, and walks out again.

Ivan follows him outside. Nell excuses herself from Jimmy and does the same.

'They've located a body,' says Kevin.

'At the Stills?' asks Nell, already knowing the answer.

'Yes. They're starting the exhumation.'

Jimmy has followed them out. 'News?'

'They've found him,' says Ivan.

'We're going out there,' Nell says, then looks to Ivan, eyes asking the question for her. He tilts his head in consent. 'You want to come?' she asks Jimmy, her tone gentle.

The old man nods. 'I guess I should see it through.'

--

Ivan drives, Nell beside him, the old man in the back seat. They take the most direct route to the Stills, south along the highway, ten kilometres, towards Jimmy's lonely farmhouse. They turn off the highway, take the driveway past the home of weatherboard and iron. She wonders at that, all those years he lived here by himself, ever since his daughter left, ever since his wife died. It's as if the accumulated sadness and loneliness of the years rests upon it. They keep moving, winding down the tilt. Nell does the honours, opening and then closing the first gate as they move into the forest. They pass the second gate, a relic now. Further on, the water starts. It's been creeping a little higher every day, a little further inland, months after the regulators were first opened and the river began to spill. They reach the once obscure turn-off onto the almost forgotten track. Now it's churned with mud, the bushes chain-sawed away, the route made obvious by the passage of police vehicles. They're driving through the water now, Ivan concentrating on getting across safely. In the back, Jimmy looks out the side window, emotionless.

The day is growing warmer, as if, funeral over, some mighty cog has re-engaged. Ivan prods at the dashboard, summoning air conditioning.

They arrive at the crime scene. The trucks, the cars, the tents, the activity—it's as if a carnival has arrived, parked outside town, preparing to erect the big top. But there will be no show; the drama here unfolded half a century ago. Over past the forensics tent she can see the shed, the hovering presence of the federal police, a Black Hawk helicopter dominating the clearing.

Blake is waiting for them, he and Carole.

'Round the back of the shed. Where you said,' he says to Nell and Ivan by way of greeting.

'Any doubt that it's him?'

'None. It's Reg Waters all right.'

chapter forty-four

JAMES WATERS—SECOND STATEMENT

IT'S TIME FOR THE TRUTH. PAST TIME. I'M OLD, CAN'T HAVE MUCH LONGER. Maybe this is why the Almighty has kept me going all these years: to give me the chance to set things straight once and for all. I'm sorry for Rita and I'm sorry for the boys, but the truth needs to be told. People need to know that it was my fault. All of it.

I always looked up to my Uncle Reg. He was always helping us on the farm, Mum and me and my sister. He'd drop in regular, giving us a bit of tea, some sugar—stuff that was hard to get. Even some chocolates for my mum's birthday. And he gave us advice too. What crops to put in, which labourers to hire, what equipment we needed. Mum would say she didn't know how we'd get by without Uncle Reg.

But Reg was a crook.

It goes back to the day that Stannard tried to molest me, the day that Gino and Alf—Eamon as he was then—saved me, the day Alf shot Stannard. There were meant to be two other soldiers there guarding the Italians with Alf, two privates called Tankard and Louth. They told the inquiry they were away from the camp scouting out a new location for the prisoners to work. Alf had deserted by then, so he wasn't there to contradict them, but the truth was that they were working for Reg, black marketeering, fetching brandy for the officers' mess.

You see, that was what Reg was up to. That was his game. The black market. That's where the sugar and the tea and licorice were coming from. It started in the first war, as far as I can make out. Reg was wounded, but he was the only one of the four brothers to get home in one piece. I reckon that the way he saw it, the army owed him, so he started to take what he could, sell what he could. By the time the second war came around, he was well set.

During the war, he flourished, but it was afterwards that he really came into his own. There was still rationing, ripe for exploitation. It lasted for years, right up until the start of the fifties. I don't know why. Seemed to last longer than the war itself. That's when Reg set up the Stills down in the forest. Well hidden. Perfect. The war finished, but he kept going. And he recruited us. I needed the money, of course. The farm Lotte and I had bought from her parents was always marginal, just like my parents' place. No matter how hard I worked it, the debt always seemed that little bit too big. I could never put a proper dent in it. So when Reg offered work, I was glad to take it. I'd spend my weekends at the

Stills. I never told my wife, I never told Tessa. Told them I was playing golf.

Bert was in on it, so was Alf, and Reg was paying Gino to source bottles through the winery. We all liked Reg, thought he was doing us a favour. What we didn't know was that he was in cahoots with Tankard. I don't know what happened to Louth, but Keith Tankard became a policeman, and I reckon that the whole time he was a copper, he never stopped working for Reg. Crooked as a dog's hind leg. He spotted Alf in Tulong one time and recognised him straight away. Wouldn't be hard, not with that eye patch and all. Didn't arrest him, though; just told Reg that he'd seen Alf swim Stannard across the river and dump his body in the regulator. Reg never said anything, not at first, but kept the knowledge in his back pocket as insurance. He had Alf exactly where he wanted him, even if Alf didn't know it.

Meanwhile, Bert had set up a little sawmill, just down the tilt from Tulong, and was making a real go of it. But Tankard, he was a smart man, cunning and conniving and able to smell out fast money, while Reg knew all about finance and mortgages and bank loans. The two of them worked out there was no way Bert, an orphan, still a teenager when he started, could have legally accessed the capital for the sawmill. Tankard deduced it was Bert who had stolen the money from the unit's safe after Alf killed Stannard. He threatened him with arrest unless he sold the mill to a mystery buyer, a big city investor. So Bert was forced to sell at a bargain basement price, even though it was probably worth two or three times what he got for it.

People say all sorts of things about Bert, how the wrecking yard was a front, that he was a crim. What would they know? He'd done his best to set up a legitimate business and been swindled out of it.

But we thought it was Tankard who was the crook, the one we needed to worry about. We thought Reg was on our side. He was a real charmer, one of those blokes everyone likes. He always had a smile on his face and a song on his lips. He had a terrific singing voice, I'll give him that, and he could play the swanee whistle. He'd put on a show when we were doing quality control on the moonshine. And he did pay us well. We were happy enough, the four of us—you saw the photo. Bert got himself on the council, gave Alf some of the sawmill money to buy the island. So by the early seventies, we thought it was sweet. And in some ways it was. Until I brought the whole thing crashing down.

The thing was, even working at the Stills, making that extra money, slaving my guts out on the farm, neglecting Lotte and Tessa, I was still struggling to stay afloat. Gino was becoming a big success, preparing to launch his new wine. Bert had finished Rita's house and had started talking of how he was going to support the boys studying in Sydney or Melbourne. I didn't say anything, but I felt a failure. We didn't even have a proper car, just the farm truck. I wished I had more money for Lotte; her health wasn't good. And Tessa—what if she wanted to go to the city, looking for work or even to study? How could I support her? She was every bit as smart as Gene or Grainger. I thought it was because the farm wasn't big enough. No economies of scale—that's what Gino said—or because I was a lousy farmer. And a lousy father and husband too, because it would get to me, the fact that we weren't doing better. I could be surly, bad-tempered. It drove a wedge between Lotte and me.

Then Gino and Bert figured it out. They were good at business, knew how to read bank statements and work out interest payments. Bert, who had never been to school a day in his life. We were at the Stills, sampling the merchandise—this was in 1973—and I started complaining about how I could never clear my debts. They looked at my papers, the ones from the bank. Bert had been on the council, knew people, could source the deeds and other information. What they found, I couldn't believe. I was glad my mother was dead. It would have broken her.

It was Reg who bought my parents' farm, you see—a distressed sale. While the war was still going and money was short and Dad was only just dead. Reg had a friend in the bank and got it on the cheap. Robbed my mother blind. My father's own uncle, my own flesh and blood. And he didn't help me get my farm. Just the opposite. He held a second mortgage over it, a secret mortgage. I'd trusted him, signed the papers without knowing what I was signing. That's why I could never get out from under: he was bleeding me dry. I was paying the bank, but half of it was going to service that bastard's loan before it serviced mine. And if it folded, if I went under, he'd have first option to buy. Reg. Jolly old Reg with the smile and the song and the swanee whistle. He was a deadset cunt.

That's when Bert and Gino went back through the records for the sawmill and established that it was Reg who had bought it, with Tankard as a minority shareholder. Alf wanted to kill him. Make it look like an accident. Or just shoot him. But Reg had his tentacles everywhere and he got wind of the sawmill inquiries. He sent Keith Tankard to warn us off, one by one. Tankard turned up at the farm with a couple of constables, bruisers toting shotguns. He said I'd lose the farm, that Reg would foreclose, that Alf would be arrested for the murder of Stannard, that Bert would go to prison for dealing in stolen cars. He would ruin each and every one of us. Never once did he mention Reg by name, but I wasn't stupid. What were we to do? He was a copper, with other coppers backing him up. I couldn't see a way out.

And then I went and ruined everything. Because of Tycho Buchanan.

He was starting to sniff around my girl, my Tessa. Everyone says what a saint he was, what a loss. And it's true, he was a beautiful boy. But he was almost twenty years old, for God's sake, a grown man, and she was fifteen. Just a girl. Sneaking out to see him, thought we didn't know, but how could you miss something like that? Her wandering around with her feet off the ground, like she was set to float out the window. No doubt she thought herself in love with him. I don't blame her for it. But him? No. I know for a fact he was working his charms on Alf's girl at the same time. Willow was her name. Lived out on the island with Alf. Smart girl, knew things. I reckon she was the one who first told Tycho about the Stills. So he came to me, all puffed up with his own importance, telling me how he was going to make the big time, go to Melbourne, become a star reporter. Wearing a fancy suit he was, a lairy shirt, telling me—me, who could barely rub two shillings together—how he was going to become a big shot.

And then he started asking about the Stills, saying he'd heard rumours about a sly grog operation being run deep in the woods, not so very far from my place. He reckoned if he could break the story, it would help him with his plan to move on to a bigger paper. I kept mum, of course. Didn't want to incriminate myself or the others. But then he had the hide to ask me if he could see my daughter, my beautiful young girl. Asking my blessing, saying that he wanted to take her with him to Melbourne. I wouldn't have minded if she was a bit older. He was a fine-looking fellow and all, and he spoke to me with respect. But it didn't matter how much I liked Bert, I knew my duty as a father. I told Tycho in no uncertain terms to stay away from her. I mentioned it to Bert, as well, asked him to rein his son in.

And then I had this brainwave. I reckoned I was a genius, but I was dumb as a doorknob. I thought I could kill two birds with one stone: get rid of Reg and get rid of Tycho. I told Tycho everything I knew about my uncle, every little bit of dirt I had on him, enough for Reg to go to prison for a long time. Tycho swore he'd protect me, that he'd never reveal his source of information, said that was a journo thing. So I told him about Tankard as well. I kept Alf and Gino and Bert out of it, of course. Tycho said with a story like that, he could get a job in Albury. Said he had wind of an even bigger story, one that would take him to Melbourne, but that Albury would be the first rung on his ladder. And that's what I wanted: Reg in prison, Tankard off our backs, Tycho in Albury and Tessa safe at home with us. She was almost sixteen, just a few months off. 'Give it another year or so,' I told Tycho, and if they still wanted to be together after that, I would give them my blessing. That's the deal I cut with him. I reckoned if it helped get him to Melbourne that would be the last we'd see of him; he'd lose interest in Tessa soon enough. Those Melbourne girls would be all over him like a rash.

So there I was, thinking myself so clever. Then Tycho went missing. I got a call from Bert and he was beside himself. He said Tycho had been going to expose the whole show, that he knew about the Stills, that something must have gone wrong. And then, a day or two later, I got the call from Rita. Bert had disappeared as well. I went out looking for him. I was worried sick, beside myself. I knew it was bad, I knew it was my fault. I went down to the Stills, thinking he might be there. I didn't take the truck. Took a horse instead, went cross-country, didn't use the track or the ford, crossed the creek further down, closer to the river. When I was close, I tied the horse to a tree and crept in through the scrub. I was almost there when I heard the gunshots. Two of them. Now, I was never a brave bloke, not like Alf or Bert, but I couldn't turn my back on this. I was scared, but I needed to know. I had this terrible feeling that I had done something beyond redemption. And so I crept closer.

I saw the two boys, Gene and Grainger, standing above a man on the ground. It was Reg—I could see that clear enough—and he was dead. Just teenagers they were, but they killed him all right. They were standing there, as if they couldn't believe what they'd done. Grainger rooted to the spot, Gene still holding the gun.

It took a long while before they moved, but when they did, they didn't hesitate. They dragged him round the back of the shed. Then I saw Grainger find a shovel. I reckon they buried Reg. I can show you where. His body should still be there. The rest of him will be in hell.

I crept back out, returned home, and I said nothing. I was trying to work it out. It didn't take much. I'd seen three cars down there at the Stills. Reg's truck, the jeep the boys must have been driving, and that flash blue car of Tycho's. Reg fucking Waters had killed Tycho Buchanan, and when Bert confronted him, he'd killed Bert as well. Just like that. As if the world still owed Reg Waters, as if he could act with impunity, that he could defile other people's families like the army had defiled his. But it was bullshit. He'd had a family: Dad and Mum and me and my sister and all he'd done was rob us blind. And now I'd cost Bert and his boy their lives.

Tankard ran the investigation. He must have worked out pretty quickly that Tycho, Bert and Reg were dead. He suspected us, of course; I'd told Alf and Gino what I'd seen. In retrospect, I reckon Tankard was a little scared: if we killed Reg, then we might kill him as well. And if he arrested us, he knew he was risking exposure. So he shut down the Stills and he threatened us, said that we should all shut up, safeguard each other. He called it mutually assured destruction: if we told anyone about him and Reg, then he would expose us. We'd all go down together. So when Bert's body was found, when Tankard told the inquest he believed Tycho had killed his father and fled, we kept our mouths shut. But it wasn't just to protect ourselves. It was to protect the boys, Gene and Grainger. So we let it drift.

Even now, I can't believe how calculating Reg was. I reckon he must have killed Tycho at the Stills, but then driven his body all the way to the regulator and dumped it there. Tankard had told him that was where Alf had disposed of Stannard's body. You understand? That way, if Tycho's body was ever found, they could point the finger at Alf, expose him as the deserter

Eamon Finucane and say he had killed Tycho as well, that Tycho was doing a story about Stannard's murder. Oh, Reg was cunning all right. But for all of that, he underestimated the Buchanans, how close they were. How a couple of lads like Grainger and Gene, polite boys who played classical music and couldn't punch their way out of a wet paper bag, would stand up to him, seek their own justice rather than relying on the police. And I was glad they did it. I created the mess, but they cleaned it up. I only wished I'd had half their guts. I never told them I saw them there at the Stills. Alf and Gino and myself, we were the only ones who knew.

And Grainger, what he did was beyond decent. It was selfless. Honourable. Tessa was desperate to keep Tycho's baby, but there was pressure on her to give it up, right from the word go. There were plenty of people telling Lotte and me that would be for the best. And then Grainger stepped in, married her. It wasn't because I was holding the death of Reg over him; he never knew that I'd seen them that day at the Stills. I was never going to dob on those boys anyway, but after he married Tessa, I would have died first. So when the fishermen found Bert's body, when they held the inquest, I didn't breathe a word. Alf and Gino felt the same; we let Tankard spin his bulldust.

But now it's time for the truth. Tessa. She rings me every week, her trapped in her house, me all alone up here. God knows why she bothers with me, considering what a lousy father I was. She invites me to family gatherings as well. Christmas and the like. But I find it hard to go, find it hard to look them all in the eye after everything I did. Yet it hasn't been good for her, not for a long time. She's got Grainger and she's got you kids, but you're all grown up now, you've all left home. She needs to know what happened. She needs to be free of it; she needs to live her life.

I can see why Rita has confessed. I'm guessing she knows what really happened. The boys must have told her what they did, how they avenged their brother and their father, and she's determined to protect them. But I can't let her do that to Bert. Smear him like that, this story that he killed Tycho. I know he's long dead and he's beyond all that now and she's taking half the blame onto herself, but I can't let her do that to Bert. It's not right.

You have to understand what he went through. Not so long after Stannard did what he did, Bucky's dad died and he was orphaned. He had nothing, not even a pair of shoes. No family, no inheritance, no education. He could have curled up and died. Turned in on himself. Plenty would have. Or worse: he could have turned into another Reg Waters, out for himself and the devil take the hindmost. Instead, he pushed back, built a life. Saw Rita, saw she was the same, took her in, protected her.

People can say what they like about Bert. Yes, he was running a shady business, but what other choice did he have, after those bastards forced him out of the sawmill? He loved those boys. They made his life worth living. So call him a criminal, but he was never a killer. And he never hurt a soul, never hurt people the way Stannard did, never exploited people the way Reg did, never stood over people the way Keith Tankard did. Never messed up the way I messed up. Because for me, he will always be Bucky, that boy in the forest, tickling trout and chasing rabbits and riding the flying fox down into the lagoon. He was my friend and I will always remember him how he was, with his cheeky smile and mischief in his eyes. He was my friend and I'm not going to let him carry the blame for my sins.

chapter forty-five

GENE BUCHANAN STARES INTO SPACE. JAMES WATERS'S SWORN STATEMENT sits on the table before him: printed, signed, tangible. Next to it are spread photographs of Reg Waters's grave. The bullets are there too, cleaned up and in a zip-lock evidence bag.

'Yes,' Gene whispers. 'I shot him.' He looks up at Ivan, looks at the phone propped up and pointing at him, perhaps realising that Nell is watching from the squad room. 'I killed him. I don't regret it.'

'Thank you,' says Ivan. 'That will make it easier for everyone.'

'I will plead guilty,' says Gene.

'That is your choice. But first, we need you to tell us what happened. What led you to kill Reginald Waters.'

Gene lowers his head into his hands, as if he is about to cry, but when he lifts it again his eyes are dry and defiant. 'There was an old car. A wreck, a Studebaker. It sat in the junkyard. It was my bolthole. It was where I went to be alone. I was in there that day when Tycho visited. That last day, when he and Dad argued. I was lying in the back seat, reading a book, so they didn't see me, didn't know I was there. I heard them coming towards me, talking as they came.

'I told the inquest they were fighting, but that's an exaggeration. And it was only at the end they argued. Before that, it was like they were strategising. Dad was pleading with Tycho to be careful, that he had to make sure he had indisputable proof. He seemed to be talking about the old sawmill, but Tycho was talking about the present. He wanted to do a story about something happening down in the forest, said that he knew all about it, but Dad was saying if he went off half-cocked it would ruin the family. That it could jeopardise the chances of Grainger and me going to uni. But Tycho sounded impatient, saying he was only going to write about Reg Waters and the Stills and nothing else. That was the first time I heard those names. Dad wasn't convinced, I could tell. He told Tycho to steer clear of the cops in Hatheson, of Keith Tankard in particular. That was another new name, but I remembered it. Tankard.

'Dad was stressed out, I could tell, and there was kind of an impasse. A silence. I thought maybe they'd realised I was there, but no, they were just consumed by their own thoughts. Then Dad changed the subject. He said Tycho should stay away from Tessa Waters, that she was too young and her dad was worried about her. And I remember Tycho saying that it had turned serious. That was when Dad got angry, said Tycho would ruin all of us, that he was in too much of a rush, that he was selfish. Tycho bit back and that's when they started arguing for real. Swearing at each other. Then, suddenly there was silence. I risked taking a look. Tycho had his back to me, but he was showing Dad something. Then he walked away and Dad followed him. By the time I figured it was safe to come out of the car Tycho was gone. I never saw him again.'

'Right. Was there any mention of the Italian mafia?'

'No.'

There's a pause. Nell thinks Ivan must be gathering his thoughts.

'Okay,' he continues. 'You overheard Tycho and your dad arguing. Then what happened?'

'Tycho went missing. The next day, the paper rang and said they couldn't find him. Dad went searching for him, but he didn't say anything, just asked us if we had seen him. Mum wasn't too worried at first, because Tycho could be impulsive like that. I told Grainger what I'd overheard, and we offered to help look, but Dad said no. He'd been out searching in the forest and had come back around lunchtime to see if Tycho had shown up or if we'd heard anything. Then he went back to the forest. He took his gun with him and we knew it was serious.

'That night, Dad didn't come back. Mum went and saw the local policeman, the one here at Tulong. His name was Hoskings, and he was old and useless. Next thing we knew, Keith Tankard was down here from Hatheson taking charge. Tankard said not to worry, that he would find them, but Mum didn't trust him, told us he was crooked, and I told her and Grainger what I'd overheard Dad say about him. The next day Grainger and I went searching in the woods. I asked Mum if she knew where the Stills were. She said they were in the forest somewhere down along the river, maybe close to Jimmy Waters's house. That gave us a general idea. Mum rang Jimmy Waters, asked him if he'd seen Dad, but he said he hadn't.

'So Grainger and I took an old jeep and went looking, heading south along the river as far as we could go, then doubled back, trying the fire tracks and logging roads further inland. We found Dad's truck first. And not far from it, we found him. He'd been shot dead. It was an awful thing to see. It still haunts me, even now. He didn't even have his gun; it was still in his truck. Someone had shot him and left him like that. We couldn't believe it. We kept going, but we took his gun with us. And now we weren't just looking for Tycho, we were looking for Reg Waters as well.

'We found the place, the Stills, and there was Tycho's blue Datsun. He wouldn't have just left it there. And then this fat old bloke comes out, all smiling and pleasant, whistling a tune. I remember that: he was whistling. It was that old Second World War tune, Vera Lynn, "We'll Meet Again", but he was getting one of the notes flat. Grainger could hear it and so could I. Perfect pitch. But apart from that, he seemed very jolly, like Santa without the beard. He said Tycho was inside doing a bit of work for him, that he'd just go and get him. Grainger waited, but I got Dad's gun. I was always the better shot. Then this bloke came out with his own rifle, started walking towards Grainger, still whistling, like it was all a merry jape. But I didn't give him the chance to raise his gun. I shot him. Twice. He fell like a sack of shit, which I figure is a fair description.

'We buried him, there by the Stills, where you found him. We searched the whole place, but there was no sign of Tycho. We found his camera, the one the paper had given him. It was open, no film. Then we went back and we buried Dad in the forest.

Said some words, a little prayer. And we decided we couldn't tell anyone. Just Mum. Then Grainger drove the truck back to the Stills and he and I winched Tycho's car onto the back. We were driving back, Grainger in the truck and me a few minutes behind in our jeep, when he came across Tessa. He told me what happened afterwards. He gave her a lift, told her Tycho was gone. Not what had happened, but simply that Tycho and Dad weren't coming back. I reckon she suspected, but never knew the details. As far as I know, Grainger never told her everything; he's always wanted to protect her.'

There is silence. And then Ivan speaks, his voice even. 'If you shot Reg Waters in self-defence, or in defending your brother, why didn't you simply own up to it?'

'Keith Tankard.'

'What about him?'

'He came to our house a second time, met with Mum and the two of us. Grainger and I were scared; we thought he'd come to arrest us. Instead, he told us that he believed Reg Waters had killed Tycho, and that either Dad had killed Waters and was on the run, or Waters had killed Dad before fleeing. He asked if we'd ever heard of Waters or the Stills, but we just played dumb. That seemed to satisfy him. And then he warned us never to mention Reg Waters. He said if Waters was investigated, then the police would find out all about the car yard and how Dad had run a distribution service for Waters's contraband. He said Mum would be implicated and go to prison and that we could lose the yard. He said provided we didn't mention Waters, we should all be okay, that he could protect us. He was really open about it, how much he knew about, how deeply he was involved. We went along with him of course; we realised it would mean we'd get away with killing Waters, that we could keep the yard, Mum wouldn't go to prison and we could go to uni. It seemed too easy.'

'So you entered into a conspiracy with Keith Tankard to hide the truth?'

'That's one way to describe it.'

'Go on.'

'We thought it was settled. Grainger and Tessa got married and moved to Melbourne, and Tessa gave birth to Greg. I did my last two years of school, had a pretty miserable time of it. But I'd learnt something valuable: there are times when you need to stand up, take on the bad guys, kick arse. I got into uni, just like Mum and Dad wanted. But then they found Dad's body and had the inquest. It opened it all up again. And it made me realise Tankard couldn't be trusted.'

'How so?'

'At the inquest he still wanted to keep Waters out of it, and so did we. I exaggerated the argument between Tycho and Dad, made it sound like a real fight. That was Tankard's suggestion, he said it would add an element of confusion. But then he used my evidence to push this theory to the coroner that Tycho had killed Dad and gone on the run. It was bullshit, made Mum mad as hell, blackening Tycho's name like that. And then he dropped us in it anyway, gave evidence that Dad was a crook, that the wrecking yard was a front. He broke the agreement.'

'Do you know why? Doesn't seem to have been in his interest.'

'Tessa had come forward, given evidence that Tycho was investigating the mafia. This was back before Mackay and all of that, and no one took her that seriously. But Tankard was desperate to keep the mafia out of it, just as he wanted to keep Reg Waters out of it. I found out later that he'd had some dealings with the mafia. That's why he was so keen to promote the idea of Tycho and Dad fighting, this idea that Tycho killed Dad.'

'And you went along with it. Once again.'

Gene just stares at Ivan for a moment, as if reflecting on his behaviour, but his response is unapologetic. 'We did. And once the coroner had delivered her finding, things settled down again.' Gene pauses, takes a drink of water. 'A year or two later, just as I was finishing up at uni, I was down staying with Mum when I heard there was a job going at the *Western Explorer*. And that was it. It felt perfect for me; it felt right. I didn't want to live in the shadows; I wanted to be like Tycho, to take the bastards on. I got the job, moved to Hatty. And so it was I ran into Keith Tankard again. He was a sergeant by then, about to retire. Had a finger in every pie. Lived in this big house, had a boat, had a new car. Just reeked of it. But he'd grown arrogant and complacent. I started investigating him, the same way Tycho had probed Waters.

'He got wind of it, and he tried to blackmail me. But he had no leverage. He still had no idea it was Grainger and me who'd killed Waters. And the junkyard was no longer operating, so he couldn't use that, and besides, he'd already told the inquest that it had been a front. So I told him I wasn't scared of him. Then he overstepped, threatened me with violence, said I'd end up in the regulator like Tycho. I asked him what he meant. He said the last time a reporter on the *Explorer* had tried to expose him, he'd ended up in the regulator. He thought he was a tough guy, and that I was just some soft kid, fresh out of uni. But Tankard wasn't all that tough. He was happy to hand out a thumping, but he wasn't a killer. Not like me. I knew what I was capable of, what it was like to end a man's life; he didn't scare me. I kept digging. He was nowhere near Millewa the week Tycho and Dad died. He didn't kill them, but he was aware of it, so Waters must have told him—a phone call I guess—because he knew where Tycho had been dumped.

'I knew he was rotten, but I was having a hard time standing up the story. Everyone was scared of him. But then I found an old bloke who lived in the forest. Alf Jones. He told me he'd been a friend of Dad's. He told me what had happened with Dad's sawmill, that Waters and Tankard were behind it. That made me extra glad I had shot Waters, and firmed up my resolve. I became obsessed with Tankard. It became my life's mission, to bring him down. And bit by bit, with some help from Alf and a few others, I built up a dossier.

'I finished what Tycho started. I wrote a story not of murder but of corruption. Tankard went to prison. It was risky, of course, but I told him to his face that if he challenged me, I would write that he was an accessory to murder, tell Homicide all I knew, tell them Tycho was in the regulator.'

'You threatened him?' asks Ivan, voice a little incredulous.

'Too right. He had nothing on us; we had everything on him.'

'He just wore it?'

'Oh, it wasn't just the newspaper report. I was working in conjunction with the Internal Affairs Department of New South Wales Police by then. They were the ones who fed me the lines about the mafia. That was you lot, police sources. They busted him the same day my story came out.' And Gene offers the hint of a smile, as if confessing he feels good. 'I don't regret killing Reg Waters—he had it coming—but I take more pleasure from putting that bastard Tankard in prison. And the day he went inside, I drove down to the regulator. Just me. I chucked Waters's gun in the river and Dad's gun in the regulator. To show Tycho he wasn't forgotten, to show him he was avenged. That we'd got the bastards.'

Ivan lets that rest for a moment, before resuming. 'One thing I don't understand. If you knew Tankard didn't kill Tycho and your father, why did you accuse him of murdering Stannard in last week's paper?'

'Obvious, isn't it? You were searching the regulator; there was a good chance you would find Tycho's body. So I wanted you to suspect Tankard and not start asking questions about Reg Waters and what happened to him.'

'Even though you knew Tankard was innocent? At least of murder?'

Gene shrugs. 'He didn't pull the trigger, but he was Waters's lieutenant. He's a long time dead. No harm in it.'

'His grandson thinks differently,' says Ivan, and lets it rest there.

—

It's late in the day when Ivan and Nell eat at the Barking Frog. It's been doing a roaring trade, serving all the technicians and intelligence officers, the police and soldiers, the journalists and the sightseers. Most of them have drifted on to the Foresters Arms, so the two homicide detectives have the place almost to themselves. Ivan is eating a chicken and leek pie, but the emotions of the day have sapped Nell's appetite and she toys with a decaf, running her spoon around the lip of the cup. Her father and uncle are in custody; Reg Waters's body is in the Hatheson morgue. Grainger, confronted with his brother's confession, has corroborated it. This isn't the feeling she wanted. She's uncovered the killer, but there is no elation in it. No joy. Her own father is behind bars.

'Will they go to prison?' she asks.

Ivan blinks. 'I'd say so.'

'It was almost fifty years ago. It seems unnecessary.'

'They shot him, buried the body, committed perjury,' says Ivan, picking at a bowl of chips. 'No judge can overlook all of that, whatever the circumstances. Imagine the precedent it would set.'

'I know. I know.' She plays with her coffee. 'How long, do you think?'

'Seven years, tops. But the non-parole period could be substantially less. They've confessed, they've been solid citizens ever since, there is no chance of reoffending. They might be out in two. Even less.' He takes another bite of pie, chews, swallows. 'It wouldn't hurt if they showed a little remorse.'

'True.' She smiles wryly. 'Wouldn't hurt if they said Reg Waters raised his gun.'

Ivan shrugs. She can see he is no happier about the outcome than she is. 'Agreed. But any decent lawyer will still claim self-defence. There's no doubt Waters was about to kill them. Clear them of murder, and the rest is relatively minor.'

'What do you think about Tycho?' she asks. 'Maybe he should have let sleeping dogs lie.'

Ivan frowns. 'And just let Reg Waters carry on his merry way? Protected by a crooked cop?'

'I don't know. He lost so much. They all did. Not just him and Bert. Rita and Dad and Gene. Mum. Greg. And Willow. Even Jimmy. They've all borne the cost of what he did.'

'That doesn't mean he was wrong. Just that he went about it the wrong way.'

'Maybe.'

They fall into silence then. Nell thinks of Rita, alone in her house, Jimmy alone in his, Willow alone in hers. What is it Nell and Ivan have achieved here? It seems pyrrhic. She hopes that, at the very least, Tessa is not alone in the house by the Murray in Boonlea, that her brothers and sisters have rallied around their mother.

The door opens. A young woman enters, dressed in a blouse and pencil skirt as if for a corporate function. She surveys the room, nods to them and leaves again.

'What was that?' Ivan asks Nell, just as she's about to pose him the same question.

They're answered by the appearance of Jack Goffing, leg in a moon boot, using crutches, his assistant holding the door open for him.

'I kind of miss this place,' he says, taking a seat awkwardly, shaking off the attempts by the young woman to assist him. Instead, he sends her to the counter to ask Frieda for some glasses. He withdraws a bottle of sherry from his bag. 'Developed a taste for it,' he says. Nell can see the label: *The River Pirate*. 'I hear you've just about wrapped things up,' says Goffing.

Nell defers to Ivan, lets him answer while she examines Goffing. He looks different without the beard and glasses. Younger, sharper, a lean face with a five o'clock shadow.

'We'll file a report with the coroner on the shooting of Gerard Stannard by Eamon Finucane,' says Ivan. 'Same with the deaths of Bert Buchanan and Tycho Buchanan, murdered by Reg Waters. And we're preparing a brief of evidence to prosecute Gene and Grainger Buchanan over the death of Reg Waters.'

Goffing nods. The assistant returns with wineglasses. She distributes them, then steps back out of earshot. Goffing pours. They clink glasses, a silent toast.

The fortified wine is sweet and strong and fruity. Nell quite likes it. 'And you?' she asks Goffing. 'All resolved?'

'Thanks to you. We've secured the weapons and smashed the terrorist group. Fifteen in custody and counting. Just in time; they were working up to simultaneous attacks in Canberra, Melbourne and Sydney. An antipodean Oklahoma City bombing. Dozens would have died. Maybe hundreds. Would have changed the country.'

'And Jean-Luc Hoffner, or whatever his real name is?' she asks.

Goffing becomes sombre, looking at his glass of sherry. 'One of the Neo-Nazis has rolled over. According to him, Hoffner was machine-gunned as he tried to escape across the river. His body was recovered a few weeks back. Washed up on the southern shore. We've been keeping it quiet while we tried to find the shed and identify those responsible, but charges will most certainly be laid.'

Nell looks at Ivan; he's avoiding her gaze. 'Is that what you were doing in Victoria? Not just checking out the destroyed regulator?'

Ivan simply shrugs, and she sees the truth of the matter in his eyes.

She turns to Goffing. 'What about Noel Tankard? How is he?'

'Making a full recovery. No permanent damage, I'm glad to report.'

'Why were they holding him at the shed? Was he one of your informants?'

Goffing's voice is low as he answers, some practised art whereby his words carry to their ears and no further. 'Noel Tankard is a federal police officer. Undercover here for the past two years.'

Nell blinks. 'You're shitting me.'

'Long line of cops. Father, grandfather.'

'But . . .' she starts, and then thinks better of it.

'But his grandfather was corrupt? Sure was. Rotten as last month's avocado. Noel and his father have spent a lifetime compensating for that.'

'I thought his father was drummed out of the force?'

'Your uncle's exposés saw to that. But he was totally clean, above reproach. He joined us instead. He's my boss.'

Ivan and Nell exchange a look.

'You owe him a drink,' says Goffing, raising his sherry to his lips. 'He's the one who called off Nathan Phelan.'

'And the one who asked Plodder to send one of his most experienced detectives to investigate a decades-old crime?' asks Nell.

'Just so.'

chapter forty-six

THREE DAYS LATER AND THE CASE IS ALL BUT WRAPPED UP. THE LAST OF THE weaponry has been shipped out and the Stills have been returned to the stewardship of the forest; the police and the army and spooks have left. The exodus of the cookers has accelerated, as they are shaken from their delusions by a remarkably well-sourced series of articles in the *Sydney Morning Herald* by Martin Scarsden. Ivan laughs when she raises her eyebrows at him, telling her that Goffing and Scarsden go way back, that the Plodder knows all about them.

'So he's happy? Plodder?'

'Are you kidding? Four cold cases cleared, plus suspects in custody for the Hoffner killing. His officer instrumental in breaking open a terrorist cell. He's over the moon. Even talking about us getting another detective in Dubbo.'

'Anyone in mind?'

'Kevin Nackangara.'

Nell smiles. 'So he gets his promotion. That's excellent.'

'Well, not quite a promotion.'

'How do you figure?'

'He's already a detective.'

She just blinks. She's never heard of that before: a detective going undercover as a uniformed officer. 'They put an Indigenous officer here to provoke the Neo-Nazis?'

'He volunteered.'

'That's gutsy.'

Her phone rings. It's Tessa, calling to say that she'd like to visit Willow, asking if Nell will drive her.

'Are you sure, Mum? It's the middle of nowhere.'

'I think I would like it. She invited me, at the funeral.'

'Let me check and I'll call you right back.'

She asks Ivan if it's okay with him. He just smiles. 'Good opportunity,' he says.

--

When she gets to Boonlea, Nell can't believe the change in her mother. Three days since the funeral and she's unrecognisable. Nell had worried about taking her mother out into the wider world, but it's like another woman waiting for her, dressed in jeans, a blue cotton shirt, a hat she has found somewhere, walking boots that look suspiciously new. And a brand-new pair of retro sunglasses, like something Princess Grace would have worn.

They drive with the wheatfields to their left and the tilt above the forest to the right, the highway like a dividing line between land and ocean. The house on the rise, Tessa's childhood home, is like a lighthouse on the cliffs. There's a television news car, Channel Ten, coming down the drive, coming from the Stills.

'I've asked Dad if he wants to stay with me at Boonlea,' says Tessa. 'It seems stupid—him stuck out here all alone, me down there in that big house by myself. Grainger might not be home for a while, and your brothers and sisters need to get back to their own lives.'

'You'll have Dad back afterwards?'

'Of course.' Her mother gives her a knowing look. 'I'm not going to throw away fifty years. And I'm grateful for what he did.'

'Burying Reg Waters?'

'Not that. Saving me. Marrying me, enabling me to keep Greg, giving Tycho's son a chance at life.'

Nell takes that on board. 'Grandpa might be a bit stuck in his ways,' she suggests.

'Aren't we all?' says Tessa, smiling, before becoming more serious. 'He's old, Nell. Ninety-two next year. He's had a hard life. He deserves to put his feet up. A little affection, a little forgiveness. He thinks he failed as a husband and a father, blames himself for everything that happened. But he did the best he could. He just had a handful for a daughter.'

Nell stares hard at the road, trying to keep her emotions in check. They've been unpredictable this past week or so, ever since the shootout and the resolution to the case. 'That's great, Mum. Truly.'

'And, Nell, can I tell you? You were never a handful of a daughter. You were who you needed to be. I'm glad you defied us, stuck to your convictions and became a police officer. I'm very proud of you.'

And now a tear does escape behind Nell's own sunglasses. She remains quiet and listens as her mother grows more and more chatty. Maybe she's trying to compensate for her anxiety over leaving the house, but when Nell glances over at her, it looks more like she's enjoying the excursion. 'Greg is going to stay with Rita for a while. He and that bloke of his, they have this plan. They're going to turn the place into a sculpture park. Can you believe that? Turn all those rusting wrecks into statues or something.'

'Seriously?'

'Reckons he can get a grant. The local council is keen. Reckons it will put Tulong on the map.'

'Ha. Good luck with that.'

'Rita will be glad to have him. Apparently, she's grown quite dependent on Gene.'

That makes Nell feel better. There is nothing Ivan can do for her dad and her uncle, but he's decided against prosecuting her grandmother for her false confession, saying it would serve little purpose. Not anymore.

They drive on into Tulong, turning off the highway and down the tilt, into the great forest, past the Clarrie Buchanan Park and the Tulong Memorial Hall, past the empty campground and out past the ruins of the sawmill. They drive along the bitumen and then the graded road and finally onto the bush tracks, her mother all eyes, pointing out a falcon hovering above the road. She can't quite believe it when Nell is forced to stop: a mother duck struts across the track in front of them, followed by a brood of puffball ducklings. Nell can't help but smile: there is something childlike in her mother's wonder, free from her domestic confines after all these years, out of dry dock and back on the ocean.

They take the track, pass the fallen tree, arrive at the suspension bridge. Nell checks: the bike is there, under the tarpaulin. Good. Willow must be at home. Nell returns to the car, sounds the horn: three long blasts. And again she wonders at the change in her mother, who has meanwhile edged out onto the suspension bridge, taking in the forest. Tessa sees her daughter watching; she smiles and waves.

Before long Willow appears, coming down the creek in her canoe. Nell helps her pull it into the bank, more a gesture than real assistance. Willow hugs her mother; they have somehow become close without Nell realising it. Like sisters. There is a hug for Nell as well. 'I might take your mum across first, come back for you?' suggests Willow.

'Take your time. Show her the forest. Show her everything.'

Willow looks to Tessa, who is beaming, before answering. 'I will.'

--

Later, the three women sit outside the shack overlooking the lagoon, talking the afternoon away. Nell finds herself relaxing, tension easing out of her, replaced with a sense of satisfaction and quiet fatigue. She realises that she and Ivan have delivered more than justice, that their investigation has created something positive. She'd been afraid of driving a permanent wedge into her family, but now, sitting in the forest, she realises perhaps it's the opposite: a long-festering wound has been cleaned out and the healing has begun.

All too soon, the shadows are extending.

'Sorry,' says Nell, 'but we'll need to be getting back.'

'Would it be all right if I didn't?' says her mother. 'Willow has offered to let me stay the night.'

Nell looks at Willow, who grins and shrugs.

'Of course,' says Nell, 'I'll come back and pick you up tomorrow before Ivan and I head off.'

'Thank you.'

'But before I go, I have something for you.'

'Me?' says her mother.

Nell pulls the small plastic box from her pocket. It's little more than a flattened disc now. 'We found this in the regulator, just before they moved the radar down to the Stills. We think Tycho might have had it on him.'

Tessa frowns. Looks at Willow as if for guidance, takes it. It's small, fragile, its edges crumbling. 'What is it?'

Nell tries to answer but finds it hard to speak. Instead, she reaches into her daypack and withdraws a clear zip-lock bag containing a ring, the metal tarnished but the gemstone clear and sparkling. 'Here,' is all she can manage.

Her mother takes it, stares at it, speechless.

'He bought it in Griffith,' says Nell, struggling with the words. 'We tracked it down. Confirmed it.'

'Oh, Nell.'

'Tycho told his father, that day he disappeared, that he was going to meet you. Gene overheard him saying it was serious, saw Tycho showing him something.'

Later, Tessa is still staring into the lagoon, eyes faraway, when Nell and Willow take the canoe back to the bridge. And then it's time for Nell to say goodbye to her newfound grandmother.

'I'm so glad to have met you at last,' says Nell.

'And me,' says Willow. 'You remind me of her, of Amber. And of Tycho. The best of them. But that's just me. You're your own woman. Go out and do everything they didn't have the chance to do.'

'Right,' says Nell. 'No pressure.'

'That was a very special thing you did back there. The ring, chasing it down like that, where it came from.'

Nell smiles. 'I have something for you as well.'

Willow turns her head slightly sideways, eyes widening with curiosity.

'Here.' It's another zip-lock bag, containing a pair of yellow swimming googles.

Her grandmother stares at them, eyes narrowing again, a squint of concentration, before reaching out for them. 'Where did you find them?'

'In the evidence locker in Albury.'

Willow blinks, says nothing.

'Did you know?' asks Nell. 'About the bodies in the regulator?'

Willow shakes her head. 'Dad never said a thing.' And she turns, looking up the creek, around at the forest. 'When we were young, the regulator was a wonderful place, or so it seemed to me—a place where the forest met the outside world. Tycho took me there. It's where I first met Tessa and Gene and Grainger. There was an afternoon there, a golden afternoon. We swam and we drank wine and Gene played guitar. Whenever I came back to the forest I'd go there, remembering. But in recent years, there was never enough water, no flow. It became stagnant, full of weeds and algae, that special place of ours, left to rot, to fill with sludge. And the forest around it, turned dry and dying.' She looks back to Nell. 'So no, I didn't know anything about the bodies, not consciously, but maybe I felt, somewhere deep down, that something was wrong, something needed to be corrected.' She shrugs. 'So I blew it up. Will you arrest me now?'

Nell shakes her head. 'No. I only do homicides.' Then she can't help smiling. 'But, please, don't do it again.'

And Willow returns that smile. 'Of course not. Detective Buchanan.'

'Goodbye, Willow. I'll see you again tomorrow when I pick up Mum.'

'You will. But before you go, I have my own gift.'

'For me?'

'For you. Go and have your career; live your life. And when you are done with it, many years from now, come back. The forest will be waiting for you. When I die, the shack is yours. My father built it, he and my mum, built it on the island that Jimmy Waters found, bought the land with the money Bert Buchanan gave them. It was my mother's and now it is mine and it should have been Amber's. Now it will be yours. So that some good will come of all we've been through.'

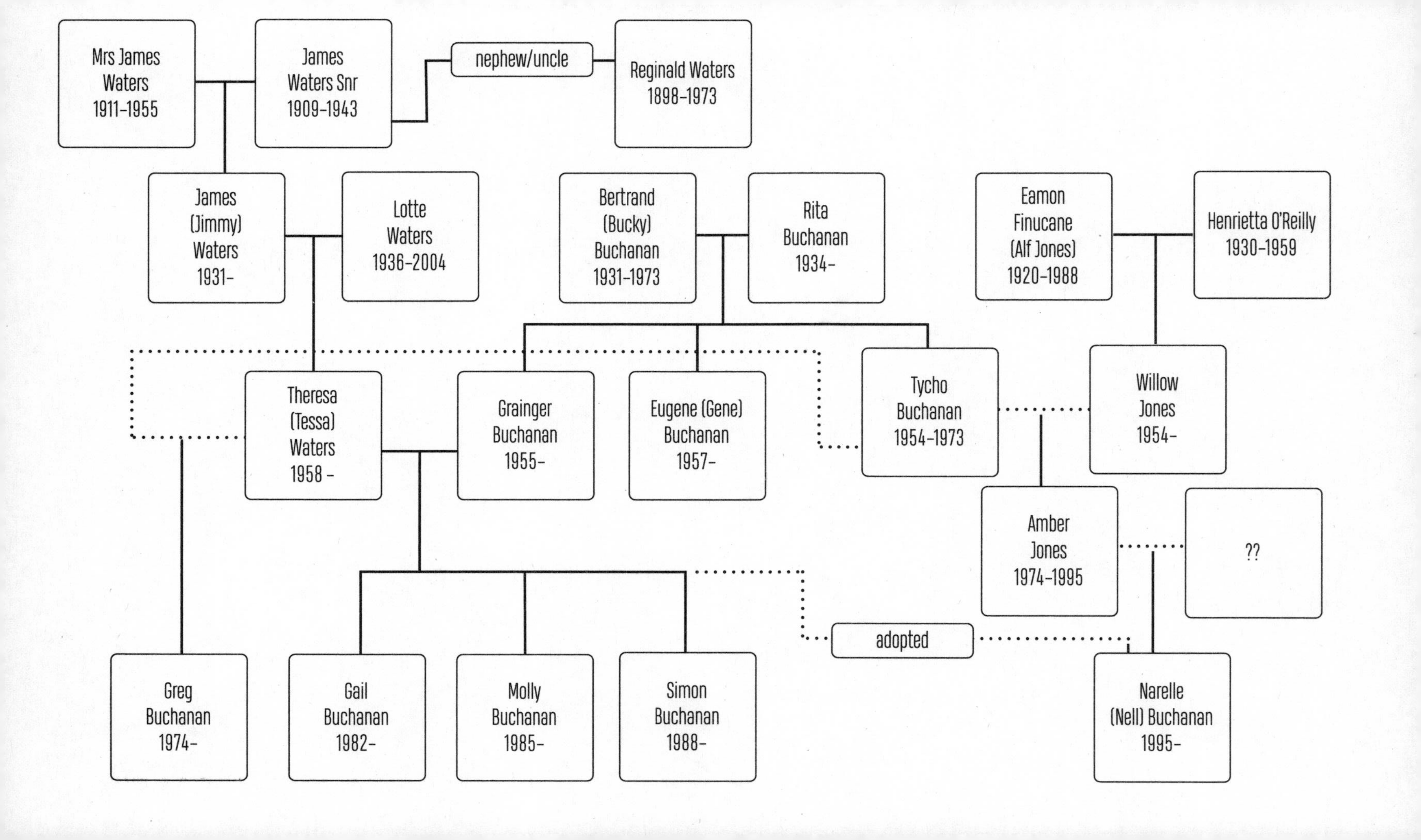
Mrs James Waters 1911–1955
James Waters Snr 1909–1943
nephew/uncle
Reginald Waters 1898–1973
James (Jimmy) Waters 1931–
Lotte Waters 1936–2004
Bertrand (Bucky) Buchanan 1931–1973
Rita Buchanan 1934–
Eamon Finucane (Alf Jones) 1920–1988
Henrietta O'Reilly 1930–1959
Theresa (Tessa) Waters 1958 –
Grainger Buchanan 1955–
Eugene (Gene) Buchanan 1957–
Tycho Buchanan 1954–1973
Willow Jones 1954–
Amber Jones 1974–1995
??
adopted
Greg Buchanan 1974–
Gail Buchanan 1982–
Molly Buchanan 1985–
Simon Buchanan 1988–
Narelle (Nell) Buchanan 1995–

Author's note and acknowledgements

THE BARMAH-MILLEWA FOREST IS A REAL PLACE, THE LARGEST RIVER REDGUM forest in the world, created by the partial damming of the Murray River by the Cadell Tilt.

I have fictionalised and modified the area's towns to better match the narrative, but their locations are accurate, as is the overall geography of the forest. Hatheson is the real-life Deniliquin, Tulong is Mathoura, Boonlea is Moama, and Anglers Reach represents Picnic Point.

I spent a week in and around the forest in the summer of 2008–09 at the height of the Millenium Drought, researching my non-fiction book *The River.* The forest was tinder dry, with trees dying and bird life collapsing. To return in the La Niña summer of 2021–22 was a revelation, the forest filling with water.

During that first visit, I interviewed local historian Tim Mannion, who told me of a summer he spent as a boy in the forest during the Second World War, minding his family's cattle. His story stayed with me and was the seed for the character of Jimmy—so thank you, Tim!—although it must be emphasised the events in this story are entirely fictitious.

I'm also grateful for information gleaned from *The Barmah Forest In Our Blood* by Nerelie Teese and Leigh Wright.

My grandfather Chas Hammer was one of the Victorian volunteers who saw service in New Guinea in the desperate days of 1942 and 1943. This provided the seed for another part of the story.

There are many people to thank, including everyone at my Australian publishers, Allen & Unwin, particularly the amazing editorial team of Jane Palfreyman, Ali Lavau, Christa Munns and Kate Goldsworthy, as well as wonder publicist Laura Benson.

Massive thanks as always to agent Grace Heifetz of Leftbank Literary and her co-conspirators Felicity Blunt in London and Faye Bender in New York.

Thanks also to the amazing team at Wildfire in the UK, including Jack Butler, Alex Clarke and Caitlin Raynor.

Aleksander Potočnik has again created an amazing map and Luke Causby another brilliant cover design for the Australian edition. Thanks to friend and photographer Robert Owen-Jones for the author photograph.

A shout-out also to audiobook narrators Dorje Swallow and Lockie Chapman, who do much to bring the narrative to life.

Huge appreciation also to all the amazing booksellers of Australia and beyond—you are the lifeblood of our literary culture!

Finally, I am most grateful for the week I spent at the writers' house Varuna in December 2021—so productive and such fun.

And, as always, thanks to Tomoko, Elena and Cameron.

If you loved *Dead Man's Creek,* why not try *Opal Country*, out now in paperback?

Opals...

In the desolate outback town of Finnigans Gap, police struggle to maintain law and order. Thieves pillage opal mines, religious fanatics recruit vulnerable youngsters and billionaires do as they please.

Bodies...

Then an opal miner is found crucified and left to rot down his mine. Nothing about the miner's death is straight-forward, not even who found the body. Homicide detective Ivan Lucic is sent to investigate, assisted by inexperienced young investigator Nell Buchanan.

But Finnigans Gap has already ended one police career and damaged others, and soon both officers face damning allegations and internal investigations. Have Ivan and Nell been set up, and if so, by whom?

Secrets...

As time runs out, their only chance at redemption is to find the killer. But the more they uncover, the more harrowing the mystery becomes, and a past long forgotten is thrown into scorching sunlight.

Because in Finnigans Gap, **nothing stays buried for ever.**

9781472273017

Also available from Wildfire

Scrublands

In an isolated country town ravaged by drought, a charismatic young priest opens fire on his congregation, killing five men before being shot dead himself.

A year later, journalist Martin Scarsden arrives in Riversend to write a feature on the anniversary of the tragedy. But the stories he hears from the locals don't fit with the accepted version of events.

Just as Martin believes he is making headway, a shocking discovery rocks the town. The bodies of two backpackers - missing since the time of the massacre - are found in the scrublands. The media descends on Riversend and Martin is the one in the spotlight.

Wrestling with his own demons, Martin finds himself risking everything to uncover a truth that becomes more complex with every twist. But there are powerful forces determined to stop him, and he has no idea how far they will go to make sure the town's secrets stay buried.

9781472255143

Silver

A HOMECOMING MARRED BY BLOOD

Journalist Martin Scarsden returns to Port Silver to make a fresh start with his partner Mandy. But he arrives to find his childhood friend murdered - and Mandy is the prime suspect. Desperate to clear her name, Martin goes searching for the truth.

A TERRIBLE CRIME

The media descends on the coastal town, compelled by a story that has it all: sex, drugs, celebrity, and religion. Martin is chasing the biggest scoop of his career, and the most personal.

A PAST HE CAN'T ESCAPE

As Martin draws closer to a killer, the secrets of his traumatic childhood come to the surface, and he must decide what is more important - the story or his family...

9781472255365

Trust

On a bright sunny day in Port Silver, ex-journalist Martin Scarsden misses a call from his girlfriend Mandy. Checking his voicemail later, all he hears is her terrified scream before the phone cuts off.

Back at the house, he finds a policeman unconscious on the floor, and Mandy gone.

So starts a riveting tale of intrigue and danger, as Martin probes the hidden past of the woman he loves. But can he trust her, once her shocking secrets are finally revealed?

9781472272942